Stellar Praise for

CAGE OF STARS

"An imaginative, heartfelt story that is hard to put down . . . Here is the great and humble thing about Mitchard's novel: When it comes to describing how searing emotions conflict with the demands of faith, it understands its limitations. Mitchard does what she can without coming across as sanctimonious."
—Associated Press

"Deeply moving and compelling . . . another winner."
—*Toronto Sun*

"Powerful . . . CAGE OF STARS is another Mitchard classic, a gripping journey into an unthinkable situation . . . a lovely meditation on faith, family, and finding peace in the unforgivable."
—*Bookpage*

"A moving, can't-put-down story."
—Susan Isaacs

"Eloquent . . . This is Mitchard's best novel to date . . . Readers are invited to get to know the Swans; they will be left all the more complete because of the experience."
—*Library Journal*

"Wonderful . . . as big and mysterious as the night sky—it's so full of love and grief and huge, life-shaking questions."
—Luanne Rice

Please turn the page for more praise for Jacquelyn Mitchard, and turn to the back of this book for a preview of her upcoming novel, *Still Summer*.

"A tale of tragedy, grief, and redemption . . . Ronnie is an endearing character . . . the reader can understand her motives and almost wants to cheer her on. CAGE OF STARS is an intense, emotional story that teaches the reader how lives are intertwined in ways you'd never expect."

—*Deseret Morning News* (Salt Lake City)

"A sweeping dramatic novel."

—*In Style*

"CAGE OF STARS explores one family's irrevocable change in an instant of violence . . . Veronica Swan narrates with the perfect pitch of a teenager forced to grow up in one horrible, shocking moment—and she rings so true that she'll stay with you after you're done reading."

—Jodi Picoult

"A compelling, suspenseful story; skillfully crafts an authentic narrative voice, and succeeds in humanizing the adherents of a religion that still suffers from widespread negative stereotypes."

—*Booklist*

"CAGE OF STARS is vintage Mitchard."

—Jane Hamilton

"Mitchard writes vividly. She has a gift for making the reader feel the emotions of her characters . . . And that's precisely what makes [this book] worth reading."

—*Edmonton Sun*

"If you thought you knew Jackie Mitchard, you're in for a brilliant surprise. CAGE OF STARS is a thrill ride of a novel—psychologically gripping, wonderfully paced; a marvelously rendered portrait of the way violence colors our lives. This is the breakout read of the year."

—Karin Slaughter

"Ronnie progresses to a young woman with considerable emotional depth, and Mitchard understatedly portrays her attempts to navigate romance and other interactions as a Mormon raised very 'of the church.' The results are sweet and solid."
—*Publishers Weekly*

"Breaks new ground for Mitchard. This time around, the plot contains a hint of suspense . . . and delves into the human emotions of revenge and forgiveness from the viewpoint of a Mormon girl . . . Mitchard succeeds in doing what she does best—developing intriguing characters in story fashion that draw you in and hold you captive. Her characters don't preach, yet convey their feelings so well they become real and allow you to step into their world for a brief visit and remain with you as more than a fleeting memory."
—*Capital Times* (Madison, WI)

"A captivating narrative about an inconceivable tragedy . . . CAGE OF STARS isn't just about murder and retribution. It examines religion and, specifically, one that's often misunderstood due to stereotypes."
—*Hamilton Spectator* (Ontario)

"Mitchard creates unmistakably vivid characters here . . . gets so much right, right down to a stunning epilogue."
—*Seattle Times*

"[Has] a taut sense of suspense and a lot to say about a world of emotional choices . . . a worthwhile and compelling read, a novel that has all the elements of good storytelling."
—*Washington Post Book World*

Other Books by Jacquelyn Mitchard

Fiction

THE BREAKDOWN LANE

CHRISTMAS PRESENT

TWELVE TIMES BLESSED

A THEORY OF RELATIVITY

THE MOST WANTED

THE DEEP END OF THE OCEAN

Nonfiction

THE REST OF US

CAGE *of* STARS

JACQUELYN MITCHARD

WARNER BOOKS

NEW YORK   BOSTON

Copyright © 2006 by Jacquelyn Mitchard
Reading Group Guide Copyright © 2007 by Hachette Book Group USA
Excerpt from *Still Summer* Copyright © 2007 by Jacquelyn Mitchard

Warner Books
Hachette Book Group USA
237 Park Avenue
New York, NY 10017

Visit our Web site at www.HachetteBookGroupUSA.com

Printed in the United States of America

Originally published in hardcover by Warner Books.

First Trade Edition: August 2007
10 9 8 7 6 5 4 3 2 1

The Library of Congress has cataloged the hardcover edition as follows:

Mitchard, Jacquelyn.
  Cage of stars / Jacquelyn Mitchard. — 1st ed.
      p. cm.
  ISBN-13: 978-0-446-57875-2 (regular edition)
  ISBN-10: 0-446-57875-4 (regular edition)
  ISBN-13: 978-0-446-57984-1 (large print edition)
  ISBN-10: 0-446-57984-X (large print edition)
  1. Mormons—Fiction. 2. Utah—Fiction. I. Title.
  PS3563.I7358C34   2006
  813'.54—dc22

                                                    2005033494

ISBN 978-0-446-69672-2 (pbk.)

Book design by Charles Sutherland

For Jane Gelfman

How many stars in your bowl?
How many shadows in your soul?

—D. H. Lawrence

"The Stars Stand Still"

Acknowledgments

I am first and always grateful to my assistant, Pamela English. Pam, you're not just the brains of the outfit, you're the heart. Thanks to my new and gleaming editor, Jamie Raab, and the splendid team at Warner Books (I hope to do you proud), and always, to my agent, Jane Gelfman, who must promise that when she is one hundred and I am ninety-five, she will still be my friend and counselor. For her help in my understanding of a paramedic's life, I thank my friend Crystal Fish. For her twenty years of friendship, her prayers in this and other endeavors, her gentle help in leading me to an understanding of the Mormon religion, I thank Kahlil Kelly and her wonderful family. Gratitude goes to Dr. M.I., for giving me perspective on schizophrenic illness, its tragedy and hope; and to Shane Baker for his dear friendship and for answering a batty mom's basketball questions. And as ever, to my pals who share e-tea and sympathy, at home and from afar, Jeanine, K.J.A.M., Anne, Jodi, Clarice, Arty, Chris, Steve, Karen, Pam, Josh, Judy, Joyce, Eliz J., Stacey, Mikail, and Melanie. I'm surprised and gratified that my majestic family hasn't left me on an ice floe. It goes without saying, but I will say it anyway, that incidents not unlike those in *Cage of Stars* do happen in the world; but this is entirely a work of fiction, and whatever mistakes made in it are mine alone.

CAGE *of* STARS

Prologue

When I set out to find the killer Scott Early, I didn't realize I was a foolish kid trying to stand in the great shoes of God.

After it was all over, everyone asked why had I done such a thing? I didn't know how to explain. Everything had gotten all turned around and confused in my mind. It had once been so clear to me that there was a way, and that I must walk in it.

It seemed so obvious. Then, not so obvious. And then, it was too late.

I opened the door that last morning, and there were the reporters, buzzing like a hatch of mosquitoes. They asked me, *Did you plan this all those years, Ronnie? How did you hold on to that anger for so long, Ronnie?* And I thought, How could anyone think that four years was a long time to "hold on to anger," given what had happened to us? Four years was a moment. People stay angry longer than that over someone stealing their boyfriend! With a few vivid exceptions, those four years, basically my whole life as a teenager, passed like a movie with the sound turned off. If those reporters had lived the way I lived, every day looking at that shed between the house and the barn, the shed Papa had been meaning to fix up for years before Becky and Ruthie died, to give Mama a better studio for her work, that sturdy old building with its gray paint beaten into powder by the punishment of the sun and the dusty wind, and the thick purple weeds bunched tight up against its walls, how would they have felt? What would they have done? Nothing ever changed the sight of that shed. It never looked different. I saw it every day, whether the pink ice plants and the rock roses were blooming in Mama's garden or the Christmas lights were up. It never went away. And it was just desolate. Like our lives were, for the longest time. No one else had been through it. So they could ask stupid questions with all the tactfulness of a big bulldozer. Another guy yelled out to me, *Did you plan in advance to kill Scott Early? He said—and he was serious—Because maybe you felt it was blood atonement. Mormons believe in blood atonement . . . don't you?*

I was so tired. I was so hungry and alone. Like a fool, I answered, "I bet you think my father has five wives, too."

The guy's eyes widened and he flipped over to a new page in his notebook. "*Does he?*" he asked.

"No," I said. "He has *sixty*-five wives, just like in 'The King and I.'"

The reporter's face got all pouty then. He knew I was messing with him. I sat down on the curb and put my head on my knees, and I didn't say a word until my father came with my uncle Andrew, who told me to say nothing at all. Blood atonement? I kept thinking. My word! It was one thing to believe that the price Scott Early paid was too small for the evil he did. I still believe that. And yes, I didn't agree with my parents that forgiving Scott Early would stop the shuddering of my heart that woke me from all those frightful dreams, my T-shirt in sweat that smelled metallic and dirty, like old pocket change. But to think I was after Scott Early's blood? Just because I was a Mormon? That was purely ignorant. Half the time, even good people think all Mormons are nuts in a cult where the church leader marries you off at the age of thirteen! Maybe some of that stuff used to go on a hundred years ago; but a few hundred years ago in Europe, Catholics went around stretching people on the rack, too. They're not doing that anymore, either!

All "blood atonement" means to regular Mormons is just that shedding someone else's blood is the most terrible thing, and "atonement" is making up for your sin. It's a metaphor, like the kind you learn in English class. Mormons think you have to do good to make up for your sins, not just say you're sorry. When I set off for California, I didn't think that Scott Early had atoned for his sins. But I didn't really know what I would do about that; I thought it would be revealed to me. I never thought about violence.

What happened . . . happened . . . just because of the tiniest mistake.

I had that to live with.

And I would always know how much I'd let my family down. My parents trusted me completely. And I betrayed their trust. I lied, and I'd never lied before. I told them only part of the truth. I told them I needed to be away from Utah. To be away from the shed. I was going to San Diego, a sunny city of young people and young dreams, to go to a good community college, where I could train to be an EMT—the work I planned to do to pay for my college. Yes, I saw the looks my parents exchanged. I knew those looks meant that they knew Scott Early was in California but didn't think that I knew. I played innocent. They believed me. But under all that innocence was a wayward heart. I might have felt very mature, even old, because of everything our family had been through. I learned something, though. Suffering and finishing high school early doesn't mean you're mature. It takes a lot more than that.

Papa told me once, right after my sisters died, that atonement wasn't something a regular person on earth can bring on someone else. He said it was between the sinner and God. He was right. But I couldn't hear it. I was pretty sure of myself. Veronica Bonham Swan, an eager girl with long twisty auburn hair that was my vanity, who loved horses and science and hated laundry and term papers. I thought one person could do what a whole system had not. Everything had come easy to me in my life.

Everything except the one and most important thing.

Which became the only thing that mattered.

And so I believed that I had survived the beautiful late fall day when Scott Early drenched our lives in blood for a purpose. I thought that if I didn't walk in the path of that purpose, when my time came to die—whether I lived to be twenty or ninety—I would pass over knowing that I'd failed Becky and Ruthie in the life hereafter as I'd failed them on earth. And I would not be able to face my baby sisters when they came running to me in heaven.

Chapter One

At the moment when Scott Early killed Becky and Ruthie, I was hiding in the shed.

It wasn't because I was afraid. I wasn't afraid to die then, and I'm not afraid now. It was because we were playing hide-and-seek. My little sisters always started begging me the minute my parents left me to baby-sit. "Ronnie, Ronnie, Ronnie!" they would tease me, pulling on my shirt while I tried to straighten up the kitchen. "Betcha we can find you this time. Betcha on our chores!" And I would always give in, warning them that if they didn't find me, they were going to spend two hours, until Mama got back, picking up every crayon and every sticker book in their room.

"This time I'm not kidding, Thing One and Thing Two," I told them that day. "*I'm* not going in there right before Mama gets home and pull all your clean clothes and markers out from under your bed."

"I promise, slalomly," Becky said. I had to laugh. Her teeth were purple from the berries she'd eaten for breakfast. Becky was as thin and fast as a minnow in a creek and seemed to live practically on air. Ruthie was as round and "slalom" as a little koala bear. Her favorite thing was to eat cookie dough right from the bowl.

They wanted to play outside, because it was a really warm, sunny day for November, not that it's ever too cold at the edge of what's practically the Mojave Desert. The purples and yellows and reds of the changing trees that day were as flashy as a marching band.

And so, an hour later, I was crouched down in the shed, behind a big sack of potting soil and a crate of clay, hoping a spider didn't pick that time to crawl up my back. I couldn't see my little sisters. But I imagined that they were leaning against the picnic table, where we ate our supper almost every summer night when the bugs weren't bad—our own tomatoes and sweet corn, sometimes with tacos and black beans—listening to the birds making their go-to-sleep sounds. Becky and Ruthie most likely had their little hands over their eyes, counting fast so that they could yell out, "Ready or not, here I come!" Ruthie would call first, I knew. She always did, and Becky always shushed her, saying there was no way she could have gotten to a hundred yet because she, Becky, was older and *she* hadn't got up to fifty. I know they didn't peek, because I'd told them peeking wasn't fair and that I wouldn't play unless they played fair.

That day, though, they never made a sound.

I figured they were counting to a hundred silently, because whenever we played hide-and-seek, Becky would count straight up as fast as she could, and Ruthie, who was only four, would say out loud, "One, two, three, four, eight, fourteen, fifteen, ten." Becky would get so confused, she'd have to start all over again.

But five minutes went by, and still, they never made a sound. When it got to be a long time, I opened the door.

And I saw my sisters, lying there like little white dolls in great dark pools of paint. I saw Scott Early, a young man with short blond hair, sitting on the picnic table, wearing only his boxers and a dirty T-shirt, sobbing as if they were *his* little sisters, as if a terrible monster had come along and done this. Which was sort of what he did think, though I didn't know that then.

It was a good thing, a doctor later said to my mother, that Becky and Ruthie didn't cry out. It meant that they died quickly. They barely felt a thing. They must never have heard Scott Early come walking barefoot across our lawn. The merciful Father shielded them from fear. Being cut across the carotid artery is a very quick way to die. I knew that, even then, from biology. But it's not over in an instant, and I prayed for months that Becky and Ruthie never had time to wonder why I wasn't there to help them.

For I was always there to help them.

Though I was only twelve-almost-thirteen, Mama could trust me to look after the little girls alone, even if she had to be out in the part of the shed that was her "studio" or at the galleries, as far away as St. George, for hours at a time.

"You are as responsible as any mother, Ronnie," Mama told me quietly one night, after the time Becky's hand got burned. Becky had been impatient that morning for her "cheesy eggs" and reached up to see if they were finished while I was cooking. She burned her hand on the pan. Mama said I had "presence of mind" because I didn't start to cry or panic when Becky screamed. I didn't try to put butter on the burn, which my own grandma would have done, because that would have made it worse. From the first-aid section of health class Mama taught me, I remembered that a burn had to be cooled down with water right away or the heat inside would keep right on burning the skin and the damage would go deeper. I put Becky's hand under the cold-water tap for five minutes and wrapped ice in a thick towel and taped it down around her hand. Then I ran, pulling Becky and Ruthie in the wooden wagon, down to our nearest neighbor, Mrs. Emory, who drove us to Pine Mountains Clinic ten miles away, between our house and Cedar City. At the clinic, the doctor, a young woman, placed a net shield and gauze under a bandage on Becky's palm. The doctor spoke so gently to Becky that I suppose it was then that I first thought I would become a doctor one day myself. I wondered if the incident meant I was called to it.

Becky had just a tiny scar on one finger after her hand healed. Our pediatrician, Dr. Pratt, said he wouldn't have done one thing different himself, except to drive her to a hospital. But there wasn't a real hospital within fifty miles of where we lived at the foot of a pine-covered ridge. Where we lived wasn't even really a town. It was a sort of settlement for people like my father, who always said he liked his "elbow room."

And so, on the day they died—unless paramedics could have arrived at our house within minutes, and everyone knew that was impossible; or unless there was a doctor already at our house, but Dr. Sissinelli, our neighbor, was at his hospital—no one could have saved my sisters.

I must not feel guilty, Mama and Papa told me over and over in the days afterward, although I could see in their eyes and hear in their voices that they felt exactly that way themselves. I was not to feel guilty for being unable to call for help until it was too late or for being unable to get Papa's gun because he was out hunting for quail, they said. By the time I opened the door on the sight that would change me for the rest of my life, it was already too late. When the police asked questions about why we weren't supervised, my parents spoke up. They defended me and their choice of leaving me to watch my sisters, telling the officers what a responsible girl I was. I had done just what I should have done. I had been brave. They said that not even a parent could have suspected that Scott Early would even find such a remote place, much less grab the weeding scythe Papa had left leaning against the barn and use it like the sword of an avenging angel, striking a death blow in seconds.

I listened and I nodded, but I didn't really believe them.

I didn't want to cause Papa, and especially Mama, any more pain, but no one could say I wasn't guilty. My cousins, and my best friends, Clare and Emma, and even goofy boys like Finn and Miko, said the same thing. But it didn't matter. Even after the panic was gone, and the worst of the agony, the guilt was always there. It could never be turned off. The guilt was like using a plain magnifying glass to focus a beam of sunlight, bringing all that heat together, turning something soft and bright into something that could hurt. Even love couldn't dim it. It was the guilt that made my anger like a burn that no one ever ran under cold water; and so it kept burning and burning down to my bones. And as time went by, and other people's cooled down, mine did not. It got hotter and became a part of me, and it didn't heal until long after. Even now, I think the scars must still be there.

Chapter Two

*Y*ou can start a story anywhere you want.

And so I don't want to start with what the police found that afternoon when they finally got to our house, and not because it's too sad. There is no way that this can't be sad. I mean, even though now I'm happy in the world, there's no way a part of me won't always belong to sadness. It's my own, like the color of my eyes. My sisters' deaths are in my genetics. I only have to think of them, of the littlest thing, of putting them up in front of me on my old Percheron mare, Ruby—which was safe, by the way, because Ruby had three gaits: standing still, walking slow, and walking a little faster—and I can still start to cry so hard, just for a moment, that I can't see my charts in front of me. I just don't want to start with "the tragedy," the whomping of the helicopters overhead, people leaning out trying to take pictures of our log house, the site of the Grim Reaper murders, the interviews about us that people gave to reporters who bought sandwiches at the general store. ("They were quiet," Jackie and Barney said of us. "They were polite. Always. Friendly, but not the kind to bother you." I've wondered since, in situations like that, whether anyone ever says anything else.) All that press stuff was such a . . . mockery, though Jackie and Barney were kind and didn't mean to bring anything unwelcome on us. I ended up having my own experiences with the compulsion to explain yourself when a reporter asks you a question, so by and by, I understood.

But none of that time would tell you about the real us. That's why I also don't want to start by telling about how I flipped out, after the story was on CNN and on the front page of the *Arizona Republic*, in letters a mile high; and people drove from all over Utah and even Arizona and Colorado to our yard. They came and stood in front of our house with lighted candles, singing "Amazing Grace." About how I kept screaming that Ruthie and Becky were ours, and why did other people get to feel good about themselves, singing and crying over my sisters they never knew?

I'd like it if you could see us, just for a minute, the way we were before then. Otherwise, we'll just be set down forever as what I kept screaming that night, while my parents tried to make me stop and come inside—just another story under a newspaper headline. A tragedy that used to be the Swans.

We were an ordinary family, a little bit more Birkenstock-y than some (my mother knitting a sweater for everyone but the horse), a little more *National Geographica* than some (my father tromping around applauding at sunsets and making teas from rose hips and his own special root beer from scratch). They were semi-hippies. Sort of cute. Not obnoxious. And they were parents who were in love. When I was little, I thought everyone's parents kissed each other every time they said good morning and hello.

What a surprise I had when I got out in the world! Most people who say they're in love are just putting up with each other because they're lonely. When I saw how most marriages were, I began to hope that I'd fall in love fast and young and forever like my folks. And it's not because I wanted to be Molly Mormon (that's what some people call it, because you're sort of supposed to fall in love young and get married young and have kids right away if you're LDS. You know that means Latter-day Saints—which is the real name of all Mormons; it's the Church of Jesus Christ of Latter-day Saints), but because I really wanted to. It makes a whole lot of things in your life easier if you have another self right by your side, for all time, for all strife, someone who remembers you as well as you remember yourself.

I never wanted to get married as young as my parents, though. They were only twenty-one, but they were pretty amazing. They did everything on their own, without help, with scholarships and working right through college. They met in high school and went through his missions without anything but letters between them; but my father said he never looked at another woman after he saw Cressie Bonham, the tall girl with her long brown hair blowing every which way in the wind. The day he came home to Cedar City, he proposed. They went to Brigham Young University in Provo together and were perfect students. They tried right away to have me, but it took ten years. And that's how Mama got so passionate about art. I think she made ceramic babies from her sadness. Here she had the perfect mate, and no soul seemed to want to come to them. I think waiting for having kids might have made them closer to each other than other parents I knew who had families right away, though. They sometimes didn't have to even speak to be able to say, *I know just what you mean.*

They weren't perfect, though. I think sometimes my father thought he was the smarter one. And sometimes my mother thought the same thing. Although my father was definitely the captain of the ship, which is how it has to be, my mother got her two cents in. They had their moments.

Once, when I was really little, I heard my father say in his big radio announcer voice, "What do you expect from this conversation, Cressida?"

She said, in a voice that was a perfect imitation of him, "To have it with a person who has an *informed* opinion on the subject."

And then, as usual when she imitated him, it would crack my father up. And then they would forget to fight.

My papa says no family is normal. And we had our share of unusual people, for sure. He was one of eleven brothers, for starters. Imagine thinking up all those names. That's how my father came to be called London, because he was close to the end, and my grandparents were getting creative. They started out with Kevin and Andrew and William and wound it up with Jackson, Dante, and Bryce (like the canyon). My grandma Swan went to college and started having babies after. That was unusual too. I'm glad Grandma didn't live to know what happened. All her sons are alive, and she wouldn't have wanted to know that Ruthie and Becky died first. She has a total of sixty-eight grandchildren and great-grandchildren, and she used to send every one a ten-dollar bill on their birthday and a book at Christmas. Every one.

The other way we were unusual was that Papa was "known" as a liberal, at least for a Mormon, in our little community. When I say "community," I'm exaggerating. I'm talking *little*. Just these few houses sprinkled around Dragon Creek, which people said ran all the way down from the mountains to St. George. (Get it? St. George and the Dragon?) For about half the summer, the creek was a dry bed that hikers could jump right over. But long ago, someone had dammed a little part; and it made a swimming hole that stayed fresh, though shallow, a little longer if there'd been a lot of snow the previous winter. We considered it ours. We built a fort next to it by bending down scrubby willows and chinked up the outside with mud. It hardened like an actual building. That was our changing room in the summer. The boys just swam in their underwear when we weren't around. It was understood that we didn't swim together except suited up or at the Sissinellis' pool parties. Where we lived, it wasn't rare that it would get to a hundred degrees, and they can tell you what they want about "dry heat," it was still hot.

Cedar City, nearer by us, was not as big as St. George, but big enough to have a college and a temple as beautiful as a Russian castle. We didn't go there often. There was our little church a mile or so up to the road (I used to run as hard as I could down the road, touch the railing on the porch, and jog back home to build my wind for basketball), a post office, a place that did hiking tours, and a general store where Jackie and Barney sold everything from cappuccino to Wonder bread, from rag dolls and quilts to ice skates and gasoline. And candy. They had, like, half the store given up to candy shelves, from the fancy gold-foil kind rolled in cocoa to the forty-pack of Pixie Stix. Papa used to say Methodism was born in song and Mormonism was bred in sugar. People in Utah probably eat more sugar per person than anywhere else in the United States. They can't have anything else, so it's their addiction, you could say. There was also an old house someone converted into an antiques and rug store, open only during the fall. And that would be it.

But even in a teeny place, there were enough people around to gossip, though they wouldn't have called it that.

What people said about Papa was that he was always questioning everything, telling people that the LDS church had so much power in Utah, it was almost unconstitutional; how the church took long enough respecting black people; how he was against capital punishment—even the "humane" kind; that he would half like to move his family to New York or Michigan, where being a Mormon would be unusual and would mean something bigger to his children than living where everyone was LDS. The talk was partly because Papa's brother Pierce was the bishop for our little ward—our congregation, if you want to call it that. Uncle Pierce was about as conservative as you could get while still being normal enough to talk to. He lived nearer Cedar City than we did, but he came down for our Sunday services and for holy days and for our special family reunion, around the time of Pioneer Days, and anytime anyone else needed him to. All of Papa's brothers (except the one who lives in Alaska and married out of the church, though we still like him) and my mama's sister and brother and all their children would come to the reunion, too. . . . Every year in early July, the first day of our family festival lasted practically all night. People tented out and cooked over fires. There was live music and dancing; and adults wore these silly old-time dresses and bonnets; and everybody invited their relatives from Colorado and Illinois and all over. The little kids had a Pioneer parade on the second day. People swam and hiked and ate and rock-climbed for four days until they were worn out and ready to go back to the suburbs—away from what was normal life to us all the time. (I don't mean the bonnets and buckskin pants!)

Obviously, a lot of our life focused around our church. That's true of most Mormons. If you have Young Women's program on Wednesday night and your family says scripture together before school and then you have church for about four hours on Sunday, it can't help but be. But when that's how you grow up, you mostly don't mind it. You see the reason that the church has a plan for everything. It makes life easier. It's not like we're sheep in a herd, all doing exactly what the Prophet and his apostles—these are his sort of board of directors—say. You always have your free will. But if you're going to believe it, you might as well do it.

There were whole years when I hardly did anything but show up at church, like a shadow walking; but I did believe.

We used that building for church and everything else, too.

From looking at it, you could hardly tell it was a church. It was small, made of simple white boards, and barely had a peaked roof. But it was beautiful inside—the floor especially. Mr. Emory inlaid circle upon circle of different woods like maple, hickory, and birch. Mama (my own mother) made a small ceramic statue at the entrance, of flowers and bumblebees surrounded by two uplifted hands, because the beehive is a big symbol for Mormons, who really are always pretty busy. It was only about three feet wide and four feet tall, but it was gorgeous. It took her nearly six months, when she was pregnant with Ruthie. Inside the sanctuary, we had movable pews, but the other rooms had folding chairs that could be set in semicircles or linked together. In the back were the offices and meeting rooms. Mama taught art to local kids in one of them. The art room was made of partitions, the shelves filled with paper, easels, and supplies for painting and drawing. It even had a little kiln and a potter's wheel that had been donated to us by the Sissinelli family, after my mother wished it out loud in their presence, saying she sculpted because she had to "feel the shape of art." It embarrassed her later, that they might have seen it as hinting she wanted to sell them something, because the Sissinellis were rich. But Mrs. Sissinelli loved my mother's vases and sculptures. She ended up owning six of them and kept three in her house by the ridge. She told Mama to think of the kiln as the answer to a prayer if she couldn't think of it as just something nice to do. My mother used it when she taught art to us and anyone's kids who wanted to come on Tuesday evenings.

We also had a really small library everyone could use, made simply out of shelves facing one another on three sides. There were rooms for Sunday school for adults and the children's primary, but they were tiny, too. Only about fifty people came on a regular Sunday. A curtain with stars on it, sewn of this lush fabric, almost like a theater curtain, separated the offices from the church rooms. Some of the kids held little shows there—like *The Divine Comedy*. It wasn't like the famous one at Brigham Young University. But some of the teenagers in high school or the local college wrote and performed a Mormon *Saturday Night Live*. They started with a prayer, but then they threw light sticks and Three Musketeers and Snickers all over the crowd, running up and down the aisles. Then, the rest was music, from Motown to techno, and skits like *The Lord of the Engagement Rings*, spoofing how proud Mormon girls usually are to prove they're getting married. It didn't get too bad, but it got a little bad. Like there was this skit with a song about how California girls wear their jeans too tight, and they'll love you but they put up a fight, or something that made the parents a little tweaked and embarrassed me, too. My cousin Bridget, who had the reddest hair in our family and could write and act, and my friend Clare, who sang like an angel, were in it a couple of times.

When the Prophet—you might call him the Super Bishop, although we don't have ordained priests like other churches, because every grown man who's a good Mormon is more or less a priest—addressed us on TV from Salt Lake, all of us would gather at the little church. If a lot of guests were in town, that would mean not much room. There would be us, counting my uncle Pierce and his wife and kids; our neighbors the Emorys from next door; the Tierneys, the McCartys, the Woodriches, the Barkens, and the Lents, who lived a mile the other side of the clinic but were still in our ward; the O'Fallons; Jackie and Barney Wilder, who had no kids; and the Breedwells. Some people had family members who weren't LDS but came, too, out of curiosity.

There were lots of gentle jokes about "Brother" Trace Breedwell and "Sister" Annabella Breedwell—"Brother" and "Sister" is what you call adults if you are one and you aren't close friends. "Elders" are big leaders in the church or missionaries, but you usually don't call them that. It's normal for LDS to have big families, but with the Breedwells, we're talking majorly big even by our standards! There are different theories about why Mormons have so many kids. Personally, I think at first it was probably because they needed a lot of us when Joseph Smith started the religion so that at least somebody would survive a lot of persecution. Many Mormons still think the more Mormons the better, to spread the word, which is what missions are for. Church teachings say it's because we all live in heaven before we're born, and we have to have a lot of children to make physical bodies for those souls, like God's and Jesus's physical bodies were made, so that the souls can come down to earth and be tested. People are tested so they can become more like God, and it goes on—you go on trying to get better and doing good—even after you're dead. You can even be baptized as a Mormon after you're dead, whether you want to be or not. The guy who wrote *The Lion, the Witch, and the Wardrobe* was a devout Anglican; and he's been baptized a Mormon half a dozen times.

Unlike most people who have a lot of kids—not necessarily on purpose—most of us turn out pretty okay even if we rebel growing up.

I rebelled.

I was always stubborn. My father said my first word was "Why?"

But I was more so afterward. I seemed to need to feed on the dark side of human life. I read *Dracula* and *Wuthering Heights* and other books that were sinister and pretty evil and while not exactly forbidden, were not encouraged. I read and loved *In Cold Blood*, which is not what my grandma used to call a story that sprang from "the life source." It was a story that sprang from hell in a human heart. But I had to know about that stuff. And my mother knew perfectly well that I was reading them.

The minorly bad stuff other kids did was more the obvious kind.

Like in our small neighborhood, one person the term *saint* really didn't apply to was Finn O'Fallon, who was nineteen and barely out of high school, although he was pretty smart. Ditto the Tierney girls, Maura and Maeve, a few years older than me, who were way too into fashion and cutting it close, with short skirts and belly buttons showing, although their older sisters weren't like that. But none of them was really bad, if you know what I mean. I know that Finn, who was named after Finn Mc-Cool, this Irish hero like King Arthur or Paul Bunyan, drank coffee and had smoked cigarettes a few times. Total no-no, but not the end of the world. Maura and Maeve had gin and tonics with Serena Sissinelli, but only once.

That doesn't sound that bad, does it? Compared with ordinary kids? Believe me, I heard stories on my basketball team that would make your hair stand up. But Maura's parents were half-crazy with worry about one alcoholic drink.

They turned out okay, though, probably because Mormons spend a lot more time (I used to think too much time) with their children. My parents weren't as whacked out about spending every minute with us as some. They had a one- or two-hour date every other weekend, plus my mother worked about a day a week outside the home. That was another thing that set them apart. She was the only mother around us who had a job besides being a mother. But it's not like she went out to be a stockbroker in Salt Lake. She did her work in her studio in the shed, where there was no heat except a space heater—although my father did put in heat and new windows after she stopped using it, maybe to try to

coax her back. It didn't work, so when I got older I would sometimes stay out there when I came home, for privacy. Back when
I was young, after spending an hour or so working, she spent most
of her time with us, cooking with us, hiking with us, or teaching
us, and she had her calling, which Uncle Pierce told her was
what she should do for service, which was the art teaching.

I thought it was a little confining when I was a kid, and I
looked forward to having friends who weren't LDS—like girls I
met when I played on the basketball team at the high school,
which even homeschooled kids were allowed to do. I *really*
wanted to have friends who were Japanese or French or whatever, to be sent to some exotic place I would have to have shots
to go to; but I would have to wait for that. You didn't find a lot
of exotic people, except the occasional Japanese tourist, in the
hills near our house. When I did finally have friends who
weren't LDS, I liked a lot of them. But I would always feel there
were things I couldn't explain—not just the things I literally
couldn't explain because you can't talk about them, like the rituals, but why we are how we are. The old saying is that every
Mormon is a missionary, but I wasn't. I just kept that part of myself to myself.

The Sissinellis were the only family around us who weren't
Mormons.

They moved here just because the hills of the Pine Mountain
range are pretty in autumn and pretty warm in the winter. You
could drive in a few hours to the Grand Canyon and places to
ski and hike. They were big rock climbers, with all the gear and
helmets and junk. It's their main home—we all thought of it as
a mansion—although they have another one. They live on
Cape Cod in the summer. Dr. Sissinelli is an anesthesiologist—
the kind who makes the most money and commits suicide the
most often, or so I read someplace. I definitely did not want to

be an anesthesiologist. He had a driver who drove his car for him all the way to St. George when he went to work, so he could sleep or go over his files in the backseat. Mrs. Sissinelli was an accountant. She worked for private clients all over the country, just by Internet. They had a daughter and a son, and the son was so handsome that he looked like Johnny Depp. The daughter, Serena, was pretty, too, and really nice, not stuck-up the way you would think a girl would be who lived in a house that had three floors and an indoor pool. She got away with a lot, though—maybe not a lot by regular standards, but a lot by LDS standards. There was the night of the gin and tonics. We were all swimming in the Sissinelli pool. It was okay that the parents weren't home because Miko, the son, was a lifeguard in the summers. His real name was Michelangelo—which he would have killed Serena for telling me if he had known. We were swimming, and Serena brought the drinks down like they were lemonade, which we all thought they were until we took one sip and practically puked. Miko was, like, I'm so not into this. He got up and told no one to dive until he came back. Maeve and Maura seemed to think that they had to prove something by finishing theirs. I just sat there and watched. That was just one time, though, like I said; and they told their parents. It was normal to tell your parents pretty much everything, even the bad stuff. When Clare and I drank the Earl Grey tea we'd stolen from one of Mrs. Sissinelli's canisters, we confessed, and we barely got punished. My father said, "Everybody kicks the gate a little." We had to apologize to Mrs. Sissinelli and write an essay about caffeine and addiction. Writing that essay, I found out that Coke and chocolate also have caffeine; and I came stomping up to my father and demanded to know why I could have Coke and Hershey bars but not coffee. He laughed and said that Hershey bars weren't in the Word of Wisdom revealed to Joseph

Smith because Hershey bars weren't invented in the 1800s. But I found out that Mrs. Emory kept a year's supply of Diet Pepsi along with her year's supply of everything else, like canned tuna and peanut butter—we have to do that, to be self-reliant—so I think she had a little dependency thing going.

Anyhow, we were pretty happy.

There were about six or seven girls a little younger or older than me around us, plus the girls from basketball, who weren't all Mormons; and sometimes I stayed over at their houses on weekends. It was nice, too, that they let me—though I was a lot younger. I didn't make out with boys, but I didn't mind seeing them flirt and kiss their boyfriends. I liked it, but basketball was totally my thing, especially since I was younger. I played point guard on the Cedar City Lady Dragons—JV at high school, even when I was only twelve. There were even articles in the *Cedar City Gazette* about me that my mother cut out and put in a scrapbook, calling me the "tiny dynamo." Coach said I would make varsity by the time I was fourteen or even thirteen because of my speed, though I couldn't hit the basket even half the time under pressure, although I was Michael Jordan at the barn alone. I was the best ball handler, though, period, better than girls on varsity. I'm not bragging. That's just true. I could dribble the ball around my feet so fast in the kitchen that Ruthie would fall over on her butt trying to get it and then go hysterical laughing because she couldn't. My parents came to every game. I had this idea I could get a basketball scholarship, but then I quit growing when I got to five feet six.

Even if I hadn't, I wouldn't have been able to play anymore. But I still love to play it and see it played.

Twice a month, Papa drove me to Cedar City, where I was a "baby holder" at The Cedars Hospital. I held little babies who were being given up for adoption or whose mothers were too sick from birth to hold them very much. You were supposed to be fifteen to do this, but Papa assured them I was experienced.

We didn't have a TV.

My teammates asked, "How do you live?" But I got used to it.

We had one when I was little, and my parents let me watch (so boring) PBS stuff of adults talking about world affairs and not-so-boring animal shows; but when they got old enough, Ruthie and Becky fought over it, so out it went. But we had about forty million CDs, and not just classical or religious stuff, but rock and country, and my father had run speakers that piped sound into the upstairs. I sewed my own clothes by the time I was ten. And by the time I was twelve, I could design and draw my own, and make them, and I was good at it. We had a desk computer and a laptop, because my father said encyclopedias were outmoded the minute you got them, and we needed the information for homework. My mother did preliminary designs on the desk model for her work, and Papa's students e-mailed him papers and questions. The little girls had games, like Zoo Builder, and a program to teach them to type. Even Becky could practically touch-type by the time she . . . died. The laptop was practically mine, and I hogged it.

At night, unless it was a Monday and a Family Home Evening, when we had a lesson that was supposed to be good for your life or just played a board game, I read and IM'ed my friends. I liked to instant message my friends, even though I could see the lights in their houses from the bedroom I shared with Ruthie and Becky. My mother once told me about a town that was right up near the North Pole. And it had only about twenty telephones, but one of them had an unlisted number! That was how we were, my best friend, Clare Emory, and me. We could have just opened the window and yelled. But that wouldn't have been private. Clare and I had computers, but our next-best friend, Emma, didn't. So Clare would call Emma and tell her what I wrote. We talked about the same things everybody talks about, clothes and boys, school projects and boys. Clare and Emma both had a crush on Miko Sissinelli, too, the way I did when I was old enough to figure out what that meant; but I was the only one who admitted it. Clare would write about her plans to be a singer. She is one, now, in New York.

Clare never gave up her passion. I did. I gave up basketball. I didn't like being stared at for something other than a good play or forcing a turnover. I guess I tried to hold on but lost my passion for playing for good after . . . well, after the verdict.

I hit the math and science then. That was what I liked next best.

My father taught American literature at the high school, even though I didn't go there. He taught me, too, in a half hour or an hour a night. My mother did the rest in two hours, and that was it. "It's amazing how much you can get done in three hours a day without all the marching up and down and the crowd control and pep rallies and nonsense," my mother told Mrs. Breedwell.

"Try teaching eight at a time at home," she said. "All different ages."

"I wouldn't think of it, Anna," my mother said. "I'd be nutty as a fruitcake." But she looked away, as if she saw something far off that caught her attention. My mother has pieces she sculpted in the Tate and a glass she blew in the Museum of Modern Art. She used to sell tons of pots and vases to tourists and collectors through galleries all over the West. Papa said she was successful even if she made a hundred dollars a year because she did it doing work she loved. She made a lot more than that.

And she did love it.

She doesn't do it anymore.

She never did it again.

This made her pieces much more valuable, but only in the money sense. She'd finished dozens of glasses and ceramics that she'd never shown. When people buy them now, she gets big checks. But she doesn't care.

She wasn't gifted in the area where she wanted to be. Not everyone is, I guess.

If I think about her talking to Mrs. Breedwell that day long ago, I have to admit my mama wasn't as happy as some of the others, in a way. The O'Fallons had six children; the Tierneys, seven; the McCartys, six. Clare had four brothers. And, of course, there were the Breedwells. Nobody had less than four. My mother just wasn't blessed in the baby area. She got pregnant, but it never lasted. Or hardly ever. There were only us three girls in our family, although at the time of the tragedy, my mama was completely over the moon because she was pregnant-past-the-point-of-losing-him with our brother Rafe. (We didn't know, at the time, that he was a boy. And I say "we" because he was Ruthie and Becky's brother, too, and so was Thor, although my sisters never got to see the little boys.)

They would have loved them.

I loved them, although I was scared to love Rafe too much at first, and my parents were, too.

Raphael was born exactly two weeks after the day my mother came home and found me, in the yard, holding Ruthie and Becky, Mrs. Emory on the house phone with the police.

I have to tell it now, don't I?

Chapter Three

$\mathcal{I}$ remember all of that day.

You'd think you wouldn't. You'd think you can't imagine what you feel like at a moment like that. You would think it would all be too big. You'd faint. Or your mind would just blink out even if you were conscious. But what's the worst is that it doesn't. Or it didn't for me. I stayed right there, unable to hide for even a moment in some kind of otherworld state like people describe—as if you'd left your body behind. I can remember precisely how there was a spill of blood from Ruthie's mouth that trickled down the front of my best Saturday shirt, my UNLV jersey, and then no more blood. I didn't know then that people stopped bleeding when they died. I could see the cut in her neck like a little mouth with puckered white lips, where Scott Early had slashed her. I remember the sound of the radio from inside, of Emmylou Harris singing "If I Needed You." I remember the smell of the tortilla stew Mama had made and I was heating up for later.

I remember Scott Early, his short blond hair and his T-shirt and boxers covered with sweat and blood spatters and dirt.

No tingle of warning from my senses told me to be afraid of Scott Early, once I'd opened the door of the shed. He was like an animal that had been hit by a car, alive but gone, completely out of it. When I ran for the telephone to call 911, I didn't even think to look behind me to see if he was chasing me with the scythe. Later they told me he'd pitched it out behind the barn, as far as he could, spinning around first as if he were throwing a discus.

The operator answered on the first ring.

"A man hurt my sisters," I said. I was sweating and huffing like Ruby did when she climbed the hill with all of us on her back; but I was trying to stay calm and make sure she understood my words. For some reason, I reached over and turned on the air conditioner. It was still on days later, when it was about fifty outside.

"Are you inside?" the operator asked. "Are the doors locked?"

"No, uh, yes, I'm inside, and they're outside, and I think they're hurt really, really bad; they're cut! You have to send a helicopter or they'll die!"

"Tell me your address," the operator said. "And lock the doors now!"

"There's no reason, he already did it!" I couldn't explain why I knew that whatever Scott Early had done to Ruthie and Becky was finished, that nothing else was going to happen. "I don't, we don't have an address. We do. We have a fire number, I can't think of it! We get our mail at the post office box. Send a helicopter or something! Medevac! It's twenty miles southwest of Cedar City, on Pike Road. We're the fourth house! You have to come now!"

"Let me speak to your father," said the operator.

"He's not home! Oh, please. Please. Help me!" I was crying hard then, getting my words mixed up. I could see outside that Scott Early was standing up and sitting down, screaming and holding his head.

"Let me speak to your mother," the operator told me.

I threw the phone against the wall and ran past Scott Early

across the yard to Mrs. Emory's door. Clare was home, but she wouldn't come out of the house when she heard what I said. Mrs. Emory did, though. She kept right up with me, and I was going as fast as I could, back to our yard, though she was puffing once she got there. Ignoring Scott Early, she knelt next to Ruthie and put her hand on Ruthie's neck, on the side opposite the cut. And then she looked up at me. I saw the whole thing in her face, plain as plaid.

"No!" I screamed at Mrs. Emory. "Go home!" I didn't mean it.

"Ronnie, honey," she began, reaching out for me.

But I kept on screaming, "Don't touch them!" Clare was standing at the edge of our yard by then, with her hands over her face. I sat down next to Ruthie and pulled her onto my lap. She was all chubby and warm. "Ruth Elizabeth!" I yelled at her. "Ruthie, listen! It's Sissy! It's Ronnie!"

Mrs. Emory was trying to call Dr. Sissinelli but said she was getting the answering machine. "Damn," she said. It takes a lot for a mother like her to swear.

When I was holding Ruthie, I thought it was unfair to Becky, so, even though she was tall for her age, I dragged her up onto my lap, too. My arms were streaked in their blood, my legs in their urine. I could smell all of it. Scott Early was spinning around, a living abstract painting done in blood, sprays and spurts on his chest and shoulders and hair. Like modern pictures of Christ.

"Who are they?" he moaned over and over.

And then my mama pulled up in her car.

Mrs. Emory rushed to stop her before she got out, but pregnant as she was, Mama was out and lumbering across the drive and the yard before Mrs. Emory could hold her back. She threw herself on the ground beside us. "Pray, Ronnie," she said. "Pray as hard as you can."

I asked her, "Mama, for what?"

She stopped. She put her hands on top of her head, pressing down her hair.

Then she said, "I don't know. That they'll live, or if they don't . . ." She sat back on her heels—Mama was always limber and strong—and began to rock and rock, holding her belly.

By the time the paramedics finally got there—and this, too, I can't stop remembering—Becky and Ruthie were already starting to get cool, especially the tips of their little noses and the tips of their fingers. One paramedic put an IV needle in Ruthie's hand; but the other one, who had tears in her eyes, waved him away from Becky, shaking her head. They kept calling Cedar City on their radios. All the people in our little cluster of houses had come out by then and were standing on their porches. My mother dropped down to sit on the ground, and she reached over and closed Ruthie's blue eyes. Then she just petted their hair, humming under her breath "All the Pretty Little Horses." She sang them to sleep with that song when they were babies.

The sheriff came, got out with his gun drawn, put it away, put a blanket around Scott Early, handcuffed him, and led him into the squad car. They really do push the person's head down gently.

When Scott Early was in the car, the sheriff came over to us.

He asked me what happened, and I told him. I told another person, a police officer who drove up in a plain car and wasn't wearing a uniform, the same thing. My mother didn't say anything. The sheriff asked my mother, where was she in the house when it happened? She didn't answer, so I said, "My mother was in Cedar City. My father is hunting, because it's Saturday and he wanted to get pheasants for Thanksgiving on a day he doesn't have to be at work. I was baby-sitting." The sheriff got red in the face. He began to write on his clipboard. He asked the names of my sisters. He asked if we knew the man who was in the police car.

"I never saw him before," I said. "My sisters, they have to get my sisters to the hospital. Do you have to ask me this *now?*"

"Do you have reason to believe that he was the one who . . . hurt Rebecca and Ruth?" My mouth opened, but no sound came out. Wasn't it obvious to him? Then, I was shocked to remember that I was covered with blood. It could have looked to anyone as if I was the one who did it.

"I was in the shed. We were playing a game. When I came out, they were lying on the ground and that man was sitting on the picnic table," I said.

"Blood is all over your—" the sheriff began.

"That's because, after I ran to get help, I sat down and held them."

"You touched . . . ? I'm sorry," said the sheriff. He meant, how could I have touched someone who was all covered in blood?

I looked up at him, and I saw that the fire service paramedic van was going nowhere. It hit me then that the paramedics weren't trying to make any huge rush to a hospital. Ruthie and Becky were dead. My stomach and my heart could feel that, but not my mind.

"I love my sisters! I love my sisters!" I screamed at the sheriff. The county ambulance had arrived, and they began trying, very gently, to open my hands from around Becky and Ruthie and lift them onto plastic stretchers. I wouldn't let go of them. Everyone except my mother was embarrassed.

"Give us a moment," she said quietly.

I told the sheriff, "I held them because I thought there might be a breath of life in them! I thought maybe they could hear me saying not to be afraid. How would you like it if your sister let you die alone? How would you like it?"

The sheriff helped my mother to her feet and looked down at his own. "Not very much, miss," he finally said.

Mrs. Emory took me inside and washed my face and arms and found a clean shirt of my father's for me to wear and sat my mother in a rocker. "I want to go with them," my mother said, trying to get up.

"In good time, Cressie," said Mrs. Emory. She started a pot of water and made herbal tea and stirred the stew. "Let's think of the baby inside you, just for a little bit, just for right now."

The paramedic van was gone, and the ambulance was about to pull away when my father rattled up in his truck. He jumped out with a slew of pheasants beaded with blood, their minky feathers dulled by death, like Ruthie's blue eyes. And he was so excited. He assumed the ambulance was there because the baby was coming early, but just a few weeks early, and that everything would be all right. "Where are my girls?" he yelled. "Why aren't you out here with Mama?"

Mrs. Emory swallowed then and opened the door. And before my father could make his way over to the ambulance, where the ambulance drivers were just standing with this horrible look on their faces, as if they were frightened even to breathe, I saw Mrs. Emory say a few words to my father. Mama got up from her chair then and went to the door, leaning against the frame.

She said, "Lunny. Dearest."

Papa dropped to his knees, letting the pheasants fall in the grass. He roared and roared and roared at the darkening sky, "Father, please, precious Heavenly Father, take me! Oh, in Your bountiful mercy, most Heavenly Father, take me, take me, take me!"

Chapter Four

The reporters started to call even before the funeral. We had to figure out what calls were coming from relatives and friends and which ones were from the press. The reporters didn't make it easy. They pretended. TV trucks really couldn't come and sit on our lawn, so they parked these big white vans with KLUTZ or whatever on it and satellite dishes on top down between the trees, where Scott Early had parked. They filmed people driving down Pike Road, even people headed up to the mountains to hike.

Because the house was filled with people, including my aunts, who pretty much were concentrating on keeping my mother in bed, and because my father was called in twice to confer with the police, I was the one who answered the phone the first time.

"Are you Cressida Swan?" asked a woman. Her voice was soft and sweet, like a Sunday school teacher.

"Veronica," I told her.

"Veronica. Veronica, you're the sister, aren't you?"

"Yes," I said.

"This is the part of my job that I hate," the woman said. "I'm from the *Arizona Republic*. And my name is Sharon Winkler. We need to do a story about your sisters' death, and there is nothing I want to do less than disturb you in your grief. But it's not fair for the whole story to be about the suspect—"

"There's no *suspect* to it," I interrupted. "That man killed my sisters."

"Well, he's innocent until proven guilty, so that's how we have to refer to him. Do you remember anything about him?"

"I thought you called about my sisters," I said.

"I want to ask you if you want a chance to talk about your memories of that day," she said, and I could hear the soft click of her keyboarding on the other end.

"No," I said, "I don't. There's nothing about that day I want to talk about."

"What were they like?"

"My sisters?"

"Yes. Someone should speak for them, you see. Nobody ever speaks for the victim."

This made sense to me.

"Rebecca was in first grade. She was a good reader. She loved to swim and race, and she could run almost as fast as me. With a little kid, you usually pretend to let them win, but I had to try to beat her. She wanted to play basketball like me when she grew up. And Ruth was just a regular, girly little kid. She liked to pretend to have lemonade and cookies for her dolls, even if the cookies were made out of mud. She'd put flowers all over them. She pretended all the time. She pretended she was a princess, and I was her lady maid, or that she was Persephone and I was Demeter, mourning and searching for her daughter after she was taken"—it hit me what I was saying—"to the underworld by Hades. Mourning so that the winter came and all the crops died."

"How did she know who Persephone was?" the woman asked. "In fact, I'm sorry. Who is Persephone?"

"The goddess of the spring, in the Greek myth? I read them to my sisters. It was part of my English work. We would play out stories when I took care of them. We believe that people who die become like gods and goddesses. Not made-up ones. Like God."

"You sound like you were with them a lot. Your sisters. Like your parents left you to take care of them a lot."

"Not in a bad way," I said, suddenly frightened, although I didn't know why. "Not very much, only once a week or less, when my mother took her pots to the galleries."

"You sound like you loved them, like they didn't get on your nerves."

"They got on my nerves sometimes. But, of course I loved them. They were my only sisters. They were very different from each other, but they were really . . . cool."

"Do you hate the man who killed them? He hurt them with a sword, is that right?"

"No, my father's weed cutter."

"Was it the most horrible thing you've ever seen?" Something about her voice sharpened. It was too eager, as if she knew she was running out of time and had to get to all the gruesome stuff.

"Obviously it was the most horrible thing that I've ever seen."

"Do you hate him?"

"I don't even know him."

"But to do that to little children . . ."

"He was crying and screaming that he was so sorry. I don't think he knew what he was doing. He wasn't in his right mind. He didn't know Becky and Ruthie. They were just there, and he came across the lawn. It could have been anyone he saw. It could have been me. I . . . I hate what he did." It was confusing, the way I felt obligated to tell her everything—even more than she was asking.

"Do you wish it had been you instead?"

"No," I told her honestly, and then, "I don't know."

"You wouldn't have fought to save them?"

"I would have done anything. I would have shot him, if I'd had to. I knew how to use my papa's gun. . . ." My aunt Jill was passing through the room, with covered dishes on a tray, right then.

"Who are you talking to, Ronnie?" she asked.

"A lady from the Arizona newspaper," I said.

Aunt Jill set down the tray and took the telephone. "Why are you doing this?" I heard her say. "She's thirteen years old. She's been through something you can't imagine no matter how hard you try." She was silent as the woman apparently answered. "No, you don't know. And I believe you might care, but you don't have to go home tonight and live with this. She does. We do. I don't think you're a bad person. This is your job. But you can't call our family and ask us to describe things that are so terribly private, right now, when we can't even begin to understand the loss of my nieces or why this young man did this." She put down the phone. It rang again. "Don't pick it up again, Ronnie," she told me. "Come and see Mama." I did, but I was nervous every time the phone rang. It rang all day long, until my uncle Bryce took it off the hook.

I slept and woke up with the first of the nightmares. But I didn't want to bother anyone. The neighbors had taken in some of our relatives, and others were sleeping in sleeping bags in our library, on the floor. I tried to go back to sleep, but I just lay there, holding my comforter around my shoulders, shivering, my teeth clicking, though the house was snug and warm, wishing it would be morning so I could go down to my mother. When I heard the clink and rattle of the adults getting out breakfast dishes, I went down.

It was like a bakery.

People from Cedar City and even from St. George, who knew Mama, and the parents of Papa's students, all of them had brought rolls or bread, but mostly sweets. I ate a piece of coffee cake, because I realized I had a headache from not eating at all the day before. Then I ate another. I looked at all the Jell-O molds. People say if it weren't for Mormons, Jell-O would be out of business. That's a joke, but in truth, I have only been at a celebration twice where there was no Jell-O. We had raspberry Jell-O fish with carrots and mandarin oranges, a grape Jell-O rainbow with mandarin oranges, an orange Jell-O in a bundt cake pan with mandarin oranges.

I've never eaten Jell-O again.

My mother was lying in bed.

When I was a baby, our house didn't have two stories. It was originally just a little cabin with three acres around it. Papa wanted to leave the little settler cabin as the "heart of the house," but he had to build a family home all around it for all the children they would have. Papa and his brothers and friends took a whole summer before Papa began teaching to put on the music room and library, the big porch that went all around, and our pretty rooms and bathroom up under the eaves. There was even a nursery—but it wasn't used for the longest time because the children came so far apart and Mama couldn't bear to have them out of *her* room because she thought they would die and she just couldn't believe they were here, after losing four. Mama drew in that room sometimes because of the northern light. It supposedly makes drawing show to the best advantage even if you're drawing not what's outside, but something that's inside the room. We also had a guest bedroom that my father called the "lady nest," because it had a duvet and lace pillows and all sorts of pictures and little collections of shells and music boxes on shelves high up so that Becky and Ruthie couldn't wreck them by winding the keys backward.

When he built his and Mama's room, which Papa said used to be a "summer kitchen," where people cooked when it was hot, he was careful to put in a huge window that showed the best part of the ridge, where there are no houses. It looked the way it would have looked to the first settlers. He wanted them to be able to see the sun go down every evening, directly across from the foot of the bed. My father loved sunsets so much, they were like friends to him. But that day, my mother was looking away from the big window, away from the little window to the side that opened, at the wall. When she saw me, although she held out her arms, her eyes were not like her eyes, blue flecked with dancing specks of gold, but dull, like puddles of slush.

"I can't sleep, Ronnie," she said. "I just lie here. If I look out the front window, I see the ridge, and remember how happy Papa was when he first showed the window to me. If I look out the side window, if I see the Emorys' light go on, I think, Now they're having dinner. Now they're reading scriptures. Tim has a cold, so his mother is giving him medicine so he can sleep. Now they're reading the little boys a story. Jamie is upstairs listening to music on the computer. Now the little boys are jumping on their beds, and James is trying to get them to stop. Clare is doing her homework. They're doing ordinary things, Ronnie. We'll never do ordinary things again without this on our hearts. Is it wrong for me to want to be free, the way I was before? I watch the lights move through the house, the ones downstairs going off. The bathroom light goes on. Amy and James are brushing their teeth. I could see Clare come over and look at our house before she pulls her blinds. The little boys would be whispering, and James would be telling them this is the last time, they have to settle down right now. It's like I'm there. I can hear them. Amy is putting on her nightgown. Now their bedside lamps light up. They're reading. She's thinking about us, but she has to distract herself, because anyone would, and she thinks about her family, too, and she can't help but feel lucky. She has every reason to believe that, when morning comes, everything will be the same as it was last night. Just like I did. I thought that, too. Why did I think that? I thought we had all the time in the world, so that I didn't have to do everything at once. I didn't have to make Ruthie a trunk for her doll clothes out of that wooden shoebox I've been saving for it, because I could do that another day. Do you know how many times she asked me if today was the day I would paint flowers on her doll trunk? And how many times I told her, Soon, Ruth, soon. Things I did or didn't do without thinking about them, the ordinary parts of every morning and every night, I took for granted. Sometimes, even when I was reading to them, I was thinking about sculpting a pot or finishing a bronze before taking it to be completed, thinking about what it was I'd done that made it look awkward and how I could fix it."

I looked at my aunt Jill. She raised her eyebrows.

"Everybody does that," I told Mama. "I sing when I'm doing my homework. It's not like I'm not paying attention."

"But I had all those moments to really look at them, give them an extra ten minutes to play in the bath, or curl Rebecca's hair because she wanted it to look like yours. And instead I put it off until tomorrow. I was going to make them an Advent calendar with a drawing behind every door. I had the paper all ready, handmade paper from a gallery in Cedar City, with little streaks of gold in it. I was going to make it in the shape of a cloud, and behind every little door would be an evergreen tree or a snowflake, each one different. . . ."

"Cressie," Aunt Jill said, "you're the most wonderful mother I know."

"I was selfish. I wanted time to myself, to draw or think."

"Every human being wants that," Aunt Jill said. "You love Ruthie and Becky more than you loved anything in your life. Ruthie and Becky and Ronnie and the baby."

"I can't watch the Emorys' house anymore, Ronnie," my mother said. "I can't watch them come out and bring things in from their truck, or watch James out planing a board on his sawhorse."

That made me want to run away, because Brother Emory was a carpenter, and I knew exactly what he was making. My sisters' coffins. My father had asked him, and Mr. Emory stopped everything he was doing for other people to finish on time. Papa wouldn't let the coffins come from an undertaker. I heard him on the telephone. Papa said he would pay Mr. Emory anything. Mr. Emory said he wouldn't take a cent; he would do this out of friendship. Or I assume he said that from Papa's side of the conversation. I heard Papa thank him. My father said he wanted my sisters to sleep in wood made from the trees around our house—and to sleep in their own sheets, with their own pillows, just as they had slept in the plain little beds that Papa commissioned from Mr. Emory when they were little.

Mama kept on talking. "I can't watch them because then I'll envy them, their lives, and that's wrong, because I love them. They're my friends. I would never want them to have to be in this . . . in this place on earth with me. But everything they do or what I imagine them doing seems so precious and special to me. Nothing is ever going to feel the same, Ronnie. Taking clean sheets off the line won't feel the same, because Becky and Ruthie won't be trying to run under them. Getting dressed won't feel the same. Food won't taste . . . I don't want to eat because I know Becky and Ruthie can't eat. I try to pray because I know that's what they'd want. They hated to see me sad, like when I lost the babies. They're with the babies now, Ronnie. I know that. With their little sisters and brothers. Your sisters are lucky because they will be in the presence of our Heavenly Father; and Papa's mother, Grandma Swan, will hold all of them tight. But my prayers feel like bouncing a ball against a wall. They come back to me the same as they were before. I know they are in paradise, but this was paradise, too! I can't imagine ever wanting to make a design. I can't imagine reading a book, or wrapping a Christmas present. I wish that they were here, even the way they are now, so I could touch them and make sure they're covered up. . . ."

Aunt Jill was crying. "Try to rest. You're overwrought. Far too overwrought. Try to hide beneath the wing for now. You know how it says in the Doctrine and Covenants, 'For I shall gathereth them as a hen gathereth her chicks beneath her wings, if they will not harden their hearts. . . .'"

"My heart is a stone, Jill," Mama said.

Aunt Jill wiped her tears on the big apron of Mama's she was wearing. She said, "I honestly don't think it's possible to feel any other way right now. Here. You have to eat some of this. It's plain garden vegetable soup. A little bread. You have to think of the baby."

"I will," Mama said, and looked straight at me. "My poor angel. Why did you have to endure this? Why wasn't I here? Why didn't he kill me?"

"We can't know that, Cressie," said Aunt Jill, and I knew she was trying not to say something my mother would think right then was stupid, like that Becky and Ruthie belonged with God. "We just don't know. Even faith doesn't give you the key to mysteries. You have to lean hard now, on us and on Heavenly Father."

My mother waved her hand as if she were brushing off a gnat. "I know that," she said. "Don't think I don't need it. Or appreciate it. But in the end, I have to face this alone. London and I can face this together, side by side, but each of us will be alone."

Each of us was alone.

The second night, the night that the newspaper stories and TV broadcasts came out, all those people, hundreds of them, gathered on our lawn and began to sing "Amazing Grace." They brought bouquets of flowers and teddy bears and put them by our door. We all sat there, except for Papa, who slipped out the back window of my room and slid down the fire ladder, the way I sometimes did to meet Clare, and went walking up on the hills.

Finally I said, "Aunt Jill, make them stop. They shouldn't be here at our house."

"Ronnie," she said, "I think I know how invaded you feel. But these are good people. They want to tell us how sad they are."

"But they're crying!"

"Of course they're crying!"

"It's not their place to cry! Ruthie and Becky were ours. Now it's like they're making them theirs, too."

"When children die—" my aunt began.

"Make them leave, please," I begged her.

"Listen, Ronnie. When children die, people give their tears as a blessing. They want to show they share the pain you feel."

"But how can they share it? What they want to feel is part of it. It's like a big show!"

"I think they mean it kindly," said Aunt Jill.

"They might mean it kindly, but I can't stand them being here. We have enough tears, just in our family."

"How can there be too many tears, Ronnie?"

I turned away from her and opened the door and stared at the crowd of people, who were by now singing "Imagine."

I shouted, "Please go home! My mother is sick and is having a baby. Please go home. She has to rest."

The TV reporters rushed on me then, just like you see in movies. *Veronica*, they said, *we heard you tried to shoot the man before he killed the kids. Veronica, do you think Scott Early should get the death penalty if he's convicted? Do you think you could have killed him? Has this changed your life forever? Will you ever be able to . . .*

I began to cry, then scream. I picked up the wooden apples my mother had carved and painted, that we kept in an old bowl on a shelf by the door, and began to throw them at the people with the cameras. My uncle Bryce took hold of both my arms, but I fought him, kicking and trying to bite him (although I later apologized). This was all on film. I looked like a hyena, with my teeth clenched and my hair sticking out of its braids. SISTER'S RAGE AT MOURNERS SHOCKS COMMUNITY.

My father came back then, and right away he drove to Dr. Pratt's house, nearly all the way to town. He almost drove over camera equipment, and the press people hollered. Dr. Pratt gave Papa pills. When my father got back, I was still screaming, "They're ours! They're ours!" I don't remember a whole lot of this. Papa made me take two of the pills, with milk. The pills tasted like the astringent I put on my face so I wouldn't get pimples. But in a few minutes, they made me feel calm. Then they made the room begin to revolve slowly. Then I fell asleep, and when I woke up, it was one o'clock the next afternoon.

My sisters' funeral was at three.

Chapter Five

As far as I was concerned, my uncle Pierce spent way too much time at my sisters' funeral trying to get all of us to commit ourselves to being good and studying scripture, and way too little time on the little girls. "Brothers and sisters, we will miss with all our hearts the sweet ways of Ruth Elizabeth Swan and Rebecca Rowena Swan, my nieces, my brother's children. But they are the fortunate among us because we know the truth. We know what has been revealed to us by the Prophet, the word we live every day, and so we can rest in the truth that they already know the joys of the most exalted celestial realm. But we, left behind, must endure to the end . . ."

I didn't listen. I didn't like Uncle Pierce then.

Uncle Bryce spoke, too, about the importance of family being like a body that helps heal the part that is wounded. That was better, but it still was about us, not about my sisters.

We sang.

A former bishop spoke.

Already, there was black rain inside me.

I stared at the plain little polished boxes with their golden hinges and thought of being in the little room outside the chapel in the funeral place where they let us look at Ruthie and Becky.

I had picked out their clothes.

Aunt Gerry had put out their best dresses on the beds the pre-vious afternoon, before all the idiot singers came. She tried to do it so no one would notice what she was doing. But I did. When I came in, after talking to Mama, I told her as gently as I could, "I'm sorry, Aunt Gerry. But those particular clothes were clothes they hated. I wouldn't want them to have to wear them . . . now."

My aunt didn't argue with me, the way some adults might. Aunt Gerry was young, the wife of my father's youngest brother. She had short hair in a shag, and she liked to dance and have tickle fights with us. She had only one baby, baby Alex, who was four months old. He was asleep between two rolled-up quilts on Ruthie's bed. Ruthie's pillow was already gone. "What do you think would be better, Ronnie?" she asked me.

I went to their closets and got out Ruthie's plaid kilt and her red-and-black "silky sweater"—the one that used to be mine when I was little but still didn't have any pills or snags on it, prob-ably because I hardly ever wore it unless I was forced to. I got out her black tights and I took off my own ID bracelet of silver beads with my initials, RS, for her to wear. My friend Jenna from the basketball team gave it to me when I was named Rookie of the Year; and though they weren't my real initials, which would have been VS, they were Ruthie's. For Becky, I found, folded on her shelf with the stuffed bear she called Blueberry, her Cinderella dress. This wasn't appropriate. But I had made that dress for her, and she tried to wear it almost every day. It was just a plain, mod-est dress with a white top and puffed sleeves, one little ribbon of gold rickrack on the neck, and a sky blue skirt so full that it would accommodate her little tummy so she could twirl. It wasn't that clean. With all of my heart, I wanted to keep that dress. It smelled like Becky—of cocoa and her soapy little head she never quite got rinsed because of the thickness of her curls. But I knew she would want to twirl and twirl and play dress-up in heaven. A little goddess should be able to wear a princess dress. With it, I placed her socks printed with black kittens on them. The colors were all washed out and the elastic stretched so when she wore them, she had to keep pulling them up. They were not her best, but why should she have to give them up now? She loved them because they reminded her of our cat, Sable. Every time my mother tried to put them in the rag bag, Becky got them out and put them back into her sock drawer. When I was finished, I brought all these things to Aunt Gerry. "Maybe the Cinderella dress isn't—" I began.

"I think you're right," my aunt Gerry said. "These are better than the ones I picked."

"I don't know if Uncle Pierce would think it was . . . like, sacrilegious or something," I said.

"Well," Aunt Gerry said, "I don't know of any rules about anything like that. I think we should just do what we think is right." She folded the clothes and put them in a box to take to the funeral place. At the last moment, I ran after her and gave Blueberry bear to her. That was even harder than the dress. I would have their books and their drawings.

But not Blueberry bear.

It had rained overnight. Papa had bagged up all those candles and wreaths and teddy bears and taken them to the Lutheran church out past the mall, off the highway. Our yard was our normal yard again. The rain had washed away the chalk marks and tattered the yellow tape. Uncle Bryce tore down the last of it just before we left, because our family would come back to our house and he didn't want them to see crime scene tape the first thing.

When we drove, I was in the backseat alone. I could see the Emorys' car in front of us the whole way.

The only thing Mama said, and just once, was, "The baby's moving."

My sisters' names were on this little board outside the funeral parlor, where they usually would put a Bible verse or something if it were a church. It was as if this were a movie about Becky and Ruthie—which is exactly how I felt, as if I were going to a movie that would be over soon. Papa had on a tie and his good black cashmere jacket, the one he wore to his brother Bryce's wedding and to services the day Uncle Pierce's sons left for mission; and Mama was wearing the long, loose purple velvet dress she wore to art galleries. Though I didn't know this, as she lay in bed, she had drawn charcoal sketches of Becky and Ruthie.

Ruthie was running away up the ridge, looking back and grinning. Becky was sitting in a circle of sunlight, holding her bowl filled with berries. Mama had stretched the sketches on little stick frames Papa must have brought to her. With my father holding one of her arms, she carried the sketches under the other arm as we walked in. All our relatives filled the place to overflowing, but they stopped hugging and touching me when the funeral man asked if we wanted our private visit.

Just the three of us.

It was cold in there, in the little room with soft pale blue curtains and recessed lights that I saw, when I looked up, were pink. The coffins were on little white stands, painted, but basically just like Mr. Emory's sawhorses. My older cousins would carry them into the chapel room when the time came.

When I saw my sisters wearing those clothes, with their flannel blankets tucked up over their shoulders under their arms and their pillows under their heads, I wanted to agree with the Arizona newspaper lady: I did want to die. There was no way to tolerate it. There was no way to lean on God. I wanted to get down on the floor and hit my head until I passed out, or scream and scream. I wanted to make it thunder. But I could do nothing that was big enough. It wouldn't be right. Later, when I looked up ways of grief, like you'd look up ways of celebrating Christmas around the world, I discovered that if I were a Muslim or an Irish girl, I'd have been allowed to scream and cut my hair and clothes. I think I should have. Seeing Becky and Ruthie with gloomy little motionless smiles, with their very same fingers that I'd had to wash jelly off of two days before holding little white roses, Becky's bear with its head on the pillow next to her, I couldn't stop crying, and not crying like a twelve-year-old, crying like I did when I was a little kid and broke my elbow wiping out on my bike. I cried so hard that I had to go into the little bathroom and throw up. When I came out, Mama was swaying as if she were going to fall, but Papa held her up. He said, "I love you, Cressie. I love our children." His mouth was squeezed tight, though, and his voice sounded like it did when he argued with Uncle Pierce. I know he was angry. I was angry, like him, but also sad, like Mama.

Mama turned down Ruthie's collar and saw how they'd sewed up the cut. It was sewn with pink-flesh-colored thread.

"It's so small now," she said to me. "It looks like such a little cut." She reached for the corner of the blanket around Becky's neck, but Papa held her hand back. We knelt down. Papa blessed Ruthie and Becky for the last time, just as he had every night of their lives and every morning before he left for school, and then he blessed Mama and me. Papa had his own way of doing things.

The funeral guy asked if we wished to kiss them or take a photograph. Mama put her fingers to her lips and touched each of my sisters' lips. "I don't want to feel them . . . not be warm," she said. The man nodded. Papa kissed the tops of their heads. I asked for a pair of scissors. The man hurried out of the room, and Mama and Papa looked at me, at first strangely, then accepting.

That Christmas, during the long days of the holiday tournament I had been so excited to play—but now couldn't because I was in mourning *and* in the newspaper—I wove together the lengths of Ruthie's auburn hair and Becky's dark brown hair into braids so tiny and tight that it was easy to form them into a ring. When I wore it on a chain, people thought it was made of some kind of exotic reed, and I never corrected them. I never told anyone, and I never wore it around my parents. I could have put it in a locket, but over time it grew as hard as deer horn. I felt that this was their wish for me, to keep. Once, on a picnic, the chain broke and I was practically hysterical until this boy I was friends with found it. People had looked for it for an hour. I still wear it when I need courage. The only time I was ever in the hospital, the nurses even taped over it so I could keep it on. I used the jewelry set I'd been given at my birthday to make a chain and I soldered the links.

That day, when I was finished cutting a lock of their hair, which still felt just as soft and real as my sisters had felt, I walked out of the room while the funeral director closed the boxes in front of my mother. I heard my mama's little shriek. I knew Papa would place the sketches on top of each coffin. I kept on walking, out to where my cousins were.

Normally, when we got together, we couldn't stop talking. Allie, Bridget, Sandrine, Bree and Tonya, Conor, Mark, Joel, and I were all the same age. Our parents usually had to scold us to go to sleep at the camp-out, and we still didn't stop, not until the stars were faint in the sky. But today, Bree and Bridgie just took my hands and led me into the room where the service would be, and they sat next to me on a big sofa. My friend Emma came and stood beside us. Bridget moved over so she could sit down, too. My parents sat up in front.

Clare got up to sing the hymn. But she didn't sing a hymn, or not right away. She bit her lip and looked at my mother and at my uncle Pierce.

Then she sang "Somewhere over the Rainbow."

Everyone was shocked at first, but then everyone except my aunt Adair cried. The birthmark on her neck got redder, the way it did when she was mad. But my aunt Gerry cried so hard, she had to get up and leave the room. Aunt Adair looked even more furious. Clare then sang the children's hymn "I Will Go Wherever You Lead Me," I think it was. Everyone sang, I think. I'm not sure. I always think of her singing "Somewhere over the Rainbow" and knowing it was for Becky and Ruthie and me, that we would meet somewhere, where all the clouds would be far behind us. This might have been okay at a Gentile funeral, but not at an LDS funeral. On the other hand, no one was going to stop her.

Papa and Mama didn't seem to notice I wasn't with them.

This turned out to be how it would be in general.

When our relatives finally went home, Papa wasn't even around the house to say good-bye.

He'd taken a leave of absence until the end of the Christmas break, and all he did was walk. He walked in the rain and in the snow and in the night. He lost twenty pounds in three weeks. Mama, as out of it as she was, said thank-yous to everyone for him. Everyone said they understood. Papa walked in the woods and over the tops of the hills until dawn that first night. And the night after that. Sometimes he'd come in at two or three in the morning. Some nights I would find him asleep in his clothes and boots on the couch. He and Mama had a little bed, for adults, that is—what you call a full-size bed. Most people's parents have queen-size or king-size. It was because they liked to remind themselves to sleep close together. But Mama was so big by then that Papa had been sleeping on a blow-up bed on the floor next to her. He would sleep there after the baby came, for a little while, until the baby was ready for a cradle in their room. On the nights he walked, even if it was cold and the wind was screaming around the house, he would come into my room, and I would almost wake when he put his hand on me and blessed me. But when I'd open my eyes, he'd be gone.

What I did was, I cooked.

That is, I thawed out things Sister Emory and Sister Finn and the others brought and put them in the oven at 350 degrees until they looked more or less done. I cut up three portions, which I put on plates. We ate whatever was in the freezer. I was glad we had a chest freezer in the barn, although I had to ask Papa to carry things out there for me or make a dozen trips. Cornbread and venison casserole. Wild rice soup. Tamales and scalloped ham, and cake, cake, cake. We had cakes enough for a hundred birthdays. Pineapple and caramel and six kinds of chocolate cake. There were ladyfingers and raspberry angel food. It got like the Jell-O. When I was in school later and craved something, it would always be salty. I ate cake in those weeks as if it were bread because there was no bread, and I couldn't drive and I didn't know how to make bread yet. I didn't like to ask Mrs. Emory, because she'd done so much.

Some nights, when Mama was asleep—she slept most of the time after taking her shower—I would climb out my back window and meet Clare at the willow fort. We'd have on our coats and mittens and wrap ourselves in blankets. Sometimes we'd break branches, and Clare would bring a log and we'd start a fire in the fire pit. Emma was sending her love but couldn't bear to talk to me, Clare told me. She was afraid she'd say something stupid. The girls from the team had sent me a ball with things written on it: "Impossible Is Only a Word." "Be Strong." "We Love You." Clare asked me if it helped. I said that it did, but it was like the singing of the strangers outside our door. I thought that they felt if you just did something nice, you got to be part of it, plus it let you off the hook. They got to give me a ball, and Coach sent a plaque that said a star had been named Rebecca Ruth by the International Star Code. A couple of times Clare and I tried to see it. The documents said it was in Orion's belt. We could never find it.

"Can we ever be friends like we were before?" Clare asked me one night. I thought about it. We were making a big fire that night in the fire pit because it was cold and we had sleeping bags, with the intention of sleeping out.

We didn't make it all night, for obvious reasons.

"Not like before," I said. "You'll always be my best friend. I don't mean that. But right now, I don't know if I can ever have fun again like we did. Where you just do what you're doing right then."

"You mean like a kid," Clare said. That was exactly what I meant. Clare always understood.

"Right now, I think I left that fun back there," I said, pointing back toward our yard, "but I'm not sure. I've never been through anything like this. Maybe you get better."

"Do you miss them?"

"I can't say I miss them. It's like they're not gone. Their clothes and toys are still there, all messed up, in our room. Every time I pick something up, I find a doll shoe or a barrette. Maybe I have to let them go before I miss them. Maybe I don't want to miss them, because once that starts, that's how it'll be for my whole life."

"My mother had a brother who died."

"She did?"

"Yes, but he was a baby. He had whooping cough, before they had the good vaccine. She doesn't remember." Clare wasn't saying something. We knew each other that well. I nudged her. "She said her mother was . . ."

"Never the same. Was she truly strange? Was she nuts?"

Clare said slowly, "No."

"She was like my mother is now."

"Yes. But she was like that forever."

"I don't think my mother will be like this forever. In the fifteenth century, when a knight died, his lady had to go to bed immediately, for six weeks."

"Neither do I," said Clare. "Your mother is the strongest—"

"The knight's lady didn't even go to the funeral. She was considered too delicate. And my mother, though she is a strong person, anyone . . ."

"Anyone . . ."

"This is beyond anything—"

"*And* she's pregnant . . . and if she loses the baby . . ."

"She won't lose the baby. It's too late to lose the baby."

"Does she wish she weren't having the baby?"

"She doesn't talk."

"Oh," said Clare.

"Would your mother?"

"Talk or want the baby?"

We heard the shouting then. Bellowing. Shouting from my house. Oddest thing, neither of us got up. If something had gone badly wrong, like my father had cut his foot chopping wood, we didn't want to know. We didn't have to say it, but we wanted the adults to take care of it. We just wanted to sit there and be twelve for a very short time.

But finally Clare got up slowly, and so did I.

My dad was shouting for me to hurry and get in the car. The baby was coming.

Chapter Six

My mother's labor was practically luxurious.

For her. Not us.

She had a lot to occupy her mind.

We had nothing to do but worry.

She got into the hospital at about eight that night, and Raphael Rowan Swan was born at midnight exactly, the first moment of December 6. Papa said it was a lucky day, St. Nicholas Day. The rowan tree is a mountain ash. Papa said it symbolizes divine inspiration and spiritual protection from harm in lots of stories and traditions. It's lucky to have one outside your house, they say, and in old legends from Finland, it's said the branches and berries are "holy." If you have one, it grows, as ours did, right into the trunks of Scotch pines and other trees without hurting them—Papa said that would be the way Raphael would grow into our family. Some nature religions use the rowan tree as part of their rituals, and I asked about that. People call it witchcraft, and real witchcraft is evil. I didn't want evil to touch the baby. Papa said that was poppycock, though; they were just a bunch of people who hadn't got to the point of choosing the power of our Heavenly Father over a tree. He said that stuff had nothing to do with how pretty the name was and its old meaning, and that the Father understood.

Anyhow, Raphael Rowan sure protected Mama from harm.

At least that night. For all three girls, Mama had been in labor almost a whole day. Not this time. She barely yelped.

I wasn't permitted to go into the delivery room, but I wouldn't have anyhow.

We were scared that the baby would be sick or have something wrong and that this would kill my mother. We were also scared it would be a girl, Papa as much as I was. All we'd ever had were girls. Whenever Papa came out and said things were going fine-just-fine, he also told me that he wished he'd let them tell him the baby's gender at the ultrasound. But now he didn't want to ask the nurses to find the doctor, for fear of alarming Mama and getting her hysterical. Both of them thought *before* that it would be fun to be surprised. I was horrified by my own feelings. I wasn't sure I could love a baby girl. Would I be able to even fake a smile? Now or ever?

I buried my head in *A Raisin in the Sun*, which Mama had assigned me for over break a long time ago and then forgotten. I kept going back to look at the poem at the beginning. The one by Langston Hughes about a dream deferred. What happens? Does it wither or corrode, or does it explode? I was thinking of my mother's dream deferred, of enough children to fill that big house with the funny little rooms. Deferred forever. Had Rafe been born three weeks earlier, my mother would have had her four children. At that time of day, we'd probably all have been over here. I wouldn't have been alone at the house. Definitely my father would have been home, as he got paternity leave for three months; and he wouldn't have gone hunting and left my mother with a newborn baby. Other ladies wouldn't have looked away, the way they did if they didn't know Mama, because they assumed that because she had only a baby and a daughter much older, she'd been widowed young or divorced. She wouldn't have had to wonder whether this look was something that was in her own mind or really there.

But the looks she would get now would be for real, if Mama told people the truth of why our family was spread out the way it was.

In the hospital, everyone already knew. I used to think of nurses like I thought of doctors, as superior people who didn't gossip or lie. But what I heard outside the room that night, from the obstetrical nurses, made me sick.

"You know Swan in 204 is the mother of those little girls that got their heads cut off."

"Get out."

"The sister was involved. My neighbor said the killer was her boyfriend."

"That's ridiculous. She was just a kid herself. Don't you remember? No, you're usually on A.M.'s. Her dad was that big, handsome guy who teaches at the high school? And he used to bring her here in the evenings to hold babies?"

"It was that kid? She was a nice kid. She would never have a boyfriend. . . ."

"Don't be so sure. . . ."

"And everyone knows Mormons don't let their kids have boyfriends."

"I heard the guy was a Mormon priest."

"There's no such thing as a Mormon priest, not the way they have in regular religions. I'm a Catholic, but I know that much."

"No, all good Mormon men are priests, and women leaders, just some higher up in our orders. We're a church with leadership in every home, as well as a council of—"

"Did you see her on TV? How the sister acted?"

"Anyone would feel like that. Lisa, her sisters were murdered."

"She didn't have to treat nice people like scum. They were just trying to be supportive."

"Mormons think everybody else is scum, no matter who they are."

"We do not. Unenlightened, but not scum." They laughed again.

My face got hot, and I raised my book to hide it.

"Do you think the baby will help her or . . . ?"

"I know I wouldn't want to have one right after something like that."

"Not that she has any choice." Laughter.

"Maybe it will be their salvation."

"I hope."

They bustled back and forth while my mother's moans rose occasionally to a cry—inside her room telling her she was doing great-just-great and outside saying things like that.

"Do you think they were involved? On TV, half the time, it's the parents."

"They're nice people."

"Anyone can look nice."

It was a small waiting room, and I finally got up all my courage and lowered my book. I coughed.

I said, "Excuse me. Please don't say these things. Everyone can hear you. I'm Ronnie Swan. Those were my sisters who died. That's my mother and father in there. My mother could hear you. Why would you think my mother would hurt my baby sisters? Why would you say such bad things about me? You don't know me. You don't know if I'm a bad kid or a nice kid. And my mother wasn't even there."

They all got quiet. You could hear a lady down the hall say a swear word. Then one nice nurse burst out crying. She started to walk away down the hall, but then she turned back and said, "I'm very ashamed. I'm very ashamed about what we said."

Another one said, "Me too. We were just being big gossips."

I said, "I forgive you. Please don't say it anymore, though. This is hard enough for us."

The not-as-nice nurse got tears in her eyes then. "Do you want anything, honey, like some tea?"

I said, in a kind of snotty way, I guess, "Just some water. Or a Seven-Up, please. We can't have tea. And it's not because Mormons think other people are bad. It's just the rules. Like my mother said Catholics used to have to eat fish on Friday. And Jewish people can't have shrimp." The not-as-nice nurse got me a can of 7-Up, and the really nice one came back from the bathroom, her eyes all red. She sat down next to me.

"Is there anything I can do to make this up to you? I have a daughter your age, and a daughter who's seven years old. I'm so sorry," she said. And then she reached out and held me, hard against her. She smelled all lemony and clean, the way nurses do; and she held me as though she already knew me. "Poor kid," she said. "You poor little kid."

Then the doctor was running into my mother's room. And I could hear my mom sort of groaning and huffing and puffing. "Don't be scared. Looks like your baby is coming."

I don't know why, but I asked, "Do you think the baby will die?"

"Heavens, no," said the nice nurse, the one who was a Catholic. "Honey, most babies are healthy. Cross my heart. Wait! I hear somebody crying! Big strong cry! Thank the Lord." We stood up. My father came out and I ran to him and he picked me up, like when I was little.

"It's a boy, Ronnie—a big, beautiful boy, nine and a half pounds," he said. "Thank the Heavenly Father." His eyes were red, too.

The nurses put a cot in the room for me that night and one for my dad. My mom started to cry only once. She said, "He looks just like Ruth."

Now, to me, he didn't. He just looked like a red, squished, little tiny man, fists held up next to his face as if he were mad. But I've observed that this is the first thing all parents say—how a baby who actually looks like any other baby is just the absolute picture of one of their relatives.

At first, I wouldn't hold him.

"It's okay," Papa said, "you won't hurt him."

"It's not that," I told him. "It's that I'm afraid he'll get bad feelings from me. That I don't love him. I'm afraid I won't love him."

"He'll teach you to love him, Ronnie," my father said. "I promise. He won't take away the hurt from losing your sisters, but he'll teach you to love him. Babies have a way of healing people. They're so innocent, and they need you so much."

I finally did hold him, when he woke up and my mother was asleep. He held my hand. I stroked his cheek with my fingers. He felt softer than the down under Ruby's chin. He had lots of dark hair and little rosy stick legs. "It's you and me, bub," I told him. But I still couldn't trust myself. There was a huge gap between him and me, not just in age. He lay there looking surprised, like someone who'd showed up at a party on the wrong day.

My parents took Rafe home the next morning. My mother was fine, and she didn't want to be in the hospital. We took this as a good sign.

It wasn't.

She didn't want to be anywhere else, either. She fed the baby and changed his diapers. But she didn't sing or talk to him. After a week, my father called the doctor. It wasn't, like, normal "blues." The doctor said Mama couldn't overcome her fear to bond with the baby.

That made three of us.

Chapter Seven

*I*t was after Rafe was born that the panic just smashed into me, like when you're fouled and it knocks you off the court and into the wall. I'm a strong person physically, but the panic was stronger than I was. It felt like I was made of little twigs. On the day of the murder, even, I didn't feel overwhelming fear. What I felt was unbelievable wretchedness and anxiety. But not fear. This new companion was someone I'd never met before. It was like what I remembered from having hives when I was little, after I ate my first and only oyster. The itch that kept at me all day, until I was concentrating on nothing except trying not to concentrate on it.

But the nights were worse. Before I could fall asleep, before the nightmares, the fear would settle like cold syrup in my stomach. I had been a sleeper. Used to dive into my soft bed. Slept like a log. I had a buckwheat eye mask because my father didn't believe in curtains ("Hell take curtains!" he would say, quoting some poet). I had earplugs because Ruthie snored. Papa once said I considered sleep a sacrament.

But within a matter of weeks, I could hardly sleep at all.

Instead, I got obsessed with security. First, it was the locks.

We had never locked our doors, and we didn't know anybody except the Sissinellis who did. They did only because they weren't there half the time and because they had valuable clothes and objects. We didn't, unless you counted people; and my father had never spent a single night away from home.

Still, that winter-into-spring, I could think of nothing but Baby Rafe curled up in his wrappie with some horrible person standing over him while my mother slept on and on and on and my father, outside somewhere, walked on and on and on. I would get in bed, set my alarm, turn on my computer, and then up would crawl this creepy idea that maybe I forgot to lock the side door. Papa had his key for the front door, since I'd taken to locking it, but he never even thought about the side door, so I had to. I checked it every night. But then I started wondering if I'd forgotten. I knew I hadn't forgotten. I never forgot. But maybe I had. Stop it, I'd tell myself.

I'd start an instant message to Clare, and then I'd have this bizarre feeling in my throat, as if I'd swallowed something like an aspirin without enough water to dissolve it. An acid taste built up on the back of my tongue at the thought of having left a door ajar, practically a neon sign inviting someone to slip into our house. My heart would start to thump. It was totally absurd. But I couldn't get that thought to go up or down. It stayed stuck. So I would have to go all the way back down there and check that screen door. And the windows. The kitchen windows and the window in the little cellar where we stored fat wood to start the stove and the one in the bathroom my parents kept cracked because of the shower steam. All of them had to be shut.

Later, much later, a teacher would tell me that the taste in my mouth was adrenaline, a physical reaction to a sound, even if it was a sound I wasn't aware I was hearing. The sound reminded me of the sound of the shed door hitting the wall the day my sisters died. That sound started me not just remembering the murders, but reliving them with my body—though I wasn't at all conscious of it. And she was right. I couldn't sleep because I was having adrenaline rushes, fight or flight.

The upshot was, I had to be content with little handkerchiefs of rest to try to wipe away the smear of the panic as it dripped, dripped, dripped down on me. I couldn't think straight. Even physically, I changed. All girls smile at themselves in the mirror, as if we're having our picture taken for magazines. We can't help it. We do our hair different ways a couple of times in one morning, even if we're not going anywhere, and look over our shoulders at ourselves in the mirror. Like, I had to make sure all my curls were distinct, because they were natural for me, but other girls had to use twisty rollers to get theirs. After Rafe was born, I looked in the mirror only to see if I was clean. I was always clean. But my face was like a mask. A mask with eyes in it that were the only thing that looked alive. My mouth didn't move. When I tried to move my mouth, it opened only a little, like a gasp with a little tip up at the corner. You don't know, until you don't have it, that expressions require energy. It would be normal for me to look pale in winter, paler because I didn't go outside anymore, into the wind and sun. But I looked like I lived underground. There was Mama, who slept like sleep was her job; the baby, who slept like a baby; and Papa and me—two other people pretending to sleep so as not to wake the others up. Except for Rafe, we were basically zombies who sometimes ate, not even together.

I tried everything in the world to exhaust myself back into my regular routine.

I ate cookies with warm milk before bed, because sugar, or so I'd learned as a child in health, quiets you down, and so does lactose or whatever is in milk. Once I got started, I ate cookies and drank milk until I sloshed. All that did was make me gain five pounds. Next, I jumped rope in my room until Papa told me I was making their bed shake. I played hundreds of games of solitaire. Finally (bad idea), I opened Becky's little *Book of Remembrances* to any page, to see if there would be a message there that would give me some peace. The page I opened read, "I aM RebBeca SWAN. A swan is like a birD, but bigger. I am a very fast runner. The faster runner in my hole class. I want a sled and a dog for Christmas. A sled dog to pull my SLID yup the mountin. Santa comes at Christmas. We have a stove but he has a way of coming through the wall. My Sister is named Sissy. She plays the hoops, but somtime she travling." That made me want Becky so bad, I had to bite my pillow. I didn't dare look at any more pages.

Sissy, Sissy! I wanted to scream.

"My Sister is named Sissy. . . ."

I read *The Iliad* to try to bore my eyes so badly, they'd have to shut.

When I did fall asleep, the dreams came. Variations of the original nightmare. I saved Becky and Ruthie; and Ruthie just cried from relief and hugged me, but Becky said, "My Sissy is so brave!" I stood there with the gun in my hand, and Scott Early lay on the ground, bleeding from the leg, like a doll growing whiter and whiter.

At night, in the lamplight, with the hall darkened, I began to see Becky peek at me around the bedroom door. Always Becky, not Ruth. I'd see the flick of her dark silky hair, the heel of her red Mary Jane shoes. I wouldn't have been frightened to see Becky—if I knew that there were earthly manifestations of people who died and that they visited the living. I'd have coaxed her into the room, gotten her to sit on the bed, tried to touch her. But though I realized I was having a sort of hallucination from sleeplessness, now Becky scared me. Everything scared me. The boiler going on scared me. A branch that hurled itself against my window with a clatter scared me. A car door slamming up at the Sissinellis scared me. One night, when a small boulder rolled down the hill (and boulders had rolled down and cracked against the ridge rocks since I was a baby), I rolled out of bed like a boulder myself and lay flat on the floor. Then I got up and surfed the Net until it got light.

When the sun rose, the fear cleared out of my room like smoke through a screen. I could breathe better in daylight. I could let go because I wasn't holding the world together by myself. I could see the Emorys and the Finns moving around outside. They could hold the world up for a while. But, of course, I couldn't go to sleep then. I had to get up and do what I was supposed to.

I knew that Scott Early was in jail. But I got my mind set on the idea that before I could stop him, he would kill Mama or Rafe. Or even Papa. I didn't think of myself. I don't know why. I just knew I couldn't lose anyone else or I would go permanently crazy. You had to have a lifetime quota. I reassured myself that mine was met; I had nothing to worry about. But the fence of my life had been breached, like the Alamo.

So I decided, my mind not quite what it was, that I would try to learn self-defense from online courses and also learn to protect my home more effectively. I asked Papa to set up a firing range next to the barn and teach me how to load the shotgun better and faster. Papa looked at me for a long time before he went to unlock the gun. He didn't say anything. He spent an evening showing me all over again how to first clean and then load it, faster than before. In the morning, he set up fat chunks of logs with a can on top of each one, the cans filled with rocks that kept them still in the wind. He showed me where to stand.

I went out there once and did a pretty good job filling the

cans with holes. Miko came driving past in his family's truck and yelled, "Hey, Annie Oakley!" But when I lowered the gun and looked at him, he stopped the car and got out.

"I'm sorry, Ronnie," he said. "When did you take up shooting?"

"It's something to do," I told him. I clicked the safety on the gun and broke it so it was useless.

"I'm used to seeing you shooting baskets at the barn," said Miko.

"That's what I should be doing, if I ever want to play again," I said. And I sighed.

"I'd shoot with you," Miko said. "Baskets, not . . . the gun."

"No," I said.

"You liked it when I would come over and play 'make it take it' with you when you were little."

"I'm not little anymore," I said. "And besides, it's not your sport."

"What do you mean?" he asked, leaning against the truck and trying to make a grass whistle. Even the holes in his jeans were perfect.

"I mean I'd trash you," I said. "I don't mean that in a bad way."

Miko put his head back and laughed. "Get your ball, little girl," he said.

"I don't feel like it that much."

"Well, now you insulted my manhood, you see."

"I said I didn't mean—"

"Come on, get your ball."

I stood the gun beside the barn and slumped over to the shed. I hadn't even opened the door of the shed once since, and my breath started to come fast just having to cross the dusty floor to where the mesh bag with my balls in it leaned against an inside wall. I will not act like a nutcase in front of him, I told myself, breathing out slowly through clenched teeth. "You go ahead and start," I told him, bouncing it to him on the hard-packed dirt.

"Ladies first," he said, bouncing it back.

I drove straight down the imaginary lane, and when Miko started waving his arms in front of me, I just turned my back and shot half over my shoulder. The next time, he was on me when I took my first step, so I faked a shot and then drove in. He used up a lot more effort than he needed to, chasing me. The third time, he leaned in, trying to pike, trying anything to stop me. He did get his hand on the ball for a moment, but I stopped and grabbed it back and pivoted away from him to shoot it over his shoulder. Swish. He was all ready to jump up for it the next time, so I faked a drive to throw him off balance. Miko retrieved the ball after I sank it, and when he threw it, he threw it hard. Since he had some size on me and a lot of upper-body strength, it would have hurt if it had hit me in the gut. But I caught it and rose up on my toes, rolling it off my fingers and sinking it from right where I was, while he stood there with his teeth in his mouth, so far away that he couldn't have guarded me if he'd tried. We stood looking into each other's eyes as the ball rolled into some weeds. He had eyes the color of strong tea. I didn't blink.

"Shit!" Miko said, kicking the dirt.

"That's five—"

"I can count."

"It's hot," I said. "We can quit." Miko was sweating, but since I hadn't done anything but basically shoot baskets with somebody jumping up and down next to me, I wasn't. Miko started to laugh.

"I can count, but I didn't count on you being so good," he said.

"Well," I said, "it's not your sport, is all."

"I could have beat you."

"No," I said honestly, "you couldn't. I do this all day, or I used to. I thought I would play in college, but I really don't think I'm going to have the height. I probably won't even get as tall as my mother, and they have girls out there who are six feet. I love the game. I wish I were taller."

"You'll be glad you're not someday."

"Maybe." I picked up my ball and from habit dusted it off with my shirt and let it rest on my hip.

"I couldn't beat a little girl. Jesus."

"No," I said, "not this little girl. I don't mean that in a mean way, either." Miko swung back up into their truck but didn't start it.

He licked his finger and polished something on the dashboard. I didn't remember him at the funeral, but I knew that he and his family must have come. He said, "Well, I would never hurt you, Ronnie-o. You know how sorry all of us—"

"We know."

"And happy about the baby."

"Thanks, Miko."

"Who are you going to shoot, Ronnie?" he asked.

"Nobody," I said. "I was just goofing around."

"Okay. So. Take care, Ronnie," Miko said softly, and drove off. I watched him and thought that if I had been any other girl, I would have let him make one point, at least; but I hadn't been in the mood to play girl. The thing was, the ball had felt so good in my hands again. When I picked up the gun, it felt like a clumsy, cold thing.

Still, I was going to go out there every day and practice with the gun; but the next day I noticed one of those white cars with the windows rolled down I could just tell belonged to a reporter.

And I thought, My word, wouldn't that make a great picture? I turned right back around and walked inside. But I wanted to so badly, it was like an addiction, how I guessed it would be to be hooked on drugs. Thinking about it all the time, imagining how it would feel, breathless from wanting to do it. I asked my father to take me hunting with him, for deer. But he said he didn't have the heart in him to hunt anymore, for anything living, even birds.

Then I started having panic attacks. I had to look them up, because if you had one, you would think your heart was stopping.

A panic attack comes from your head but isn't imaginary. You really can't breathe until you blow into a paper bag and recycle your own carbon dioxide. You really can't stop your heart from feeling like it's a device stuck on one speed. I found yoga exercises on the Internet; and still, I would be somewhere—in the kitchen, in the bathtub, feeding Ruby, anywhere at night—and one would just happen. It was a good thing I wasn't out among people, because I must have looked like a nit breathing into the Snackster's Custard bag I kept in my backpack.

Finally, I was all out of ideas.

I needed to be a child, I guess.

I thought, maybe, since my mother needed her little girls, I would try to be one. So I started to slide in bed next to her to read. I asked her to French-braid my hair—which I actually never could do for myself. It felt reassuring to me, since I was always so cold, just to touch her and feel the textures of her hair and her shawl, to warm my body against her back, which reminded me of the flannel-covered hot-water bottle she gave us when we were sick. But, though we had always been loving to each other, a good mother and a daughter who wanted to be like her, though we had fun and believed we were very much alike, too much had happened for me to crawl back onto my mother's lap. It was sad. Grace is but glory begun, they say. At least I tried.

If I'd been able to be my mother's child again, I might not have done anything else. But it didn't work.

I stopped trying after I began to feel that my spontaneous hugs or my dropping down on the end of the bed for no reason was annoying to her. She didn't act that way, but she couldn't suppress a little "poof" of irritation if the baby was lying on the bed when I lay down there, too. She was afraid I'd wake him. I could tell it was a strain. Maybe I just never was little-girl material, because it did seem that I'd been "big" ever since Becky was born.

I will say that my mother tried, too. For one thing, when she planned her lessons for Family Home Evenings, Mama searched for ways to make the stories about kids who used drugs and hit bottom real to me. But one night she smiled and dropped her hands in her lap and got out a game, like chess, that she wanted me to learn because she had a theory that it developed the left side of your brain. She said, "This other stuff has got to apply to you somehow, honey, because none of us ever goes through life without being tempted. But I don't see it. I feel like I'm trying to teach the Mormon Tabernacle Choir to hum 'Yankee Doodle Dandy.' You're so sensible, Ronnie. You have a gift of common sense."

She was so wrong. I was just a scared kid, and nothing made sense to me. I had lost my common sense along with my sisters.

I wanted to tell her then about the panic.

But how could I?

Literally weeks before, she'd touched her little girls in their coffins. She had a new baby whom she held in her arms like he was laundry. How could I put one more thing on her?

But as I said, she tried, too.

One morning, she came up and brought me cocoa and cinnamon toast, and she reached down to nuzzle my neck. Then, I could more or less feel her stiffen as she caught sight of the places on the floor where Becky's and Ruthie's beds had been. She hadn't spent a lot of time in my room since their beds were taken down. She put down my cocoa and toast and left. She had almost been smiling. Tears splattered my papers, blurring the ink, and I decided then that I would have to pull myself out of whatever well I was in. I should have talked to the bishop, but he was my uncle, and so crusty and old, or to Sister Tierney, who taught Young Women's. But I didn't. It would have helped, but I wouldn't.

I knew there had to be something that would make me normal. And being LDS, it had to come from the Heavenly Father. Why hadn't I thought of this before?

A teacher would come to our house after church once every month—not a schoolteacher, but someone from church whose duty it was to check in on us, to see if we were doing okay. Not just for bereaved people. They check in on normal people, too, and if there was an old person who was sick or didn't have enough food, there would be a family assigned to them to make sure they were okay and got what they needed without being embarrassed.

The lady and man who came to our house were husband and wife, and the wife helped with Young Women's. They were Brother and Sister Barken, and they lived so far down the road, we hardly knew them except from church. But I had always admired her, because she dressed so fashionably, in clothes she got from Europe every summer, when they took their four daughters to Italy or France, where they stayed in farmhouses. Sister Barken wanted each of her children to learn languages, even though they were only little, and not just because they might be sent to Spain or Germany on their missions. She once said in Young Women's, while I was still going, that learning another language was like learning music.

While her husband talked with my parents about the archaeology of the Golden Plates that were given to Joseph Smith, Sister Barken took me aside. The tradition among Mormon kids is, run when the teachers come; and I had. I was in the little laundry room, folding towels. Although I knew better, all the white and pale blue towels were a little pink, because I was a little distracted and one day I put everything in with my red uniform shorts, the ones with the white dragon on the rear end. The dragon was a little pink, too.

"You've been doing all this yourself, haven't you," Sister Barken said, but not in a mean way.

I lied. "No," I said, "just this load." I didn't want her to think my mother was mental. She *had* just had the biggest tragedy of her life, and a baby, within a month.

"Ronnie," said Sister Barken, "we could look at a passage of scripture that might help you. I had one in mind, from Isaiah. But I think what you really need is . . ." She put out her arms, and I collapsed into them. In her tight, fancy black skirt and jacket, she just sat on the floor of the laundry room, among all those pink towels I was trying to bleach out, and held me until I stopped crying. Then she asked, "What are you worried about?"

"Everything," I told her. "The baby. The laundry. My soul. My mother."

"The scriptures say that Heavenly Father never gives us a burden that we cannot carry," said Sister Barken. "But I don't take that to mean He thinks we have to carry it alone. What are you doing for Christmas, Ronnie?"

I shrugged.

"You could come to us," said Sister Barken. "All our family lives so far away. My girls look up to you so much. They think you're like Michael Jordan!"

"Personally, I'd really like that, but I don't think my parents are up to it, Sister Barken. I don't know if we'll even make it to church. We haven't yet." We had things in the mail from Grandma Bonham and Grandpa Swan, and little things from other relatives on a side table. But we had no tree; and Papa had given all the presents in pretty paper that Mama had gotten for Becky and Ruthie to Uncle Pierce, for other children who wouldn't have had presents. We couldn't have stood it to look at them.

"Well. You know, this year I'm putting makeup kits that I got in France in all my girls' stockings. They're very small still, except for our Lauren, who's your age; but I thought I would keep the other ones sealed up with our stored things until Caitlin and Stacy and Tonya were bigger. You know, the Prophet says it's important for a woman to be well-groomed on the outside as well as on the inside. And the funny thing is, a little bit of gloss on your lips and a little mascara is nice. It gives a shine to your face. It helps you feel happier." I didn't know where this was going, but I smiled. I usually used Vaseline on my eyelashes because it helped them grow long and not break off as well as making them glisten. "The thing is, I bought an extra, in case one broke; but none did. I would like to give that one to you, Ronnie."

"That's very nice, but no, of course not, Sister Barken. It must have been very expensive."

"Well, isn't that supposed to be something you let grown-ups worry about? It's a gift to me if you accept it, really. I'll feel happy." I didn't feel happy; but I'd also never had a makeup kit before, and I was curious. "You . . . stay here, and I'm going to run home and get it. You can put those towels through the wash again. I'm going to change out of this suit and we're going to give the house a spit-and-polish, okay? And then I'm going to teach you how to put on a little makeup so it doesn't look as though you're wearing makeup at all."

That was what she did.

She dusted, and her husband and my father swept and polished the floors. Sister Barken took the feather duster to the backs of all the books. She ironed my sheets and my mother's, before Mama got into bed, so they'd have that crisp, hotel feeling. And then, when Mama was asleep with the baby, she sat down and put a mirror in front of us and showed me how just a tiny bit of shadow that you could barely see made my green eyes look deep and mysterious, and how Frenchwomen put on their colored lip moistener with brushes, just a little at a time. It wasn't your normal church visit.

While we worked, Sister Barken talked to me, just a little at a time.

"Ronnie, you can't expect to make your parents feel happy," she said.

"I wish I could make them feel anything," I admitted.

"They will, in time, but, and I know this is hard for you to believe, it's even harder for them than for you. Having your child die before you is what all the philosophers called the only unendurable grief," Sister Barken said.

"Because the parents should have died first?" I asked.

"Yes, and because you have an entire life on earth ahead of you. You don't know it now, but that life will be full."

"How I feel is, it will be full of time to remember this."

"Yes. But in time, those memories of terror will be replaced by memories of sweetness, and anticipation for the reunion with your sisters, who have . . . ascended as martyrs."

"I thought martyrs died for their faith," I said, puzzled.

"They were innocent, and I would think Heavenly Father would consider them martyrs."

I said as gently as I could, "They were in primary. They barely knew their first Bible stories, especially Ruthie. They were ordinary kids."

"The way you speak of them, and your love for them, doesn't make them sound ordinary. They sound very special."

"Then why would God let this happen to them?" I knew this was a dumb question.

"It wasn't an act of God. It was an act of a human being. Heavenly Father had to let wicked human beings hurt and kill His only Son, our Lord Jesus, not only because there was a plan for this, but because human beings have to have mortal agency. Free will. That's what makes bad things happen, that and Satan working away at people all the time. God cries with you over this, Ronnie, and just because you can't come to programs right now doesn't mean you're not good. Don't punish yourself. None of us is as good as we can be, but you're pretty close."

I felt better than I had in days. And I kept that makeup kit until every tiny flake and lick was used up. The brushes I still have, and I wash them every week. Sister Barken said they would last for years, and they have.

When I showed it to my mother, she smiled.

"Sometimes we just need a small something you'd never think of," she said. "And Sister Barken knew what it was. It doesn't hurt to have a little beauty, even in sadness. And she was right, Ronnie. Your job is not to try to see the meaning in this, but to pray to get beyond meaningless suffering to meaningful grief, good grief. I hope you get the space to do that, with everyone looking at us."

My father came into their bedroom then and said, "I pray that they'll look at us with compassion, not as though we were freaks. Maybe we should consider . . . leaving, Cressie. Leaving here."

"But, London, we would take ourselves wherever we'd go," Mama said. "You can't run away from you. Ruth's and Rebecca's graves are here. Our home is here. Look at the blessing Sister Barken brought Ronnie, and all of us, today. I think we have to stand in our place and wait on the Lord."

"I see that," Papa said, "but I'm restless."

"You always were," Mama said, and turned her face away.

Later that week, I went with Papa to run some errands.

"Ronnie, I just want you to know this isn't the end for our family. You've been so terrified. I've seen your worry. I haven't known what to say. I haven't been there for you," Papa said then.

"Pops, it's okay. I know," I said.

"It's not okay," he said. "You want to lead your child. But I don't see the path yet."

I thought of the maps that my mother had once asked us to make of our lives, of the places that made up what we thought of as home. The little girls just drew trees and circles; but I worked hard on mine, including the church, the general store, the road to the high school gym, the mountains where I rode Ruby, my own room, and my own desk. If I had put my old map over a new one—one that basically made a skinny, empty triangle of my house, the barn, and the church building—it would have looked as though my world had disappeared. Scott Early had taken away not only Becky's and Ruthie's lives, but all of our lives. Barely in his forties, my father looked like a trembly old man, his raggedy head in his hands, his milkshake separating like slush.

And so I didn't tell him that they'd forgotten my thirteenth birthday.

Chapter Eight

There would be no trial. Scott Early had written a full confession and added to it over time.

So there was no need for anything but a judge's decision.

But there was an investigation. The sheriff visited us more than once. He actually was a pretty nice person. The psychiatrists and medical doctors for the defense lawyers and the prosecutors interviewed my parents and me, asking us if Scott Early had demonstrated signs of pain, if he seemed to walk unsteadily or had a seizure. They were all the same, and they were as curious as dogs. I told them that Scott Early held his head and moaned, but that was all. After regular doctors did a thorough exam, including pictures of his brain, it turned out that Scott Early didn't have a physical disease that made him unable to think.

We waited for the decision. Days passed, then weeks.

That was the silent-movie period at its worst. I simply walked through my days, trying to be me. I went to Clare's recital with the Emorys. I set up a fan that would keep me from sweating through my sheets as the nights got warmer, but even the air-conditioning didn't help. I began doing full-out wind sprints from our house to the church, then jogging up the hill to the Sissinellis and back, so I would be conditioned for summer basketball camp. None of it was any fun. None of it was even satisfying. I had always wanted to be super-slender like Clare, and now I was, but it turned out to be a chore to take in the waists of my pants. Lessons had no effect on me, and I simply endured things I used to enjoy. Family Home Evenings were no fun without my sisters. Some nights we only played Monopoly, pretending the board was heaven. There were a lot of visitors. Relatives and even some of my mother's gallery buyers dropped by or came to stay. I could see the shock on their faces when they saw the beautiful Cressida Swan with baby oatmeal stains on the shoulders of a dirty man's striped shirt, wearing a pair of my father's overalls three sizes too big. I was sad for her, but people made my skin crawl. I hoped the sight of my mother would make them stay away. Finally, they did. You're obliged to mourn the mourning of your brothers and sisters, but people can stand only so much.

The Sissinellis were in their summer home on Cape Cod, all but Miko, who was spending his last summer before college in Utah with friends. He was off camping most of the time. I walked Ruby past their house more than necessary when he was home, sitting out on the porch without his shirt with his friends. They waved to me once, but Miko said something to them and they put down their hands. I guess he told them about my sisters, and they acted like most people did when they found out—like they had something to be ashamed of.

A few days after Miko left the first time, Mrs. Sissinelli called and said the lady she asked to come in and clean had quit, so she asked me if I wanted the job. I cleaned their house to earn money. The pleasure I felt in dusting the Florentine glassware, my mother's ceramics, and the inlays on the picture frames had no envy in it, but the space and silence were magnificent. I hung around long after I had to, though I didn't charge Mrs. Sissinelli for the extra time. I felt like the custodian of a museum, able to touch all the jewels and even lightly brush my finger over the textures of the paintings in the galleries. Once, after I'd polished it, I slid all the way down their curved banister. Once, I put on one of Mrs. Sissinelli's furs and stood in front of the mirror, savoring its softness like a spoonful of dessert, seeing myself as I would look as a wealthy woman who had six of these. Once, I turned on all the speakers and played Vivaldi while I danced on the floor of the foyer, the sun through the patterns of stained glass making my arms and hands into the sleeves of a harlequin costume. It was cool in there, cooler than our window air conditioners ever made our house; and I found extra things to mess with, cleaning the grout in the kitchen with a toothbrush. What I really longed for was to curl up in their deep sofas and sleep forever. There was a time when I did fall asleep, almost jumping out of my skin when Miko and his friend came banging through the back door. As I walked out into the furnace of the afternoon, I was grateful that all he said about me was that I was "the kid down the road," not other things, even though they might have been more interesting.

Serena wrote me to see if I wanted to come out to visit; they would send me a ticket. I very much wanted to go, and my parents encouraged the trip because I'd never seen the ocean, but there was still that itchy shadow garment all over me. I wrote back to tell Serena I hoped she would ask me again, any other summer, and I would come. I was needed at home now.

At night, when she could bear the heat enough to be out, I walked Ruby down to stand in the cool mud of the creek bed. The mosquitoes were like a veil on my face, and Ruby's haunches quivered with pain and annoyance, no matter how much natural repellent oil or WD-40 I rubbed into her coat. I knew that since she was nineteen, Ruby was ready to go for what I'd always hoped her last years would be, as a therapy horse at Guiding

Gait, a place in Cedar City where little kids with cerebral palsy and even adults got lifted onto the backs of quiet horses to let them have fun and to build their confidence. I arranged with Papa for her donation. On the day they came for Ruby, I cried harder than I had at the funeral. Papa cleaned her stall for me, washing every corner with water and mild soap, laying the floor with fresh shavings. I couldn't bear to do it alone. Ruby's broad back was the last bridge between my sisters and me. Now they were square on the other side.

Not having Ruby to look after left my evenings idle. I started doing a little church work, mostly mailings, because it would let me be alone. Clare and Emma asked me to come with them to a study group about changing women's roles and whether they could work within the context of the church. I said I didn't want to go. Mama made me. So I went, taking the bus. About twelve girls met in a room at the Cedar City Public Library, with a woman who was LDS but also a playwright. She'd written all the words and music for a play about Noah and the Ark that had been shown and acclaimed in London's West End district. I was getting into a discussion one night about whether a woman could legitimately work and raise a family if her work was a service to humanity rather than simply a way of increasing her family's wealth, works on earth being a way of attainment in heaven, when I overheard two ladies outside the open door say, "That's her. That's the girl who was there when the little kids were killed. The Grim Reaper murders."

I never went back.

Mama said the decision was being held up because Scott Early was being examined over and over by psychiatrists from Salt Lake and Phoenix and even an expert from Philadelphia; and they were also talking to people from his own hometown, Crescent City, Colorado, and his university friends and professors.

Papa still roamed. He wore out his boots and had them resoled. He was so thin, he looked like Abraham Lincoln; and he forgot to cut his hair until the principal reminded him when the term began that the kids were the ones who were supposed to get in trouble for having long hair. At night, when the bugs were fierce or the air too thick even for him to stand it, he paced our halls. Or he glued and sanded and polished everything in the house, replacing screws in doors that hadn't closed the right way since I was a baby. Mama confessed it made her crazy trying to fall asleep listening to him rearrange the silverware drawer in tidy little divided containers. We almost giggled. Papa made Mama a button holder from one of his old tackle boxes and separated all the buttons according to size and color. Then he made me one—from the wooden shoebox Mama had intended for Becky's doll clothes. I couldn't see how he could do that, if he knew what the boxes were for. Maybe he didn't know. I guess he needed activity more than he needed to seem sensitive.

I spent all the time I could with Rafe, until you could tell he was reacting more to me than to Mama.

Poor Rafe.

Mama didn't start to love him, really love him, until he could sit up and crawl.

I look back on that long, long year. She never exactly ignored him, and she made sure he was clean and sweet smelling; but I never heard the murmuring and singing from their bedroom that I heard when Becky was tiny. There were other odd signs. When he was only one month old, they moved him to his nursery instead of keeping the cradle in their room. I liked my privacy, but I kept our two doors open, so he could hear me breathing or typing, my music playing softly, and know someone was right there. Mama treated him like a nice little puppy, something dear she would pet, but as if she weren't all there. She really wasn't all there. It was no one's fault, my father said. Dr. Pratt said the same thing.

But, thank Heavenly Father for His mercies, I couldn't resist my little brother. When I came into a room, it was as if someone had flipped his switch. His eyes locked on mine like a pair of hands and pulled. He wriggled and gurgled and chuckled like a sweet little seal. Papa was right. Rafe tricked me into loving him. How can you not love a miniature human being whose greatest joy was to lie on the table while you blew bubbles on a fold of chin pudge at his neck? Who thinks it's completely hysterical when you set a Tupperware container on your head—not just the first or the second or the fourth time, but the twentieth time? He was so fat and utterly cheerful—almost as if he had to be, to win us from Ruthie and Becky—that even my uncle Pierce said this boy was a joyous spirit with a purpose on earth of creating mirth. At six weeks old, Rafe had astonished Mama by sleeping from seven at night until eight in the morning. I was the one who went into Rafe's room and poked him to make sure he was alive. He was the human equivalent of the locks on the doors I had to check.

For Mama barely did anything except sleep, still. I never woke her; I figured she went in her dreams to feel her hands making a pot again, or wiggling Becky's loose tooth, or trying to brush out Ruthie's hair.

You could tell that waking life was an obligation for Mama. She was never unkind, but she didn't initiate a thing, even eating. Mrs. Emory tried to get her to help reach out in the primary, but I could see from Mrs. Emory's face that she repented asking right in the middle of saying it. She then suggested Mama minister to women in homeless shelters, to teach their children to draw; but Mama said she honestly couldn't be with children at all. She helped by making packages from home for young people on their missions, filling them with books and jams and hand-made shirts and scarves. Parents were supposed to do this them-selves, but some had so many younger kids that the packages got scarce.

Mama had once taken me places, like museums and univer-sities, to help make history and biology living subjects. Now, she simply assigned me my readings, if she remembered, and told me to do Internet research for my papers. She had seemed relieved when school ended; and she had ended school early that year, in mid-May, marking my exams and sending in my report to the school district.

We got a letter informing us that I had enough credits that I was already a high school sophomore. But I didn't feel knowl-edgeable, the way I had when she'd taken me to plays to under-stand the reason Shakespeare wrote his plays in speech that made the King James Bible sound like a comic book. I started looking at my old *Book of Remembrance*, a kind of personal scrapbook of photos and meaningful objects from nature, as well as my own observations and descriptions of me from adults I knew ("devout and loyal, but stubborn"). I began to add to what I'd written when I was little. As I worked on my writing and pasting, I would watch Mama at the table, her hands busy with knitting sweaters and caps for Rafe for winter, simply staring at the shed—as if the power of her look could make it go up in flames. It was almost as if she had forgotten how to play and didn't know that Rafe needed it. She simply tied her empty thread spools together with bright-colored yarn but didn't bounce them or set them up in towers on the floor.

I did that.

Every morning that fall, before I got out my books, my mend-ing, or my computer, I would hear Rafe signal me with the tinkling of his bells. I would peer in, and as soon as he caught sight of me, it would begin, the roly-poly gyrations all over the cradle. Rafe wriggled so much before he could roll over that he wore off a patch of his thick black hair. He had a tiny little bald spot Papa swore was the baby version of the one his brother Pierce had.

Rafe was the thing my parents had the biggest argument over that I'd ever heard.

It had to have been summer then, because I was in basketball camp, catching a lot of grief from Coach when we'd scrimmage, and why wouldn't I? I'd be driving up the lane and then my brain would blink out and I'd pass right into the hands of the opposing center. He would start to say, "Where's your head, Swan?" But then he'd stop, and I could see he was half-ashamed and half-mad that he had to make allowances for me. I tried to concentrate on the drills, and there still was nobody who could take the ball away from me if I was on my game or catch me if I had it. But way too often, I was throwing it away or letting it drop as if it were a gum wrapper or a penny.

Finally, I quit. I was very sad.

Basketball seemed to me to be the one sure way back to a sort of halfway version of the Ronnie I had been. All my team friends had been so glad to see me, so glad to give me back the job I always had—that all point guards have, of sort of being the brains of the team, making sure everybody was where she was supposed to be. They didn't care that I was younger. They'd missed me. They said the team wasn't the same without me. A couple of them told me, during drills, that they wanted me to be captain next year. But a point guard has to think, fast and on her feet. Just like Becky wrote, I didn't even realize when I was traveling. I would have been an asset to nobody on varsity. When I finally told Coach, he and the assistant just hugged me. Nobody tried to talk me out of it. I came home crying the night I quit, taking the bus from Cedar City to about a mile from our house and then walking. I could hear them before I walked in. Great, I thought, this is just great.

"He's your son, Cressida," my father was saying. "He's a blessing come to us in our sorrow. You act like he's a burden."

"And what do you do? London, you're never here. When you're home, you're not here. You're alone in your thoughts. I can't get in. We don't pray together. We don't talk. I hear you pacing and . . . fussing all night."

"That'll end when the verdict comes in. My emotions are all over the place, Cressie." Because he was a teacher, I guess, Papa always sounded like he had prepared remarks and was talking about the themes in *To Kill a Mockingbird* or something.

"And so are mine. Where does our baby fit into that?" my mother snapped back at him. "At the hospital, you convinced me that I would have all your support in binding this little boy to us. . . ."

"I don't mean our family in eternity. I'm sure we'll be just *fine* in eternity. I'm talking about earth, London! We're not doing so well on earth!"

"Cressie, it hasn't even been a year!"

"Tell Raphael that! I try," she said, and I could hear her begin to cry, "I try to give him the same . . . love I gave the girls. I pray for the strength to overcome grief with love. . . ."

"I read once . . . I read it to you, honey. John Adams and Thomas Jefferson on the holy purposes of grief? Adams wondered to what end we endured the sensations of grief. Remember how he said that? He used the example of the couple with everything going for them, the way we had. And he wrote, wait, let me think . . . 'Through one of the accidents allotted to humanity,' one of them died. Why would it happen? And if it did, why would we feel such misery? Finally, he said that the more sensitive we are, the deeper we grieve. His opinion was that the purpose was to drive us deeper into reflection, to make us stoics and Christians."

"Well, that's nice, London! That's a wonderful intellectual conjecture! But this is real life, just a little bit south of hell on earth! Am I stoic? Is stoic getting up and bathing the baby and brushing my teeth every day? I must be stoic, because what I really feel like doing is lying in that bed until I dry up and smell. What I feel is like a Rachel, lost in the wilderness, but all my tears are dry. I could blow away like a leaf. There's no purpose for my grief, London! I'm not Thomas Jefferson. My grief just leads back and back and back on itself, then—"

"I'll do better, after this. After the verdict. I will, Cressida."

"After? You'll turn back to your family? We have a date for that then?"

My father was quiet. No one heard me open the door.

"Yes," he said.

"And what about Ronnie? I already abrogated my mother-hood to Ronnie to indulge myself, when that time belonged to my children. . . ."

"That's not true, Cressida. Your gift is from the Heavenly Father as surely as your motherhood is."

"If I had been here!"

"The result would have been the same. Unless I had been there, standing literally there, with the gun loaded and pointed."

"No. It was me." They were competing for being the worse parent. I wanted to run, to Phoenix, to Salt Lake, to Labrador. "I believe it with my mind, but everything else spits it back in my face. My own selfishness cost Rebecca and Ruth their lives. My pottery! My *art*!"

"That's not how God works, Cressida. I know that. It's my deepest belief that God does not punish us for impulses that He also gave us—"

"Stop it! Don't lecture me. I was talking about Ronnie. *Ronnie* is bearing guilt that should have been mine and only mine! Or yours, if you want some of it. And now she's mothering Rafe. She's taking up slack for me. What am I making of my daughter? She's truly earning a higher realm right here on earth; but it's not fair to her. I forget to cook meals. Ronnie does it. She watches me like a hawk. You know when she said she didn't need a new swimsuit for next year? It's not that she's self-conscious. London, I think she doesn't believe she'll ever be able to leave this house again! That she'll never be able to leave me here alone! We forgot her birthday, London! We forgot her birthday!"

"No!" my father cried. "No! That's not possible." He was quiet. "We did. We forgot her birthday." *Only like seven or eight months ago*, I thought. "Maybe, Cressie, maybe she needs time away. I've even thought she should go away, board with one of my brothers in Salt Lake and go to school," my father said.

Oh, mercy, I thought. *They're going to give me to Aunt Adair. I'll be like Jane Eyre.*

Then he added, "That's why I walk, and I can't rest, Cressida. It blots out everything. I'm afraid I'll break a window or smash a chair. Their faces are in front of me when I teach. I lose track of what I'm telling the kids in the middle of a sentence. I'm talking about Hawthorne and I'm thinking, *Were Rebecca's eyes blue, or were Rebecca's eyes gray?* Their faces are in front of me when I'm doing church teaching. Their faces are in front of me when I try to speak in meeting, when I try to open my heart to take sacrament. I forgot Ronnie's birthday. I forgot my daughter's birthday."

"It's wrong," my mother said, "it's wrong, wrong, wrong. Not just what he did. Scott Early has such a terrible hold on our family. Lunnie, I'm sorry. I'm sorry I shrieked at you. Actually, I had to. I need to shriek."

My father's words were muffled. I knew he was crying. I assumed that Mama was holding him against her. Rafe began to whimper.

"My son," Papa said, "my little son. And Ronnie, so alone."

It was sort of sweet, I guess, a kind of release for them, but I tell you, it scared me. Your parents are your rocks, and mine were crumbling. I truly did feel like one of those boulders worn loose by erosion, pitching away from its strong source. I wanted to shriek, too. I wanted to cry like a little kid with a flap of skin hanging off her toe. But I was afraid that I'd make a fool of myself, or—worse—no one would notice.

"Perhaps," Mama said, and I could tell she was giving Rafe his bottle, "perhaps there is a reason." Dr. Pratt had told her months before that our baby wasn't gaining enough weight and put him on formula. Mama knew it was because she couldn't eat enough to give Rafe the proper nourishment. "In some way, we are meant to be more mindful, to treasure these children more than ever, because of our loss."

"No one could have treasured Becky and Ruthie more," Papa said. "They were hard to come by. We never took them for granted."

"*These* children, Lunnie. Ronnie and Rafe. We can always do better. We can always minister to our children more completely."

I was thinking, as I crept upstairs, that it was the first time I had ever heard them speak his name. Scott Early.

Of course, I knew it, from the newspapers, from the pictures of him that Clare taped with the VCR and I watched on her TV. I knew more about him than I did about some of my cousins. I knew he was a graduate student in pharmacy, that he was twenty-seven years old, square-jawed and handsome when he was cleaned up, that he was married to a school counselor, that just a few weeks before he started driving from Colorado to Utah, he stopped talking to all his friends. His wife would find him crying on his knees in their room. He went to church twice a day at the end. He talked to the minister. But what he said made no sense. He said he was hearing voices and the voices got louder and louder, but that his wife would die if he went to a doctor for help. In the newspaper, the wife said, "Scott is a gentle person. He's been a gentle person all his life. We've known each other since we were juniors in high school. He's just as he was before now. He doesn't understand why he did this terrible thing." The interviewer wrote that the lady, Kelly something, was asked if Scott Early knew what he did was wrong and that she said, "He knows it was wrong, but he doesn't know that the Scott he really is, did it. I can't really explain."

But someone had to explain. Someone had to account, or we would live like faded photographs in a box for the rest of our lives. We would be stuck like the old people in the nursing center we read to and sang to at Christmas, who kept telling us about the toys they'd hidden for their children—toys that had been new forty years ago.

I was sleeping when the call finally came.

The judge was ready to see us.

Mama got me up and fixed me a breakfast so big that I practically gagged. It was too hot for pancakes. And I didn't want to go, but my parents insisted. I put on my long green summer skirt and a short-sleeved pullover. My mother said to put on a long-sleeved pullover instead, not because my shirt was immodest, but because of the reporters, so I did. Just a few days earlier, a woman had come from the Sunday magazine in Arizona, just showing up at our house with a photographer, who snapped pictures of the outside while the woman, who was petite and pretty and Asian, asked if she could do a profile of our family as it was now, with the new baby as the focus of new hope for the Swans. My mother, horrified, didn't exactly slam the door in her face; but she said firmly that it would be a kindness to leave us in peace, that we had done nothing wrong, and that we were trying to rebuild our lives. Those few things Mama said, and some silly descriptions, the lady made into a story a page long, with photos of the picnic table—arrows sketched in on the places next to it where my sisters died. My father had burned the picnic table that night, despite the heat.

On the morning of the verdict, we left Rafe with Sister Emory and drove to the courthouse in town.

My father put out his arm like a boy running with a football and pushed his way through the reporters.

What do you think the judge's decision will be, Cressie?

Do you think he'll get life? Veronica? How do you feel right now?

Are you afraid the Reaper will come for you if he ever gets out, Ronnie?

I know that there are good and thoughtful journalists. But they were like pigs fighting at a trough for garbage.

The courthouse was freezing. I was glad, although I looked like a prissy-poo in my long-sleeved shirt and braid, that I had something over me. Mama put her shawl around my shoulders, too.

The judge came in. We all stood. I heard Scott Early's chains clink as he struggled to his feet. The judge's name was Richard Neese. He was a young man, a lot younger than Papa and handsome as a movie actor. Maybe he was too young to be a judge. He had dimples. You think of judges being crusty, like my uncle the bishop, not having dimples. I felt sorry for him, having this hard a job. And this particular part of that job had to be the worst.

The first thing he said was, "I've been on the bench only one year. This is the most horrifying set of circumstances I've had to consider in that time. I confess there were times I despaired. But I thought it best to take a long time, though I know this time must have been excruciating for you, to study these reports. I've also done my own independent study, in coming to this decision. There are so many choices. And the easiest is obviously to sentence Scott Early to be confined in Draper at Point of the Mountain until he is an old man. That would guarantee the safety of the community, and Scott Early's safety, in that environment, would not be our concern. But he would certainly die there. What he has done would make him an instant target for inmates who consider their own heinous crimes trivial next to killing a child. And perhaps that is what the fair thing to do would be. But it would not be the just thing.

"I have read the many reports from physicians involved with this case, and the conclusion from both those retained by Scott Early's family and those retained by the state is that Scott Early suffers from schizophrenia, which is a complex disease and can arise from many causes, internal or external. The fact that the administration of medication instantly stopped his auditory hallucinations and compulsions further confirms this diagnosis. Since his treatment began, while he has been confined to the county jail, Scott Early has been able to write about the circumstances of the murder of Rebecca and Ruth. But he has also written more.

"He has written, and I'm quoting from his journals: 'At first, my belief was that it was inevitable that I should die for the horrible thing I had done, that it was the only fair penance for such an egregious sin. Obviously, I was afraid, as any human being would be afraid, and saddened to think of the effect this would have on my wife and my family. But as my thoughts became more lucid, I realized that a dead man cannot make restitution. A dead man cannot do anything, in this life, to contribute anything good to the world, even to help those like himself, or to help children afflicted by grief, or help people to understand mental illness—which, as a pharmacist, I understood could be a matter of brain chemistry and not of will. And so I talked with my attorneys about what I could do, incarcerated, to, in some small way, encourage the treatment of people such as myself, to encourage the understanding of mental illness. And I began to hope that I might do that, not because it would be less frightening for me, but because it would be a more difficult task. I do not think these thoughts arose from a selfish desire. I think they arose from my long hours of prayer and contemplation. I thought about what I had done, and how that could have been prevented. I thought about the particularly heinous nature of taking the lives of children, whose entire futures I erased with one act. I thought about the families, the Swans and my own, I had devastated, and how that could not be undone. The anguish of this line of thought is indescribable. But I had to consider that taking my life could not restore the lives of the Swan children. So, while I believe that it would be right to condemn me, I do not believe it would be useful. And, before this happened, I wanted very much to live a useful life.'

"He goes on. But this is sufficient.

"Obviously, in this situation," the judge went on, "our first duty is to the community, in this case represented by the Swan family. We may have seen a change in Scott Early, from a man who clearly fit the legal definition of diminished capacity, to a man who is thoughtful and concerned. But we can't know, at this point, whether that is a durable change, whether he poses a danger to himself and society. We must assume that he does. And so releasing him with treatment is not an option at this point, as it would be if he had a physical impairment, a tumor that impaired his impulse control that had been removed, for example.

"Our other concern must be compassion, which should be on the mind of any court in the making of decisions. The Romanesque statue of Justice is depicted weighing the scales—the scales of evidence—but she also is blindfolded. This has been, in many descriptions, said to portray impartiality, that is, 'blindness' to anything but the facts. However, what this blindfold truly signifies is that justice should not be influenced by any outside force, social or political.

"However, in this case, we must be influenced by compassion. That compassion must be directed at the Earlys as well as the Swan family, because although the Earlys are innocent of any wrongdoing, they raised a good young man who became terribly ill, so far as we can tell, without the influence of substance abuse or family mistreatment or trauma, but, from what our investigators can gather, the combination of his parents' genes or simple bad luck. We cannot overestimate the role of mental illness in the commission of crime; and Scott Early is a signal example of that phenomenon. Before November nineteenth of last year, he had never been given a parking ticket. He had no history of violence at all, much less violent crime. He has asked for the opportunity to allow us, the community of justice, to learn from him how such a man could do such a thing.

"Perhaps it is idealistic in the extreme to believe that by refusing to exercise the ultimate punishment available to us as a culture for the commission of such a crime, we can 'learn' from individuals who commit such crimes. In the case of the murders of Rebecca and Ruth Swan, capital punishment would not, in fact, be an option, since Scott Early's crime clearly was opportunistic, not premeditated or in conjunction with the commission of another felony. Indeed, he has repeatedly stated that he continued to drive until his car ran out of gas to prevent himself from doing exactly what he did.

"And so, under ordinary circumstances, Scott Early would be guilty of manslaughter in the second degree, an act that, while it appeared voluntary, was in fact not his choice, but which ended two lives. He could serve two sentences that consecutively might amount to more than two decades.

"However, the circumstances we face are not ordinary. A verdict of not guilty by reason of mental disease or defect is difficult to justify. Scott Early did know that what he was doing was wrong, gravely wrong. But though he knew the difference between right and wrong, he did not, at the time of the deaths of little Rebecca and Ruth, know the difference between the real world and the world no one but he could see or hear. He did not believe he had a choice.

"Therefore, instead of sentencing Scott Early to a prison term, which would do us no good and him harm, I am placing him in the custody of the maximum security facility for the criminally mentally ill in St. George, Utah, at Stone Gate, for a period of no less than three years and no more than seven years, to include the time he already has spent in the county facility, where he will receive treatment and cooperate both in his own therapy and in the study of his mental processes before and after the crime. He will receive periodic evaluations of his mental capacity and condition and, at which time when he is released, it will be under close supervision by community mental health authorities, and under the provisions of the statutes that make it mandatory for those in his locale to know who he is and where he lives, and for the Swans to be kept apprised of this knowledge for the rest of their lives as well.

"I realize that this decision may not satisfy everyone's desires in this case. I realize it may be a source of controversy. But I am confident in having reached it with the sincere cooperation of both the state and the attorneys for Scott Early, with the expert advice of medical doctors on both sides, with testimony both from the Swans and from those who know them best, with the Earlys, including Scott's wife, Kelly Englehart, and those who knew them best, and with my own conscience. I offer my condolences to all involved, and I genuinely wish I could offer more, especially to London, Cressida, Raphael, and Veronica Swan, whose lives are forever reduced. Mr. Early will be transported to Stone Gate tomorrow. And this court is adjourned."

We stood, and my mother held on tight to one of my father's arms as I held on to the other. I know that all of us were thinking the same thing: We had never considered the possibility that Scott Early would ever see the outside of an institution again. We felt as though we had been punched in the stomach. As he was led away, Scott Early looked at me; and what I saw in his eyes, before I looked away, was not any kind of relief, but pure pain and pleading. Then, I did look away. I didn't want to be tempted, even in the Christian sense, to pity him.

When we walked out onto the courthouse steps, the press clustered around the attorneys and around Kelly Englehart and Scott Early's parents.

We were invisible. But we knew that we wouldn't be for very long.

We ran. The pictures of us from that day are of our backs, as we ran away.

Chapter Nine

More than ever, with the story in the paper, Mama didn't want to go anywhere. She refused again to go to church. Papa brought food home when he came back from school.

Another birthday passed that no one except for me remembered. My mother hurried up and got me a new winter coat—wow, I thought ungratefully, from Sears by *mail*!—when she noticed that I'd gotten cards from my grandparents and aunts (and a hundred bucks from the Sissinellis).

Months went by. *Anything* would have been a relief. I kept thinking that if it got dry enough, there'd be a fire on the mountains, and I could watch the smoke jumpers parachute in, as I had once when I was small. It was a wicked wish, because a wildfire meant wildlife and people could die; but I wanted the world to feel the way I did—like a fire in a trap, secret and snared, but so hot that only a bigger blaze could overtake it.

Then, slowly—and she later told me that it was because she prayed every night for hours for the Holy Ghost to guide her hand—Mama began to really notice Rafe. He was talking by then, saying everything he could to get her attention. She started to teach him to use his shape sorter and point out the ball and the apple in his little books and make noises like the cow and the horse.

By then it was late fall, almost the second anniversary. That was the very first time I felt safe to leave the house. I'd left before but had been a wreck the whole time until I could get back home.

Clare and I put our feet into the icy water that was now filling Dragon Creek's pool. Then we lay in the sun, on the prickly dry grass. Despite our dozens of conversations, Clare had never asked me straight up what I felt about the verdict. I don't know why. I would have told her. Maybe she was frightened to open wounds she didn't realize were nowhere near closed.

But that day, suddenly, she seemed to draw herself up straight and it all came out, everything she had wondered about for months on end.

"Did you think he should have gone to an insane asylum?" Clare asked.

"Maybe," I said, "but forever."

"What if he was cured?"

"What would that matter? If I killed someone because I was sick, and then I got well, would that mean I didn't kill them?"

"No, it wouldn't," she agreed, "but it's different if you don't know. Joseph Smith said that God does not look on sin with allowance, but when men sin, allowance must be made for them."

"I get that," I told her. "And you sound so prissy, no offense. But what about after you *do* know? Then you should pay for it."

"Don't you think anybody's ever legally crazy?" Clare asked, checking her top to see if she still had a tan line. "Who's crazy and gets better?"

"Retarded people," I said. "Not people who are getting a PhD in pharmacy. People who were insane all their lives—like born that way."

Clare said, "Huh."

"What does your mother say?" I asked.

"Same as you."

"What does your father say?"

"Same as you."

"What's the matter with you, then?"

"I just think you aren't responsible for what you do if you don't understand it. I think you should try to hate the sin, not the sinner."

"That's not very loyal to Becky and Ruthie."

"Come on, that's not fair," Clare said, "I'm totally loyal. I just think that *nobody* could have done that if they knew what they were doing. Unless they were crazed out on drugs or, like, a paid executioner. That's why I agreed with what the judge ruled. I didn't say I liked it."

I sat up and hugged her.

"At least it's over now," I said, "and if I decide to go back to the basketball team, maybe everybody won't stare at me. Maybe my mother will come out of her daze. Maybe Ruthie and Becky are more understanding than I am, because they had to have known about this."

"That's what I think," Clare said.

I longed so badly to *be* normal, to sound normal—even though I didn't feel normal. And there's only one way a teenage girl can do that, so I asked, "Do you like David Pratt?"

"We weren't talking about David Pratt. We were talking about forgiving and how you felt about the verdict."

"I know," I said miserably. Should I tell her? I thought. What I really think? We'd always been almost each other's mirror image, since we were little girls in primary. She deserved to know.

"Clare," I said, "I could shock you so much with what I really think."

"Nothing you could say could shock me."

"What I really think is he should die, or even better, he

should have his wife killed in front of him, so that he can feel what we feel, now that he's well enough to understand feelings."

Clare breathed out slowly through her teeth, "*Shhhhhhhh*," and I realized she was doing a singing exercise to calm herself. "Ronnie, that's wrong," she finally said. "But it's also a totally normal way for you to feel. The one thing is, he's sorry. He repents."

"What do you mean? I don't care. I don't want him here on earth with Rafe. I don't want him on earth with me."

"Do you want him in paradise with Ruth and Rebecca? Because if he was truly sorry in his heart of hearts, that's where he'd go. That would be a release, an escape. Or do you want him sitting there, having to understand what he did and talk about it and think about it every day, every time he closes his eyes? Which would you think would be worse?"

"I never thought about it that way," I said.

"Well, it seems as though it's really you who has what she wants."

"I never thought about it," I said, "him thinking about it constantly."

"It must be a torment," Clare said quietly. "Now, as for me liking David, well, I like all the Pratt kids."

"I don't think I can talk . . . friend talk now, after what we said."

"I think you couldn't have talked friend talk unless we'd said what we said." That was Clare. Even when she didn't approve, she always understood.

Finally, and in a pretty feeble way, I asked, "Well, I meant, do you *like him* like him?"

"We're way too young for that, Ronnie-o."

"I like . . . I like Miko."

"Are you *nuts*?" she said, and for just those few moments, we were two teenage girls giggling together. It was so good.

"He's . . . totally out of the question! He drinks coffee. I mean, he's a coffee addict! And he's not at all church material. He's probably had sex ten times!"

"You don't know that! Coffee's not a sin if you're not LDS. And he only drinks the fancy kind, that's mostly milk. It probably has about half an ounce of coffee in it. His mom has that machine."

"It's still a sin," said Clare. "That's like saying if you only smoke one cigarette, you're a little sinner."

"It's not a *sin*," I told her. "It's a lifestyle thing. I'm not saying you can ignore it. But it's not going to keep you out of heaven! *Joseph Smith* said that when Judgment Day comes, a lot of people won't go to heaven, and that some who don't will be Mormons! Anyhow, he'll give it up for me. He'll have decaf mochas. He'll convert, and then climb to the top of the tower and wait for me to let down my hair and twine a dark red love knot into it, and carry me off, and marry me, and we'll start a practice together and both be doctors."

"I, uh, hardly think Miko Sissinelli is going to be a doctor!"

"Why? His father's a doctor! He's going to college!"

"Ronnie. He's a goof-off!"

"Your brother Dennis is a goof-off."

"He's only twelve. He thinks putting toothpaste in his hair is a good joke."

"He's still good in school. He called it the Morbid Tabernacle Choir, right there, during the Christmas concert," I said. "And he's still a smart kid. A goofy kid is still a normal kid." We always went with the Emorys to the temple, to hear the choir and take the little kids to the Santa events in the city, every Christmas, except the first one after the murders, when Rafe was only three weeks old. You might have heard records, but you can't imagine what it's like to actually hear them. It's like hearing heaven. The Christmas I was away in California, Clare sang "Silent Night" as a soloist with them, because she was their scholarship student.

Clare said then, "Can you imagine anyone marrying *Dennis*? Ever?"

"I can't imagine anyone marrying anyone. I just want to . . . get out of here. Not away from you. But away from everything, including . . ."

"The shed."

"But not just that. It's mostly that. But I'm not sure I'll ever get away from that. For me, Becky and Ruthie and that day are, like, forever. Like a bad knee. I've stopped thinking that I'll ever 'get over' it, and around here, people will always see me differently. We're totally in each other's pockets constantly—I don't mean you. Everything feels small. Nothing really matters. I want to move to New York and be an actress."

"And a doctor."

"Yes. And a stuntwoman and a detective!"

"I really am going to move to New York and be an actress," Clare said; and I would think, ten years later, of this moment, down by the creek, of two skinny girls with potbellies and size AA cups in our bathing suits and sweatshirts, when I got the tickets in the mail and Clare was playing Beth in the musical of *Little Women* on Broadway. She hadn't even told me she was up for the role; she let it be a surprise. I could never have held something that big inside me.

"I can do it," she said. "I can get a scholarship. To Juilliard. If I study hard."

"Don't you need a . . . I mean, you're wonderful . . . but a professional voice teacher to get in places like that?"

"I've been saving my baby-sitting money. Your voice doesn't

really start to develop, unless you're a child prodigy, until you're . . . you know, in puberty. I've saved two thousand dollars, Ronnie."

"Get out!"

"I have! I made, like, sixty dollars a day dog-sitting the Sissinellis' Yorkie. And I baby-sit the little Finns with my little brothers every day in the summer until noon, while my mother and their mother do their relief stuff. They insist on paying me."

"And you're going to use this . . ."

"To take lessons. I found a studio that a lady has in her house. She's sung at the Met, *in* New York. I can take the bus there. She charges twenty-five dollars for a half hour. If I take one lesson every two weeks, and practice all the time, because she lets you make tapes, I can really train."

"You planned this all out."

"Since I was eleven. There's a huge LDS temple across from Lincoln Center."

"Talk about eyes on the prize." I was referring to a lesson that Brother Timothy had taught us, during his visit, about determination. "I admire that. I'm just yakking. About me. I'm not smart enough to get a full scholarship to college, much less medical school. I'll have to take loans it'll take me until I'm forty to pay off, if I do it. My parents can help some with college, but not much."

"Maybe *you* should marry David Pratt, the doctor's son," Clare teased me.

"If you move to New York and I move to somewhere like Hawaii, we'll never see each other again."

"We'll have the private planes!" Clare said.

"I forgot, of course," I told her, almost laughing.

"And we'll e-mail every day," she said.

"This isn't for years, though," I reminded her.

"But you'll be the one who leaves first," said Clare.

I don't know why she thought so. But as it turned out, I was.

Chapter Ten

*T*he big thing that happened that next spring, when I was fifteen, was that my cousin—named after my mother, but always called "Ceci"—got married.

A month before the wedding, Ceci visited us with her mother, my aunt Juliet, and her fiancé, Patrick-the-Professor. He was handsome, a returned missionary, and already an instructor at NYU. My father said right away, "She hit the trifecta," and Mama gave him a narrow glance. Though I didn't know what the word meant, I knew Ceci supposedly had landed a good catch. Everybody knew that returned missionaries were the best husband material, or so the older girls, like Alora Tierney, said. Alora hated school and worked her brains out to get the grades so she could get a scholarship to BYU only to "land her big fish," as she put it. This infuriated my father, who said BYU was a "meat market" and that if Heavenly Father didn't intend women to understand economics, why did He give them charge of households, and if women weren't intended to understand philosophy, why were they the first teachers of the word, and if they weren't intended to practice psychology, why did the Lord intend they should be mothers?

Patrick came for lunch. He was staying with Uncle Pierce's family, and Aunt Juliet and Ceci were staying with us. Everyone was so dippy and excited. Ceci was twenty, and "the esteemed professor," as my father immediately began calling him (but only around my mother and me), was thirty-three. He was also really bossy and had opinions about everything, especially about women and "immodesty," and "material culture," and what Ceci would be expected to do for him—which sounded like everything from being a cordon bleu chef to a CPA. He said right away that he had "interviewed" my cousin carefully, as if she were trying out for a job. But because he was handsome and "proven," my girl cousins and other girls from the ward were all nodding and willing to listen. To me, he looked like a guy wearing a cardboard suit—pretty good, in other words, unless he stood up close in bright light. My mother asked politely what his area of instruction was.

And, poor soul, it was American literature.

Now, you don't get crosswise of my father on the subject of American literature.

Papa hit Patrick with his Opening Question right away: Did he believe that students should read everything, including Poe, with his dark imaginings, and Hawthorne, with his "morbid emphasis on sin"? Or should text studies be restricted to doctrine-promoting books and poetry, such as those works by Emily Dickinson and Theodore Dreiser? And it was like watching someone walk into a fan. Patrick didn't believe that Hawthorne and Poe or, for that matter, F. Scott Fitzgerald should be read by impressionable students.

"You think that perhaps their faith is not strong enough to withstand the process of discernment?" Papa asked mildly. "Or are you worried that yours isn't strong enough to guide them?"

"Not all students' faith is at the same level of commitment, Brother Swan," Patrick said. "And in any case, there is so much good literature available to us that to dwell on darkness, to introduce it to young minds, seems itself a risk not worth taking."

"Risk?" Papa asked. "Isn't being LDS a risk every day? Isn't the very existence of our religion based on risk, on bold choices to reject the commonplace and embrace the truth, even if the whole world is wrong? Shouldn't students be taught to understand others' points of view, in an environment that promotes inquiry and righteous discernment, or be swayed by them later in life?"

I honestly felt sorry for the guy as Papa invited him to take a walk, because Papa was banging one fist against his open palm by the time they were halfway across the front yard, and Ceci's fiancé looked like he wanted to sprout wings and fly away.

Still, we were glad to be alone, we women. Ceci had her wedding dress with her, which had been Grandma Bonham's and then my aunt Juliet's. All my girl cousins had to try on the wedding dress. It *was* something else, gorgeous ivory satin, with one hundred covered buttons up the back, each with its own little satin loop. It was also teeny, like a big doll dress, but so was Ceci—she weighed about a pound for every button. I couldn't even get it up past my knees, and I'm not that big. Clare got into it, but it wouldn't button. You got to wear your wedding dress for your wedding only if it didn't have short sleeves, a low neck, or was pure white, not ivory. Which I didn't think was totally fair. At a Mormon wedding, only family members who are LDS go to the ceremony. It's very sacred and private. Other friends could come to the reception.

The visit was also really good for my mother.

It was the first time Mama had seen her sister since the funeral. She was very close to my aunt Juliet; they wrote to each other, real letters, not e-mails, almost every week. And they would have been closer if my aunt's husband, Arthur, ever let their family travel. He was afraid to fly and didn't want to drive all the way from Chicago, where they had lived since Ceci was my age. I guess it was all right with my uncle for my aunt to come alone, since if she died on the plane, there would still be one parent for all the younger brothers and sisters, including my aunt's other daughter besides Ceci, who was named Ophelia. We called her "Lee-Lee." I understood the Shakespeare names, but to me, naming your daughter Juliet or Ophelia was like naming her "suicide," and that, I never got.

My aunt was the first person I ever knew named Juliet.

That night, when my mother and her sister were downstairs talking, I wrote to Clare.

"U think he is so hot?" I wrote.

"CC's lucky," Clare wrote back. "MSS love their testimony more than the rest of us. U can't argue with that. Someone who's done his MSS has been through the fire. He's seen the way R faith is treated."

"In *Milwaukee*," I answered. "Come on."

"Like there R no people who need 2B taught the truth in Milwaukee?" Clare asked.

"Maybe, but it isn't Rwanda," I wrote. "He acts like a hero."

"PU here," Clare signed off, meaning "parental units" were in the room.

I was just being a pain.

But the way most girls fluttered around guys was still kind of embarrassing. It was okay with other parents, but not mine. Another weird thing about us, about my parents. Of course, we were excited for Ceci. The wedding was going to be held in Salt Lake, in the *big* temple, and Patrick's family was wealthy. They had given Ceci a pearl necklace and were planning a catered dinner at a restaurant and a professional photographer—only black-and-white shots, Patrick said, and sniffed—all very uptown for Mormons. Usually a Mormon reception was not as big as Gentile weddings, but nice anyhow. Sometimes, it's even in a church basement, with Jell-O and cheese and crackers, but

CAGE *of* STARS

sometimes it's at a fancy hotel. Depends on the family. We were all looking forward to Ceci's, in part because it would be fancy and we'd all have an excuse to make or buy new clothes.

As for Patrick, the more time he spent at our house and church, the more I saw my father's point. He said all the right things, calling us "cousin" and so on, but he didn't act like he was really crazy about Ceci. He acted like *she'd* won the lottery. When I complained about this to my mother one night, she said only, "Marry someone like your father." She gave me a look with her eyebrows raised and added quietly, "Most girls do. Ceci is."

Still, we had a great time. Ceci loved our baby—you could tell she'd be one to have a baby right away—and made a big fuss about him. Rafe was at his cutest, doing things like following the flight of a fly with such fascination, he finally got dizzy and fell over. For the first time, I got to show off my very own little brother, to let others see what I knew—that I loved him as much as I'd loved my sisters. It was even okay that we had to take Aunt Juliet to visit the graves and I had never been. When we pulled up, it touched me to see that Papa's and Mama's headstones were apart, with Becky and Ruthie between them, and that Mama had arranged somehow for two little sculpted hands made of stone to connect Becky and Ruthie to each other. Another person might have found it creepy, but it was very comforting to me. I hated to see everyone go, even stuffy Patrick, because I knew we would go back to being how we were after they left.

Then, just a few days later, a few months after my fifteenth birthday—for which my parents had given me *another* winter coat—my father got me up early and called me out to the barn. He was standing next to Ruby's old stall with a goofy grin on his face. He'd never stored anything in there.

He must have planned it all along.

I named her Jade.

She was a buttermilk beige Percheron, three years old, already green-broke and gentle as a lamb, with one brown and one green eye. "She reminded me of you," my father joked, "because you always seem to have your mind in two places." I wanted to get right up on her, but the lady from Cedar City who'd raised her said she'd never been sat by anyone she didn't know. Still, I wanted to try. The lady held her halter, and I blew into her nose and talked into her ear and stroked her side, the way mother horses lick their babies (horses hate it when you slap them on the neck, so I don't know why everyone does it). Then I sat on the side of the stall and put one leg over. She quivered but let me sit on her right away, there in the stall. The lady was pretty surprised. But Jade was trusting, and we understood each other right off. This obviously wasn't like my other birthdays. I couldn't believe how thoughtful a gift it was. I went running into the house to get Rafe so he could pet her nose.

Jade brought new life into my days. She wasn't like my sweet Ruby, as comfortable (and eventful) as riding a coffee table. I never even put a bridle on Ruby, just a length of rope around her neck that I would touch gently if I wanted her to go one way or the other, which was mostly for Becky and Ruthie to hold on to. Angel horse though she was, Jade had a mind of her own; and I spent hours as spring turned into summer teaching her ground manners, getting her comfortable with a bridle, and training her to stand perfectly still to be washed and picked. Jade wasn't exactly resisting, but all these new things kind of puzzled her. And when she was puzzled, she'd either stop on a dime and pout or have a shaky-shake fit all over, which would have made me laugh if it didn't sometimes wiggle me off a horse that was seventeen hands tall. Jade never went up or bucked, but she was such a wiggler, I finally put her under saddle until she settled down. It didn't take long.

I think I rode Jade every day that summer. I had the best inner thighs in my neighborhood. When I rode at night, it was natural that I remembered having the little girls up in front of me on Ruby, when I'd take her for a stand in the creek, away downstream from the swimming area. One night, Becky told me she wanted a telescope when she grew up, so she could look at every star "in person." We would lie back on Ruby as if she were a sofa, and I would point out the stars in Orion's belt and the handle and cup of the Big Dipper. Becky argued that it was not a cup at all; cups were round, and the dipper was square. And she said she could see a tiny baby star living inside it. Ruthie and I never could. "That's because your eyes are round, and mine are sharp," Becky told me once.

When I took Jade to stand in the water, I tried not to think of them or to wonder if they saw me, if the tiniest stars were *their* eyes. Jade was good in water, and a lot of horses shy from it. I thought someday I might trailer her somewhere we could swim.

In June, before it got too sweltering hot, I rode Jade up the hill to the Sissinellis. I'd seen a car up there, and though I didn't know if the whole family was in town, I thought I'd go over just in case. I couldn't wait to show Jade to Serena. If it turned out that only Dr. Sissinelli was around, the way he sometimes was in and out in summer for a case or a seminar, he'd give me my key so I could start summer cleaning. Having just finished washing Jade and squeegeeing the water out of her coat, I pulled my hair into a braid so I'd look half-human, but I didn't bother to clean up. I was wearing Papa's old flannel shirt tied up in front and my jeans that were almost too small to close and so short that I had to pull them down like hip-huggers.

What I didn't count on was that I'd never ridden Jade on such a pebbly path as the one up the ridge, and she didn't like it one bit. The sound must have bothered her. Though I wasn't scared, she spun around on me twice, and once, her foot slipped. Then she got all spooky and started to sweat so much, I was scraping it off with the reins. I could've taken her home then, but that would basically have been teaching her a vice, so I slowly urged her forward. We weren't really in danger, but she was irritating the heck out of me. Finally, I hauled off and gave her a kick, and she took off running all the way to the Sissinellis' porch. I was bareback and just dug my fingers into her mane along with gripping my reins. When we got to the grass, Jade just stopped with all four feet as if she'd run into a wall, and I went right over her head onto the lawn. I wasn't hurt, except for my butt and a nick on my palm from a piece of gravel, but I was surely embarrassed. No one came out, for which I was grateful. There probably was no one home. Just to make sure, I got up and knocked on the door, rubbing my rear end where my jeans were ripped. As I was heading back down the steps, to where Jade was lazily cropping the Sissinellis' flowers and looking at me with her long-lashed green eye, the door suddenly opened, and there stood Miko. He was barefoot, eating a sandwich the size of my head. He beckoned me inside. I didn't think a thing of it. He had the stereo on so loud—it was Vivaldi, *The Four Seasons*—that I couldn't have heard him if he'd said anything. He kept on eating the sandwich. When the section ended, he said, "Aren't the speakers cool?" He wasn't bragging, just delighted.

"I hear them all the time," I said, "remember? I'm the cleaning lady."

"Bet you didn't think I liked classical, though."

"No, I figured you for vintage Van Halen, through and through. What are you doing here?"

"I needed some stuff, and I like being here alone. Helps me think."

"*You*, think?" I teased him. "Now, that's news."

"Every day is a winding road, you know, Ronnie. Never know what's around the bend." He leaned over and, with his thumb, put a dab of mayo on my nose. "How old are you now, Ronnie?" he asked. "Let's see, Serena's almost sixteen, so that makes you fifteen. Fifteen years old."

"I'm almost sixteen," I said. This was baloney, of course.

"I wish you *were* sixteen."

"How come?" I asked, although I knew. I could tell by the way he was looking at me. And although, if you're LDS, every date is potentially a mate, and that was out of the question for Miko and me, since he was a Catholic and worldly, and nearly four years older, I still wanted to know.

He drank his whole glass of water and said, "Because you're beautiful and you're not a simp."

I was suddenly aware that we were all alone in that big house; and it must have shown on my face, because Miko said, "Don't worry, little saint. I'm not going to ask you for a date or anything. I'm too old for you, and I know you don't do that." He stopped and then said, "She's beautiful, too."

"Who?" I asked.

"Your horse. What's her name?"

"Jade. She has one green eye."

"You have two."

"One of mine is glass, though," I kidded him. "I got her for my birthday. I thought I'd show her to Serena. Is Serena coming?"

"No, my sister has a job this summer that already started. Lifeguarding. Family tradition. Aren't you going out there? She said you were."

"In August, if she still wants me to." I was excited about the trip to Cape Cod. Serena had told me boats took you five miles out into the ocean and that she'd seen humpback whales with their calves.

"You smell like a horse," Miko said. "You took a mean spill. I saw from upstairs. Are you hurt?" I held out my dirty palm. "Now, Miss Swan, this looks like a pretty serious abrasion. Let's see. I'm premed"—he took my hand—"and in my esteemed opinion, I think you'll live. But you better wash it off. Have you had a tetanus shot?"

I said, "Duh."

"Never hurts to ask."

"You can ask anything you want," I told him. And the air between us changed.

"Well, can I ask to kiss you?" Miko said.

"You can ask anything you want," I said again, and he kissed me. He didn't try to grab me or anything, and though I figured that this was probably wrong, I kissed him, too, putting my arms around his neck. It was a real kiss, and it didn't feel sinful. It felt safe and clean and natural as the sunny day outside. I haven't kissed that many boys, and at that time, I hadn't kissed any. I figured Miko had probably kissed a lot of girls, but somehow, I was certain he hadn't kissed them the way he kissed me—as though I were one of the globes and vessels of priceless glass on the mantel, precious and rare. Your first kiss is your first kiss, after all. It made me realize a couple of things. One was that life would continue for me, that there was a chance I would feel something other than mourning and determination in my time. The other was that I had probably loved Miko, in some way, since I was about ten years old and that I would probably, in some way, love him for the rest of my life. That was sad. But at least I *felt* it.

We stood back from each other then, in the silence that danced with little particles in the sunlight from the big cathedral windows, and Miko said, "Let me wash off your hand." He did, at the sink in the kitchen, and though this was an ordinary friend thing, it felt different. It felt unbearable. For the past two and a half years, I'd been crying for no reason about ten times a day, my emotions all over the place; and I thought I might start to cry if I stood there very long. I figured I'd better get home, quick, and I told him I was going as soon as he was done cleaning my hand. Even how gently he put on the Band-Aid made me feel as though I might faint.

Although I probably saw him twenty times over the next few years, Miko and I never spoke about that day, about how he gave me a foot back up onto Jade's back and waved good-bye, with neither of us saying another word. We didn't talk about it until after I'd come home again from San Diego, before I went to college, after everything had happened. Miko was really involved with a girl from the University of Colorado by that time, but he still considered me a friend, the way the rest of his whole family did, and was worried sick about me.

I still think of it as the only purely happy moment in my life between the day my sisters died and the day of my wedding.

I kept it to myself.

I didn't tell Clare, or even Serena. It was like a lucky pebble kept in my pocket that got so shined up from rubbing against the denim that no one could tell it had ever been an ordinary stone. Just as the ring twined of my sisters' soft hair came to resemble something else no one recognized, still, I would always know what it was, and that it was mine, something that time, and even eternity, could never change.

Chapter Eleven

Coming home after visiting the Sissinellis in Cape Cod was difficult.

It wasn't because of Miko, who wasn't even around.

He'd decided to go canoeing with his college friends somewhere in Canada during the time I was out there.

I think he knew it wouldn't be a great idea for us to be around each other, and I was kind of relieved when Serena and Mrs. Sissinelli picked me up at the airport and told me Miko was away. Relieved, but also almost sick with disappointment. Still, I was sensible enough to know that Miko might as well have been from Saturn for all the likelihood of his being my . . . well, my crush. Most girls who go to school with kids who aren't Mormons (and even in Utah, some kids aren't) have the experience of wanting to date a boy who's not of the church. I guess if you grow up with something that's not just your Sunday life, but your Monday-Tuesday-Wednesday-Thursday-Friday-Saturday life, you can want to put yourself against it for a time and see if it holds up. People do it different ways, I suppose.

Anyhow, I was glad that Miko wasn't there, because I was having enough trouble putting him out of my mind. I prayed every morning to forget that June day at his house; and every morning, the memory got more vivid.

What was actually more difficult about coming home was

that visiting the Sissinellis made it pretty easy to get spoiled, just in two weeks. It was also not that difficult to forget my life and what my life meant.

On Cape Cod—in fact, from the moment I left Provo—I was only Ronnie Swan, a curly-haired girl from the Wild West who rode horses and never went to school a day in her life (that was what homeschooling meant, for all Serena's friends knew).

It was *fun.*

It was fun not being "poor little Veronica" or "that one whose sisters were killed" or "London Swan's oldest" or "poor Cressie's girl." I felt free of the two little stone hands on my sisters' graves that locked me to their deaths as surely as they locked them together in their graves. And I didn't feel guilty. For years, I had been in mourning, a mourning as visible as if I'd been born in Victorian times and had worn a long black skirt and bonnet. Plus, I had been *watched* in my mourning, described, like a character from Dickens, even photographed by newspapers and magazines that did "one year later" stories about the murders and about Scott Early's sentence—such as it was. At least right then, I hoped that I might be ready to come out into the light and to see the way others lived. It wasn't that I minded being who I was and always would be; I didn't want to be anyone else forever, or even for long. My parents knew that. They knew I wouldn't be transformed, any more than a missionary is transformed, not forever. I would take this journey and make it part of me, as missionaries did, but I wouldn't become part of it.

The night before I left, my father again quoted some poet, about leaving home in order to return to it and see it with new eyes. "There's nothing wrong in that, Ronnie," he told me. "It's healthy."

He understood, though I had never told him, how all the freedom I had once felt on our land, in our hills, had been trashed by Scott Early. Once upon a time, that little map, of our house and my room, our church and Jackie and Barney's store, had been all the world I'd ever needed; but now it felt broken and soiled. I wanted to see who I was outside the limits of our private world at the foot of the mountains, to see if I could restore some of that sense of it being where I belonged, settled among those who'd watched me growing my whole life.

The Sissinellis were part of that world, but they weren't *of* it. And the airplane ticket they had sent to me was a ticket to discovery. My parents had objected, politely at first, to their paying for it; but the Sissinellis insisted that I had gone above and beyond in my care of their house (as I had, with all that polishing, for my own pleasure). It was like extra-duty pay. It would be their joy, especially given what had happened, they said; an early birthday gift. My parents finally gave in, gracefully.

And so I had my first flight on an airplane. When we traveled before, we drove to Florida to see Grandma (a really fun experience, since Ruthie was about three the last time and had to stop to go potty every twenty minutes) or to see my aunts and uncles in Salt Lake or Mesa. I knew how long the flight would be, almost coast to coast, so I brought a biography of Charles Lindbergh and a novel. But I never opened either book.

I was so distracted by the passengers, the movie, the bag lunch, and even the peanuts that the ride seemed to pass in minutes. The little eight-seater plane that took me out from Boston to Barnstable Airport was supposed to be scary, but I thought the fact that it flew so low was absolutely awesome. You could see everything, all the little lakes and waterways, sailboats like wings on the ocean, flying far from the harbors. I loved the feel of the air under the plane, even when it pitched, rose, and dropped. I imagined that this ride was as close as I'd get to knowing how it must feel to be an eagle.

Once we got to their home, which was as nice as the one in Utah but not so big, the Sissinellis showed me to my room, where there was a bed with a mattress the size of the Great Salt Lake and more pillows than we had in our whole house. I fell into the bed and slept ten hours.

I didn't dream. I didn't wake drenched in sweat. I woke to the sounds of birds and the sight of sky painted with small, shredded white clouds through the open skylight over my head; and I turned over and slept another half hour. It was like being at a spa.

The next morning, I went with Serena to her job, where I watched her teach little kids to dog-paddle and float in the "ponds," which is what they call lakes out there. Serena in this setting was a different person for me. She was so pretty and gentle and kind. The little kids all seemed to trust her, even the ones who were scared of water. They ran to her when she appeared in her red swimsuit and her long sleeveless shirt that read WELLFLEET REC, her straight black hair looped up in a knot. I would have expected Serena to have a summer bikini that left barely anything to the imagination. But it turned out that the Sissinellis were actually pretty strict parents, and the stuff Serena had done around us in Utah was mostly to impress us—and mostly when she was younger and having what she called "the traditional eighth-grade rebellion." Her bathing suit was two-piece, but pretty modest (not for me, but for her). While she taught, I swam all the way across the lake and back. My shoulders felt like they were going to come out of the sockets. Playing in our little creek was nothing like this; I was lucky I had muscles.

For the first time that night, I ate lobster (I'd forgotten that I got hives from oysters, but I had no problems) and decided this food had to be some kind of special blessing. My stomach literally protruded when I was finished. I'd brought my own traveler's checks taken from my savings, but the Sissinellis just paid for everything as if money were a thing they didn't think about.

They told me why they lived there part of the year.

Mrs. Sissinelli, who asked me to call her by her first name, Gemma, had grown up in Boston and met her husband there. But he'd spend his summers working on an uncle's ranch in Arizona when he was a boy. So they'd compromised, once they could afford to do that. "The property costs so much out here, you have to be, like, a movie star to afford a house on the water," Mrs. Sissinelli said, "and when the children were small, I didn't want to worry about them wandering to the drink!" That night, as we sat in the restaurant, we actually did see a movie star, Dennis Quaid, with his son. Even Serena was impressed.

"Do you think he had a face-lift, Pops?" she asked her father.

"Pretty sure," said Dr. Sissinelli.

"How can you tell?" I asked.

"He wouldn't really have a rim of the white of his eyes that shows when he's not trying to open his eyes all the way," Dr. Sissinelli explained. "That's kind of a clue that a person has had a brow lift. They're a bit more common among men who have to depend on looking younger than they are for their jobs; but you'd be surprised how many regular businessmen have cosmetic surgery, too."

"Do you do that?" I asked him.

"No," he said, laughing. "This is my ordinary old face, Ronnie."

"No, I mean do you do anesthesia for cosmetic surgery?"

"I do," said Dr. Sissinelli. "But I do that for a special reason."

"Why?"

"Because if people are determined to take such a big risk as having general anesthesia for such a relatively, well, trivial

reason, they should have the best of care. You can die just as easily from cosmetic surgery as you can from surgery to remove an
appendix or remove a tumor; and it would be a terrible blow to
a family to lose a parent or a young adult for that reason."

I had never thought of it that way. "You wouldn't think of
your doing that for a humanitarian idea," I said.

"Just for the bucks, huh?"

"No, I didn't mean that at all!" I said, and blushed.

"I know you didn't," he said, and Mrs. Sissinelli slapped his
hand. "I actually teach cosmetic surgeons about the importance
of anesthesiology in pain control and blood loss during these big
operations, such as liposuction or skin tucks. That's what I do in
Boston, in the summer. So I essentially have two jobs."

"You can't only do cosmetic surgeries. People in Utah don't
have cosmetic surgery," I said.

"You'd be surprised, Ronnie," Dr. Sissinelli told me, wiping
his lips with his napkin. "But of course, I do my work in all kinds
of surgeries, planned and emergency."

Later, we all sat on their deck; the sea air, even inland, was
like a warm bath that never got you wet. "This is amazing," I
said. "The air feels like . . . it's so soft."

"You're not used to humidity, Ronnie," said Serena, laughing.
"You're going to end up looking like an old cowpoke if you don't
use moisturizer."

"I use hand cream after I work in the barn," I told her.

That night, I got introduced to washing my face with grains
and putting on moisturizer. And Serena was right, it did make a
person look glowy and clean, as if I had on blusher from my little French palette when I didn't. Serena was pretty impressed
with my Parisian makeup. It made me feel sophisticated that she
was. I liked the softness of my cheeks and the sweet almond
smell of Serena's moisturizer and sunscreen. When I looked at

the bottom of the jars, though, I saw the stuff cost fourteen dollars for a jar half the size of a pint of milk. Still, I thought I might save for it. It wasn't the same as glitter eye shadow. She also introduced me to sports bras, which made running a whole lot easier, and gave me a pair of her, like, ten pairs of running shoes, to keep. I'd been running in my basketball shoes.

On the first Friday, I saw the ocean.

Serena drove me to the National Seashore. We took bikes and a picnic lunch. The dunes were like massive waves of the palest maple sugar and led down to something I had seen pictures of, but I could never have predicted how it would actually look—vast and in bright blue motion. There was something about its endlessness, its patience, and its . . . I can only say its face, changing with the light and the time of day, ruffling and swelling, delivering shells and sweeping them back with its indifferent hand. Serena was used to seeing it and wanted to go on riding toward the lighthouse, which she said had a light that would shine fourteen miles out to sea. But I couldn't move. I laid down my bike and sat on the ground for so long that Serena said she'd grab me on the way back and pedaled off. And I sat, the sun burning my neck and forearms in a way I'd regret later that night, forgetting even to eat my lunch, until I felt the waves were inside me, their rise and rock and break and fall in rhythm with my breathing. I would have sat there all night, listening to the roar and the hiss. "I don't think I could handle this all the time," I told Serena when she got back. "It's too much for a person. I don't think I'd ever do anything else."

"Maybe you'll live by the ocean when you grow up. This one's the scary one, the North Atlantic, the one that's cold and rough. Down there"—Serena gestured—"there are a hundred wrecked ships that got driven into the rocks. The Sound, on the other side, is warmer. We can swim there. Have you seen the

Pacific? I guess it's scary, too, sometimes. But California, it's different from here. The weather and the people are more gentle. More nuts, too."

"I've never seen either one before now."

"I can't imagine never having seen it before."

"I can't believe that I am."

One morning, when everyone else was asleep, I went into Miko's room. There was a pile of clean clothes on the end of his bed and swimming trophies from when he was little on a pyramid of shelves. His closet door was open, and I recognized one of his old leather jackets and put my hand in the pocket. There was nothing in there except a flower, a purple clover, dried up. I opened his top bureau drawer. There was change, and a ton of arrowheads, some baseballs and a cologne bottle, a Scout knife and a bunch of little parts of things, like the insides of phones or speakers, and a couple of CDs out of their cases. In the raised part, where an older man would have cuff links and rings and such, Miko had an envelope of photos. I shook them out into my palm. I knew it was like looking at his diary, but I wanted to see a picture of him with his girlfriend, if he had one. They were mostly of his friends, skiing, either blowing powder or wiped out, laughing, gigantic, red, male smiles, and one of this blond guy I had seen a lot at their house sitting by a stone fireplace with a pretty girl on his lap looking mad at him.

But the next to last one in the stack was . . . me, on Jade, shot from one side and above.

I almost didn't see it, because it was turned backward in the pack, facing the others, out of the usual order. I had to guess he took it from his bedroom window that day in June, because I was wearing my cutoffs and Jade was under saddle and going up the path to the ridge. I was sitting with the reins in my lap, trying to knot my hair up in back. From the light, it looked to be late afternoon. The scrub plants were smudges of gray and green, with a vivid yellow streak here and there. If it hadn't been me, I would have thought it was beautiful, like a calendar photo. I didn't know what I wanted to do with that picture. A part of me wanted to take it, as if it were proof of something. But it was Miko's, and I would never know why he took it, if it was just to use up the roll. Still, something inside me hummed like a tight guitar string as for a second I let myself think about Miko focusing his camera on a girl with tangled red hair, her bare legs milky above her cowboy boots, tucked tight against the mare's honey-colored coat. I put it back into the envelope just as he had left it.

I won't say I didn't think of it again, especially when Miko called and they put me on the phone with him. He asked how I liked the Cape, and I said, like a dumb little kid, "I saw the ocean for the first time." I could hear him laughing the way you would at a child, and I gave the phone back to Serena.

But there were more than enough wonders to keep my mind busy. Out on a whale-watching boat, I saw a whale roll and looked into the great ruddy cave of its mouth, not thirty feet from me, as Serena told me about how this huge creature nourished its massive body by scooping up little shrimp smaller than my fingernail like a giant sieve through the thicket of tissue it had instead of teeth. When Serena's father got us up at four A.M. to go fishing, I saw a whale shark longer than Dr. Sissinelli's boat and almost fell out of the boat trying to take pictures. I saw crabs blurt and burrow into the sand and seals with their soft eyes and humanlike heads rise up to look at me as I looked back at them. There were miles of cranberry bogs and marsh grass that smelled of vinegar and lime. I saw more BMWs in one place than I thought there could be anywhere on earth except Germany, and more food in the Sissinellis' fridges than I'd ever seen anywhere but on the shelves of our "year's worth" of beans and peanut butter. I remember trying to explain the food stock to Serena and her friends, some of them just as nice as she was, but some who were stuck-up. It took a whole evening by a beach campfire. It wasn't paranoia, like the people who holed up with guns and didn't pay taxes, I told them, but a sort of way of remembering the pioneer ideal, how they had to put by for winter and surviving disasters. Mama also always said it was a great idea in case someone got sick or lost his job. "Why wouldn't you just go to the Stop and Shop?" asked a girl named Jessie. I could hardly look at her, because the only thing on her breasts covered by her swimsuit were the nipples.

"If it was destroyed, there would be no Stop and Shop. There would be no electricity, which is why we have a wood stove and a coal burner, and lamps that run on oil, but a regular stove that uses gas, too," I told her. "It's a tradition. If you are prepared, you are never lost, I think it says. It's part of our commandments."

"You mean your Ten Commandments?"

"No, we have those, too," I said, almost laughing. "These are . . . social things, requirements that are part of our covenants, not really scripture, but sort of based on that and made into practical life."

"Do you believe all of it?" a boy called Cameron asked me. I knew he was Serena's boyfriend, although they hadn't really had a date. He held her hand as they sat on the blanket, with his face, with soft lips as beautiful as a girl's, made sharp by the shadows.

"I guess I don't question it," I said. "I mean, we're not robots. You can be a Mormon in pretty wide limits. My dad is. The way I think of it is, anybody's church beliefs would sound as crazy to us as ours do to you; and some of it is based on things that happened over a hundred years ago, passed down from the early prophets who started the church. It's a pretty new religion. Some of it makes sense in the light of day, and some of it doesn't. Some people say we're not even Christians, because we believe that Jesus was a person who became a god, just the way Catholic saints became saints after they died. I grew up believing it because it's a way of life. The older you get, and see how your church affects you, the easier it gets. It's like a shield. It keeps you safe. Like, we don't have to decide whether to smoke, because you just . . . don't. It's a pretty healthy way of life."

"Except for the sweets," Serena put in.

"Got me!" I said. "Mormons wouldn't be Mormons without their desserts. That's what 'Deseret' means. Pound cake." Serena punched me on the arm. "I'm kidding."

I got some funny looks, but you're used to that around people who aren't LDS. Generally, the other kids were just curious. Most of them didn't go to any church, though the Sissinellis went to Our Lady of the Waves. Serena's friends seemed to kind of get a kick out of a girl whose whole life was planned out—well, not planned out, but more or less the same as every other Mormon girl's life anywhere in the United States, right down to the lessons we learned on Family Home Evenings. Only one guy, this surfer dude, a guy Serena didn't much like (though she had when she was younger), said, "It sounds like you have no freedom at all."

"But that's the thing," I told him, "you do. You have free will, and the gift to you is that once you're old enough, you choose it. You don't have to be a Mormon because you were raised a Mormon. It's like Jews who don't practice their religion but they're still Jews. Some people don't. They're called Jack Mormons. . . ."

"Like Catholics who don't go to church except on Christmas," Serena said.

"In a way, yes," I agreed.

Overall, I learned that New Englanders had a certain pride about being tolerant of anyone's way, as long as no one was hurt by it—toward gay people, for instance (I practically fell over when I saw the men in Provincetown, six feet tall and dressed up as Cher). They accepted me, asked me and Serena to come swimming at their pools, and one, a boy called Lucas, even got a mild crush on me. I didn't feel the same toward him, though I liked the attention. I used the excuse that I was younger than Serena, too young for dates, because he was a nice boy.

The two weeks were over in an instant.

Before I left, Serena and her mother gave me this box, and it was filled with the lotions and creams Serena used, enough, it seemed, that it would last until I grew up. "But you didn't have to do this," I told them, shocked by their generosity. You never felt with the Sissinellis that they were trying to impress you; they just gave as if it were totally ordinary, a funny kind of tithing.

"You have a beautiful face, Ronnie, and beautiful skin," Mrs. Sissinelli said. "That climate out there can punish it. And there's skin cancer, too, if you don't protect yourself from the sun."

I was so thrilled—it felt like Christmas—that I hugged them. "This has been the best time, the best rest, I've ever had in my life."

"You deserve it," Serena said with an undertone of sadness in her voice, like the cello's sound in the orchestra. "What will you remember most? From this time, I mean? I'm not saying that we never want you to come back."

"Definitely the first time I saw the ocean," I said. "Definitely. But so much else. Catching fish that weighed fifteen pounds. The picnics. Being in the water more often than a seal. Just . . . so much."

When it was time to leave, everyone hugged me and Serena said, "Couldn't you stay longer?"

But by then I was homesick, not for Utah, but for Rafe and my father. I hugged them again; they felt like family to me. "This is probably the farthest from home I'll ever be in my whole life," I said.

"A whole life is a long time," said Serena's dad. "I've heard you want to study medicine. There are plenty of good places here to do that. And there are Mormon wards in Boston. Utah is your home, but it doesn't have to be the only place you live."

I had known this, of course, but never entirely taken it in. I could live somewhere else and still be myself. Leaving for college had always been something out there, like a house being prepared for me to move into. But I imagined I'd go to BYU—like everyone else. Now, I reconsidered: I didn't have to. I could study hard and get good scores and maybe get a scholarship to another place, a place where Becky and Ruth hadn't died. A place where I could be both the Ronnie I was there and the Ronnie I was here. I could work until I had enough money for a year of college, or win a scholarship; and I could go away—at least for a while. It might be healing. It might be acceptable. It wouldn't mean that I wasn't a good Mormon girl. It would mean I was different, like my mother, but not in a bad way.

On the airplane home, I thought about it, examining it from one side, then another. I thought about how I would explain this to my parents to avoid hurting them. There was no hurry; I had years to think this over, weigh it, change my mind, and change it back.

Still, it was exciting and frightening, yet reassuring.

My parents were quietly happy to see me so healthy and tanned, and Rafe was so excited that he ran under the security rope and jumped into my arms. I think they expected me to babble all the way home about what I'd done, but I was quiet. I wanted to ride Jade and see Clare and my other friends. I loved my family, but I felt as though I were sinking back into the mourning, the sad life edge that was like a dark border around stationery.

When I got home, I saw an envelope, unopened, on the hall table; and a terrible tang came up in my throat when I looked at the return address. It was from someone named "Early."

"It's not him," my mother told me quickly. "It's from his parents. I haven't been able to open it, either," she said, glancing at the plain gray envelope as if it were a scorpion. "But I think I should. I have no reason to believe that they want anything from us, Ronnie. I think it's just that, as parents, they feel as much grief, of a different kind, as we do. I think they must have wanted to reach out; imagine if your child had done such a thing."

"I'd just burn it," I told her, carrying my clothes to the washing machine.

"That wouldn't be fair," my mother said. "I'm going to pray about the wisdom of reading this letter. And when I'm ready, I know there'll be an answer."

And there was, but it was an answer so far out beyond what I expected that, for the first time in my life, I wondered if my parents were sane.

Chapter Twelve

Since the course work for my junior year was already finished, I spent the time before Christmas getting ready to take my college exams. With my mother, I reviewed the essentials of all I learned in algebra I and II, geometry, and precalc, as well as biology, chemistry, and physics. With my father, I reviewed vocabulary and the differences among words: *A raccoon is to a polar bear as a Muslim is to an Islamic extremist. A carpenter is to an architect as a choreographer is to* . . . You get the picture. I studied a flip book of words no ordinary person ever uses in real life: ascetic, amalgamate, amortize. We went over the hero and the antihero, the protagonist and the antagonist, the individual's relationship and obligation to society, the individual's knowledge of and abuse of power, the individual's relationship to nature, the individual's alienation from society as expressed by his search for harmony with nature, the individual's journey inward as represented by his journey over the course of the novel—as in *The Adventures of Tom Sawyer*. I was madly bored by the individual.

So stuffed with knowledge, I felt like a carrot-spice muffin— a treat made from stuff that would otherwise be too good for you to enjoy.

Once I got my dates, I went to my father's high school on two different days and chewed my way through six pencils.

We waited for my scores. My father said, "You'll shine, Ronnie."

I said, "Dad, there were words on those tests, like 'deleterious,' that I never saw before in my life. I should have studied Latin. I couldn't even find a root word to work from, except 'delete.' It sounded like a side dish on a deli menu."

"But that was the right root word. Deleterious means having a harmful effect on someone, subtracting something," my father encouraged me.

Since I was a minor and they were addressed to my parents, when the scores for my tests came, I had to wait, both times, on pins and needles, until my father got home. Right away, both times, I knew from his face that there was something to celebrate.

I got a combined 1500 on my SATs and 34 on my ACTs.

"Well done," my father said simply. But he was beaming.

My mother said, "Oh, Ronnie, my sweetheart. My bright, beautiful girl."

Rafe said, "Go, go, Ronnie," and we all laughed at him. Mama insisted on calling my grandmother.

Grandma said, "Veronica, I'm not surprised. You are a survivor."

Since that summer, I'd been turning the away-from-home thing over and over in my mind, and I figured this was as good a time as any to bring it up. "I've been thinking," I told my folks, "that I might not go to BYU. I might . . . With these scores, I might apply to some other places."

My mother looked a little alarmed. "Far from here?" she asked.

"Maybe," I ventured. "I really liked the ocean."

"You don't go to college to look at scenery," my father said. "On the other hand, there's nothing wrong with considering other places. I wouldn't suggest Berkeley, but there's Yale. . . ."

"Yale?" my mother squeaked.

"I'll get a scholarship," I told her. "And since I'm young, I can work a whole year before I start. I can save up my money."

"You're not going to save up Ivy League tuition baby-sitting and cleaning the Sissinellis' house," Mama said.

"I thought I might train as an emergency medical technician, and work at that from when I'm eighteen until nineteen," I said.

"You've given this thought," Papa said.

"It's a worthy thing to do, Papa," I said. "And in cities, EMTs can make more than twenty thousand dollars a year—so with that, and my savings, it might take me a little longer than most people. . . ."

"Is being a doctor something you feel is your destiny?" Mama asked me. "Or is it just a glamorous idea?"

"I've known I'd be a doctor since I was a kid," I told them. "I've known since Becky burned her hand."

"It's not easy to have such a demanding profession and raise a family," Mama told me.

"But people do it," I told her. "I might not get to have so many children, unless my husband stayed home or we switched off working—"

"Whoa!" my father said. "That's something you really have to think through. If the mother is the sole breadwinner in a house, wouldn't the man feel diminished?"

I looked my father right in the eye. "Not if he was like you," I said.

He looked at me right back. "You know, you're right," he said.

A few months later, just as it got warm, for my sixteenth birthday, my mother came up with an idea that knocked my socks off.

She hosted a dance.

For me.

As if I were the Pine Mountain equivalent of a debutante.

It was a sweet, goofy gesture on her part. It just wasn't their style. It wasn't anyone's, but ours especially. I know she meant it to make up to me for . . . so much, for the past, the coats from Sears, the silence when I left my childhood and turned thirteen. And probably also a reward for doing well in school, a combined graduation and "nice job" gift, for all the meals I'd cooked and diapers I'd changed, for cleaning the house and ironing Papa's shirts, for the hours I'd spent searching the Net for what I was supposed to be learning in my sophomore year and part of my junior year and then basically teaching it to myself, giving myself tests and sending in the scores. It was as if Mama'd slowly awakened from a coma or from a long sleep—she started responding to questions by blinking her eyes, then learned to sit up and then walk. It was strange having her around, humming, making biscuit dough and pies. Whenever she'd walk into the kitchen, on good days, fully dressed and with her hair done up, I'd jump.

The recovery started with little hints. Mama got out projects, not just the knitted hats, which her hands made without thinking, and set to work on them. She made blankets for new babies expected in our family, a wedding quilt for one of my father's nieces, whose husband had died many years before in a farming accident and who was about to marry again. She went to work, and Relief Society, even to the center in town that distributed food to the needy. She would still stop, sometimes in the middle of a sentence, and stare out at the shed, but then she wouldn't go blank and leave the room, to slip back under the quilts. She would begin to cry. The crying seemed like a comfort. She would cry and pet the sketches of Ruthie and

Becky she'd drawn for their funeral, which my father had matted and framed. When my father came in, she would kiss him. He seemed very relieved, and the walking at night slowed down. There were times I could hear him down in the kitchen, also crying—the big, sloughing sobs that men do. But I would also hear Mama come out and say, "Lunny," and lead him into their room.

They were slowly returning to normal, and I thought that I was, too. I'd convinced myself that my mourning was about to become sweet memories, and that might have happened if things had gone along as they were.

The party just seemed like one more proof we were turning the corner.

I didn't know how to react.

Our lives for the past few years had been quiet and very private, deliberately.

Only this last summer, for the first time since my sisters died, had I gone down to camp out with my friends and cousins near the creek at the Pioneer Days reunion. The previous two years I'd stayed away, and my cousins Bridget and Bree had respected my space. I didn't go anywhere except with Clare, and then only once in a while—Christmas shopping in Provo, lessons, Sunday school, Young Women's if I was interested in the topic. I did my service at Guiding Gait, the rehabilitation stable I donated Ruby to. Ruby remembered me, and when she saw me, she would clomp over to me and whicker like a filly until I climbed into the paddock. And then she would lay her big head on my shoulder. It was always hard to leave her, but I had Jade.

The only bad thing about the party was that I didn't get to dress up for it until after the first surprise, when about fifty people took my picture with my mouth hanging open like a fish on land and burdocks sticking out of my hair. I'd been grooming Jade. To make it a real surprise, my mother had told me that when I was finished, I should stop and ride Jade up to the church building and bring her back a UPS package someone had left there for her by mistake. She didn't know how big the package was, she said.

I got to the front step, and suddenly all these people came running out of a tent set up in back and yelled, "Surprise!"

I about fainted.

Then I made Jade wheel and kicked her up to a trot back to the house and set the land speed record for taking a shower and changing into a long skirt and the Pima cotton peasant blouse I'd bought on Cape Cod. I washed my face, put on moisturizer, eye shadow and blush, and lip gloss with a brush, then shook my hair down and twisted each piece around with my fingers. There were pictures of me then, too, looking pretty. But the first pictures of my only birthday party were of me in my Lady Dragons T-shirt, all dirty from bathing my horse. And in time, I treasured them even more.

With Clare's help and me having no idea, Mama had invited every boy and girl I knew, including any available cousins my age, some of them all the way from Arizona. Serena came, though Miko was away in Europe for his school break, and she gave me a forest green DKNY sweater—real cashmere, which I still have—from both of them. I danced with everybody. I opened so many presents, it was like a baby shower. My parents gave me an iPod. Clare had gone to a mall in St. George and made me a CD of her singing every song that was special to me, from "Respect" to my favorite hymn, "O My Father," to "Somewhere over the Rainbow" to "Everybody Hurts" to "Il mio tesoro." My cousins pitched in and gave me a portable sewing machine; it weighed about six pounds, and with it I could sew anything. I got boxed CD sets and Gap jeans and two hand-knit mohair scarves from Sister Barken. And my grandpa Swan, totally out of his quiet character, sent me the sweetest thing of all, my grandma's wedding gown. It wasn't like Ceci's, because my grandma Swan had been a bigger woman. She'd died in a car accident ten years before, when, as Grandpa wrote, he'd thought she was as good as living forever. But she'd always wanted one of her granddaughters to wear her gown, and Grandpa figured I was the one. Instead of satin, it was sewn of old watermarked silk; and with its long puffed sleeves that gathered tight at the wrists and its train that could be caught up in a loop, Grandpa said it was meant to look like a riding habit, because Grandma had horses in her blood, just as I did.

Everyone seemed to want this to be the happiest birthday I'd ever had

And it was.

There was even a deejay, who played everything from Motown and Abba to bleeped hip-hop and techno classical, and my father's famous root beer, and a cake the size and shape of a sunflower, with golden candy beads all over it. It was past midnight before the last guests went back to the cars they'd hidden all over the place and drove away.

"Why did you do this?" I asked my mother the next morning after church.

It was Sunday, so we would have to wait to clean up the tent they'd borrowed until the next day, so as not to violate the Sabbath. But that was fine with me. I liked the Sabbath because after church I could lie around and read, as long as it was something decent. And in recent months, it had been a time I spent alone with my mother, while my father took Rafe on short walks.

As we sat together, she explained, "You deserved a treat, a celebration of just Ronnie. You never faltered. You never used the tragedy as an excuse for stepping over the line."

"Is that it? Just because I did what I was supposed to?"

"Grace under pressure, I guess."

"Thank you, Mama," I said.

But that wasn't all there was to it. My parents were telling the truth about rewarding me. But it turned out that they had what you would call, if my parents were a different kind of people, an ulterior motive.

They had two.

I don't mean to suggest they would really have tried to ease a shock with a bribe. But I know they hoped it wouldn't hurt.

On Monday, my mother let me sleep in, and when she woke me up, she sat down with me for some chamomile tea. I made toast and gave Rafe a bite every time he ran past me. He had a face full of frosting with little gold sugar beads in it. My mother said, "He got into the leftovers of the cake. I'll never figure out how. You couldn't open Tupperware until you were four. I still have a hard time."

Then she took my hand.

She said, "Ronnie, in September, Dad and I will be married twenty-five years. I'm almost forty-five years old. You're almost a young woman. And so I wanted you to know before I told anyone else: We're having a baby."

Floored for the second time in forty hours, I said, "Are you past where . . . ?"

My mother said, "Yes. It's a boy. He'll be born right around, well, the due date is November seventeenth."

I gasped. "Did you plan that?"

My mother laughed.

She *laughed*, and before I was pleased, I was completely disgusted.

"No," she said. "We didn't *plan* it at all. I thought I was having menopause. I'm not even sure we have the dates right." This verged on too much information, so I changed the subject.

"But won't it remind you?" I asked, my voice like the ring of flint.

"Yes," she said, "and that's hard. But I believe that Ruthie and Becky had a hand in this, honestly. That they wanted to send Rafe and this new soul to us from their position in paradise, knowing what we can't know."

"How do you know it's a boy? Because you're not . . . you know . . ."

"Showing. I am, but I wear all these smocky things. And I had a test called a CVS." I knew she wouldn't have had an abortion for any reason.

"You wanted to know it was a boy to prepare yourself."

"Yes, I guess. It's easier. I would have welcomed a little girl, a little girl like all my girls, but I wanted to be prepared for how I'd feel."

"I'm glad you're happy, Mama."

"Aren't you?"

"Of course," I said. "I just all of a sudden feel disloyal to them. To Ruthie and Becky. Being happy. Having a party. Going on with our lives."

"Do you think they'd have wanted us to grieve forever?"

"No. But yesterday morning, before I knew about the party, I rode Jade to the graves, to bring flowers. And I had the sense that there was something I should know that I didn't. I guess this was it."

My mother got up and poured Rafe juice into his sippy cup. She had never regained the weight she'd lost after my sisters died, so even with a thread or two of gray in her dark hair, she looked younger than she was. She still carried Rafe everywhere on her back in a pack, and he was a big boy. Now she would have to stop that. But she never let Rafe out of her sight. There was no question of his going down to the stable with me, as Ruthie and Becky had. She would never have let me take him up on Jade. I was worried she'd make him a scaredy boy, keeping him so close. I supposed another baby would help. I still couldn't quite believe it.

Then my mother said, "I don't think that's what they wanted you to know."

"What?" I asked.

"I've imagined myself telling you this a hundred times since we decided, Ronnie. And I still don't know if I'll find the right words."

"Go on," I said. "Are we moving?" I was hoping she'd say yes.

"No. We're . . . going to forgive him."

There was no question about whom she meant. Stunned, I let my hands fall in my lap. For some reason, I thought of my iPod and my sweater, and of how all of it was meaningless stuff now, blasted into ash by one sentence. I thought of my weeks on Cape Cod and all the college applications I'd sent for, all meaningless paper. But I still had to know what she meant, so I asked, "How?"

"Don't you want to know why, first?"

"If you want to tell me. I have to be totally honest, Mama. I don't care."

"Right before we found out about the new baby, your father was awake, trying to read, just in torment, sitting down and getting up. I was watching him, and I could tell there was something he wanted to say but was afraid to. Usually, it doesn't do any good to try to pry information out of your father. But I decided to try. I asked him to share with me. He sat down on the bed and said, 'Cressie, we have to forgive him. We'll never be free unless we do.' And suddenly it made perfect sense to me. The letters from his parents are so filled with contrition and bewilderment. They don't understand what happened any more than we do. And I don't want you to think that they suggested this. They didn't. It's our choice."

I couldn't speak. All the old feelings kindled inside me, like firewood that had dried, and went up in seconds. Scott Early had already been let off the hook. Now we were going to make sure he felt all better about it.

Those little graves. Jade cropped the grass while I'd placed a Mason jar of wild geraniums on it, which probably were dead by now because it had been so dry. I'd talked to Ruthie and Becky, my hand stroking the ring of their hair on its thin silver chain, telling them about my wish to be a doctor who helped children and how they had helped me make that choice. Telling them about the huge whale in the ocean, with its gentle murky eyes. Assuring them that they would be next to my heart as long as I lived and when I finally lay down beside them to wait for that waking-up morning, as the old gospel song said. How could anyone look at those tiny headstones and have the desire to *forgive* the man who made them necessary?

"Mama," I finally choked out around a lump made of anger and tears I would not allow myself to shed, "don't you think this is a betrayal of Ruthie and Becky? Can't his own family take care of him? Are you so happy that you feel like forgiving everyone for everything, because of the baby?"

Are you off your nut? I really wanted to ask.

"I struggled with those very questions after we decided, Ronnie, and I still struggle," said Mama. She quietly folded and smoothed the quilt on her lap. "But I can't mother Rafe and this baby and you with this . . . this shard of hatred in my heart. I don't expect you to understand, until you pray and study it, that we're doing this for ourselves, not for him. He's . . . a good person, Ronnie. For the past few months, he's been going out . . ." I gripped the table, and my mother added quickly, "Not alone. He goes with other patients, and has visiting privileges; he wears a bracelet and stays over with his family, and his wife—"

"I don't want to hear this," I said.

"I told you, Ronnie, this is for us," she pleaded.

Not for me, I thought, definitely not for me. Not for me, who held my sisters as they changed from cuddly little monkeys to stiff, cold little dolls.

"I hope the Heavenly Father can help you see this, Ronnie," said my mother. "I can't see into your heart right now." Lucky you, I thought, because it is a coal, and you are at the center of it. "We know that this is the right choice for us, and we've spoken with the mediator at the hospital. He's setting things in motion. There will have to be a period of preparing, for Scott Early and for us. We're not the first people who have ever done this. Not by far. It's becoming a way to replace revenge with reconciliation. As the procedure goes forward—"

"Count me out," I said flatly.

"Ronnie, this is a decision we've made for our family," Mama said, a hint of the Bonham steel in her voice.

"Thank you for the party, Mama, and the iPod, and Jade, and all your love. Thank you for Rafe," I told her. "Thank you and our Heavenly Father for Ruthie and Becky. My sisters.

Your daughters. And Scott Early's mistakes. I guess he's over them. I'm not. Please, Mama, don't speak of this to me again."

As I walked away, I could hear the quiet catch of breath that meant she was beginning to cry. Cry, I thought. Go on and cry. I didn't look back.

Chapter Thirteen

"You should go with us, Ronnie," Mama told me. "You of all people need to be released."

I didn't answer her. I just kept working on the scarf I was beading for Clare's birthday. Hobbies. I had about four hundred hobbies all of a sudden. Jade shone like her name. I made earrings. I whittled. I made brooches from antique buttons, taken from the box that was to have held Becky's dolly clothes. My Christmas presents were almost finished.

"Veronica Bonham," Mama said.

Ignoring her was not okay. In the rest of the world, our teaching at Family Home Evening had said just the week before, it was wrong that young people set the rules for everything—what people wore, what they said and how they said it—that ours was a culture of young people. My father said that people used to want to grow up, and now they want to grow young. I could lip off to my mother, but not like a kid on TV. I couldn't say what I thought, which would have been, "This sucks."

She didn't know that was why I wasn't opening my mouth.

"Ronnie?" Mama finally said sharply. "Answer me."

"You didn't ask me a question."

"All right, miss. Why are you refusing to do something that is so important to your father and me? Except that it will make you uncomfortable? Do you think *we'll* be comfortable? Do you think it will be like a picnic? This is going to be the hardest day of our lives."

"Honestly, I'm sorry for that. But I can't go," I said. "It would be a lie. It would violate my beliefs, as I understand them. You didn't raise me to be a liar, even to make you happy. And on top of that, I'm afraid."

"There'll be an armed guard in the room at all times."

"I'm not afraid of him," I said, shaking my head. My mother was so wise, but she could be dense. "I'm afraid of seeing him. I'm afraid of the memories. The dreams are bad enough. They had stopped, but now they're back. You were not there. You were not there alone at first."

"Darling, that hurts me. Do you think we want you to suffer? It's just the opposite. Don't you think we fear the same things?" my mother asked me. "But we think that this is the only way that we can get rid of some of those feelings. Clean them away."

"Mama, every person carries things in a different way," I said, my scalp tightening. "They say you don't dream in color, but I do." I decided, for the first time, to tell my mother about the nightmare. "Like last night. It was the same as that day, only I got the chance to save Becky and Ruthie. Scott Early comes walking across the lawn, and he's shivering. I throw him that old coat we keep for going to shovel in the stable. Then I point Papa's gun at Scott Early, and though in all the other dreams I've shot him, this time I just hold the gun on him until the sheriff comes. The little girls are crying because they were so afraid, and saying who is he, Ronnie, I was so scared, Ronnie, is it okay now, Ronnie, but it is okay because they're fine. He apologizes, and I'm so relieved . . . and then I wake up. And they're dead. And you're going to tell Scott Early that's okay with you." My mother sat down with Rafe. "I've looked up post-traumatic stress syndrome on the Net." She nodded. "When you're so anxious you can't sleep because you're afraid of having recurring dreams . . . then that's what you have. I keep thinking that if I face my memories, I'll work through it and not have to take pills or go to therapy or anything. I thought time would heal the pain, but it didn't. Grieving helped. But it didn't heal. And this cut away everything I've done to try to move on. I'll be, like, twisted, forever. And it's not your fault. You have to do what you can live with. It's his fault."

"But what if it goes the way your father thinks?" Mama asked. "He was the least likely to forgive, Ronnie. And he roamed and roamed and prayed, and the answer came to him—we can make some of those feelings go quiet, if we forgive him. We're trying to end his influence over our lives. I didn't mean that to sound like a speech."

"I can't forgive him."

"Ronnie, you can."

"Not now. Maybe after death."

"He's doing well."

"You said that! I don't care about the way he was, or the way he is, Mama! I don't care that he's doing well. That's the difference between you and me! I don't care that he can have a real life if he stays on medication, and we can't. There's no medication we can take that will bring Becky and Ruthie back. Or me. The part of me that's gone, too, Mama! But you didn't notice! You spent two years asleep!"

The way I was going on scared both of us, I think.

I didn't swear at her, but I was yelling. This wasn't like reading a book with sex or swear words, like *The Catcher in the Rye*, where the kid is actually a great kid but swears all the time because he feels insignificant and the bad language is what he uses to hide how much he cares. I felt like he did, except all the little kids had fallen off the cliff, with the killer coming through the rye. I was a fool to think I could ever outrun my parents' infernal goodness and Scott Early's curse on me.

Anyway, my mother just got up slowly, holding her stomach, but not like she was looking for sympathy.

She didn't take off on me for what I said.

She left me alone until the day of the reconciliation came.

But late that morning, she came slowly up the stairs to my room, where I'd been hiding out since morning. She sat on the bed. I started setting up my pencils on end in a little row, exactly side by side, like soldiers, on my bed table. Sense out of chaos. Line upon line. Since I'd waked up with a little scream, before it was light, I'd been trying to fake an ordinary morning. But all the while, I'd been thinking: I'm giving Rafe his yogurt and Cheerios, and then my parents are going to go sit in a room next to Scott Early. I'm making my bed, and then my family is going to go offer Scott Early their forgiveness. My team, the Lady Dragons, the seniors, Alison and Mackenzie and Dana, are in the quarterfinals at State in Salt Lake, and I could have been with them, if I could have kept my head together; and my parents are going to see my sisters' killer and see how nice they can be to him.

Mama put her hand over mine so I'd have to stop arranging the pencils.

She said, "I see your side, Ronnie. But life isn't fair. I don't mean, 'Oh, dear, this is so unfair.' This isn't like losing a job when you did everything right. It was an outrage. I might not see our motives any better than you do, if I were your age. I thought I needed to make you do this. But I won't. I won't force you." Mama gathered up Rafe, who came running in, smiling that little crazy elf smile. Rafe's dark hair stuck straight up, which I thought was hysterical. It was like he had a teeny Mohawk. Mama still treated him like a baby, which you couldn't blame her for. She rocked him to sleep every night.

Rafe said, "Boo, dragon!"

"Boo, dinosaur," I said to him.

"Ronnie Dragon, don't cry," he said.

"I'm not, Rafiesaurus."

But I was, and not from sadness. From fury. From being clean exhausted. From pure frustration.

"Why am I named 'Veronica'?" I asked, to change the subject.

"There was a little girl I knew, probably in first grade, and her name was Ronnie. I thought it was the coolest name," Mama said.

"But Veronica?"

"Well, it's Hebrew for 'True Face,' and when I saw you, I thought, even though you were a baby, you were already you. We had a book of baby names. That's why the bishop gave you the sunflower for your flower. It looks as though it has a face."

"I'm thinking of changing it legally to 'Ronnie.'"

"Okay." I'd expected an argument about that, but she didn't blink. "It's your name. Let's talk about the here and now."

"Why didn't you name me 'Titania' or something from Shakespeare?"

"I don't think the nickname for that would have been flattering."

"It could have been Tanya."

"You know how kids are, Ronnie."

"You don't," I mumbled, "or you would leave me alone. Please, Mama, leave me alone."

"Okay. Titania," she said then, buying time. "I actually did think of that once, when we thought we'd have a baby born in midsummer. But you were a winter baby. We thought of other names . . ."

"Did you ever tell me other names you thought of?"

"I might have— Viola. Miranda . . ."

"That's why I remembered it, I suppose," I said, beginning to relax.

"But that name, Titania, sounded like a heavy metal in the periodic table. Not like the name of a beautiful child. We named Rebecca partly after a name in *Ivanhoe*, though actually Sir Walter Scott was kind of a bigot. And Ruth. Ruth . . . I had always wanted a little girl named Ruth. But about the mediation, please, Ronnie. Pray about it. There's still time. We don't have to leave until after lunch. If you want us to pray with you, we will. In fact, either way, that would be best."

"You'd do that anyway. You never leave without praying over me. I have prayed about it, Mama. Remember what you said after Becky and Ruthie died, about your prayers bouncing back at you like rubber balls against a wall? That's how I feel. There are times when I've felt I received the Holy Spirit when I needed help so bad, just to plain live, but I don't feel that way now. I can't get to peace about this mediation thing, Mama."

"Maybe you're forcing it, instead of just clearing your mind. Maybe there's a different way to receive."

"Maybe I am, but if it was right for me to go, I'd know it."

"Sometimes the right thing is the hardest thing. What would it hurt?"

"Mama, it would make me sick. I'm glad you're not going to say it's basically an order, because I wouldn't go if you dragged me." I was shouting again.

From their bedroom, where he was dressing, my father called, "Ronnie, have respect."

"I am respectful," I answered. "Of what *you* want to do. I even understand why . . . No, that's not true. I want to, but I truly don't understand why. But I'm not trying to *stop* you. I'd like to stop you, but I won't try."

"When we first considered this, we told you we believed that a good person can do wrong unintentionally," Papa said.

"You think Scott Early is a good person?"

"I think there's good in him. Now that I know how he lived before this."

"No!" I told both of them, more violently than I meant, because Rafe popped up, his eyes and mouth round, his little feet in his Weeboks sticking straight out. He never looked more like Ruthie than right then. "If there's good in him, there was good in Hitler! There was good in Pol Pot."

"It's not like that. They were madmen. They wanted to destroy, eradicate whole races of people, Veronica!" my father scolded me.

"So you're saying one person isn't as important as a million people. If one person is just as important as a million people, then *he's* a madman."

"No," Papa said, "he acted like a madman. He was sick, not just his ego, his whole mind, his spirit. He thought he was acting under orders from someone outside him, and he knew that whoever was giving the commands wasn't God, because he's a believer, so he was terribly frightened. And this being, in his head, was commanding him to do this terrible thing, and now he knows—"

"I've heard all that. I've heard all that until I'm sick of it. It just lets him be irresponsible for his actions. You can do whatever you want if you have a disease that makes you do it. Okay, he was sick and now he's well. Then he should go to trial again, now that he knows and understands this, and be condemned and executed as a so-called sane person would have who did this. That's what would happen to me if I'd done it."

"Ronnie!" my mother cried out. "Ronnie, don't!"

"Would that bring your sisters back? His being executed?" My father was almost roaring. "You know it wouldn't. And, Ronnie, Scott Early isn't 'cured.' He will always have this disease. He has to take medication for it the rest of his life, or—"

"Or he'll go and kill someone else? Do you think he doesn't want to? Once he gets out . . . who's going to make sure that he stays nice, kindly, happy Scott?"

"Kelly is. His doctors are," my mother said.

"Kelly! You talk about her as if she were your friend."

"In a way, she is. In a way, she understands this more than anyone else, more than my brothers or sister or Aunt Jill and Aunt Gerry, more than my friends. She understands, and she feels it with her entire soul. She's a good woman, Ronnie. She takes full responsibility, and she knows what she's—"

"You can say that on the basis of some letters?"

"And meeting Kelly. She's a steadfast young woman."

"Where did you meet her?"

"She came to see us. When you were in Massachusetts. . . ."

"That long ago? You let her in our *house*? That's why you were so happy to let me go see Serena, and not have your unpaid housecleaner for two whole weeks."

"Apologize, Ronnie," my father called from downstairs.

"I'm sorry," I said. "But I'm even more sorry you let that person in my house."

"She didn't do it," said Papa, who'd come up to my room.

"Look, I can't believe any of this. I'm in a house where Scott Early's wife came? Did you show her the ground where they bled? Did you show her the graves?" I was about as close to hysterical as I'd been the night of the TV cameras. "How could you? And not tell me? How could you look at someone who could love Scott Early? Who could touch Scott Early?"

Mama sighed. "*Because* she can love him. Jesus could love the sick that others wouldn't touch. She can love him despite what he did, because she knows that what the judge said was true, that he didn't have the capacity to—"

"That's just an excuse!"

"You still think that!" Mama was shocked. "Nothing you heard three years ago made you see that this illness was real. . . ."

"Yes! I still think he should have been in prison, and then the other prisoners would have killed him!" I knew by then much more than I ever wanted to about how prison inmates feel about child killers.

"Ronnie," my mother said sadly, "that's so lacking in everything I believe about you. You're so compassionate. You understand that schizophrenia is on a gene that's born in you. It's not a choice. It's not something you develop because your . . . because your parents abused you or because you weren't raised to know right from wrong. Scott Early's parents raised him, in their way, just as we raised you."

"As if you know that."

"We have their letters. His father was a dentist. His brother works with his father. His mother and father could be our parents, Grandpa Swan and Grandma Bonham. How do you think his parents feel, knowing what their son did?"

"Don't say that! Mama, please don't. Stop talking or I'll get up and leave."

"You need to know," she went on. "He studied hard and went to church, and he didn't get into trouble. And he got sick. You don't have a choice. Would you hate him if leukemia made him do this? Or a brain tumor?"

"That's not the point! You're saying what Clare said!" I knew what the point was, but I couldn't find the words. "Just go! Leave Rafe here and go."

"We thought, if you didn't want to go with us, we'd take him, because you're so upset," Mama told me.

"Are you afraid to leave Rafe with me?" I heard my voice go flat. "Are you afraid for the same reasons that—"

"Ronnie, mercy, no! I just thought that you'd want to be alone, or be with Clare, if you had to think of us going to Stone Gate. . . ."

"Okay, then, take Rafe with you. He looks like Ruthie. Let Scott Early see my brother."

"Ronnie!" my father said sternly.

"Go ahead. I'd rather go to hell!" I screamed, and then threw myself down on the bed, pulling my comforter over me.

There was a silence then, as though someone in the room had pulled a gun.

After a long time, my mother said, "Leave her be, London. She has a right to her own feelings. The Heavenly Father will help Ronnie. There are things human beings cannot do." There was a whole continent of heaviness in her voice.

I IM'ed Clare after I heard them pull away.

RU There?
R they gone?
2 C him.
Not U.
Not if I was going to hang.
I wouldn't either.
Do U want me to com over?
Maybe.
R U doing the alone thing?
Rite now. Maybe later.

Actually, I fell asleep. The discussion with my folks had worn me out.

And when I woke up, it was dark and I could hear them talking in the kitchen. I went down, because I was starving, and took out some tortillas and melted cheese on them in the toaster oven. Then I sat down at the table. I knew they wouldn't say anything to me unless I started it.

"So," I said finally with a huge sigh, "how'd it go?"

My mother's face was all rosy and young, and her hair curled around her face. "It was wonderful!" she said. "I mean that, Ronnie. It was terribly sad, but in a good way."

They told me about the room where they met. It wasn't like a regular visiting room, more like a living room, with a sofa and soft chairs. A guard brought in Scott Early, who was wearing handcuffs, and then the mediator, who brought cups of water and joked that he would have brought coffee and stuff. The first thing Scott Early did was give my parents a journal he'd copied on the machine in the institution's library—the thoughts he'd written over the years. It started back when he was first battling with what he'd done, and then it went on later, when he could analyze his disease with what he knew about brain chemistry. Then he went on to his responsibility. He said the journal explained more than he ever could; he wasn't good at speaking his feelings, like his wife.

"And then?"

"We took our turn to talk," said my father. "We talked about our family and about that day, and the year after. He listened, and his face was so drawn and . . . awful, Ronnie. As if he were being whipped. Every time we'd stop, he'd say, 'No, please go on. I need to hear this.'"

"He agreed to this mediation for us, not for him," said my mother. "He said he was never going to get over what he'd done. For him, that wasn't the point. He said he wanted to dedicate whatever time he had left on earth to trying to heal what he'd done to us. He said that what he'd done, he'd done to the whole world."

"Nice of him," I said, getting more tortillas.

My mother said, "Scott Early said that once his medication took hold, he had dreams. They were of that day. He was wearing only ragged underwear and walking across the lawn, but instead of slashing at your sisters, he was telling them not to play with the scythe, that it was dangerous. Then he was picking them up and throwing them up over his head, and they were laughing. And you came out and asked what he was doing, saying that he was a stranger and to leave the little girls alone. But you smiled. He asked for a drink of water and you gave him one, and he said it was the best water he'd ever drunk. He'd been so thirsty, his throat was like dust, but after he drank it, he felt strength. You threw him an old pair of pants. He wasn't cold then. He thanked you and he left."

"He's just putting himself in a Bible story to make himself feel better. 'I was thirsty and you gave me drink. I was naked and you clothed me,'" I quoted.

"'As you did to the least of these my brethren, you did it to me.' Surely a murderer is the least of your brethren, Ronnie. It's the same dream you had. Admit it," my mother said. "Except the gun."

I had to think about that, because basically she was right. It gave me the willies.

"Is that all?" I asked them.

No, it wasn't. The mediator asked my parents to talk about their anger and about their memories of Ruth and Rebecca. He asked my father what he would have done if he had come home while Scott Early was there. My father said he would have shot him, if not to kill him, then to disable him. There was a lot of other stuff. The mediator asked Scott Early what remorse meant to him. They asked my family what repentance meant to them. They agreed that it meant you had to become a new person and that if the new person ever committed the sin again, then the repentance was void.

After that, Kelly, his wife, was let in. My mother hugged her, because, as Mama said, her agony was all over her face. She told them about the hate mail she got and how, at first, she wanted to leave Scott Early and run as far and as fast as she could, but that her marriage vows said in sickness and in health, and they didn't mean just the physical kind. They had met when they were sixteen. She had known Scott Early almost half her life. She looked forward to every visit she had with him. But before her first visit, she was scared that she might not be able to hug him and hold him and be with him. She was afraid she might look at his hands and think of what he'd done. Kelly said it had to have been a different person—that this was why schizophrenics were once described as split personalities. She hoped she would be able to be truly loving to Scott Early. All she knew up to that first visit was that she would be able to be kind. She was trained to be kind, even with mentally ill people. She didn't know if that would work when the mentally ill person was her own husband.

The thought of all this love and attention focused on Scott Early made my mouth fill with saliva, the way it does when a person is nauseated and tries not to throw up.

At the end, the mediator asked if my parents wanted to exchange some gesture with Scott Early. They were afraid to. It was the moment when they had to stack their faith against his crime. But finally, my father reached out and held Scott Early's forearm; and my mother took his hand. And they told him, *We forgive you, in Becky's and Ruthie's names.* He cried, and Kelly cried. He said he didn't deserve their kindness. He asked if he could write to them, and they said he could.

"It was one of the most stunning moments of our lives," Papa said, "because we meant it. We felt free. We felt as though the huge burden of our hatred, that I carried on my back all those nights I walked and walked, was lifted. Not the grief. But the anger. We saw through him, to the person he had been before."

They told me that the doctors were considering letting Scott Early out in a year or so, but that it would be our legal right to always know where he was, and in every neighborhood where he lived, the neighbors would be told what he had done.

I was thinking about how great it would be to get Christmas cards from my sisters' killer. But I told them I was glad for them. I kissed them good night.

When I was back upstairs, listening to music quietly and trying to fall asleep again, I had a flash.

They hadn't forgiven him in *my* name. I was free, but in another way. There were to come months of thoughts and plans that I made and put aside. But I guess that was when I decided.

Chapter Fourteen

I think every religion must have been started by a person who loved someone who died.

Even Heavenly Father must have grieved terribly for Jesus, His only son. He must mourn for Him even today. No matter how I try, I've never fully understood how a father could sacrifice his *child* for the sake of wicked people. If the Father had made the grave decision to atone for the sins of humanity, why wouldn't He offer Himself as a sacrifice? Any other parent would have. There must be an answer. But I've never found one so far that makes sense of that first choice, to let Jesus die in agony and disgrace and to have to watch. That's probably sacrilegious. But I know how barbaric it was to see something much quicker and more merciful happen to people I loved. And knowing what that was like, if I had the choice now, I honestly wouldn't select my sisters for that fate to save myself or even to save the world. I know people still die all the time for ideals or allow their children to go to war. I knew that the founder of our church, Joseph Smith, suffered horribly as a little boy, with four operations on a lame leg and no anesthesia. When he got married, they lost baby after baby to diphtheria or typhoid or one of those old diseases we don't get now. Everyone yearns for heaven, and nothing binds you to the hope of eternal life like that kind of defeat on earth. Maybe it's not a defeat. Perhaps you must be divine to see the meaning. But as the mortal I am now, I know this much: When someone you love that much leaves you behind, so all at once, there isn't as much of *you* left to die when your own time comes.

I'm sure of it, and that's regardless of all the good that has been God's gracious gift to me, in the face of my hardheaded foolishness. My mother would say that I ignored the magnificence of God's plan for me, though she loves me all the same. But I'm not sure that what I did wasn't part of that plan—for me—as what they did was part of the plan for my parents.

I look back and realize that Becky's and Ruthie's deaths really were like the eclipse I saw when I was six. For a while, everything else was blotted out. And then the sun returned, and the sun hadn't changed; but we had. We were people who had lived in the darkness at noon and knew even the sun was something that wasn't necessarily to be counted on. Their deaths were more profound than the sum of all our lives to that point. All crime victims think of their lives divided neatly into two segments. "Before" is always a summer day. If I have a sore throat and, even so, a double shift ahead of me, or have a sore back—when I've said, "One, two, three, lift," and the other two people holding the sheet were looking out the window—or if my life seems to want more love or work than I can give in the hours that make up a day, I sink back. I tumble back, and it *is* a windy summer day. I know that it seems sunnier to me now than it did when I thought it was just an ordinary part of a not particularly dramatic childhood. Memory is a trickster. And yet.

Suddenly I am back there, with Becky and Ruthie up in front of me on Ruby, clumping down the path, then all of us jumping down to splash in the creek. Becky is trying to catch the little sunfish in her two hands.

I suppose what made it worse for me that last year at home was my certainty that no one except me seemed to recognize that the eclipse changed everything. It was not just because my mother was wearing maternity jeans and dancing to Marvin Gaye while cooking and tickling Rafe and sprucing up the house—things I'd longed to see for years—but because my parents were bathed in the comfort of having forgiven Scott Early. It couldn't ever have been the *same*, really; but that act of glorious faith, or foolishness, wiped away the chance that we could ever be anything like the family we were, unless there ever was another event that changed our lives utterly.

And so I began the first steps of the plan for my own reconciliation. Not retaliation. I didn't think of it that way.

I took driver's education from an old man who delivered cheese to Jackie and Barney. He'd once been a PE teacher, and though he couldn't see very well, he still taught a few private students. Serena helped me, too. Whenever she wasn't at drama club, or I wasn't working at church for my job, unpacking and stacking big boxes of cereal and toothpaste, we drove around the hilly roads like two wackos in some old seventies TV show. Serena had a little Honda CR-V that her parents had given her for her seventeenth birthday, but she was more gifted in doing pedicures than the three-point turn. At least, though, she could do it and survive. I could sew, and I could teach a horse to back up, but I couldn't get that car into four-wheel drive to save *either* of our lives. We would end up sliding backward into little ditches, two 120-pound girls pushing two tons of car.

"Now, Ronnie," Serena would say once we were back in the

seats, belted in and sweating as if we'd run a mile, "remember. Small corrections on the turns, tip, tip, tip. Don't jerk it like you're trying to steer the *Titanic* around an iceberg."

It was better when we took to the highway and drove to Cedar City. I discovered I had one genius for driving. I could parallel park like an army sergeant. The fact that Serena's car was about the size of Rafe's Little Tikes mobile didn't hurt.

Since I was barely speaking to my parents, except to ask politely if they needed help with something or to answer a direct question, I couldn't enlist my father. On top of our not speaking, my father would have used our practice sessions in the car to try to convert me to their point of view about Scott Early. Given his ability to talk the birds out of the trees, he might actually have been successful. And if he got me to agree with him, it would have had the effect of making me more than angry with my father, which would in turn have been a terrible heartbreak. I *loved* both of my parents equally, but I *liked* my father more. That he had been the brains behind the mediation session at Stone Gate hadn't done much for that feeling.

One day when we were on the way to get Jade feed, I was driving the pickup and my father said, "By the way you're shifting gears and checking your blind spots, you seem pretty comfortable behind the wheel. . . ."

"I am, Papa," I said. "I'm ready."

"I always imagined I would be the one who taught my eldest how to drive," he said wistfully.

"We've hardly been together," I said. "You know that."

"That's been your choice."

"Yes, it's been my choice," I said.

"Are you a good driver?"

I used one of his own phrases. "Good enough for government work," I said.

"Then I'll schedule your test," he said. "Although this isn't the way we do things. . . ."

"As Mormons or as us?"

"Us," he said.

"There isn't a way we do things anymore, Papa," I said, "and I'm as sad about that as you are."

He told me the news then.

Scott Early was about to be released. He had been successful on his home visits—very successful, I thought in an ugly way, given that his wife was already pregnant. And they were moving, somewhere out along the coast. He would continue to study library science—a program he had begun in the hospital—until he had a master's degree. "Scott" had never had another "incident."

An incident, I thought, and hit the gas a little.

"Slow down," my father said. "Get a ticket now and you'll never get a license."

I thought about the other ocean. The warm one Serena had told me about. Papa began to tell me where Scott Early was living, since the law required that we always know Scott Early's whereabouts; but I asked him to stop. In all honesty, I was concentrating on remembering the road signs and pedestrian awareness and the way to yield at a four-way stop. In due time, I would learn. I thought of the ocean and its eternal, imploring calm.

But it was my father who finally drove me to Cedar City to take my test.

He sighed as he signed the papers certifying I'd done my practice.

The tester at the bureau was the twin of the little old guy

who delivered cheese to Jackie and Barney. I passed on the first go.

And then it was a matter of getting a car.

I had savings from work, birthday money, Christmas gifts, enough for a couple of semesters at a technical school, where I had decided I would learn to be an emergency medical technician, either for a private ambulance company or for a fire department. The course catalogs I'd sent for, from Boston and Arizona and Chicago, described the job as stressful, requiring long hours (but with a flexible schedule) and the ability to face life-and-death situations. This was supposed to warn you off, but I figured that stress and long hours were my natural habitat. And no one could know more about the sight of people who were injured. At least in this job I'd get a chance to change the odds.

In cities, a person could earn twenty-five thousand dollars or more a year at this work. It wouldn't take me too long to save enough for college if I lived in a rooming house or at the YWCA. And some colleges, such as UCLA, allowed EMTs to earn their way through school by working for emergency medical services on campus while they were earning their degrees in microbiology or public health—on their way to medical school! What could possibly be better?

One evening before bed, I asked Papa if Jade belonged to me or to our family.

"She's yours, Ronnie," Papa said. "And you've trained her beautifully."

"Papa," I said, tears teasing my eyes, "I'm going to sell Jade."

Before he could stop himself, he cried, "No! You love that horse! That horse brought . . . you back!"

"I know. I love her. But I'm going away, and you knew that, to earn money for college, and then to college. No one here will ride her. I have trained her beautifully. She'd behave for anyone, even a child. She's bombproof. And, I need a car. I know that with the baby coming and with Rafe, you don't have that kind of money, though I know you would if you could. I need a safe car, Papa. And Jade deserves an owner who'll be there for her every day."

Mama came into the room, lumbering. She looked bigger than she ever had when she was pregnant. I wondered if the baby really was further along than they'd thought. It wouldn't be long now until the baby came and until the . . . anniversary. "What's all this?" she asked, taking out a plate and filling it with molasses cookies.

"Ronnie has made a decision," my father said.

It wounded her; I could see it in her eyes, although her mouth said plainly that it was up to me. "Ronnie, we'd set aside funds to help you with college . . ."

"But you didn't count on the baby."

"No."

"And I can do this. I know I can."

"You've always been . . . resolute," she said.

As a gesture of goodwill and because I needed my father's touch, I asked him to pray with me to find a good owner for Jade.

I hoped it would take longer than a week. But that's what you get when you pray.

A mother from St. George answered my ad. Her daughter was thirteen and had been taking lessons since she was eight. They came twice to see Jade, and Jade behaved like a movie star. They paid me eight thousand dollars. That would get me a car with some left over.

On the last night that sweet Jade would be mine, Clare and I rode her, twin bareback, down to our old willow hut. Years had blown away the mud we'd chinked so carefully, and branches had dried up and popped free until there were holes in the walls. We hoped there would be water in the pool, but it was dry. "We brought our dolls here," said Clare, "and our wicked tea."

"Oh, weren't we bad? We acted like it was cocaine. All the nights we slept out. Remember hearing a coyote sniffing around the outside?"

"I think it was a cougar," Clare said as Jade stepped daintily into the creek bed. "I still think it meant to eat us."

"If it meant to eat us, it would have," I told her.

"I've been accepted to the Boston Conservatory," Clare said. "Full tuition."

"Oh, Clare, Clare!" I cried in honest joy. "You'll see the Atlantic Ocean! You'll learn to be . . . everything. Oh, Clare. Are ever going to do a mission?"

"No," Clare said, "Maybe. I've plenty of time for that. I might take time off after college and go then. I think it's best that I . . . take this step now, while I have the courage."

"I didn't know you'd gone to audition."

"I didn't. I sent a DVD we had made in Cedar City. It cost me two hundred dollars, Ronnie! I sent it to three schools and BYU; and Boston offered me the best scholarship. And anyone would want to go there . . . except for . . . leaving you . . . and the little boys, home . . ."

"That's what growing up is, Clare," I said, feeling no braver than she did.

"It hurts," she said, and we hugged, both of us on the edge of tears, knowing that the willow fort would either blow away altogether one windy night some years from now or be rebuilt by Clare's little brothers or the little Tierney kids.

It was not ours anymore.

How I wanted to tell her then, and how I wished my own fate was not so dark and complex. I wished I could tell her that I knew I needed to face Scott Early in my own way, how I would have to get my feet under me and do it on my terms. I wanted Clare's absolution for a monstrous lie to my family, a sin of omission, letting my parents know and yet not know. How sick it made me to wonder whether they would fear for me or fear for him. I wanted terribly to tell Clare all about it, ask her what I should say to Scott Early and to his wife, how I could get them to see that my pain, as distinct from my parents' absolution, deserved attention, how I still wanted to punish him. I wanted to ask her, in her purity, whether what I felt I must do was simply an illusion, sent to seduce me by Satan, or if it was like the verse my Bible opened to, Isaiah 30, which I had almost memorized: "Thine eyes shall behold thy Teacher, and thine ears shall hear a word behind thee, 'This is the way, walk in it,' whether thou turnest to the right or the left." In the fading sunlight, Clare looked like Lewis Carroll's Alice, her blond sheet of straight hair swinging forward, a purple coneflower between her hands, as if she could disappear in a moment, like a magical, innocent creature, down the rabbit hole.

"I wish we were sisters," she said. "And I don't mean in God's way."

"Me too," I confessed. "Do you know that Becky would be almost as old now as I was then?"

"She'll always be little to me, her rear as big as a teacup, and her jeans falling down," Clare said.

And then, just as before—just exactly as before—we heard my father shouting. We knew the baby was coming. But we looked into each other's eyes, and neither of us got up to answer him; and soon we heard the van start and pull away up the gravel drive. Hours later, after we had prayed together and sat for a long time in silence, until Jade's green eye shone like a cat's in the dark, Clare and I walked back to my house arm in arm, the way European girls do—although I didn't know that then. We did our own special hand touch at my door as I walked Jade, closed fists, then palms, then a clasp. "BFF," said Clare.

"Always," I said. "Best friends forever."

It was past midnight.

There was a message on our answering machine. Rafe was at the Tierneys' house, because my parents hadn't been able to find me, but was probably already asleep, so no need to fetch him until morning. I had a healthy little brother, Jonathan Thoreau Swan, whom we would call "Thor" as he grew up because he was so burly and strong, like a little Norse prince with his ruddy hair. He weighed nine pounds nine ounces.

While my parents were at the hospital, I found my mother's button box and took out the letters from Scott Early's family, from his wife and him. There were more than a dozen. I laid them on the kitchen table, making sure they were out of Rafe's reach.

When he was asleep, I asked the Heavenly Father to guide me as I opened a search engine and asked for a list of good technical schools that offered emergency medical technician training. If the one I found was not in California, I would know I must not go there, and I would feel limp with relief. When the page opened, I closed my eyes and put my finger on the screen. The name of the town was La Jolla, pronounced "La Hoya."

I looked at the return address on the letter from Kelly

Englehart, Scott Early's wife. It was in San Diego. I plugged the names of the cities into a map search. La Jolla was 13.2 miles from San Diego. I put my head down on the table and cried.

Chapter Fifteen

"We're going to begin with the emotional side of the work you've chosen to do, or that you *think* you've chosen," the instructor told us.

A woman about the age of my mother, she told us she'd put in twenty years as a science teacher and then became a paramedic. We all watched this crisp, compact little person as though we could inhale what we needed to know through our eyes. A class of more than thirty people, we didn't look like the ordinary college types. I was the youngest, but some people were older than the teacher. Many of the students had full-time day jobs and could take only the intensive night course. We'd start our practicum on the streets after only one semester of jam-packed classes. The day students at La Jolla Tech took other courses, too, and ended up after two years of work with associate degrees that included an EMT certificate. We would get only our certificates. Class began at five P.M. and lasted each week-night until eight. This instructor was one of three, a firefighter who worked day shifts.

She told us, "What you will see, as a basic-level emergency medical technician, will be situations that will certainly frighten you, and may be unlike anything you've ever seen before. How many of you have seen a person die?"

A young Asian guy raised his hand. I looked at my list. Kevin

Chan. His name was next to mine. I sometimes still wonder if that was just chance. We'd gotten a list of everyone's names, phone numbers, and e-mail addresses the previous day, and we were told to learn them as part of the bonding essential to our work. Some of us would end up on crews together. We were urged to study together and to learn one another's strengths and habits until we understood one another instinctively. We'd had a picture taken together first thing, all of us grinning with fists held high. Each of us would get a copy, and one of our exercises would be, within a week, to take that photo and write everyone's name on the back in five minutes. One day, all that knowledge might help us save a life—maybe even our own.

"It was my grandmother," Kevin Chan began, "and she died when she was eighty-nine, of pneumonia. All of us were with her. It was as though she took a long breath and then simply left. Quiet. Peace."

"And how did that affect you?" the instructor asked.

"Naturally, I was very sad to lose Grandmother. I'd never known any life without her. But I could see that she was not in pain, and she had lived a long life, and all of us had outlived her. It helped me decide that I could do this, for some reason, that I could try to save people, and prolong life, and face death, that I could be a paramedic someday. That seemed to have more meaning for me than teaching English, which is fine, by the way, but this seemed to combine a little bit more of my sports life—I play hockey—and my head life. It sounded like I just said 'head lice,' didn't it?"

The rest of us began to laugh, but the instructor's voice sliced through. "What if your grandmother had been shot in the thigh, and the exit wound tore apart her abdomen?" she asked. "What if she was in horrible pain, and you and your crew had to unload a backboard in seconds, and everything you would need to try to stop the bleeding, and what if your hospital destination told you to divert, that they were full, and you had to call the medical director for your station house, and get an advanced life support system unit to intercept, and still your grandmother bled out before you could get her to the hospital? And what if it weren't your eighty-nine-year-old grandmother, but a thirteen-year-old boy or a seven-year-old girl who'd been playing with her father's gun?"

"I'd be . . . terrified," Kevin said.

"Well, good, because that's the appropriate response to that kind of situation. That, and the thrill of the challenge of trying to intervene in a life-and-death emergency," said the teacher. She sat down, perching one lean hip on the corner of the desk, for the first time since the class had started ninety minutes earlier. "If you weren't adrenaline junkies, you wouldn't be here. Most of the time, EMTs save lives. Sometimes no one can save those lives. From now on, you will encounter death. Death will become familiar to you. The families and friends of those who have died will be no strangers to you. Their suffering will break your hearts. You will feel anger, moments of hopelessness, even worthlessness. That's normal, unless it lasts. After a 'bad call,' you won't be able to get over it on your own. You shouldn't try. Everyone involved, from the police to the firefighters to the paramedics to you and your crew chief, will be pulled in a few days later, the next day if possible, and gather in a room with professionals who will talk you through those emotions of pain and fear, because otherwise what would happen?"

Without pausing to think, I said, "You'd relive them every night of your life."

"Exactly. . . . What is your name? Veronica," she said. "You'd relive them, and you'd ask yourself over and over, Did I do the right thing? Did I do what I was trained to do? Did I do enough? And your heart would start to pound, and you might feel you couldn't breathe. That's why a CISD, a critical incident stress debriefing—which is just what that meeting is called—is essential. Once you talk through what happened and why it happened, and why it wasn't your fault, you'll be able to resume a normal life in a profession that exposes you to the side of life we don't consider 'normal.'

"You'll have to learn that high levels of stress come with the territory. And you'll have to learn how to cleanse yourself of that stress, through talk, exercise, prayer, whatever it is you do. Not only will you experience stress because you'll have to work on Christmas Day, and you will, and not only because you'll be rolled out of bed in the middle of the night, and you will, or because you may have to keep going with no sleep for many, many more hours than anyone else you know. It will come because there could be a child in your arms who could go south on you in seconds if you can't clear whatever's blocking that child's airway. Because the subject you're watching, as you wait in hiding across the street for the go-ahead, is armed and could turn your way; and you could see that man taken down by the police, and then go in and try to repair what the police had to do to save your life and the lives of everyone else on the street. Because you might come into an accident scene and the injured may be a kid you knew from high school who pulled out of a blind drive and got creamed by a cement truck. You'll see hundreds of car accidents in your first year on the job. You'll see, perhaps, dozens of fatalities. The stress will come from what you see and touch and smell and feel. There's no sense in denying those feelings, because those who deny them end up trying to drink them away or medicate them away. You have to face them, but you'll have help, every step of the way. If you don't know that you can do

that, and still go out dancing with your friends the next weekend, become an accountant."

We all laughed then, again, but it was more like a release of
tension.

"You came here because you want to help other people," she
went on, "but the first thing you have to keep in mind is that to
help other people, you have to take care of yourself first." Her face
softened as she added, "You have to override your instinct to dive
right in sometimes. If you come into a scene where there's been a
domestic incident, or there is one in progress, even if there are injuries, stop. Don't intervene. The cops will do that. Think of the
people you'll never save if some crazy husband brains you with a
baseball bat. Keep your own safety and well-being in mind, first,
at all times. Assessing a scene will become second nature to you;
you'll feel danger if it's there. But if you try to be a hero in a
threatening situation, you could end up being the one transported
to the ER." She began to tell us about our other instructors, their
names and backgrounds and what they'd teach us.

I knew what she was saying was essential, but I drifted for a
moment, wondering what other people in the room would think
if they knew how I had first encountered death. I was already
spent, halfway through my second day of classes, overwhelmed
by the information in my books. I'd only glanced into my big
text, slamming it shut after learning that I'd have to memorize
the names of all twenty-eight bones in the human foot, from the
calcaneus, to the five metatarsals, to the cuboid and the talus,
not to mention a couple of hundred others, along with a thousand other things about the way the human body worked and
how to make it work that way if it was in trouble. I'd had to
jump right in after a two-day drive, a sleepless night at a cheap
motel, a day of searching for a place to stay, looking at a dozen
studio apartments I couldn't afford.

At last, I'd found one that I could.

The last possible address I'd circled had been a tall, lavender Victorian near the beach. It was unlike any other house on the street. A big willow hamper of afghans sat on the porch, along with several rocking chairs. Flowers in bloom climbed the porch rails. I wanted to just stop and sit on the steps and listen to the waves. But I rang the doorbell. The lady who answered the door was gorgeous, if it's possible to say that about a woman who was probably, when I met her, seventy-five. She had white hair, truly white, that foamed back into a perfect thick wave caught at the back with a tortoiseshell comb. Her face was soft and as pink as one of her hollyhocks. "I'm Alice Desmond," she said in an accent I didn't recognize then but would later learn was Australian. "May I help you?"

"You have a room to rent, I think," I said.

"I do. That's already in the newspaper, is it?"

"Well, I need a room. I'm going to school not far from here." I put out my hand. "My name is Ronnie. Veronica Swan."

"Hello. You seem very young to be in college."

I pretended to laugh. "Everyone says so, but I'm older than I look."

"I take great care with my rooms and my guests."

"Well," I said wearily, and sighed, "I do, too. I take great care with everything I do."

"Come in, then," said Mrs. Desmond.

The room was at the very top of the house, two flights up. Except for a thick comforter with a gold-and-blue quilted top, with squares of shells and lighthouses, it was entirely white. White bookshelves, empty but for a single shell or starfish, marched nearly to the ceiling in one corner. The walls were white, and there were picture frames on the walls that had no pictures in them, with perhaps a sprig of sea oats stuck in one corner. I liked that; it reminded me of something my mother would do. All of it was so spare and serene. White metal hooks caught back gauzy curtains, and from a window seat I could see a corner of the misty blue fan of the harbor. There was a button board counter with a tiny half-size refrigerator and a little stovetop. The room had its own tiled bath, with a deep claw-foot tub, and I nearly began to cry when I saw the stack of thick towels.

"This is exactly what I'm looking for," I said. "And thank you for showing it to me. But I can't afford it."

"How do you know?"

"Well, I've looked at eleven other places, so I know the going rate," I said. "You're very kind to have shown me."

"Well, you look shattered. I'll give you a cup of tea, at least. I was just making some."

I would learn that this was Mrs. Desmond's first response to anything that puzzled her; and in time, I would find that reassuring. She poured boiling water into a china pot through a tiny, egg-shaped tray of aromatic leaves. Carefully, she folded a blue linen napkin over a plate and placed six iced lemon cookies on it.

"Do you like biscuits?" she asked.

"Oh, my word, yes," I said.

"Do you take sugar?"

"I just . . . I can't have tea. I'd love a hot drink, but I can't."

"Are you allergic to it?"

"I'm not. I'm not able to have caffeine. I'm a Mormon."

"I see." She sighed and reached into her cupboard for a tin. "You can have Ovaltine? I don't know. Are you the polygamy bunch, then, or the ones who make the quilts?"

"Yes, sure," I said. "About the Ovaltine. I can have that, and I'd love some. . . ."

"Though it is rather like chocolate, and chocolate has caffeine."

"We just . . . We can have Ovaltine."

Without thinking of how embarrassed I would be, I ate all the biscuits myself while she boiled the water. Mrs. Desmond smiled and laid out six more.

"Now, the Mormons," Mrs. Desmond continued as she carefully prepared her own tea, pouring the steeped tea into a cup over milk and sugar cubes. I watched her with the fascination of a dog watching its dinner scooped from the can. I was so tired, and Mrs. Desmond's movements were so precise and yet measured, it was like seeing a ballet in slow motion. I think I could have fallen asleep at that table, and I think she could tell.

Finally I shook myself and said, "I think you're thinking of Amish people. They're famous for quilts. As for modern-day Mormons, we only marry one person. That, the polygamy, was something that happened, only for a bit, a long time ago. Some of it was just a pioneer marrying women in name only, because single women couldn't inherit property; and if their husbands died, no one might look after them and their children. The people who do it now are breaking the law. They're sort of crazy, too. No one I know supports them. My father is a teacher, and my mother stays home with my two little brothers. One of them is almost four, and one is just a baby."

"And you."

"Yes."

"You're quite a bit older. . . ."

"I had two little sisters. They died."

"Oh, my dear," said Mrs. Desmond.

"Thank you for the cookies. I was famished," I told her.

"So you don't drink tea. Do you have a great, shedding dog? Do you smoke?"

"Oh, my goodness. No!"

"Do you bring men home?"

"Not unless my father comes to visit," I said. "It's . . . We're pretty conservative that way."

"Well, the rent for that room is . . . eighty-five dollars a month. If you dine with me, that's another five a week, and of course, you can cook small things in your room. There's a laundry in there, on the first floor, and—"

"Eighty-five dollars a month?" I couldn't believe my ears. And I also knew that she was fudging, that she could get a lot more than that. "Are you sure?"

"Well, yes, I am," said Mrs. Desmond.

"I can afford that!" I told her. "And I have references. . . ."

"My eyes and ears tell me all I need to know. They haven't failed me yet."

"I could be anyone."

"But you aren't, are you?"

Veronica was a lady in every sense of the word, Mrs. Desmond would later tell the newspapers, *and I'm utterly certain she still is. She wasn't typical of her generation.*

I moved in that night. She showed me a spot right behind the house to park my little Civic.

In class two days later, I was daydreaming about how gratefully I would sink into my snowy expanse of pillows when the same Chinese guy whose grandma had died elbowed me gently. He whispered, "Is this all kind of a lot to you, or is it just me?"

"It's all kind of going right through me," I wrote on my legal pad. "And I thought I knew some of this stuff."

"I think we're finished," the teacher said. "You look as though you've all had enough for one evening."

I began to gather up my thick text, which I'd bought just that morning, my various lists and handouts and forms, and to stuff them into my backpack. I'd spent the day getting my student ID and paying the first installment on my class. And that had left me just about broke.

"I was going to ask you, do you live around here?" asked Kevin Chan. "Do you want to meet and study? I think some of the other people here might know each other, but I was majoring in English at UC Davis until this year . . . and I'm afraid I'm not going to make it. There are no doctors in my family. My father runs a restaurant." I sized him up to see if he was trying to flirt with me, but he seemed to have nothing in mind except someone to help him wade through the organ systems.

"Sure," I said, and smiled at him. "What kind of restaurant is it?"

"A Chinese restaurant," said Kevin. "What else would you think? There are more Chinese restaurants in California than there are in China!"

"I've never had Chinese food," I said.

"Get out. Everyone's had Chinese food. You know, like fried rice or beef chop suey or that junk?"

"I really never have had Chinese food."

"Are you, like, kosher or something?"

"No," I told him as we walked out into the California twilight. Weather here seemed to roll from one endless and seamless day of golden perfection into an exact replica. "I'm from Utah, and I live in a little town . . . it's not even really a town. I'm sure they have Chinese restaurants somewhere, in the cities, but we just never went to one. The only restaurant food I've had is lobster and Mexican."

Kevin laughed. "That's quite a contrast. But you'll have to come to The Seventh Happiness."

"What's that?"

"That's our restaurant. My mother oversees everything in the front, and my dad in the back, and my mother's father cooks and my mother's mother cooks and my mother's sister cooks and my sisters wait on the tables and my little brothers clean up. When we can get them to."

"Why's it called The Seventh Happiness?"

"I think because there are only six," he said.

"Six happinesses?" I asked.

"Yeah, but don't ask me what they are because I don't know any more about that than I know how to speak Chinese."

"You don't know how to speak Chinese?"

"What are you?"

"I'm a Mormon."

"Oh. Well, I'm a Methodist. But I didn't mean religion. I meant, what are you? Irish?"

"I'm English and Danish. I have no idea why I have red hair."

"Well, do you speak Danish?"

"I get it. But I just assumed, since you had a restaurant and you called your grandmother 'Grandmother,' that you were *Chinese* Chinese," I said.

"Context clues. But no, my great-grandfather was Chinese Chinese, but I'm ordinary American. I probably know five sentences in Chinese, mostly how to say thank you. Look, what's your name?"

"Ronnie. Veronica in class."

"Ronnie, when did you get to town?"

"A couple of days ago. I haven't even had time to buy milk!"

"So why don't you come tonight? I have to go over there and work anyhow...." He saw my hesitation. "Okay. I'm sorry. You're new here, and you don't know that all of us in California treat each other like we've known each other all our lives from the minute we meet. It's a So Cal thing." He saw my stare. "Southern California? So Cal? I mean, I could be an ax murderer for all you know." I winced then, and he held up both hands. "Ronnie, I was just trying to be nice. I have a steady girl-friend who's at UCLA film school, and I'm just used to being the all-purpose big brother to my sisters' friends. No biggie. Okay?"

"Okay," I said, breathing out through my teeth the way I'd taught myself to do when anything scared me. I hiked up my book bag. And then I thought, How could I have been frightened of this kid? He's no older than Miko.

"I'll see you in class," Kevin said, getting out his keys.

"Okay," I told him. He bounded down the steps. Kevin would remember afterward, when reporters asked him, that practically the first thing he'd said to me was that he could be an ax murderer. *No wonder it freaked her out,* he would say. As I watched him spring out to the parking lot, for some reason I yelled after him.

"Wait," I told him when I caught up. "Listen. I don't know how expensive your restaurant is, but I can afford one dinner out. Right now I have Ritz crackers and peanut butter in my house, which isn't really even a house, just a room full of suit-cases and boxes, and I haven't had anything since breakfast, which was one boiled egg in a cup my landlady made. And the landlady is really nice, but I don't want to impose on her by asking to have dinner the second night I'm here. Not to mention that she probably ate her dinner hours ago. So if you'd like to bring me with you . . ."

"I wouldn't expect you to pay for it!" Kevin said, grinning. "The most you'll have to do is wash dishes!"

"I'm a champ at that! I've washed plates and forks for my whole church!"

"Geez, Ronnie, I'm kidding about that, too! No, come with me and meet my parents and the kids, and you can take home Chinese food to last you the next week."

The Seventh Happiness was only twenty minutes' drive from

CAGE of STARS

the college. Kevin parked his car in back and we went in through the screen door, where a tiny old man was sitting on the steps, smoking a little cigar and muttering and pointing out things in the air. "This is my uncle Torrance, my father's oldest brother," Kevin said. "Uncle Torrance, this is my school friend Veronica." The old man waved and kept on muttering. "He drinks," Kevin said. "We let him think that he's working here, but this is mostly what he does, get tanked and sit on the back steps and talk to his wife. She left him about forty years ago. He's Torrance, and my uncle who's a police officer is Barstow, and my father is Carson, after Carson City, California."

"This is so funny!"

"Yeah, it's nuts. This was my grandmother's idea."

"No, what's nuts is that my grandmother did the same thing!" I said happily. "We thought she invented it! My father's name is London! And his brother's named after Bryce Canyon. We're probably the only two people in America whose grandmothers were nuts in exactly that way!"

Kevin shook his head. "I knew I was right to ask you over. Must be the red thread," he said.

"What's that?" I asked him.

"Well, that is one Chinese legend I do know. It means if two people are meant to meet in life, they're born connected by an invisible red thread. And no matter where they're born or how far apart they live, eventually they'll meet, because they're already connected."

He pulled me inside, where everyone in the hot, scrubbed-bare little kitchen was screaming and banging on the lids of big pots and vats. There were maybe six people in white coats and hairnets in there, bashing away at a huge stove and steam table. Racks and colanders of sliced vegetables glistened on the sideboards, where a woman was chopping in a gleaming of flying cutlery. Overhead, plucked ducks hung from their necks on twine. As we stepped in, the woman cutting vegetables wadded up the little white hat she was wearing and began screaming at one of the men working at the steam table, using her big knife as punctuation.

"What's wrong?" I asked Kevin, hanging back.

"What? Oh, nothing! That's how my family talks to each other. Nobody talks in a normal voice if they can yell. That's my aunt Rose. She's mad at her husband because he bet money on the ponies. Mom!" Kevin yelled to a tall, pretty woman who looked like a model in her sandals and sundress. She slipped her apron off over her head and came toward us, smiling. "Mom, this is Ronnie from my class. She's never had Chinese food in her entire life!"

"Well, Ronnie, I'm Jenny Chan, and though I'm deeply shocked, I'll get over it if you have some of ours," she said. "Are you going to be an EMT also? We worry about Kevin doing this work. We thought he was better off with the idea of teaching literature. We think it could be dangerous." Kevin's auntie Rose was banging on the chopping block with her knife at that moment, pausing every couple of minutes to wave it in the air. I looked from one woman to the other.

"I think he'll be able to handle it," I said.

Kevin and his mother rolled their eyes.

"Point taken," said Mrs. Chan. "Rosie!" she cried. "That's a good knife. Wait until home and fight with your own cutlery!" The older woman reluctantly went back to her supercharged chopping, the knife a twinkling silver blur. I was surprised she still had fingers.

That night, I learned that Chinese food was one of the Lord's blessings on earth. I sat at the bar next to the kitchen window and ate shrimp with lobster sauce and black prawns and gingered rice and Kung Pao chicken, which The Seventh Happiness made with so many hot peppers that I also drank three root beers. Kevin's sister Marie was my age, and his sister Kitty was a year older. They turned up the radio and danced in the hall between the kitchen and the dining room while they waited for orders to be ready. Kevin's little brother Scott, who took away the dishes, was only thirteen. His other little brother, Conner, who folded knives and forks into napkins and put a little decorated tape on each one to keep it together, when he wasn't coloring with crayons on the place mats and playing Connect Four with me, was nine.

Jenny Chan, Kevin's mom, was one of the kindest people. She asked me all about my family and told me how brave I was to go so far from home on my own, how frightened she would be if Kevin went to another state for school, how she had painted the plates for the restaurant herself, and how angry she got at Uncle Torrance every time he dropped and broke a whole stack of them, "although I'm very sorry for him, of course." Kevin's father was also a nice man, tall and polite like Kevin, but distracted and perpetually rushed. I could see why. Two hundred people must have come through the beaded curtain over the door at The Seventh Happiness during the hours I was there, from the sort of sunbrushed blond family I'd come to associate with La Jolla—one in which the father and mother looked similar enough to be twins—to long-haired girls and boys who wore dreamy smiles, ripped T-shirts, and sandals, to big Jewish families coming to eat after services.

"I thought Jews couldn't have pork," I whispered to Kevin when he got a chance to set down the phone for a moment. As soon as he put it down, it rang again.

"Only Chinese pork," he explained. I would learn, until one night, that almost everything was a joke to Kevin.

On the third night that I fell asleep in California, I could still hear those pot lids clanging, but by then I had more on my mind than my happy stomach. Kevin drove me back to my car and followed me until he was sure I was on the right street. Mrs. Desmond was sitting on the porch when I got home. It was after ten.

"You're out late," she said quietly.

"A nice boy from my class took me to his family's restaurant for dinner," I said. "Normally, I wouldn't have gone with a stranger, but I had a sense about him."

"People are very trusting here," she said. "And generally kind. That part reminds me of home."

"It must," I said, sitting down on the steps.

"How are you adjusting, Ronnie?" she asked.

"It's too soon to tell. There's too much to take in. The classes. The ocean. Chinese food. My mother said when I called home after I got here that I sounded as though I were sleepwalking. And I practically am. I should go in and sleep for twelve hours, Missus Desmond. But how do you manage it? When the air is like this? I've never felt air like this. It's like . . . lotion."

"Would you like a cup of tea?" Mrs. Desmond asked. "And perhaps a biscuit? You look a bit shattered."

"I don't think I could eat another thing," I told her, showing her my little cartons of leftovers with the red dragons stamped on the sides. "I'd be grateful for a cup of herbal tea. I'm just . . . I guess my father would say I'm overstimulated, like my little brother gets before Christmas. Everything is so different. The sounds and the crowds. I've never been in so large a city," I said. "To stay, I mean. I've been to Cape Cod, and Salt Lake City, but only for visits or a day trip. . . ."

"It's chamomile tea," Mrs. Desmond said. "It will help you drop off to sleep." I felt a pang. My mother gave us chamomile tea, with scalded milk, when I was little. Mrs. Desmond must have seen something change in my face. "Are you feeling home-sick, Ronnie?" I nodded. "Would you like a shawl? I have dozens. I just wrap one more around me as it gets darker. I like to watch the water change as the light disappears."

Mrs. Desmond lifted an afghan out of a big hamper on her porch, and I put it over my knees. She went to get the tea, and by the time she came back, I had dropped off. I shook myself awake, slapping my hands, which had fallen asleep.

"Come up here and have a chair," she said.

"I'm used to sitting on the floor," I said. "My father says I wasn't born to live indoors."

"Then put one of those lap robes beneath you and lean on my chair," Mrs. Desmond said kindly. "I've got too many daughters to feel comfortable with a tired child lying flat on a damp porch floor."

We watched as couples passed us hand in hand—heading for the pier, I supposed. California was apparently open all night. They were, most of them, impossibly beautiful people, like gazelles or some other exotic creature of the plains, people who moved with a sort of grace I thought must be particular to *Hominidus californius*. They had the longest legs and necks.

"Do they all look this way?" I asked.

"It seems so, doesn't it," Mrs. Desmond said, and then asked, "Ronnie, why are you really here?"

My neck muscles gripped. "I'll be getting a job in . . . in San Diego, but I don't have one yet. I'm going to school at La Jolla Tech, studying to be an EMT. I told you. I came for school."

"Why would you want to do that? That job?" Mrs. Desmond asked.

"I . . . well, I want to be a doctor one day, and this is a good path," I said.

"It's very gruesome," she said.

"But not if you help save a life," I said.

"Paramedics came when my husband died," she told me, "but it was far too late for him. He'd had a massive heart attack."

"How very sad," I said.

"Not really." She smiled. "I suppose it was *sad*. In a general way. But I moved here with the wrong fellow, you might say, although I knew he was the wrong fellow forty years ago, when I married him. My children still live in Brisbane. Someday, when I get enough energy to pack up this place and sell it, I'll move back there. I thought I was in love, I suppose. He was an American pilot. I was, you might say, an old maid, a governess if you can believe that! We have three lovely girls, but once he'd set his mind on moving back here, after he retired, and it was just him and me . . . Ah, well, that was fifteen years ago. He died the third year. I go home at Christmas and in summer, which is winter there, of course. That's why I take in boarders, not because I need the income. So that there would be someone to look after the place while I wasn't about."

"Who lived here before?"

"A young woman, well, not as young as you. But she was a nurse and had left a marriage that didn't go well for her. A lovely girl. Filipino. She finally did marry again. She lived here for three years. Ancaya," said Mrs. Desmond. "She was good company. A crack card player. Do you play?"

"Chess," I said.

"We'll have a game."

"I would like that. I played with my father."

Mrs. Desmond was quiet for a long time. Then she said, "You'll find I say what I think, Ronnie. Not everyone likes that. I have a feeling you do. What I meant before was, why are you here really? Beyond the studies?"

"No reason," I murmured.

"I thought perhaps you were starting over. People come to California to do that. You told me about your little sisters. I hope I'm not being untoward, but to have two sisters die . . ."

"It was an accident."

"A car accident?"

I sighed. "They were murdered, Missus Desmond."

"In Utah, by a man with a pitchfork. . . ."

"A weed cutter. You read about it, then."

"Quite a long time ago now, wasn't it? I remember the incident. Yours is an unusual name. I'm an avid reader, particularly about violence. Don't let that shock you. I'm fascinated by inhumanity in all its infinite variety. I'm amazed at what people will do to one another. You're not old enough to be in college."

"I've graduated. I'm seventeen, almost eighteen, Missus. Desmond." I thought she would feel better if I told her I was almost eighteen, so that was what I told her. Later she found out, of course. "Please, don't tell anyone about this. I just want to do my work and live quietly."

"I can see why you needed the distance between you and that incident," she said, but not like a busybody. "I'm very sorry, Ronnie. Perhaps this is why you chose this work. To save others when your sisters could not be saved."

"Thank you, Missus Desmond. I don't know. That must be part of it. I don't mind your knowing. But I don't think I can talk about it. I think I'll just turn in?"

"Do, Ronnie. I'll put the house to sleep after I've watched the boats come in for a time." She called it that, putting the house to sleep, turning out the lights and locking the doors. She raised one hand in a little wave and said she'd pick up the tea things.

She didn't say anything about Scott Early living in San Diego, then or later. But she knew.

Chapter Sixteen

On Saturday, I drove into San Diego—thinking every moment of Serena as I fought the traffic, small turns, tip, tip, tip—and bought a telephone book for a dollar. I went to the zoo and sat at a table. It was the most beautiful zoo I'd ever seen. I drank lemonade and was mesmerized by the most amazing performance. Two girls—I suppose they were ballerinas—wore green face paint and leotards covered entirely with leaves to make them seem as though they were vines. Decorated, leafy stilts extended from their arms and legs so they towered, twelve, fifteen feet tall and moved like giraffes. They walked among the children, who didn't seem to know whether to be terrified or charmed as they looked into those heavy-lidded, gorgeously immobile faces, and then twined themselves gracefully around the trees, where they blended, as if they really were vines. I watched them for an hour, imagining how much grace and training it must have taken to do this. Then I stood in line to see the pandas, because one was the only one-year-old cub in the United States. The cub was nearly as big as the mother, but he pestered her so much—hanging from her legs, poking her ears—it was easy to tell he was a baby.

Finally, unable to put it off any longer, I sat down again with the phone book to look up their address.

Even paging through the E's made me break out in a sweat. But there it was, on Monitor Street, just as the envelope's return address had said. I thought, then, that I would try to find their church. Knowing what I knew of Scott Early's family and what avid churchgoers they were, they would immediately have established themselves with a church, in the way I'd read that alcoholics, in a new town, find an AA meeting right away to help them adjust. On top of that, the neighbors would have had to be notified about what Scott Early had done. So it was natural that they would seek out a church, where people would presumably try to be forgiving. They were Lutherans, so I looked for a Lutheran church near Monitor Street. I hadn't even looked up a church for myself, and here I was searching for Scott Early's!

I was soon discouraged. There were, like, fifty Lutheran churches in San Diego and about five near Monitor Street. How would I go to forty Lutheran churches in a semester? Or a lifetime?

I decided to gamble, and the next morning, I went to the ten o'clock service at St. James Lutheran Church, only two blocks from where Scott Early and his wife lived. First, I drove slowly past their house—a big pink duplex, two apartments one on top of the other—with sage-colored doors. No one came out while I was watching.

I'd never been in a Lutheran church, and it was mammoth. The hymnals were filled with songs I didn't recognize, except for "Rock of Ages" and the Christmas carols. I sat in the back and sat and stood when everyone else did; but it was strange not to hear The Book of Mormon or the King James Version of the Bible. The Bible sounds all wrong without the thees and thous. The juice and bread they passed around for Communion looked safe and okay, so I took some. It was when I was leaving that I saw him. He was carrying the tiny baby in a sling, and he looked right at me without seeing me at all. He was a big, open-faced, handsome man with blond hair cut short, barely recognizable as the skinny, pale thing I had seen screaming and writhing in my yard. He looked like a farmer, all tanned and muscular. I hadn't expected him to recognize me, because I was sure he'd had about as much interest in watching the news as I had. And it had been so long ago. But the old metallic taste soured my tongue, and I felt my hairline pop with drops of cold sweat. I couldn't breathe. I wanted to throw myself under the padded seat I was walking past and hide. Then I saw her. She was adorable. Kelly. I had never seen Kelly in person. She was little and blond, with a Dutch-boy haircut. She came up next to Scott Early and took his hand. A lot of grandmotherly types surrounded her and him, pointing at the baby and making googly noises. All you could see of the baby was a rabbit tail of toffee-colored hair. Kelly looked right at me, too, and she did a little bit of a double take. She must have seen me on television at some point and in court, but I had been three inches shorter then and twenty pounds lighter. Still, I was who I was; but I supposed it was like seeing your bishop at the movies. You don't recognize the person if she's out of place.

How could I have found them, I thought, in the first hour of my search?

As I watched, entranced, Kelly hung back and posted a notice on the corkboard near the entrance of the church. It was on stationery surrounded with flowers, and it read:

JULIET NEEDS SOMEONE TO WATCH OVER HER: Day nanny wanted, four days a week and occasional weekends, to care for adorable seven-week-old girl. Mommy must go back to work, because her students need her, and Daddy is studying to be a librarian. Good pay for the right person. Ten holidays. Flexible hours and references a must. Call 672-3333.

She tacked it up. The worshippers flowed around me, greeting the minister in his lush, satiny robes.

I waited until almost everyone had left. Then I took down the notice, folded it, and put it into my pocket.

On the way home, I bought myself a corkboard. I put the notice on it. I tacked up my class picture next to it. And for the next three nights, I tried to shut my mind off to the one while I studied the other. It was Scott Early's phone number I ended up committing to memory.

Chapter Seventeen

$\mathcal{I}$ never knew how much my hair really meant to me until the Monday night after class when I went to a salon and let someone chop it off and dye it brown. I had to steel myself not to scream at every whicker of the scissors. My hair was part of how I thought of myself, Ronnie Rapunzel, the girl with the curl; and as I watched strand after strand drop, it was as though I were shedding my skin. Except for my mother's trims, it had grown for ten years untouched by human hands—tended by me as if it were a rare bonsai or something. Before I had a blow dryer, I would hang my head over the heat register in my room, twining the curls around my forefinger, sometimes for fifteen or twenty minutes. By the time I finished high school, it fell to below my waist, and while I wore it looped in a bun for sports or most practical things, or tightly braided, I wasn't unaware of the looks I got when I let it hang down to go swimming. It was my crowning glory, as it says in the Bible. A few years back, I'd actually stood in front of my mirror in my underwear, with my hair over one shoulder, and let myself think that my hair was prettier than Lindsay Lohan's, though I could see my butt was twice as big.

The stylist was careful to bind and bag it for donation to Locks of Love, an organization that would make it into wigs for little kids who had cancer. Seeing my long, rusty curls in her hand was like seeing a severed limb (although this was before I'd actually *seen* a severed limb). I couldn't look in the mirror as she applied the dye and foiled in a few artful streaks; and I felt like hiding my eyes when she asked me brightly, "So, how do you like it?"

I opened one eye. I peeked.

I didn't know what to say. There was a nice-enough-looking young woman there in front of me, but I surely didn't know her.

"We usually go the other way. I never met a redhead who wanted brown hair. A natural platinum blonde once, she wanted red," the woman said.

The stylist wasn't a jerk. She'd feathered the hair around my face so it was slightly shorter in front than in back. At least, given how springy my curls were, I wouldn't look like I was wearing a clown wig. And the style was modern, very "not country" girl. My eyes were suddenly enormous, and my chin came to a point in a way I'd never noticed. The color didn't look fakey; I looked like an adult, a city chick. It wasn't ugly or anything. I just wasn't the kid down the road anymore. But my head felt as though I could float up through the ceiling, as if I'd been carrying a gallon jug strapped to my forehead all those years.

"It's great," I babbled to the stylist, who had a purple streak in her own shoe-polish-black hair. "It'll be so easy to take care of, and you know, I have to keep it up for my work anyhow, so this will really help. . . ." I couldn't wait to shove the forty bucks into her hand and get out of there.

"There's twenty inches of hair here," she called after me. "This is the most we've ever donated!"

Wow, did that make me feel great. Another loss courtesy of Scott Early. He might as well have cut it off himself.

After class, I phoned Kelly and introduced myself.

"This is Rachel Byrd," I said, "with a 'y.' I saw your ad?" I had chosen my name carefully. Rachel, who cried out in the Bible for her lost children, and Byrd because Becky had written, "A swan is like a birD, but bigger." I wouldn't forget it, even in an emergency. Kelly asked if it was possible for me to come over right away, and did I have my résumé with me? "I don't actually have a résumé," I told her. "I don't actually have a printer at present. My parents are sending it to me when they can find a used one they can afford. I'm an emergency medical technician, or at least I'm studying to be one. But I can give you letters of reference. Lots of them. I was a volunteer baby holder from when I was only twelve years old; and I basically helped raise my baby brother because my mother was ill after he was born."

The whole time, I was panicking, thinking, reference letters from where? Would Clare send a letter of reference that didn't have a postmark from Utah? About "Rachel Byrd"? If she would, how would she? And would she send it to Scott Early's wife? No, of course, she could send it to me. I could say I was going to use it for lots of applications. I could redo it on a printer at school. But who did I know who didn't live in Utah? My aunt Jill in Colorado? My aunt Juliet in Chicago? Did relatives count? Would west-y locations make her suspicious? No. That was ridiculous. This was California. California was in the West. But I had to think of a way to get around the name thing. White it out, something. I just had to stay calm. Be Rachel with the light brown hair.

An hour later, I parked in front of the big, pink-colored duplex. Kelly and I shook hands. She said immediately, "An EMT. So you must know infant CPR."

"I do," I said. "All the baby holders had to; and I'd learned it in health, too, at home." In a few weeks, I knew I'd learn it again, in our section on airways. I'd looked ahead in the syllabus.

"And so much experience," Kelly said. She spoke in a soft, breathy voice, assured yet almost childlike; and though she was pretty, she looked a whole lot older than she had in the courtroom, or even that Sunday morning in church. There were circles under her eyes, badly covered up by a smudge of makeup, and she was too thin, though her face was puffy.

"Yes," I said. "There's pretty much nothing about a healthy baby I don't know how to do, even in a crisis." We were beginning to learn about how a little child's organ systems were so small, the head so much larger than the body, that it would be perhaps the trickiest part of our job, being delicate but thorough with the presses and pushes and insertions, to avoid doing more harm in the cause of good.

"Do you want to see Juliet?" Kelly asked. "I wish you could meet my husband, but he's at school. We only moved here just a couple of months ago, before Juliet was born."

I said, "My aunt's name is Juliet."

"Isn't it the most beautiful name? But it's sad, too, isn't it? When you think of her in the play, being only fourteen. I can't bear it when I think of that. Scott chose her name. I really objected at first. I thought it was bad luck. But now I love it, too. Here she is, my girl!" My skin prickled as if it were something tight I'd outgrown. It was just what I'd always thought about my aunt's name.

Juliet, though, was a gorgeous baby, maybe the prettiest baby I've ever seen. Her lashes were as long as the end of my pinkie fingernail, and she had soft apricot skin and masses of buff-colored hair, between brown and blond, just like Jade's. I almost said how much she looked like my little sister when Becky was a baby.

But in truth, I hardly remembered anymore how Becky had looked as a newborn.

"She's spectacular," I said. I'd picked it up from Mrs. Desmond, who said that about everything from chocolate-chip cookies to TiVos of *The Price Is Right*.

"She is wonderful, isn't she?" Kelly asked. "We never thought we'd have her. My husband was . . . sick. My husband was very sick, and he was in a hospital, for almost five years."

Not even close to five years, I thought. It was only four years. Actually three years and eleven months.

"Is he better now?" I forced myself to ask.

"He's totally better. He's absolutely fine. He didn't know what was wrong with him, and he . . ." Kelly leaned over Juliet's basket and tucked her little pillow behind her back. It was like the stabilizing pillows we were learning how to place in class to keep people's heads from moving when they had a possible spinal injury, except it was tiny. Then she said, "I don't know how to say this. Scott had a mental illness. Now, don't be frightened. He's not dangerous or anything like that. He did something . . . unbelievable when he was sick. He doesn't remember it, but when he realized it, he was . . . suicidal for months afterward. Don't worry. You'd never be able to tell now. He's a wonderful father. He adores Juliet. He's studying to be a librarian. He was a graduate student in pharmacy before he got sick. It was . . . very bad. He hurt a family's feelings so terribly."

I wanted to slug her.

I wanted to hug her.

Hurt a family's *feelings*? I could taste that tang on my tongue, and I struggled with the snag in my windpipe.

But, really, I thought, what was this poor woman supposed to say to a prospective nanny? My husband murdered two children? And it's okay because he takes medicine and you won't have to see him much?

If she'd told the truth about Scott Early, would anyone except for me on earth have had the guts to work in this clean, spare apartment, with its bouquets of fresh flowers and its few humble, carefully chosen photos and ornaments? Wouldn't anyone else have run like a deer? Kelly had come here with a purpose, just as I had, but hers was to flee all that was familiar. Perhaps, in a sense, that also was mine, at least in part. I had to make sure if my . . . plan, undeveloped as it was, would hold up in the light of day. But Kelly believed she was at the end of her road to Calvary. She thought that my parents' forgiveness and her move would make it all better, make it all go away.

What I couldn't grasp at all was why she was even here. If Kelly had given birth to Scott Early's baby and then left him, I might have been able to understand her. She would have been able to have the best of the boy she'd loved before, but not have had to live with an evil man. I could see, already, why my mother considered Kelly a kind and decent person. But she *hadn't* left him. She'd hung on like those women whose husbands led them away from their faith, saying they loved them anyway, as the men destroyed the families' lives through drinking or cheating or gambling or even heresy. Was it lust? Was it a misguided loyalty, a promise even our Lord would never mean anyone to honor?

But Kelly was a saver.

I was, too.

And some people didn't deserve to be saved.

This little girl did, though.

And that would be my job. I just wasn't sure how, but an idea, light and shifting as a cloud of steam, had begun to float about in my mind.

"What do you do for work?" I asked Kelly, though I already knew. Good job applicants asked questions.

"I'm a school counselor," Kelly said. "You wouldn't believe the issues kids have today. It seems they're even worse here than where we come from. They tell me everything from . . . oh dear, their uncle trying to, well, be too familiar, to their mothers worrying that they're too fat! Well, I guess you would know about the problems teens have, wouldn't you? How . . . old are you?"

"I'm eighteen," I said. "I'll turn nineteen on December tenth. I know I look younger. I always have." My first overt lie. It was at least my real birthday. "My parents are teachers, too." This wasn't a lie. My mother had taught us, hadn't she? "They don't make much. I have to earn my way. We live in a rural area north of Phoenix."

Well, it *was* north of Phoenix. So was Canada.

"Why California?"

"Well, it's just so beautiful, isn't it? Sunny all the time, not so hot and dry, and the ocean . . ." I tried to sound like a kind-hearted but not too intellectual girl. It was easier than I thought. "I've just never seen a more perfect climate than here! I want to learn to surf! And I'm hoping to go to school here, so I . . . wanted to establish residency, to pay in-state tuition? I'm not sure I'll be able to afford it. It's expensive here. But it's possible. I can guarantee you the semester, probably the whole year, at least." Anything was possible. "At least I could give her a good start."

"San Diego is something, isn't it? The most beautiful city I've ever seen," Kelly said, looking dreamy. "It makes you feel as though the people who live here must be happy all the time."

One wasn't. The baby chose that moment to wake. She cried sharply, and instinctively I gathered her up. "Hello, princess pea," I said, and turned to Kelly. "I think you're going to need a new stretchy here; this one's a little damp."

"I have to stop nursing her now, though I'll pump," Kelly said, wide-eyed, mournful. She went to a drawer in a bureau they'd painted with polka dots and got a diaper and a stretchy one-piece with a monkey on the front. In a few deft motions, I put it on, first carefully wiping Juliet clean and folding the diaper into a neat little package.

"Even a few weeks of nursing is better than nothing," I said, remembering Rafe and my mother. "The colostrum is important.

It's powerful stuff. She'll do just fine, won't you, Miss Juliet . . . I don't think I got your last name?"

"Englehart," said Kelly. "That's my last name. We . . . used my last name for her. Not because we're so extra-modern. It just fit. My grandma said it meant 'angel heart' in German. That's just so nice, isn't it?" I knew exactly why they'd chosen that last name. There were plenty of people who knew who Scott Early was. "Well, what you'd need to do is this: I work from nine to three. My husband goes to school at eight most days, and he sometimes doesn't get home until five or six. So, I'd need someone to work from about eight to three, four days a week. Scott has Fridays free. And sometimes, not very often, we like to just go have a salad or see a movie . . . so if there was ever a night you could work later, or on a weekend?"

"I could," I said. "I do need the extra income, though I have to study pretty hard. But I could study, if that's okay, during her naps."

"Oh, yes, I don't expect cleaning or anything from you. Just looking after her things, maybe running a load of wash with the baby detergent. We go through her clothes so fast! And you could have your lunch here. We'd buy whatever it is you like."

"Well, thanks," I said. "I could do that. My training is very intensive. And starting in about six weeks, I'll be doing practicum, and ride-alongs, so I won't be free every weekend. But my classes are all at night, because I knew I'd need a day job—except on Friday!"

"That really works out!"

"I hope you didn't mind my picking her up," I told Kelly. "I should have asked first. But I used hand sanitizer before I came. It's like a way of life now, that and my rubber gloves!"

She looked at me oddly then, and abruptly she said, "Do . . . Have we met before?"

I felt my heart accelerate into its familiar staccato. Did the brown hair make me look like my mother? Did Kelly recall a photo from a newspaper or a TV shot, of our family, me growling at the TV reporters, or pale on the courthouse steps? Were my looks so distinctive?

"I don't think so. But I did pick up your job advertisement at Saint James Church . . . Do you know where that is?" I asked innocently.

"Oh, that's it! We go to Saint James. Do you?"

"I usually go to church closer to where I live, in La Jolla. I totally wanted to live right by the beach! But I've been to Saint James." By my reckoning, I hadn't told more than one complete lie yet, except my age. Even my name. My father had once told me that it wasn't illegal to call yourself Donald Duck—movie stars changed their names all the time—unless it was to commit a crime.

To commit a crime.

"That must be where I saw you," Kelly said. "The people there are so kind. Little miss here has all kinds of grandmothers in the nursery. I can actually concentrate when I'm in church, and . . ." She let out a long breath. "I need that."

"Me too," I said.

"Well, I start back to work in two weeks, Rachel," Kelly said, "and I'm going to interview two other girls. But I really don't think I need to look any further after meeting you, if you can work for what I can offer, twelve dollars an hour to start. I'm sorry I can't offer benefits except holidays off with pay. You'd be a freelance contractor and responsible for paying your own taxes. . . ."

"That's okay with me," I said.

"Then could you possibly come for a practice this week, and meet my husband, and then start on Monday two weeks from now?"

"I could do that," I said, a physical sensation, not unlike the pain that travels outward from a sting or a burn, creeping up my arms at the thought of "meeting her husband." We shook hands, and I patted the baby's cheek. This is best, I said to Juliet with my heart. I had known all along I would get the job. The red thread, I thought.

I wrote my aunt Juliet that night and asked her to send a letter to me describing my skills in caring for little ones, but leaving out my name, as I didn't want anyone to think anything strange about me in case they recognized "Ronnie Swan" from the murder case. I'd learned that people tended to judge you if you'd had something bad happen to you, no matter how nice you were. I wrote to my cousin Bridget, who was in college at the Art Institute of Chicago, saying the same thing, asking her to refer to me as "my cousin."

But before I could do anything more than mail the letters, Kelly called me. "I don't need any references, though I'll be happy to read them. Some things you just know," she said. And I thought, sadly, how right she was. "I spoke to those other girls, and, I don't mean to sound unkind, but I wouldn't have let them take care of my cat, if I had one! They were, you know, black nail polish, and one even smoked, though she said she would go outside! And who would be watching Juliet while she was outside?"

"Well, children are the most important thing, and I guess some people take it too lightly," I said, sort of hating myself for deceiving her.

After class on Friday, I went back to "meet" Scott Early.

It was stunning.

He truly was that nice, hearty man I'd seen in church. He had a confident, gentlemanly manner and a strong handshake. It didn't change anything, but I was overwhelmed by the power of medical science. *Medicine* had done this? I had to remind myself that what I needed to do didn't have anything to do with Scott Early as he was at the moment—but what he had done before and might do later. He looked flat into my face, and I knew he didn't recognize me from Adam's off ox. "Are you going to take good care of my little girl?" he asked.

Like you took care of mine? I thought. But I said, "Of course. You don't have to worry about a thing." He *didn't* have to worry about a thing, either.

They went to a movie. I gave Juliet her bottle, and after opening the window to the soft, salty night, I began studying and memorizing the names of all those bones. I worked for forty minutes, and then, because I couldn't stop myself, I began to open drawers. For seventeen years, I'd been respectful of others' privacy. My parents had never even opened the label on a catalog of exercise clothing with my name on it. But in just a few months, I'd become an expert and eager snoop, combing Miko's room and now this.

I started with Kelly's closet. She had a few work outfits, some jeans and shorts and T-shirts. The shorts and shirts were faded. Even Clare had six or seven pairs of shoes, but Kelly had only four: black heels, brown heels, walking shoes, and a pair of sandals. I went to her chest of drawers. I found sweet, clean underwear, with sachets of lavender tucked in among her bras. Exercise clothes. A wedding veil in a special airtight box. A sexy little red teddy. Birth control pills and some Valentine's Day cards. There was a plain blue book of handmade paper on top of her sweaters, in the next drawer down. I grabbed it. What did I expect to find? A book of horror stories? A gruesome notebook filled with newspaper clippings? It was just Juliet's baby book, with her little footprints. "Juliet Jeanine Englehart" was calligraphied on the first page, which was decorated with little silver stars. Kelly had written so much about the first month of her baby's life that even the borders were filled with her neat, tiny handwriting. I lifted a pile of sweaters. And I saw it then. I knew what it was. A buck knife, the kind used by hunters to gut a deer. My father had one that he hid on top of the cabinets, too high even for my mother to reach. I didn't touch it, but my hands started to shake. I thought, Here is proof that even she doesn't trust him. I put the sweaters back carefully.

Scott Early's side of the closet wasn't very interesting. He had a plastic set of drawers, like the kind from Sears, with his underwear and socks in it. Jeans, polo shirt, loafers. His bedside stand had two drawers. In the top drawer was a book, a novel about a man who sold his wedding ring and spent the rest of his life trying to find it again, a book about sailing, and a box of tissues. Pills in a carefully marked series of containers: "Morning," "Lunch," "Bedtime." A newborn pacifier. In the second drawer, there was a diary. I sat in the rocking chair. The journal began with Juliet's birth, but some earlier pages had been cut out. I could see the edges, stiff as a mown hedge.

This is the beginning of my real life. Juliet is awesome. She's a rose. She's an angel. There has to be something in my life, maybe the mercy of God, that allows me to have something like this happen to me, because I don't deserve it. We were having dinner at Sambucco when Kelly's water broke and the contractions started right away. I had to have the ambulance come, and poor Kels was so embarrassed because it's "our" restaurant. She was crying and saying, We're never going to go back there. I wrecked the chair! They took us right up in the elevator. By the time we got to the maternity floor, the nurses were hurrying us up because Kelly was already six centimeters dilated. A few pushes and there she was. It was probably much worse for Kels than she says it was. I wanted to name her "Jewel," because that's what she is. But Kelly said that was a country-western name. I thought of Juliet, because it sounded a little like "Jewel," and Kelly didn't like that much, either, but she gave in. Maybe she was just tired out. I hope I didn't force it on her!

The next entry was from September:

Juliet is becoming a real little person. I know she can see, because she looks right into my eyes. I think her eyes will be dark blue, like the ocean. I'm so glad we came here. Colorado is so dusty and dry. I want to teach Juliet to swim. I can't wait for her to say "Daddy."

I read the next entry.

I feel so guilty. Kels has to do all the work to support us, and she doesn't make that much. She hasn't had a new dress in years. I feel so good, and I'm learning so much, but she comes home all depressed because the kids she sees at school are so troubled. I can't believe parents can be so lousy. They don't even think about how their actions affect kids. Kelly told me one father had his daughter going to buy him cigarettes!

I shut the book, slipping the little lock into its place, making sure it opened easily and didn't need a key. Scott Early's outrage over parents smoking cigarettes was about all I could take.

Juliet started to whimper, and I changed and fed her, gradually calming myself down. I began to sing to her, "Hushabye, don't you cry. Go to sleep, my little baby. When you wake, you shall have all the pretty little horses. . . ."

They came home, relaxed and laughing, at nine.

They paid me and hired me.

I thanked them. I promised I would always do my best for Juliet.

When I went downstairs, I thought I heard a faint ribbon of music. I looked back up at the big window at the front of their apartment. The two of them were dancing, holding Juliet between them. My mother danced with Rafe standing on her feet, spinning him around the way he wanted her to until he was so dizzy, he fell over laughing on the rug. But what loomed over me as I watched them was a memory: I was little. Maybe I was six or seven. My mother was dancing to her Motown music and holding the baby's arm out as if they were partners in a tango. The baby would have been . . . Becky, if I had been that small. The little girl who was me was jumping up and down next to my mother. I could hear my father laughing. *What you want, baby, I got . . .* My head throbbed, though I never got headaches. I thought of the next line: *What you need . . .* Scott Early and Kelly looked so happy. They had everything they wanted. The past was the past. For them. The little baby in my mother's arms was buried in the cemetery now, her quick little legs quiet forever in their black Sunday tights. But Scott Early's little baby girl was healthy and strong. No one would ever hurt her. I could hardly remember that kind of happy, a happy without an "in spite of" like a rock in the middle of it. Denial was built into human nature, but surely they must think of the murders all the time. They must. They'd had less than a year together since he got out of Stone Gate. Every day must be a gift to them. A new surprise package to open, despite how "guilty" Scott Early felt—guilty because his wife had to earn the living, not because he'd taken two little lives in the time it took to write down that sentence! Every day after he'd done that was a package to open for us, too. A package of obligation, tied up in dirty brown paper. We hated to see the sun go down and dreaded seeing it come up. We barely spoke for a year; Scott Early and Kelly were dancing!

And now, I thought, even my parents were happy. Heavenly Father had given them the mercy of forgiveness and allowed them to let Ruthie and Becky go like balloons released to the sky at a parade. They'd been able to move ahead. Did *they* think of my sisters every day?

Was I the only one who kept this vigil? Why did Scott Early have a right to his "jewel"? What was amiss with my faith that I couldn't let go?

I turned away and drove home.

Mrs. Desmond had left a note for me and a plate with a stuffed pepper and mashed potatoes on it for me to warm. It was her bridge night. I loved stuffed peppers, but I simply cut up the food with a fork and flushed it down the toilet, rinsed the plate, and put it in the dishwasher, afterward scribbling a note of thanks. I knelt next to my bed and prayed for the rock to be a ball of ice. I prayed for it to melt.

I got into my bed, shivering, and opened the laptop my father had insisted on giving me. Mrs. Desmond had high-speed cable, to e-mail her daughters daily. I opened Google and searched out places in Texas and Arizona called Second Chance and Safe Haven, where scared girls too frightened or ashamed to tell their parents that they'd given birth could leave their babies to be found and adopted—no questions asked. The programs worked. The babies weren't dumped in trash barrels; and sometimes the mothers came back, but sometimes they didn't. After a few months, good parents were found for the little abandoned ones. As if someone had whispered the instructions into my ear, I knew exactly what I was going to do.

Chapter Eighteen

On Monday, Kelly gave me a key to their apartment so I could take Juliet for walks in her stroller on nice days—and they were all nice days. We met every morning at the door, and Kelly gave me a list of things Juliet would need during the day and money if I needed to pick up anything at the corner market. Then she flew out of the door with her briefcase under her arm and her backpack over her shoulder. I watched her put on her mascara in the rearview mirror.

Juliet was an easy baby, and Kelly kept her as clean as a rosebud. Every day, I warmed the milk Kelly had pumped and stored the night before and tickled Juliet's cheek to start her sucking. The first time she smiled, I rummaged through Kelly's desk and found a disposable camera with a few shots left and took pictures, leaving Kelly a note.

The next day, Kelly met me at the door and hugged me. "I wasn't here for her first smile, but you saved it for me! Rachel, thank you!"

And that was the first of about thirty times my own craftiness nauseated me. But after that, unable to stop myself, I took pictures of Juliet whenever I could and delighted in finding just the right socks to match her dozens of bite-size outfits, "capri pants," and "miniskirts." She was like my own little doll. Holding her tiny hands, playing "doing crunches" by pulling her up to a sitting position, I forgot for hours at a time why I'd come to California. But then I'd be sprawled with Juliet on a blanket in Belleview Park, recognizing patterns in the shadows the leaves made on my hands, making shapes for her with my fingers, when suddenly I would see those intertwined stone hands in Pine Tree Cemetery. And a black film would creep over me, staining me, reminding me that I wasn't really Rachel Byrd, normal girl, happy in her job, loving school.

I would try, then, to think of Juliet's new family, who would have waited so long for her, a couple who couldn't have babies of their own, their joy after I left Juliet, carefully wrapped, fed, and dry, in some safe, lighted space. These havens were protected from the weather, not patrolled by a camera but checked three or four times a night by volunteers. It would all be fine.

Of course, I was as naive as a bale of hay; I didn't think about the fact that the FBI would have been all over a kidnapping like white on rice, within hours, and that in all likelihood they would have found Juliet and me, if Scott Early didn't find me first. I would have been charged with a federal crime and gone to prison—facing a fate that Scott Early never had. But as my thoughts corkscrewed and drifted, it seemed then that no one would ask questions, or even locate me, since I'd be long gone, back to Utah, my hair again its normal color, my soul its normal viscosity. I thought I'd leave Juliet's pram in Belleview Park so it would look as though someone had taken her *and* me. Smart thinking! That I was registered at school under my own name, and that any idiot would connect Scott Early and me in about ten seconds, didn't occur to me. I was almost seventeen, but ever so much older and younger. I didn't know anything about how the world worked. And I supposed I didn't want to think too hard about it.

When the forewarning of Kelly's heartbreak crossed my

mind, as it did sometimes, such as when I did her laundry (for which she was so grateful), hanging up T-shirts that read JULIET'S MOMMY!, I'd turn my mind's eye to the paint on the shed, and the other black paint, that pooled on the ground and sprayed the picnic table.

Juliet wouldn't be dead, her life cut off in a moment, like my sisters.

She'd be free, free of Scott Early and the taint of his vicious presence.

But had *his* presence ever been vicious? Or his disease the only part of him that was terrifying? Whenever I saw him, he was all gentleness and kind humor, but couldn't that change? I knew that mentally ill people sometimes felt so good that they simply stopped taking their meds; and Scott Early could do that, too. Otherwise, why did Kelly have that huge, sheathed hunting knife? There had to be a reason. I knew she would stop at nothing to save Juliet. But what if she couldn't? What if only I could? As it said in the Bible, there was a way for me, I reassured myself, and I had to walk in it. A path for me set forth by our Lord.

Still, I looked forward to the breaks, the times when I didn't have to think about it, when I could "play normal" and do all the things other girls did.

Kevin and I met before our bones exam at L.M.N.O. Tea, a little shop near Belleview Park—which was walking distance from Kelly and Scott Early's house. He picked Juliet up easily and held her and said he had about ten little cousins. "What a cutie!" he said. "I can't wait to have one of these." He got a whiff of her then and said, "On the other hand, I can wait. Speaking of . . . Ronnie, *what* did you do to your hair?"

"It fell out," I told him, grinning.

"You, like, colored it. My girlfriend says all the time she'd give her left pinkie for curly red hair, and you . . . what did you do?"

"I wanted a change," I said. "New state. New job. New life."

"Maybe I should dye my hair red," Kevin said.

"Maybe you should tell me the main bones of the head. How many temporal? How many occipital?"

"I know that hope is the thing with feathers that perches in the soul—"

"Be serious! What are you going to do when she asks about your ethmoid?"

"I'll say I'm Chinese American."

"Ouch," I said, and socked him. It was as though a fly had landed on his forearm. "Kevin! Come on!"

"Do you mean the paired facial bones?" Kevin asked. "Those would be the lacrimals, nasals, zygomatics, the maxillae, the palatins, the inferior—"

"You knew them all!"

"You know Asian people are smarter. Don't you watch TV? The Chinese guy always figures it out." Kevin made me feel like a kid again. Why was that? I was a kid. I just . . . hadn't felt that way for so long.

One night when I came home after classes, Mrs. Desmond handed me a letter. I took it, shocked. The only letters I ever got were cards from Clare in Boston and Emma back home and big fat packages from my parents, with drawings Rafe made of me.

There was no name on the return, only an address, also in Boston. I read:

Dear Annie Oakley,

I just found out that my sister hasn't written you one time since you left! Leaker! Well, I'm no writer, but I thought I would drop you a note. Maybe you could write back. Medical school is nothing like college, I can tell you. I don't have time for the brewskies and the babes (except one, more about that later). I have to hit the books every night. It is Boston Univer-

sity, so I'm not complaining. I'm not what you would call a natural. I was
out at the pier the other day, and you'll never guess who I saw. Clare! She
was in town for just three days, doing a concert with her vocal chorus
from Juilliard! How could two people from the middle of nowhere end up
bumping into each other in Boston? She was the one who gave me your
address. She's looking beautiful, not that she was ever anything but. I
guess all her time is taken up with lessons and musical theory and stuff,
too. We had some coffee. Don't worry! She had lemonade. She said you
were pretty lonely. Why don't you take up surfing? Afraid a shark will eat
you? I'm dating a girl. I guess it's pretty serious. She moved here from Colorado just to be with me. We don't exactly live together. But she works
near where I live. She wants to get engaged. I'm not sure I can take that
on right now. I'm thinking, maybe, ten years! But I really like her. Serena
is good. She's going to Cape Cod Community College, because my parents won't pay for her to go to a real college until she figures out what
she's going to do. Clare said you're studying to be a firefighter? That's
weird. But I can see you driving a fire engine! Well, here's my number if
you ever want to talk. Or you can drop me a line sometime. I'm working
on my fade-away jump shot.

> Your old friend,
> Miko S.

I crumpled up the letter and felt like I might start to cry.
But why?

Miko was happy. He was in love. I was sure Clare had told
him that I was studying to be an EMT, not a firefighter, and that
he just wasn't paying attention, probably because he was too
busy staring at Clare, who I knew was already practically engaged to Dr. Pratt's son, just like I'd teased her when we were . . .
little girls. Well, not little girls. Just a few years ago. Why did it
seem like a century? I was the only one still . . . stuck. I
smoothed out Miko's letter and nicked the address off with my

fingernail. I ran to the corner and bought a card picturing the beach. "Here's where I spend most of my time! I'll call! Maybe after my surfing lessons! Later . . . Ronnie Swan," I wrote.

On Thursday night, after class, I met Kevin's girlfriend, Shira. I guess I expected her to be Chinese, too, but she was a teeny-weeny little Jewish girl. She was making a film, and she had decided to shoot footage of the restaurant. It was called *Americas* and was supposed to be images of immigrants. "So they're not really immigrants, so what?" she told me. "Neither are my grandparents, but they look it. Good enough!" She had long wavy hair, but ashy brown. Kevin had told her about my hair.

"Excuse my asking, but why did you cut it?" she asked as we shared an order of vegetable subgum, since Shira was a vegetarian.

"Just for something new," I said.

"With those green eyes?" She tapped her chopsticks on her plate. "Kevin told me it was killer. The way he sounded, I was jealous!"

"You're jealous of everybody!" Kevin broke in.

"Well, I'm two hours away, buddy!" He picked her up like she was made of feathers, and she kicked until he put her down. "One of the demerits of being small. That and having to shop in the section of the store where the shirts have kitty cats on them! I was so grateful when the Gap started having size two. But it turned out that two is really six and six is really eight! Back to the kids section." She smiled at me, and even though she'd just made me feel like a tanker truck, I couldn't help but smile back. "Listen, girlfriend. The hair. Let it grow out."

But I couldn't let it grow out. Every few weeks, I dabbed the roots with peroxide and some henna Mrs. Desmond told me about, better for the hair than dye.

The other reason besides her movie that Shira was in town was to see Kevin's hockey game. He played semipro for the San

Diego Sailors. Every time we'd studied, all the way past bones and into the circulatory system, into the heart and its functions and malfunctions, he'd invited me to come to a game with his friends and some of the other younger people from class; but I always said I didn't have time. The truth was, I wouldn't have known a hockey stick from a pogo stick, and I didn't want to look like an idiot. This time, they asked me again. I thought through what I had to study: ischemia, angina pectoris, AMI, ventricular fibrillation, tachycardia, asystole.

Then I said, "Sure, why not?" With Shira there, I thought I would be okay. If she could understand it, I could, too. There were two ends to the rink, that much I knew, and a net at each end. How complex could it be? Shira explained the basics, and though I never got the hang of icing, it seemed pretty similar to a breakaway, although it was evidently illegal. By the end of the first period, I was standing up and yelling every time Kevin knocked the other team's shot out of the goal and dancing to "Surfin' USA" every time they scored. A person had to be amazed at the strength and agility of Kevin's legs and reflexes, as time after time he knelt and dodged and threw himself on the puck. "I couldn't do what they do walking," I told Shira. "I don't see how they can do it on ice!"

"He's played hockey since he was three," Shira said. "It *is* like walking to him."

"You wouldn't think, with no ice around . . ."

"Yeah, but his father played in college. In New York. His father went to college in New York. He was going to be a doctor."

"Kevin said there were no medical people in his family."

"Well, Kevin's grandfather died. He was hit by a drunk driver. And his grandmother had the restaurant. And that was that. Chinese are like Jewish people. Family comes before anything else."

"It explains a lot of things. Kevin loved English—"

"But he's going to do this instead. It's complicated, but I guess it makes sense. Like playing hockey in California," Shira said with a shrug.

"I suppose. Where I grew up, everyone knows how to ski before they know how to read, but it's usually seventy degrees in the winter, except up in the mountains."

"Now that, I could never do. Ski," Shira said.

"It's easy," I told her. "All you do is crouch down and let gravity take over."

"It's easy if you grew up in Idaho or wherever, not Brooklyn."

"Do they . . . approve of you? The Chans? Not being . . . Methodist?"

Shira burst out laughing. "I thought you were going to say not being Chinese! They were a little weird at first, but Jenny said finally it all comes down to the same thing. . . ." My shoulders drooped a little. "What? What?" Shira asked.

"I don't know. Nothing. I got a letter from a guy. He grew up where I did, but he's Catholic, and I'm a Mormon. And it's ridiculous anyhow. He always thought of me as the little kid down the road who had a horse. . . ."

"But you thought something else."

"Not really."

"I can tell you did," Shira insisted.

"He's in love with somebody. He's totally happy."

"You wish it was you. So, why don't you . . . whatever? Tell him."

"I could never do that. Anyhow, I can't . . . We don't usually . . ."

"Marry out? Neither do Jews. Kevin would have to convert."

"Would he do that?"

"He says so. We'll see. . . ."

"Well, this guy is Italian, he's so Catholic. And he doesn't think of me that way." I remembered the picture of me on Jade, coiling up my long hair.

"I'm not convinced, pardon me," said Shira.

The Sailors beat the Coronado Corsairs three-zip. We went out afterward for beers and one 7-Up.

"No alcohol?"

"I'm underage," I said.

"And if she wasn't, it wouldn't matter. She can't have tea or coffee," Kevin put in.

"Kevin's become an expert on the Word of Wisdom," I told Shira with a smirk.

"You can't do *anything*!" he practically shouted.

"I can do anything I need to. Nobody needs to put crap in their head to rob their brains!" I said, pointing at Kevin's stein of beer. Everybody laughed then, and Kevin blushed.

"She can have Coke, though, and it has caffeine. . . ."

"But it has to be specially blessed," I said. Everyone laughed again.

"I give up," Kevin said.

Shira said, "I would. Quit while you're behind."

I liked Shira. In little more than a month, I'd made two friends, plus a handful of acquaintances from class, and Mrs. Desmond, who somehow made an extra portion of dinner every night but kept forgetting to charge me the extra five dollars. And so far I'd successfully avoided anything but the most passing contact with Scott Early. Kelly left my money in an envelope propped against the lamp, and Scott usually went out rowing on Fridays and then to a church group he ran for the children of homeless people. So we hardly ever saw each other.

Then, one afternoon, he asked me to bring Juliet to the library where he was volunteering. I couldn't say no. All the ladies there made dove noises over the baby, passing her from arm to arm like a special piece of rare embroidery.

"And you must be Kelly!" one older woman said.

"No!" I shouted so loudly that library patrons turned their heads. I stammered, "I mean, I mean, how could a kid like me be this sweet baby's mother? I'm just the baby-sitter. Kelly is just as pretty as Juliet." It was a natural mistake, given that I had brown hair, the same as the baby's, though Kelly was so blond.

Scott Early apologized after the ladies drifted away. He was helping decorate the children's section of the library for Halloween. He held Juliet on his lap and tried to get her to slap at a little paper bat.

"You wouldn't believe the stuff I see here, Rachel," he told me softly. "There was a mother in here, and obviously she was hurrying home from work, and her little girl was having trouble deciding on a book, and she slapped her! Maybe she was just stressed out. But I couldn't believe she could do that to a little kid. I can't imagine slapping Juliet just for being slow, you know? Or slapping her for anything, for that matter." He held Juliet close to him. "Sometimes I don't know who's under more stress, the stay-home moms and dads who come in here or the ones running by on the way home from the office. No doubt about it, being a parent is stressful in a world like this, everyone in such a hurry. . . ."

He went on, but I didn't hear.

My hands went cold, so cold that I had to jam them into the sleeves of the hoodie I'd bought for a few bucks at Goodwill. Scott Early was absolutely sincere. He really thought that his having witnessed a woman slap a child was horrible and wanted to share this with me. I shook my head and murmured something. I told him I had to get home; my day was finished, and I had class. Then I ran all the way back to the apartment, arriving just as Kelly pulled up. "I didn't know that was a jogging stroller," she said, laughing.

I hid in the safety of my car, freezing in the late afternoon lavage of San Diego sun, until I could stop shivering enough to drive safely. And for the first and only time, I skipped class. My car seemed to want to drive to the back of the purple Victorian. I cut the engine and fell asleep in the seat, still shivering. The tap on the window sounded like a firecracker. I nearly jumped out of my skin, and I hit the horn.

"Veronica!" Mrs. Desmond scolded me. "I saw you out here, and I thought you were sick."

"I'm sorry," I said. "Maybe I am. A touch of something."

"Better come inside. I'll give you some tea. I must say, you look like you've lost your best friend," Mrs. Desmond said.

"No, I just felt under the weather. Too tired for my class. With it, and my job . . ."

"Your job. You take care of a baby?"

"Yes."

"Is that difficult for you?"

"Why?"

"Because of your loss."

"No. I do have little brothers."

"But it must make you think of—"

"I try not to."

"The man who did this thing. Is he still in prison?"

"He never went to prison. He was incompetent. He was mentally ill."

"So he's in an institution," Mrs. Desmond prodded, oddly persistent.

"No, he's not. He got out after a few years."

"That doesn't seem fair."

"No. But that was the judge's decision."

"And does your family know where he is?"

"Yes."

"Did you ever feel the need to see him?"

"No," I said honestly, "I never feel the need to see him."

Mrs. Desmond looked right through me. "I would have taken you for someone who'd want to know."

"Know what?"

"Everything, I suppose. Where he went. What he did. What he was like, now."

"I sometimes feel . . . I sometimes feel I already know more than I ever wanted to know." Mrs. Desmond nodded. And I went up to my room and took three Tylenol and slept until morning.

The next day in class, I was working with Kevin and Shelley—a tall black girl with beaded braids who made me think of how an African princess would look—studying the workings of the defibrillator. Those of us who wouldn't do cadaver training were working on a life-size rubber dummy.

"Imagine having to really use one of these," I said.

"I've seen one used," she said.

"You have?"

"On my mother. She had a heart attack."

"Did she survive?" Kevin asked.

"No," Shelley said.

"I'm so sorry," I said just a half second before Kevin said the same thing.

"All of you," Shelley said, "you're like little kids playing doctor. You have no idea what the real world is like." I felt my scalp tighten.

"Don't be so sure," I told her. "Nothing will ever shock me."

"Why's that? You grow up in a railroad car? Because I did."

"Just . . . nothing will," I said, and shut my mouth.

"What did you mean?" Kevin asked me later when we met at L.M.N.O. Tea.

"I'm just not very shockable, Kevin," I told him. "Mountain life. Let's forget it."

"Shira said you lost your boyfriend."

"Funny, 'cause I never had one."

"She said a boy from home—"

"Just a friend. I had a crush on him when I was, like, twelve."

"Chas, the forward on my team," Kevin said, "did you meet him?"

"He's a great player."

"He's a great guy, too."

"I know you're going to say he's a Mormon, Kev. I'm not going to necessarily like a guy because he's the same religion."

"He's also a nice person."

"Well . . ."

"We have our team picnic next Saturday. You could meet him. Shira's coming down."

"Maybe."

"Ronnie, you have to live a little."

"Don't go trying to fix me up," I pleaded with him. "Promise, or I won't come."

He crossed his heart. He did it anyway.

A dozen of us had a picnic at the gorgeous Balboa Park, some of the team members and some people from class. We'd finished our first stage of classwork and were ready to begin our practicum, actually riding with and working with licensed EMTs and paramedics under the direction of a medical supervisor. So there was plenty of cause for celebration. Kevin's team was in the playoffs, and all but two of our class had made it through. We ate chicken sandwiches and sweet rice balls courtesy of The Seventh Happiness, and then we played Frisbee. It was when I dived for a catch that I felt my necklace strain and pop. It didn't have a real clasp. That had broken years ago, and I'd replaced it with a series of loops I made with scraps of my mother's art wire and my father's needle-nose pliers. Desperate, I dropped to my knees and began searching the grass. Dusk was coming on. How would I ever find a loop of brownish hair in brownish yellow grass in the dark? Chas, who actually was very cute once I saw him without a helmet on, got down on his knees to help me, as did Shelley and some others.

"What was it? A locket? Was it your mother's?" Chas asked me.

"Like that. I have to find it. It can never be replaced," I told him.

"Don't worry," Kevin finally said. "I have an idea."

He ran to get one of the ever present service people who zip around the park in golf carts. With the lights of two carts shining directly on the turf where we'd been playing, Kevin assigned us grids we walked shoulder to shoulder, from one section of fence to the section on the opposite side. It was dark and I had given up when another guy from the team, Dunny, shouted, "Is it a long silver chain with some kind of ring made of thread or something?" I leapt for it, nearly tearful with relief, hugging Dunny, then Kevin. The braided ring hadn't even come off the chain, but a link was torn away. Then I turned to Chas and kissed him. There was a big silence.

Then Kevin whistled.

Chas said, "Well, I guess I can ask you to go to the movies, now that we've been introduced."

And so we started dating. We went to museums and once to a theater for a production of *Our Town*. Mrs. Desmond, who was about my height but skinny, lent me this long black skirt and a black crepe top from Italy. All night I moved around as if I were a porcelain doll, for fear I'd rip it. I'd never seen the play. Chas loved it. But I cried all the way through it, imagining Becky in Emily, seeing Becky being eleven, being my age, being a grown woman.

Afterward, Chas drove me up to a peak where I could see the whole city of San Diego spread out beneath us, twinkling like the Christmas diorama they used to have in Salt Lake. He kissed me, on the lips, on the chin, gently on the neck. And then he talked about his mission, in the worst of the projects in Harlem, where he said he'd been happier than he'd ever been anywhere. He wanted to go back there to teach school once he got his degree. "But I'm being scouted," he told me.

"Scouted?"

"By the pros, for hockey," he said. "The Blackhawks. It would be hard to turn down."

"I know," I said. "I used to play basketball. I used to dream in basketball, like it was a language."

I thought of my father talking about hitting the trifecta—back when Ceci was marrying the stuck-up Professor Patrick. Hmmm, I thought. A former missionary who could also end up a pro athlete. But I couldn't feel what I wanted to feel about Chas. No string thrummed in my stomach when he kissed me. Still, he was respectful and admired my wish to become a doctor. He listened to me as if I were the most interesting person on earth. Maybe the humming would come in time. Kevin was clearly ultrapleased with himself, having found what he believed to be the only two Mormons in California, never mind that there were hundreds in the ward I attended in La Jolla alone. About every other weekend, when Shira came to stay, we would go to the beach and have a campfire. I would lie in Chas's arms, under the riot of California stars, and feel romantic: How could anyone feel anything but? Except I'd watch Kevin through the orange, popping flames, watch him scoop Shira beneath him, stroking her body beneath their blanket, moving them out of the light; and I would think not of Chas, but of my own arms around Miko's neck.

Meanwhile, my work was becoming exciting. Because I was under eighteen, I couldn't start practicing officially after forty-six class days, the way the others could. I would get to do everything else, though. And finally I got the chance for my first ride-along.

Everyone expects the first ride-along to be nothing. And we all hope it'll be a three-alarm fire—not because we want anyone to get hurt. Otherwise, it's like getting dressed up for a formal and then spending the evening playing cards with your aunt in the kitchen. I'd learn the routine of a firehouse, but I could do that anytime. I thought maybe I'd be able to watch as the EMTs transported an elderly person with chest pains, to see them assess the vital signs, which I could do by then in my sleep. I'd help try to take a verbal history as they administered nitro if the systole was less than 90. We'd bring the patient on in, and she'd be fine. Someone might ask me to hand him something. That would be it. For me, I thought, that would be it. And it would be cool, exciting enough.

But on my first ride-along, I went through what everybody used to joke about, calling it C-Spine Immobilization 101, the short course, because I was the only one there who could do it.

That would have been enough.

But then, that same night, something else happened, something I still don't fully understand.

Almost the instant we sat down at the firehouse where we were stationed, the first call came. One of the EMTs hadn't yet shown up for his shift. It was a head-on collision on a beach road, with numerous possible head and neck injuries.

The crew chief looked around more in annoyance than fear. "Come on, Swan," she said to me, "kid games are over." My mouth went dry.

We got to the scene and were assigned to this . . . kid. He was younger than me. He was lying in the road on his back, blood just foaming from his shattered lower leg, where a tooth of broken bone poked through the skin. "That's the least of our worries," the chief said. "What you can't see is always worse than what you can."

And she was right. The kid was alert and responsive, although he quickly began to get sweaty and agitated, sure signs of shock. While one of the EMTs took his pulse and looked at his eyes with a penlight, the chief pulled me aside. "We can't wait for an assist," she said. I nodded. "We're going to have to immobilize him and run with lights and sirens straight to the ER at Loyola." I nodded again. There were six of us, including Shelley, the girl Kevin and I knew from our class. She watched as one of the regular crew applied pressure to the wound with a huge bandage, trying to get the bleeding stanched for transport, but every big wad of gauze was soaking through. The chief then told me to hold the kid's head still, without touching his ears. I slipped from my brain into my body and let all the words I'd heard in classes take over.

"If you need to tell me where it hurts," I said, "or answer my questions, don't try to nod or shake your head. Promise? Say yes or no. You're going to be just fine, but you have to stay still until we get you on the bed." The boy was looking up at me, his brown eyes transparent in the van's headlights.

"Yes," he said. Then he said, "My mom was driving." I saw tears begin to leak out of the corners of his eyes. "We were fighting about my grades. Is she okay?" I knew his mother was bad off. Another truck arrived.

"Don't move, sweetie," I said as if I were years older and he a child. I saw a girl named Douglas, whom everyone called "Doogie," who worked for another unit, doing chest pushes on a woman lying in the deep grass at the sandy verge of the road. "I think your mom will be fine, too," I told him as my chief and the others lifted him onto the backboard and put the immobilizing pillows in place on either side of his head. Shelley's eyes locked on mine. I knew that she was thinking the same thing I was. At that instant, I realized what this work was about. This boy would have to live seventy years knowing that his smart-ass remarks might have cost his mother her life. Whatever his body had endured would heal. But unless that CPR worked, he would leave Loyola wearing a cast that would one day be removed and an invisible yoke across his shoulders that never would. I could give him only two things, a safe ride and ten more minutes of the life he still understood as his. I also knew that the edge of things, as the instructor had called it, where so much could be changed in an instant, was where I wanted to work for the rest of my life— maybe because I knew how that ground felt under my feet. I prayed for his mother to live as we rocketed through the silent streets.

We weren't at Loyola for ten minutes, and the chief barely had time to give her hands-off report, when we got another call.

"Damn," she whispered. "Is there a full moon?"

We were not even two minutes, straight shot, to the Pacific Ice Palace.

En route, we listened to the dispatcher flatly describe the victim as a young Asian male whose heart had stopped after having been struck in the chest with a puck. A player for the San Diego Sailors. He'd been in goal. There were three goalies. Only one was Asian.

"No," I whispered, and the inside of the van darkened as if we were fish in an aquarium of ink. I reached out, totally unprofessionally, and took Shelley's hand. Then we turned away from each other and began our equipment check.

We sped through the side streets, flickered past the silhouetted figures of girls in short skirts standing outside coffee shops, men unloading the backs of trucks, a teenager walking her dog toward the beach, all distinct signs that there would be a tomorrow, that the player whose heart had stopped from the blow was not Kevin. Mechanically, we tidied up the unit, slipping on fresh gloves and disposing of a used bandage roll in a red hazard bag, spraying down the backboard and wiping it clean. Outside, people continued to flip past the windows—shoppers, runners, kids skating, an old man with a cane—as if the world outside were a picket fence and we were the stick running along it. I realized why veterans called people outside "civilians." They saw an ambulance, and to them it meant everything would be okay. We saw a hole in the world.

Then the driver hit the brakes and it was all sensation. Thought would have been a luxury of time we didn't have.

I remember crashing through the doors of the auditorium, our sneakers finding purchase on the ice. Politely thanking the coach, who'd been giving CPR and doing mouth-to-mouth. One of the regular EMTs checking for obstructions before she hyperextended Kevin's neck and inserted the oral airway, attaching the bag, the BVM—bag valve mask—device. Leaving me to pump the bag while she connected the portable oxygen unit, watching it begin to inflate. Chas from somewhere, saying my name, speaking to me from somewhere. The noise of the rink receding, muted, distant, as the chief cut open the Sailors jersey. The bruise an impossibly perfect circle just south of Kevin's perfect left shoulder. Listening for the charging of the AED, the automated external defibrillator. The shock. Carrie Bell, our chief, taking an anxious inventory. No rhythm. Charging, ninety seconds, and shocking him again, the horrible rag doll leap of Kevin's body as the unit's jolt slammed into him. No rhythm. Another round of oxygen as we loaded him onto the backboard and lifted the backboard onto the collapsible wheeled support cart. Charging. Leaning clear. No rhythm. The voice of the driver: "Loyola, this is La Jolla unit sixty-eight, how do you copy? We are less than five minutes out with a subject, Asian male Kevin Chan, age twenty-one, pulseless nonbreather, chief complaint arrest due to trauma. Subject is unresponsive to repeated defibrillation attempts. He was struck in the chest with a hockey puck . . . administering oxygen, followed by defibrillation attempts. Continuing CPR."

As if I were the only one there, I prayed aloud, "Heavenly Father, in Thy tender mercy, help us, Your clumsy servants. We beg You, spare Thy servant Kevin Chan, who is good in the world. Let him live to be of service, to work Thy word." The whine of the AED. The thump. Kevin's arms reaching up as if he were pleading, then flopping back.

"It's been fifteen minutes," Shelley whispered. "If we did get him back now . . ."

"No," I said. "Let me give him another two minutes of oxygen."

"If we did get him back—"

"No! Not yet!"

Carrie said, "Ronnie. He might have been gone when we got here."

But mine was a child's voice, begging. "He's one of us. Try once more, please try once more."

The chief sighed. There came the whirr. Charging. And then, before our crew leader could administer the shock, another voice spoke, muffled and indistinct.

"Ronnie?" He reached up and fumbled at the airway. Shelley, although she wasn't supposed to, removed it. "What are you doing? Where am I?"

Shelley gasped. "Jesus almighty. Kevin?"

"Yeah?" he said, his voice a rasp.

"Do you know what day it is?"

"Uh, Wednesday. Why . . . am I here? What happened? Is the game over?" Kevin asked. I reached over and felt for his pulse; it was steady and slow.

"What did you do, witch girl?" Shelley asked. "That boy was gone. You some kind of saint?"

"Saints are in heaven," I said, and knelt on the floor of the unit, my arms wrapped across my chest. I knelt as the others flung open the door. With two ER doctors and nurses waiting, they ran with Kevin, the rattling cart disappearing beneath a light, yellow as the blink of a firefly in a jar, through the doors that swung open with a hiss.

Chapter Nineteen

Kevin's family closed the restaurant the following week and feasted the team and the ambulance crew.

Kevin's sisters carried out platter after platter of the most expensive dishes on the menu. Nothing was spared. The story had traveled, and word had it that I had something special—a sense some EMTs have. The whole night, Shira sat next to me and kept petting my hair. Jenny Chan hugged my shoulders from behind every time she crossed the room. Finally, Mr. Chan made a toast to crew sixty-eight. "When Kevin brought Ronnie to meet us, we thought she was a special girl. When he was in the hospital, Kevin said he had told her about the red thread. But we had no idea that the red thread that bound Kevin and Ronnie was a lifeline." We all clinked our glasses. "The red thread is destiny, in legend. It connects people who are meant to have a meaning in each other's life. You can't always understand your destiny, but it always knows you. Ronnie, you have our thanks . . . and our love."

"It wasn't me!" I told them all, laughing and blushing. "Everyone, including the manager of the rink, saved Kevin. We just did our jobs."

"Don't say it was just your job," Shira said. "We know what happened."

"It was my job," I said. "But it was also . . . it was *Kevin*.

Everyone who was there would do anything for anyone that we did for Kevin. But Kevin helped us save him. Whatever else happened wasn't because of me, Shira. I think your sweetie is meant to be around for a long, long time."

Shira and Kevin gave me a bracelet she had made herself from black jet beads, with a slender red thread of garnet beads running through the middle. It must have cost a lot just for the beads, not to mention the time spent. When they helped me put it on, everyone clapped.

I was pretty thrilled.

I also was pretty terrified.

I thought that my name would somehow show up in the paper; but the story, though it did make page one of the sports section, only mentioned "La Jolla paramedics" and quoted our crew chief, Carrie Bell, saying, "Sometimes, when it seems you have to give up, there's one more try left in you. We had some hotshot young people out there, and I'm proud of all of them. Some were on their first ride. And three lives were saved that night." I sent my father a copy, and he wrote back, thrilled. Serena wrote, too, sending a card in a bright yellow envelope. The front read, "It's always about YOU, isn't it?" Inside, she'd written, "I'm so proud of you," and enclosed a picture of her and me that summer on Cape Cod. She told me she'd sent Miko a copy of the story, too.

The week after the banquet, Chas dropped me off and kissed me good night on the porch. I still hadn't figured out my feelings about him, and I knew he felt the same way. He told me once that my mind was always somewhere else when we were together. I blamed school, but I knew he wasn't convinced. Mrs. Desmond had met him and said she thought he was a bit "skimmed milk" for me.

"You expect me to show up with the Mormon Russell Crowe," I kidded her.

"That's right, Veronica," she told me. "A nice Australian. I'll keep my eyes open when I'm away in a few months." She was expecting me to watch the house for her. As it turned out, I barely had time to return my key.

So many good things had happened that it would have been easy to lose track of the reason I was in San Diego at all. And I wish that I had. Juliet was getting bigger, laughing aloud now. I could pose her, sitting up, like a little frog, before she rolled over on the rug. I would get her all propped up in a tripod position and run for the camera, and by the time I got back, she'd be on her tummy, waving her legs and arms, doing the swim. Then one morning when I showed up, Kelly made me stop and shut my eyes. When I opened them, she showed me that Juliet, easily a month before most babies, could turn herself over entirely, back to front. Before I could catch myself, I clapped my hands, and Kelly hugged me. When I drew away gently, I saw the puzzled hurt on her face.

"I'm sweaty," I explained. "I just had time to splash and towel off after my run." When she smiled her upside-down smile, I realized that I cared about her feelings.

But the days sailed past, until just before Kelly was to leave for a two-day conference in Las Vegas. Scott Early would be deep in his finals. I knew Kelly was worried, from little things she said about making sure Scott got "time to study," even if it meant "extra hours at double time" for me. She was afraid, she said, that the extra stress might cause him to slip, or despair, or give up. And Scott seemed distracted, too. Feeling dirtied even by the thought, I realized that the time was now. Juliet was attaching to her parents, even to me. She was doing everything she could to woo our eyes, to get us to see her, flirting and mugging, struggling to take her place as a part of the human race. If I waited too long, she would be frightened and disoriented. All this, only to hurt Juliet? No. I loved my job. I'd grown to care for my friends—especially Kevin, who'd been especially tender to me since what Shelley persisted in calling "the resurrection," and comforting Mrs. Desmond. I even liked San Diego. But it was too clear that I had to do this thing and then go home, to where I could take back my name, the color of my hair, and the texture of my soul. For the first time since I'd come, I felt real fear. What color would my soul be, afterward?

I was about to unlock their door on the morning Kelly was to leave when I heard them, Kelly's voice raised in anger.

"I can't leave you alone with her for a minute! I worry constantly!" she shouted.

"Kels," Scott Early pleaded.

"I mean it, Scott! It's bad enough that I have to be away from her for two days without—"

"It's not like that," he said.

"Yes, it is! I lie down for a nap because I'm exhausted, and I wake up and she's been sitting in poop while you watch the Discovery Channel! When I say you have to change her, I mean *more than once a day*!"

My breath escaped in a rush. They were an ordinary couple, arguing about ordinary things. I leaned against the door, annoyed to tears at how life mocked me just as it seemed about to prove my point. I waited until Mrs. Lowen downstairs came out to get her newspaper and waved to me, until I heard Kelly begin to sob quietly. She said, "I hate this."

"Kels, please, I'm sorry," Scott Early was saying. "I know this isn't about her diaper. It's about that you can't go anywhere without worrying about me. You can't go to a conference without thinking I'm going to fall asleep and forget we have a baby. I'm not, Kels! You're driving yourself crazy with this! And you're like the little girl who wants to be friends and watches everyone else down the street at the birthday party. We can't go anywhere without people knowing it's me. No one asks us to join the bowling league. You hear the other teachers talking about the cookout and you—"

"I don't even care!"

"You do care. Anyone would. And I'm so ashamed. I feel as though I have a big red sign around my neck that says, '*Run!*' You must be so ashamed. I should move somewhere so far from people—"

"No," Kelly said quietly. "We've come this far."

"I will, Kels. I'll go. Juliet doesn't even know me. She doesn't ever have to see me again. It's not myself I feel sorry for. . . ."

That's a comfort, I thought.

"Scott, we've been over this. I don't blame you. I blame—"

"I am the disease, Kelly!"

"No, Scott."

"The first time I touched you, you started to cry. . . ."

"And I'm ashamed of that."

"I don't even remember. . . ."

"And you don't want to remember. You don't. You couldn't live with it. You're too sweet."

"Kelly, I love you."

"I love you! Scott! Why won't you believe it? Why did this have to happen when I was going to be away? Now you'll be more stressed, and I won't be able to pay attention," Kelly said. If she didn't hurry, she'd miss her plane.

I coughed so they'd hear me turn the key in the lock. Kelly, her eyes streaming, opened the door before I could. "I bumped my leg on the bed. Right on the shin? You know how that kills?"

"It kills," I said. "Put some ice on it." I stared at Scott. He picked up Juliet and carried her into their bedroom. Kelly put ice in a towel and laid it across her eyes for a few minutes.

"Better," she said. "Wow, am I going to be late!" She started to walk out, then came back for her overnight bag. "Look out for things, Rachel," she said, searching my eyes.

It might have stopped right then. But I heard Scott singing to Juliet, behind the bedroom door. "When you wake, you shall have all the pretty little horses . . ."

I pushed the door open with my foot.

"Why are you singing that song?" I asked him.

I fell back in time as if my shoulder had been shoved, to the sight of my mother, crouched in the dust, crooning and stroking the tangled hair of her two little girls—already beyond the sound of her voice. Only four years ago. Only four years.

Scott Early looked up at me, his eyes red.

You sorry piece of trash, I thought. You poor lost soul.

Then he said, "You sing it to her all the time. I never heard it until I heard you sing it." He smiled.

I turned and left the room, the irony of it curling my hands into fists. In the kitchen, I had to consciously unfurl each finger from gripping the sink. "Leave the car seat today, please," I called, and made up an excuse: "I'm thinking of going to Balboa Park with some of my friends, from my school. Is that okay with you?" I heard the rustle of the sheets as he laid Juliet in her basket.

"Okay," he called. "Is your car open?"

"Keys are on the hall table," I called back.

If only she would leave him, I thought. None of this would be necessary. But Kelly would never leave if she hadn't already. She would never take Juliet away. But how could I take Juliet away from Kelly? Just as Scott Early had taken Ruthie and Becky from my mother, only in a decent, kindly way. Would they have other children? What if they did? That wouldn't be my concern. Or would it? Was I really convinced that I had come here to protect Juliet? Or did I want only revenge, the knowledge that Scott Early and his foolish wife would feel exactly what we had felt? The-end-of-the-world pain? The knowledge that tomorrow wouldn't be better? Would I wish that on another living soul? How could I call Kelly foolish? Nothing about this was Kelly's fault. But she could have left him! She had free will! I recognized what was happening. I was "cascading," as they said in class, contradictory emotions flowing over me like driven water.

I picked up the telephone and called True West Airlines.

Chapter Twenty

$\mathcal{I}$t was dark when I tucked Juliet's blanket around her and began walking back to the apartment.

I'd never gone to Balboa Park, of course—never intended to. What I'd done instead was make a false start to the airport and then ask the driver to turn around. Instead of going straight back to the apartment, though, I had stopped at the tea shop. I wanted to see Kevin once more, and I knew he'd be there. He usually was on Thursdays. It was open mike night, and he liked hearing the musicians. Now that it wouldn't matter, I wanted to tell Kevin who I really was and why I'd come. I wanted to tell him my feelings about Miko and why no one would ever be hurt by the things I'd planned but would never really do.

I guess I wanted to be understood.

"Ronnie!" Kevin called when he saw me, motioning me over to his table. He was alone that night, all his buddies busy with other matters. He'd told me once he preferred listening to music alone, without chatter—that for him it was like meditation. "You missed a guy who was really good, even though he didn't sing much of his own stuff, just Josh Groban covers. . . ."

"Kevin," I said, "I have something I have to tell you."

"What?" he asked, distracted. The next guitarist was setting up.

"I might not be . . . ," I began, but I chickened out. "I was just going to say a lady complimented me on my bracelet today. She said she'd never seen anything like it."

"Shira's pretty talented at jewelry."

"You think you'll get married?"

"That's a long way off," he said. "You want some tea?"

I don't know why, but I drank about a quart of chamomile.

I doubted I'd be able to walk the ten blocks without having to pee. My mouth was cardboard dry, the way it is just before you have to speak in public or just after you've almost missed your foothold climbing a rock wall and narrowly avoided plunging down to the end of the rope. I guess the latter was more or less what had happened to me.

Finally, I gave Kevin a hug—for the last time, unbeknownst to him. I thanked him again for the bracelet. He looked surprised, like why was I bringing up the bracelet again, right then? I wanted to tell him that the red thread would connect us forever. But that would have aroused his suspicion that something was up with me. I promised I'd call him when I decided whether I was going on to full paramedic studies, as he was. When I got to the door, I looked back at him. Something about what had happened with Kevin was a lever that moved me to ask that cabdriver to turn around. I just didn't know what it was.

I did know that I was beat.

All I'd done the whole day was to rush around—getting ready to board the plane for Texas with Juliet, my baby, my "lap sitter," as the reservation lady called her.

I'd gone back to Mrs. Desmond's and left her a note and the next month's rent. She'd find my keys and the iron she'd lent me and everything else in my room. Then, as Juliet napped in a nest of pillows on my floor, I'd stuffed my duffel bag with my laptop, my makeup kit, my cell phone, and all the clothes too nice or too useful to throw out, leaving behind only trinkets and books.

I'd loaded the car, which I planned to leave on a side street with-out the plates. With any luck, teenage punks would strip it back to the paint by the time anyone found it. I had cash for a cab ride to the airport and cash for my airline ticket. The semester had ended the previous week, and Juliet was three months old, old enough to drink formula, old enough to travel. It was now or never.

And so I'd stashed her pram in the bushes at Belleview Park and set out.

But before we were even halfway, I told the driver to turn around, asking him to stop so I could retrieve the stroller and then to drop me at the tea shop.

I felt a curious sense of relief and regret. Scott Early would never know that there hadn't been an all-day picnic at Balboa, as I'd told him. He'd never know about the plane reservations. He'd just think I'd hung out late with my friends, and he wouldn't worry about Juliet, not while she was with me. Once he found the note I'd leave behind, he'd think I'd resigned without giving notice. Young women did it all the time. They'd be dis-appointed, but not horrified. No one would ever be the wiser.

I walked faster. My bladder felt like a submarine. I could pee in the bushes, but with my luck, a bunch of runners would come past the moment I slipped down my jeans. I also wished I could just leave Juliet in the lower hall, fast asleep in her stroller. I'd dump my duffel bag into the car and head for the airport alone. I'd leave my car in the lot, change my ticket, and then sit in the lurid comfort of the lounges and eat Danishes and read about the dumb lives of movie stars until the dark morning brought an air-plane that would take me as close to home as I could get. The cab ride had cost half as much as the plane would have.

But I didn't dare leave Juliet unguarded. Scott Early could be asleep. I had to put Juliet into her bed, make up some goofy note about some emergency at home, leave their keys on the table, and go. I knew that one of my cousins would road-trip back with me to get my car. I was too diminished to hit the midnight roads alone and try to drive to Utah. I'd rather have spent my last dime. In fact, I would be spending my last dime.

Why had my nerve failed? I had been sure when I left the apartment.

I had to be alone to think this out, link by link.

I tried to connect the dots between my role in Kevin's survival and what I wanted to do to Scott Early and his wife. But I couldn't find the words to make sense of it. Had I been placed in the enormous position of having saved a life to see clearly the consequences of "saving" Juliet, albeit destroying her parents? Was I intended to see that what I was doing in full knowledge, Scott Early had done unknowingly? Was the magnificence of Kevin being spared some kind of sign that Scott Early truly had repented, turned entirely around in his life and proceeded from darkness into light? Or were the things connected only in my tired, tattered mind? I turned things one way, then another. The very thing that had outraged me to the point of action, Scott Early rocking Juliet and singing to her the same song Mama sang, had tugged at me, like a line reeled out to the end of the reel and then pulled taut, as I'd set off with Juliet in my arms.

One thing was suddenly clear to me: I'd stayed so long at L.M.N.O. Tea not just to be with Kevin, but because I wanted it to be too late for me to catch any plane at all. I didn't want to give myself a chance for a last-minute change of heart.

More than anything, I wished Kelly were back. If I'd been able to tell her, face-to-face, that I needed to leave, she would have been sad, but she would have taken over. I didn't know if

Scott Early could. The greatest irony of all would be to leave Juliet and have my worst fears come true.

Finally, I made it up the hill to the pink stucco duplex, feeling as though I had a hot-water balloon in my abdomen. It was dark. Every window was dark. Even the soft yellow light from the baby whale lamp in Juliet's little room—the light they left on until I put her down the few times that they went out on weekends and I looked after her—was turned off. So I put my duffel in my car and carried the stroller and Juliet up the six stone steps, got out my key, and opened the outer door. I held the apartment key between my lips while I made my way down the hall to the elevator. Up we went, with a bump, and I maneuvered everything down the hall. But when I put my hip against the door and inserted the key, the door simply swung away silently, into blackness.

And I was frightened.

I wasn't frightened of Scott Early, though he had avoided my eyes when I passed him on the way to the car that day, with my excuse about going with friends to the park. That was easily put down to embarrassment over my hearing their fight. What I feared was that he'd gone out to study and someone might have seen me leaving, and then him leaving, and believed the apartment was empty. Someone could have come in to rob it and might still be inside. I was in real pain now bladderwise, so I turned into the bathroom and peed for an absurdly long, blissful interval. At least, if I was going to be tied up and robbed, I'd be comfortable. Then I went back to see to Juliet.

The sensible thing would have been to back quietly out of the door, go down and find my cell phone somewhere at the bottom of the duffel, and call the police.

But before I could, I heard something—not quite a moan, more like a muffled cough and then a knocking noise, as if someone were hitting something against a heavy object. It came from Scott Early and Kelly's bedroom. And so, leaving Juliet in the doorway, I flipped on the light, and I saw it.

Against the hall lamp, where Kelly always left my checks and the sweet, silly notes and cards she sometimes gave me, was a plain white envelope. On the envelope was written, "For Veronica Swan." My arms tingled the way your arms do when a foolish driver comes peeling out of nowhere and only by swerving do you avoid getting creamed on a stretch of indif-ferent California concrete. As if I'd tried to stick in a plug with a bad wire. He knew me. My mind darted out at me, like a dark thing from an underwater hole. *He knew it was me*, and that meant he was in here and the lights were off because the only way he could free himself forever was to kill me, too. But how could he think that—would he imagine that my parents would forgive him a second time, take his hand, pray with him, wish God's blessings on him, if he recanted on his promise to do no more harm, only good, forever in this life? Could he imagine he could put this down to an illness? Of course, killers don't think of such things. They don't think at all. But I did. I thought of how Mama and Papa would feel, knowing I'd gone and done this and died for it. I turned to run, but I heard that whack again, and Juliet began to fuss. Pressing my hand on her tummy, I rocked her gently back and forth until she blinked out again, her perfect mouth working around her passie. Using my fingernail, I slit open the envelope. There was a single sheet of paper inside.

Why would Scott Early write to me if he were intending to ambush and kill me?

Then again, if he had gone off his meds and waited for this time, lain in wait until Kelly was hundreds of miles away, it would make sense to him to send me a message, an explanation, to tell me in whose name and on whose orders he was acting this time . . . but I read:

Dear Veronica,

I know that you are not Rachel Byrd. I don't know why you came here, but I assume it was to take my life. It is a life I owe to you and your family. When I first learned who you were, when a funny card from a friend back home fell out of your backpack, my first thought was to run. But I can no longer run away. I can never ask your forgiveness, but now I have to face what should have been my punishment before, and Kelly will be grateful forever that you didn't hurt Juliet. You treated her . . .

I threw the note to the floor and ran for the bedroom.

Scott Early had tied a plastic bag around his head, and it was misted with his shallow breaths, sucked in against his open mouth. He'd wrapped his wrists with duct tape—ten, twenty times around. And the whumping sound was his kicking against the footboard of the bed. I don't know if he was entirely conscious. Open bottles lay empty on the floor—the clonazepam that helped him blot out his dreams. They were probably the same dreams, old, misty dreams that still surprised me, especially after a bad call, waking me with the force of a collision. Like a robot, I walked back out into the hall, brought Juliet's stroller inside, lifted her out, held her against me so that she didn't wake, and laid her carefully on her side in her cradle. And then I sat down on Kelly's desk chair and waited, watching as Scott Early's breathing grew quicker and shallower and the agonal kicking of his legs slowed to a twitch.

This was his wish.

This was his atonement.

He had chosen this, coward that he was.

I had not done this.

But on the desk was a photo, taken on Halloween, of Juliet dressed in a felt bunting made to look like a carrot. I remembered her newborn's wrinkled little face. In just a few months, it had taken on curves and characteristics. Her cheeks that had been flaps now were rounded velvety little globes. Scott Early was on one side, with his own cheek pressed against Juliet's, and Kelly was on the other, smiling at both of them. I'd taken the picture myself. They looked . . . like they had seen heaven. In Kelly's face was the certainty that Scott was again, forever, the boy she'd loved at Colorado State, the boy she'd suffered with as the voices grew louder and more demanding, the husband she'd cleaved unto when hate mail asked her how she could bear the touch of the Grim Reaper. In Kelly's face was the purest love, not love of her own dreams recovered, but unconditional love for Scott Early and their beautiful baby.

I waited a full minute by my watch. Five more minutes, and Scott Early would suffer irreversible brain injury. Five minutes or less. How long had he been this way? He was already hypoxic. I could see that by looking at his lips. After his brain winked out, he would be just an electrical impulse, a heart waiting to stop. He would cross over and perhaps be at peace.

And perhaps so would I.

I jumped up and ripped open the plastic bag, using the nail scissors Kelly kept in her drawer to cut the pink ribbon he'd bound it with. He'd vomited, and I grabbed his shirt and wiped the acidic stuff away from his mouth. Then I filled my lungs and put my mouth to the mouth of Scott Early and blew in—long, measured, timed breaths, summoning all my training. I sat back on my heels and looked at him. He was immobile, his face still bluish. My hands crossed, I slammed my fist down on his chest. I felt for his pulse. It was patchy, irregular. I took in more air and breathed it into Scott Early's mouth, again, and again, and again, again, again, until I was dizzy, swaying and clinging to the headboard. Then, finally, he coughed, and I held him up while he vomited the sour white contents of his stomach on the chenille spread. I pushed him onto his side and slid his pillow under his back. I dialed 911. I gave them the address. Yes, Scott Early was breathing. No, he was unresponsive to questions. Yes, he had overdosed on a nonspecific number of Fluanxol tablets as well as clonazepam and Halcion and, although the label was ripped off, what I thought was the anti-Parkinson's drug Artane. Yes, I had administered emergency resuscitation. No, I was not a doctor, and I was not his wife.

Here I was, calling for emergency medical help. Calmly and clearly, in detail, an act of desperation now second nature, my training displacing my emotions. And yet Ronnie the young woman was a transparency: It was possible to see through the overlay to a terrified long-haired kid screaming for help, throwing the phone to the floor, running across the hard ground to Sister Emory's door.

It was impossible. Life was not tracing paper.

Calling for help to save Scott Early.

Calling for help to save us from Scott Early.

To pass time, I pictured what was happening on the other end. People who'd been sitting around the station house playing cards or stirring chili leapt for their gear, checking to make sure that there was glucose, a board, oxygen. I could taste the adrenaline in my own mouth, just as my fellow EMTs would do as they slammed into their truck now. They were me. I was them. I forced myself to check Scott Early's pulse one more time, then sat back down in the chair, gripping the arms so as to will myself not to fly out that door. His pulse was steady now and regular. He was beginning to moan, but you could not call it verbalizing.

I couldn't ask him to describe his condition. In less than three minutes, I could hear the sirens. Quickly, I wrote down the telephone number and name of the hotel where Kelly was staying. I also wrote down her cell phone number and then, finally, a note to her reading, "Sorry for this pain, and my needing to leave, from Rachel, with love to Juliet," just one sentence. I relented then and added that the suicide attempt had been stopped early, and he would probably be fine. With a piece of tape, I attached these to Scott Early's filthy shirt.

The unlocked door hit the wall as the paramedics slammed into the apartment. I stood in the bedroom doorway while they threw themselves on Scott Early, opening his eyes and examining his pupils with their penlights, clearing his mouth, inserting an airway. Then, from the telephone in the kitchen, I called Mrs. Lowen downstairs and told her that Scott Early was sick and might well be taken to the hospital. I asked, "Is it possible for you to come up and look after Juliet? Just for an hour or two? I'm sure Kelly will come back tonight. I'm so frightened. I have to leave or I'll miss my plane." It wasn't a lie. Well, it strained the definition of truth. Mrs. Lowen didn't know how sick Scott Early was, or why. But in fact, if I didn't get out of there right then, there would be a million questions, and I would miss any plane altogether, even tomorrow. I had to get out of that place.

But I did lie. The lie was that I was frightened.

I had never been less frightened. I was too numb for fear, numb to my lips. But knowing that Mrs. Lowen was going to grab her purse and run down the hall and up the stairs made me bold. I knew someone would show up shortly to investigate this, but there was no choice for me but to vanish. My fingerprints were all over that apartment, but since no Rachel Byrd existed, neither did her fingerprints.

When I walked out that door, I would become Veronica Swan again.

I walked out the door.

It was not until hours later—when I had driven to the airport, parked in long-term, and purchased a ticket for the morning plane to St. George; when I was lying on a thin mattress in the Red Roof Inn a block from the airport, listening to a group of truck drivers overhead cheering for the Giants—that I realized I had forgotten his note. I had left behind Scott Early's note to me, right on the floor near the hall table where I had dropped it. And the woman at the airline counter might know where I was. I had been the only one to show up there at midnight, disheveled and dirty, smelling of puke, asking to change a reservation and if there was a clean but inexpensive motel nearby. There was only one ticket counter for True West.

She would remember.

And still I was not frightened. I had done nothing wrong, unless thoughts counted. But now I would have lost my anonymity. It would all come out. Kelly would be there within hours. And when she got to the hospital, she would be asked about the circumstances surrounding Scott Early's suicide attempt and the disappearance of her nanny. She would tell someone who Ronnie Swan was and what my connection was to them. The police would be suspicious. Who wouldn't be? Even *Kelly* might suspect that, with her gone, I had tried to hurt Scott Early and made it look like a suicide attempt.

My cell phone rang.

I didn't even try to dig for it.

It rang again.

This time, I plunged my hand deep into my duffel and pulled it out. Without even looking at the callback number, I flipped it open.

"Veronica," said Mrs. Desmond, "are you hurt? Are you safe?"

"Yes," I said.

"It's on television," she said. "Would you like me to come for you?"

"No, ma'am," I said. "I've caught you up in this too much already. I'm sorry, Missus Desmond. I'm so sorry."

"But the report says there was a call from an unidentified young woman who saved Mister Early from a suicide attempt."

"Yes."

"And the baby is unhurt."

"Yes."

"This is absurd. I'm going to come there now. . . . Where are you? You poor child. At least I can wait with you until . . . Is your father coming for you? We can go to one of those awful Denny's and have some soup or something. I would think they would have herbal tea."

"It's okay," I said. "I'll sleep."

"I don't feel safe with your being alone. You didn't do anything wrong, Ronnie."

"I . . . hope not," I said. "I should never have come."

"Good-bye, dear," said Mrs. Desmond. "I'm not sure I shouldn't come. Where are you?"

"Some motel. By the airport."

"I'm not sure about this," she said.

The phone went dead. It was out of juice.

I lay sleepless in the dirty room, where the air conditioner blasted relentless chemical-smelling air. I put on my hoodie, then my jean jacket. I lay down again.

Did thoughts count? *Had* I tried to hurt him, with my thoughts? Of course I had. I had hoped and hoped, for years and years, had stopped just short of praying, hundreds of times, that Scott Early would fall, fry, crash, choke, trip, slip, seize, freeze, drown.

Thoughts did count. But did all of them? The hatred *and* the pity? The awful moment when the pity outweighed the hate? Did thoughts count to the world . . . or only to me? Legally, was I liable for anything that had happened? Had I . . . assaulted Scott Early just by reminding him of what his mind would not ever allow him to remember?

Only I knew why Kelly kept the buck knife in her drawer. Even Kelly, who had loved him so long, would die before she let Scott Early harm her baby. I'd looked at Juliet in her basket and thought of her as a tiny princess Moses, to be set on clean waters. I had seen her as an earth angel I would send on a journey down a river of hope, to bring to someone unknown the very joy Scott Early had stolen from my family. But I had also watched the Scott Early who rocked baby Juliet and helped tiny children find their books at the library. And he was not the man who had killed Becky and Ruthie. And yet he was. He had once had a personality of surpassing sweetness. And it had been stolen from him by an illness. Perhaps this was why I had not been able to do that huge and terrible thing. My convictions weren't really convictions, only half-baked promptings, leftover rage to kill, or to feed.

Did Becky and Ruthie know? Were they like the hungry ghosts Kevin Chan had told us about, on moonless nights, around campfires at the beach, trying to spook us with his tales? Were they spirits of people who died in the wrong way, who were cruelly hurt or who committed suicide? Kevin's grandmother, his father's mother, despite her tendency to say "Gotcha" and "A-okay," put out rice and fruit for these ancestors so they wouldn't do mischief, like pull down the laundry or dump ashes in the rice. But how could such a myth be real? Ruthie and Becky were the Heavenly Father's chosen. They would not have sought revenge. Kevin's face wound past me. He would be well and live a long life, but he would never understand.

What had made me come here?

I had never, not even on the day of the murders, felt so alone.

Looking up at the grubby light, I wrapped my arms over my heart and prayed for answers. But the Lord is not Alex Trebek. I prayed until sweat collected under my hair, at my temples, in the freezing room. What was vengeance? What was justice? Had I even known what vengeance would mean? I was a sinner, I told my Lord. I knew I had sinned. But was it possible, I prayed, that I had ended up administering justice along with artificial respiration? Justice was based on a word in Hebrew that meant giving people what they needed, not what they deserved. Had I freed Scott Early or condemned him to a life of knowing that it was I, the witness, who had spared him—forcing him to reckon every day with the burden of my forgiveness? Could my old, banked rage have led me to grace?

And then a truth washed over me like the momentary flash of sunlight off the harbor—a brief, piercing illumination. I remembered the passage in Doctrine and Covenants 3, the revelation of the Lord to Joseph Smith after Joseph Smith trusted his foolish friend with translations from the Golden Plates. The friend lost them, or his wife hid them. And Joseph Smith warned, in his rewriting of the revelations, against anyone "Who has set at naught the counsels of God, and has broken the most sacred promises which were made before God, and has depended upon his own judgment and boasted in his own wisdom." I remembered it from Sunday school: "For, behold, you should not have feared man more than God. . . . Yet you should have been faithful; and He would have extended His arm and supported you against all the fiery darts of the adversary; and He would have been with you in every time of trouble."

Father, I prayed, this is my truth. I feared Scott Early more than I feared You. I trusted my own wisdom more than Your divine counsel. My heart burst. How could I have expected God to comfort me?

I don't know how long I prayed, or when I fell asleep under the garish light, or what time it was when I woke to the whirl of revolving lights outside my window and the banging at my door. I got up and brushed my teeth while the police shouted, *Open up, open up!* I checked myself the way I once did before a basketball game, to make sure my soul and body were in it together. They were. As for being in grace, I accepted that we aren't given that to know.

When I opened the door, I was composed, even as the lights blinded me. It was just like what Clare once said, quoting some baseball player, déjà vu all over again. I stepped outside and held my arms up over my head. *Ronnie,* someone called, *Ronnie, how did you feel when your sister's killer tried to kill himself? Ronnie, did you come here to murder him? Are you glad he's in a coma? Ronnie?* I sat down on the curb and curled over myself.

"Veronica Swan," said a man's gruff voice. "Are you Veronica Swan?"

Suddenly I felt someone's arm fall lightly across my shoulder.

"I am Alice Desmond," I heard a voice say. I looked up. She was holding up one of her black umbrellas, though it was not raining. "This child is a minor. Her father says you are to leave her alone until he can come for her."

Chapter Twenty-one

Once I had wished with all my being to clear out of the little hollow below the ridge at Pine Mountains.

And now I wanted that little hollow, with its red barn and blue house, more than anything else in the world. I wanted to be there—curled up on Sunday mornings in my teenager's bed, running my fingers along the grooved, scrubbed-to-satin butcher block that smelled of cinnamon and cloves, turning up the wood stove in the morning to warm my mother's slippers before I slipped them on to start my breakfast, her worn scuffs that always seemed warmer than my own.

Mrs. Desmond had told my father the honest essentials. I was spared what I knew would be his moan of concern and shock and my mother's voice piping in the background, "London, what's wrong? Is Ronnie hurt? What happened?" We sat in the lobby of the Red Roof Inn with a police sergeant, because Mrs. Desmond insisted that the officer phone his commander and ask under what authority I would be brought to the police station and questioned without the presence of a parent or guardian; and the officer said he would wait.

"Uncle Andrew is coming with me," Papa told me when we called him the second time. "Not that I can think of any trouble you might be in, with the law, that is. Try to stay calm. I just think we're going to have to explain things to them. And you're going to need to explain things to us. You are very lucky your landlady was so kind."

"I will try to explain," I said. "I don't think they'll listen. Maybe you will."

"Don't try anymore," he said. "Just sit quietly."

I just sat quietly.

No one seemed to know quite what to do with me or Mrs. Desmond. I wasn't under arrest. But after a while, a police lieutenant came. Kevin came, too. But they would not let Kevin talk to me. The lieutenant said I was a witness to a suicide attempt, so he had to make me wait for various reasons, including my own safety, until one of my parents showed up. After a while, I put my head down on the back of the scratchy green motel sofa, then on the arm of the sofa. When I woke up, there were my father, wearing a corduroy jacket over his flannel shirt and jeans, and my uncle, in a business suit, and Mrs. Desmond, still with her umbrella, looking down on me. I'd never seen anything more beautiful. My father held me tight.

And then he asked, "What happened to your hair?"

My uncle Andrew identified himself to the lieutenant as an attorney and asked if he could have a moment with his niece.

"Papa, it's a long story," I told him after the officer moved away.

"And you can share it with us, but not anyone else, Veronica."

Uncle Andrew asked me, "What have you said to the police?"

"That I came home to the place where I worked and the man who lived there had tried to commit suicide and that I gave him artificial respiration and called 911."

My uncle asked, "Did you tell them you knew this man?"

"No," I told him, my voice unnaturally slurred and slow to my ears, "they already knew that, from calling Kelly Englehart."

"Okay," my uncle said, taking a little notebook out of his breast pocket. "Was the baby ever in danger?"

"No, she was with Mrs. Lowen the moment I left. I made sure."

"Did you tell them why you'd come here?"

"No, because I don't know," I said. His face seemed to slacken with relief, and he gave a slight shake of his head. "I honestly don't know anymore."

"Ronnie, we're going to take you home now. We'll go talk to the lieutenant, and then we'll go home. But you have to promise to let me do the talking."

Anyone could tell the police officer was confused. There was something "off" about all of it, he said, but he couldn't figure out where any criminal activity fit in. He seemed to be totaling it up in his mind: I had used a false name, but it wasn't anyone else's name. I had concealed my identity, but not for any gain or to perpetrate a fraud. I had worked in the home of the man who killed my sisters, but even his wife didn't have a bad word to say about me. Finding out that I was Ronnie Swan had prompted Scott Early's suicide attempt, but I hadn't told him; he'd found out on his own.

"My niece, furthermore, instead of allowing the man who murdered her sisters to die, saved his life," my uncle said mildly.

"There's that," said the officer. He looked me over from top to bottom and said, "Well, you're free to take her. But leave a telephone number where you can be reached." We got up, too.

"Why did you do this?" the officer asked me suddenly.

"I think from what I can discern," Uncle Andrew said, "it's that Veronica wanted to see with her own eyes that Scott Early was not a threat to his wife or child, as he had been to her little sisters. I don't think she could fully believe her parents' account. She's always wanted to know the truth, no matter what it was, since she was a child. And, as a child, four years ago, she went through a terribly traumatic experience."

"Is that true?" the officer asked me.

"Veronica, there's no reason to say anything," my uncle told me gently.

"It's all true, though," I said softly. "He's right."

In the parking lot, Mrs. Desmond shook hands with my father and gave him the rent check I had left. "You have a beautiful child," she said.

"Thank you for watching over her," my father said.

Mrs. Desmond and I didn't say a word to each other. I just held her and she held me. And we parted. I've never seen her again. She wrote me when she moved back to Brisbane. I have no doubt she will be alive when I get the time and money to go to see her.

When I got home, it was dark. They let me sleep for two days straight, and then my parents gave me the grilling of my life.

"How could you?" my mother asked me through tears, pacing with baby Thor over her shoulder as I held Rafe in my lap. "How could you put yourself in danger? How could you open yourself to accusations? Why didn't you trust us, Ronnie? How did we err? Not with Scott Early, but in raising our child? How could you have lied so straight-faced to us? And don't say that leaving out part of the story didn't constitute a lie because you know it did. You did this in direct contradiction of us. You did this in direct contradiction of what we believe."

"Mama," I said softly, "I did it in accordance with what I believed. I'm not saying it was right. But it was my agency to do what I believed was right at the time."

"And now you are suffering for it!" she cried. "And bringing down on us all the same attention you brought . . . I didn't mean that you brought . . . that was brought on us four years ago, I meant, you are bringing down all that attention again."

"Wait," Papa said. "Stop now for a moment, Cressie. We're going too fast. I think Ronnie knows full well that what she did was wrong. And I think the issue here is really Ronnie's soul and heart, not what some fool might write in a newspaper, that will be forgotten in a week, the next time an actor on *Friends* gets married or a politician cheats on his wife."

Mama looked at him, then at me. "You're right. I didn't mean, Ronnie, that you brought that on us. People sometimes think that there are no mistakes. You say what you truly believe even if you regret it later. But what you say when you're in stress is all mixed and inside out. If you get up from that table thinking your own mother believes you had *anything* to do with Becky's and Ruthie's deaths, my life really will be in vain. And your father is right, it's foolish to worry about what people think, Ronnie."

I said, "Nothing would surprise me, Mama. I know you love me. But I'm not the same kid I was."

"But all those nights that you wrote to us about the house where you were staying, and your friends, and about all you'd learned, all the while working in that house, lying to her and to him, intending to take their baby?"

"She never intended it," my father said. "Ronnie *does* what she intends. She intended to go, and she thought she might do something wrong, but instead, thank Heavenly Father, she did something very right indeed. Perhaps she was in the right place at the right time for reasons we don't know. She saved Kelly more heartbreak than she caused her, in the end."

"Please, Mama. You can punish me forever, Mama," I said, "and I'll do whatever you want. But you can't punish me more than I'll punish myself."

Friends came up to me in the days following, at church, on the road; and all of them looked as if they wanted to say something but couldn't think of what to say. For a week, as Papa predicted, there was a column in a collection of *News from*

Around the Nation on what had happened; but this, too, was in-conclusive and odd. My friends in California were quoted. They were puzzled but called me smart and loyal and kind. Mrs. Desmond, in line with her personality, said in a *San Diego Sentinel* story sent to me by Kevin that it had certainly made for a cracking few months. In general, at first, even my relatives stayed clear. I went to speak to Uncle Pierce on my own and told him how the memory of the Prophet's words struck me in the motel room that night. He sat for a moment, tapping his finger-tips together.

"Ronnie, I know you think that I am severe," he said, "but I love you, not only as a child of God, but as a child of my family. I'm simply not . . . demonstrative. I'm more like our father is than how our mother was. And I can't presume to improve on the lesson given you by our Heavenly Father. It was precisely correct. In the end, Ronnie, we teach ourselves. A sunflower may look like a withered and broken stick in the winter, but in the spring it will rise up new, and turn its face to the sunlight, and grow tall."

One night, I opened my computer and IM'ed Clare. We were too old for little-girl things such as instant messaging, but some-how it felt like comfort.

"Hi."

"A L! D U want me to come?"

"I can't wait," I wrote.

I heard her door bang open, and I was standing with *our* front door open when she tripped over the step and practically fell into my arms. We held each other up, and I breathed in Clare's sweet lavender scent, leaning against her and into her warmth. "What happened to your hair?" she asked. (We were *so* deep.) I thanked God she was home for winter break.

We sat in my room, and I told her all of it. Everything. From the certainty to the doubts, to the fear, to the recognition. "I don't want to say that I told you so," Clare began.

"But you will," I finished for her, hugging her again, not quite daring even the whisper of a giggle. I couldn't believe she was real, flesh. I had been away a mere three months. I felt as though everything was changed—as if outlined in black marker for emphasis, the way I'd done with my geography as a little girl.

"No, I won't," said Clare. "I can tell by looking at you that you already know. Were you absolutely terrified the whole time?" She hugged herself and trembled. She looked so grown. I wondered if I did, too. She didn't have to ask what had happened to me. What my father called the "tribal telephone" had been at work on that for days.

I told her, "Not at all. Some of it was scary, but only for a moment. The first time I saw Scott Early. Obviously, when he tried to kill himself. But not talking to the police. Not the things you would think would frighten you."

"What about the EMT stuff?"

"*That* is scary," I said. "I love it. I'm going to St. George Community College and finish my full course in becoming a paramedic, so that I'll be able to administer medication, even painkillers, through IV lines and do more complicated medical procedures en route to the hospital, and real assessments. . . ."

"You don't sound like this . . . other thing . . . affected you at all," Clare said in wonderment.

"It did. You can't know how much," I tried to explain. "But not all in a bad way. I saw what I'd done, and I helped Kelly. . . ."

"But you almost killed—"

"Clare, no. I didn't!" I said, and wondered, Would everyone think what Clare thought? "I didn't do a thing to him." A vein in my head began to pound. "Yes, I should have stayed here. I never should have gone there." I tapped my headboard, thinking, and then said, "But I have to tell you that it may not be until this moment that Scott Early fully appreciates what it's like to nearly leave behind the people you love or what it would be like to be left behind." I didn't want to tell her what else had happened to me: a new set of recurring nightmares of Scott Early's livid face behind the glassine hood of the freezer storage bag, of the apartment door swinging slowly open in the dark, the thump—so like the sound of the door hitting the shed those many years ago. I could do nothing but pray and hope these would fade in time. I put my hands over my face. "Just because I'm happy to see you doesn't mean . . . I'm totally happy," I told Clare.

"But I want you to be happy," she said. "You can't blame me for wondering, though. So was it right or was it wrong?"

"Could anything be both?" I asked.

"I don't know."

"I'm not sure, either. I know I'm glad he's safe. I mean that. But I'm glad I'm safe, too. I'm glad I'm home."

"That, of course, is the thing I prayed for hardest, when I heard," Clare said.

"Let me, just, be me for a little while, Clare. Me with you, here. I don't want to remember it now."

And so, for a while, we allowed ourselves a break from the drama. Clare told me about dating David Pratt; they'd even done some making out—strictly outside the clothes. "I don't know what will happen when I go away again," she said.

"If it's meant, it'll last," I said. "My parents lasted."

"It's a different time from when your parents lasted, Ronnie. He could have anyone."

"*You* could have anyone."

"Did you like a boy down there?" she asked.

I thought of Kevin. "Like a brother," I said, "not like a love. I did date a boy. He was LDS."

"Did you like him?"

"Sure. But not enough. You know?"

Clare nodded.

That weekend, we went to church as a family; and carefully, a little at a time, our community accepted me back into its body. By the time I turned seventeen, it (except for the occasional stare) was as if I'd never been away. Sister Barken sent me a card with a picture on it of someone standing on his head, along with a long mohair scarf in my favorite color, periwinkle blue. Inside it read, "Chin up, Ronnie. People may not understand, but they believe. They believe in you. We believe in you."

One night, all four of the Sissinellis came to our house unannounced. Serena and her parents hugged me, and Miko squeezed my shoulder.

"We came," Mrs. Sissinelli said, "to give you a birthday present, Ronnie." She handed me a small box. It was a pair of gold earrings, each with a huge pearl. "Catholics read the Bible, too," said Mrs. Sissinelli, "and St. Matthew speaks of finding the pearl of great price, which I know is part of your doctrine, and which we believe is the glory of the blessing of Jesus, even hidden in a hostile world. That's more complicated than I meant to get. I just thought it was appropriate. We just saw these as for you."

"Thank you," I told her. "They remind me of the sea, and you gave me the sea."

Miko asked, "What did you do to your hair?"

I said, "I didn't want to look like the kid down the road anymore."

"Well, you sure don't," he said, shrugging.

"I'm gradually washing it out," I told them. "It was stupid. I loved my hair. But at least kids with cancer are going to get pretty wigs they'll never have to curl." Serena's eyes filled, but Miko looked down at his shoes. My parents shook hands with the Sissinellis and thanked them for welcoming me home.

It was fear of the dreams coming back now that I was home again that kept me up all that night. I fussed with completing all the bits I'd gathered in advance to make presents—little things such as plain wooden photo frames or old wooden boxes I'd bought at a thrift shop and mailed back home. Now, I decorated them with shells or wrapped bits of sea glass I'd gathered in California or painted on them with stars and half-moons. In the darkness, I went out to fetch some of my mother's old art supplies and her hot-glue gun. To get them, I had to open the door of the shed and see the spot where I'd knelt when we played hide-and-seek. All the windows were new and the paint fresh. There was a bright, cheerful light. Old boards had been replaced and new ones caulked. No troublesome drafts. The supplies had been organized on shelves that smelled freshly sawn, with our canned goods stacked neatly beside them. There was a plain but newer futon in there, with a soft mattress. But I could still, from one window, see the place where the picnic table had stood. When my heart began to flutter, I grabbed a fistful of wires, the hot-glue gun, and the tackle box in which my mother once kept the jeweler's supplies she used for her artwork, and fled.

It was four in the morning when the pebbles hit my window. I looked out, expecting Clare. But it was Miko, standing down there in his old leather jacket. I put on my jean jacket and went outside in my pajama pants.

"What were you doing?" he asked.

"Making Christmas presents," I said. "Sewing. What do you want?"

"I wanted to know why anyone I thought was as smart as I

thought you were could do something so goddamn stupid," he said.

"I don't know," I said. "If I've said that once, I've said it a hundred times. It *was* stupid. But I felt it was the right thing to do. We don't have to understand everything in this life."

"You really think there's another one?"

"Absolutely. That was one reason why," I said. "Because I know I'll see my sisters again. I'll have to be accountable. That's why Mormons get married in the temple for time—which is now—and for eternity, which is forever. So they'll always be together. My parents will. I will, when I get married."

"Damn it, Ronnie," he said. "You did something nuts. You worried me. And you also never called me."

"It wasn't like you cared so much. And I was busy."

"I'll say," Miko said with a grimace. "Listen. You're like . . . a little sister. Always there. Shooting baskets. Shooting *guns*. Riding Jade. I thought about you a lot. When I heard about this, I practically puked. I thought, how can she be serious?"

"I'm serious. I'm a serious person," I said.

"I'm serious, too, Ronnie. You don't think of me that way. You think of me as some rich asshole who flies back and forth from one fancy house to another. But I am a serious person. I will save lives someday."

"I already have," I said.

"Little Miss One Up," he said.

"Maybe I don't think you're a serious person," I said. "What do you care? I'm the kid who cleaned your parents' house, who you laughed at with your stupid friends. I'm the kid you noticed because she was in the middle of a tragedy, on the news. I'm the little kid down the road you saw hundreds of times but only really saw once."

"I know when you mean."

"I know it, too."

"But that's not the only time I really saw you, Ronnie. I'm standing here in the middle of the night, and I see you." He pulled me to him and kissed me, not as he had years before, but drawing my body against him, the way Kevin had with Shira.

"Not here," I said, glancing over to see if my parents' light was still off.

Holding hands, we ran down to the creek. "I never went into the girls' changing room," Miko said.

"It's utterly glamorous," I told him, leading him inside. As I'd hoped, younger kids had chinked up the walls with mud. It looked almost as it had when I was a child. "It's very dark. It's probably also completely soaking with mud on the floor." But the floor was dry and covered with a tarp of plastic. A new generation, I thought. We lay down inside the willow fort, and Miko held me. He kissed me and ran his hands along my ribs. I put my hands under his shirt against his hot back, and none of it felt wrong. The cord in my belly sang.

"Ronnie, you're a Mormon!" he said finally, sitting up.

"So?"

"I can't . . . You're a Mormon! You think an angel came to some kid with bad legs and told him about a new book of the Bible."

"You think an angel came to a girl and told her she was going to have the son of God."

"I've never thought a virgin could have a baby."

"Right."

"I've never thought Jesus made this big appearance in New York State, either, like Eric Clapton on a comeback tour, the way you guys think."

"I've never thought a priest could change regular crackers into the actual body of Christ."

"Come on, Ronnie," he said, dodging that one. "What could make people think that little Joseph Smith was thinking about religion so much, when he was just this fourteen-year-old kid— that he went out in the woods and saw holy visions! Give me a break."

"What about Saint Bernadette, a poor little French girl, seeing the Blessed Virgin—"

"They didn't start a whole religion about a kid's hallucination!"

"No, they just believed the yucky water from the little spring where Bernadette went would cure people with . . . cerebral palsy and cancer and leukemia—"

"Cancer and leukemia are the same thing," Miko said.

"Joseph Smith wasn't perfect. But he said that whatever was exalted or good or wise from other religions, Mormons wanted to bring into our religion, too," I said. "Why are we having a religious argument? This is stupid."

"Where's that written down?"

"What?"

"That Mormons wanted all the good stuff from other religions."

"I'm not sure. Do you have the whole Catholic service memorized?"

"No," he said, "I haven't gone to church except on holidays or when my parents made me since I had First Communion."

"Well, then what's the point? I have. And what does it matter if Joseph Smith was loony? What he started turned into a really good thing, in time. Our way kept a lot of people off drugs and drunk driving and smoking and getting STDs. . . ."

"I didn't mean to insult you," Miko finally said. "Every religion is crazy. Yours is crazier than most. And I guess some of it, only some, makes sense. Like, I've never thought that you could make yourself all cozy with God just through going to confession and saying the rosary. I always thought you had to do good stuff. Like walk the walk, not just talk the talk. I . . . guess."

"And I always thought Catholics had it too easy. All they had to do was say sorry and pray a little and everything was so fine again. I believe you have to do good things. All Mormons do. It's just sensible. So what does it matter if stuff some of the early Mormons did was nuts? I'm not nuts."

"That's, uh, debatable," Miko said. "Given your recent behavior anyhow." I pretended to ignore him.

"My family isn't nuts," I finally said. "Clare's not nuts. There are people who call themselves Mormons, and they really are nuts. It's just that when it's so-called Mormons who do the bad things, it gets on the news. Look at all the stories about Catholic priests molesting little boys. Does that mean all Catholic priests are child molesters? Or make people wonder how anybody could be Catholic?"

"Do you have any relatives who are polygamists?"

"Is your uncle in the Mafia?"

"Catholics don't go building gigantic temples all over the place no one can ever see!"

"No, just Notre Dame! And the Vatican!"

"Anyone can go in the Vatican!"

"Well, people use those temples constantly! And you don't have to pay to go in! If you go to Salt Lake on, like, even a *Wednesday*, you'll see people taking wedding pictures in every doorway. They sign up months in advance to—"

"Let me kiss you," he said, interrupting my speech. "It's more fun." He took hold of my shoulders, and my necklace popped out of my sweater.

"What's that?" he asked.

"Something I made a long time ago."

"What is it? Is it made from plants? Or hair woven from Jade's tail?"

"Not that, but something like that." I didn't tell him for years what it really was, and then only in a letter.

He kissed me again, pulling me closer. "Don't keep this up, Miko," I said. "I'm not a game you can play."

"I'm not playing."

"We're too different," I said.

"But I want you," he said.

"That's . . . just being young and alone in the dark. With a girl who was on the news."

"You really think I am that shallow, then," he said.

"I guess," I said, thinking, Miko! Don't let me get away with being snotty! It's just . . . like me playing defense down at the barn! Don't let me let you go! But he only shrugged.

Finally I said, "For what it's worth, I . . . want you, too. But you're right, that's not the same as love."

"Who said anything about love?"

"No one. And so that's why we have to go back to my house now. And be friends."

"We will," he said, stroking my cheek from my hairline to my chin. "We'll always be friends, Ronnie-o." It wasn't supposed to end this way, I thought.

I got into bed and cried myself to sleep. But beneath the tears, a part of me was thrilled, even in my gloom. It had happened. What we'd both felt was love, no matter what we said. And I didn't care what came of it in the end, or so I told myself. The experience itself was so unexpected and exhilarating that it stopped the nightmares. As I drifted between sleep and waking, I imagined riding Jade to Miko's house—only with both of us the ages we were now. I jumped off Jade's back, and he took me into his arms and kissed me, the way he had that night, not like the kid down the road. I slept for eleven hours. No dreams.

Chapter Twenty-two

$\mathcal{I}$ did finish my full paramedic training before I went to college. It wounded my vanity that I wasn't the youngest freshman at Harvard—the youngest freshman at Harvard was, like, thirteen. But as Miko later said, I was undoubtedly (except for the thirteen-year-old) the only virgin.

Studying harder than I'd ever studied in my life and working on the campus emergency services didn't leave me much time for a social life. Our crew chief, Ian, was full-time. He'd done the work for fifteen years. Ian began as a student majoring in business but loved working on the campus so much, he never finished his degree. (Imagine! Being accepted to Harvard but choosing to work there instead of going out into the world and making the big bucks! I respected him for it.) He told me once, "I think this job makes me feel more alive than bloodless corporate warfare. My buddies love that crap. It makes them feel alive. I tell them what I do sure makes the kids who overdose feel more alive, if I get to save them." He appreciated having me on his crew, because I was a paramedic, and he knew I could have gotten a city job for more money. But all I wanted was to make sure my scholarship was funded and have a little extra to spend on CDs and clothes and my cell phone bill (huge).

The kinds of trauma we saw were different, on campus, from what I'd seen in California: drunken kids falling off statues where they were posing for dumb photos, getting concussions and greenstick fractures, a case of meningitis we caught just in time, an abortion in a dorm that ended with the girl losing a third of her blood through internal bleeding, and those sad and painful attempts at suicide Ian had described (mostly over grades or busted relationships).

"I don't know why they can't go on just long enough for it to feel a little better," I told Ian. "Why can't they have enough hope to wait just a little while?" He knew what had happened to me.

"They don't know it will ever feel better, Ronnie," he said with his perpetual melancholy. "You had your faith. It's funny. So much misery, here among kids who supposedly are the brightest kids from all over the country, from all over the world. Brains are no guarantee of happiness. There are times I think brains make it worse." I was, probably for the first time, humbled, not just appreciative, that my upbringing simply ruled out that kind of self-destruction. If it hadn't, I might have done what those girls, and they were usually girls—only three boys in all the time I was there—did. I knew that I fit the profile: emotional, impulsive, obstinate.

There was one case. I shouldn't call her a "case," although most of us got through by distancing ourselves that way. She was a gorgeous Latina girl who'd almost finished her degree when she blew a critical test in her major, organic chemistry. One test. It would have meant taking the class over, because she failed. But that was all it would have meant. Taking one class again, one more summer at school. It was spring. The chestnuts were in bloom, and the hydrangea. I thought she could have held on. But instead, she found a vein and used a syringe filled with air, and, well, she knew where to give herself the shot. I thought, Heavenly Father, help me; this girl used the food of life to end her own life. She wrote in the note she left, "My parents worked long and honorably to help me go to Harvard. I let them down. Mom, Dad, Lucinda, Jorge, Luis, your big sister loves you so." I can close my eyes and remember her tranquil, bluish face, her fan of dark hair, the immaculate orderliness of her room, the stack of textbooks to return left in a pile with a Post-it note on top. One of the other girls, who was on her first crew, became hysterical. She hyperventilated. I was one of the people on her debriefing the next day. I had to get out of a class for it, and for once, I didn't care.

There were car accidents, but most of them were minor, big dents in the Beemer.

I saw only one other fatality the whole three years, that of an old law professor who died quietly, and well into his eighties, during a lecture on torts. Kids later joked that he died from boredom. But I found those jokes cruel, and so did a few kids in my ward who were majoring in law. It isn't a *tragedy* when an old person dies. But it's not a joke. Mrs. Sissinelli had once told me that Catholics prayed to the Virgin Mary for a peaceful death. I got the sense of that, for the first time. If you die doing what you love, well, that really is a blessing.

It was also a blessing that there was a nice Mormon ward in Cambridge. But although there were some nice kids, guys and girls, whom I liked, they weren't "like home." And in any case, I wouldn't have wanted just to hang out with Mormons.

I had other friends.

And that was why, although I'd received a full-ride scholarship to the University of Chicago, too, and to Brigham Young, I chose Boston. I felt better being closer to Clare, who was, of course, in New York, and to Serena, who finally decided to major in art at the Boston Conservatory.

And Miko was there, too, in medical school.

We had remained friends. As much as I'd hoped for, well, more, I was thankful for his familiar presence. He *was* like a big brother, taking me to the farmers market, helping me avoid the tourist boutiques. And because we set a lunch date—usually for sushi—a couple of times each month, he became a closer friend, the kind of person in your life to whom you can tell anything. I even went out to the Cape with him and Serena for a few weeks, the summer after my freshman year. They all said later they could see everything just by looking at us, though Miko never laid a hand on me.

He was all about Diana.

When I went back to school, Miko met the guy I had been seeing, Eric Lock, who was majoring in business. He called Eric a head on top of a suit. I told him that I thought Diana Lambert, who was majoring in Miko, was a boom-boom body attached to a head. We were both goofing around, of course, but not really. It was more what Papa used to call "kidding on the square."

There were some nights when neither Eric nor Diana was around. Miko and I sat alone together on the Commons and talked and talked, as we had before dawn that one night, watching the water tangle down through the rocks above Dragon Creek. We never had a real date. But after a while, it became clear, without either of us saying anything, that something that had begun in the hut near Dragon Creek was intensifying between us. We didn't make out. We didn't even hold hands. But it was as if we did. Miko started to throw pebbles at my dorm room window at night. When I'd come down, he'd say, "I was feeling homesick. I wanted to talk to the kid down the road." And we'd talk until the sky went gray. We talked about his internship coming up. He wanted something in the Pacific Northwest, Washington or Oregon. Some of those hospitals were major resources for people in Alaska, who didn't always have access to the best medical care. "Imagine having to fly in to some remote place and take care of a kid with a burst appendix, or e-vac him to a hospital. It'd be so cool. I know I'll do my share of looking at sore throats and bad backs, but that's what I think about when I think about going out there." I knew just what he meant. It was why I did what I did.

Miko also told me that he'd spent half his life near Boston, and he wanted to see that other ocean. I certainly understood that. After one of those long nights, I'd get up for school feeling as though I'd been knocked on the head with a baseball bat. But I still got my grades.

The following spring, he got his match: Harborview Hospital, his first choice. I was the first one he told. I was happy for Miko and miserable because the first thing that crossed my mind was that even with taking a full load during summers, it would be a year or more before I graduated.

Lectures? I gave myself hundreds. Why do you care, Ronnie Swan? What's it to you? You aren't really going out anyhow! Be glad you ended up having fun together as long as you did. But then other thoughts would come stealing: I could apply to the University of Washington Medical School. It wasn't really my first choice. Yale was my first choice. Yale! Get over it, I'd tell myself. We were just Ronnie and Miko, pals. Well, not really. But neither of us was giving in to feelings we probably both had and dismissed as impractical for several hundred reasons.

Then, one night, Miko yelled for me to open my dorm window. "I've got a pebble down here I want you to catch. Remember? The girl with the great basketball hands?" The pebble he threw up to me was a diamond, set in a simple platinum swoop of a ring. I ran downstairs and jumped into his arms, wrapping my legs around his waist. He said, "I figured I might as well get it over with."

"How terribly romantic," I told him after we kissed, each of us in complete relief. "Like catching my first striped bass. In fact, catching my first striper was more romantic."

"Ronnie," he said, pulling the combs from my hair until it filled up his hands and spilled down over my shoulders, "you knew damn well guys don't ever get over their first redhead."

"It's just lust, then," I said, kissing him again and again and once more.

"Who said anything about lust? I'm in love with the kid down the road."

He got mad when I left him standing there and ran upstairs to call Clare. I *was* only twenty years old.

Two summers later, after we were married in the temple at home, we flew to the Cape house for a short honeymoon before my classes began. My mother-in-law had filled every room with white roses and jasmine. I can close my eyes and remember the enchantment of that overpowering bath of scent. And years later, I only have to touch Miko's shoulder while he sleeps, and my body remembers everything else. There's one picture of us, black and white, that we have above our bed. It's me in my grandmother's wedding gown and Miko in gray morning clothes, looking into each other's eyes and laughing as if we'd both just medaled in the Olympics. That was how we felt.

The time apart until I graduated was brutal. Miko made me feel complete, and stolen weekends didn't fill the lonely void they left behind. There were times I almost dreaded going out to see him, that huge trip for two sleepless nights together. I was already missing him before I got on the plane. It was like being married and not married, not at all the same situation my parents had together at BYU. Once, when my mother visited me, I asked if she ever thought Miko and I would be together. She said, "I hoped you would." And I was surprised.

"Even though he was a Catholic then," I said.

"Love doesn't care about those boundaries," she said. "I prayed that he would see the right way for both of you, and that you'd have all the happiness as a woman you didn't have as a child." She held me, with my head on her shoulder. "You'll get through this time, Ronnie. You'll get through this time because you're the most determined person I know."

Naturally, I applied to the University of Washington Medical School. Then I prayed as if I were mounting an assault on heaven. And I was accepted. When I got the letter, I sent Miko red, white, and silver heart balloons at work. Everyone thought it was his birthday. Later that night, over the phone, he said that a muscle in his neck that had been tensed for months had finally relaxed.

The apartment we found was really only a big room, a converted attic with ells and nooks made over into a kitchen and a bedroom—not unlike the one in Mrs. Desmond's house. Though it was hardly lavish, the tiny slice of a view of the Sound from the front window made it feel luxurious. We draped slant-roofed corners with fabric stretched on bungee cords for makeshift closets. Every vertical space was crowded with traditional student brick-and-plank bookshelves, except we painted the cheap pine planks to match the blue wall and used glass bricks that seemed to capture more light and, seemingly, more space. One wall was periwinkle blue, covered with my father's photos of the flowers and mountain meadows, and a single glad shelf displayed my mother's favorite porcelain, a sinuous, milky vase with the shape of a thistle curved around its narrow neck. She'd given it to us for a wedding gift. The kitchen was so small that I couldn't stand in the middle and extend both my arms straight out. But everything seemed to expand on those rare occasions when we had friends over and filled the twenty-five-CD changer to the max. The bathroom had the same kind of big claw-foot tub I remembered from San Diego. And I could sink into it, down to my nose, when my feet were swollen, as they were most nights, especially after we learned we were expecting. It wasn't exactly planned, but it wasn't exactly prevented, either. It was sort of the way Miko and I happened, fate ignoring human objections. And, like our marriage, it was certainly welcomed.

Dr. Sissinelli wanted to buy us a house then. He wanted at least for us to let him rent a big three-bedroom apartment. But we wanted to make it on our own, or almost, because my in-laws did help out with tuition. We simply draped another corner and made a stamp-size extra room. We painted purple-and-yellow polka dots on the walls and got ready for the little one everyone had hoped we'd put off for a while. All the parents wanted me to take a year away from school to be with the baby, but I'd seen other women manage a baby and medical school. I could do it, too. And I did, although I felt some days as though I were running in wet sand.

None of our parents could get there in time for the birth, because the baby surprised us and came just a few weeks early. Selfishly, we were almost glad about that. I felt the first bite of labor coming on while we were at the movies, but we waited until the end of the film before we set off for Harborview.

Miko was all so over-the-top proud that his child was born at "his" hospital, where the obstetrician in the labor room called both of us "Dr. Sissinelli." I'd wanted a midwife, but Miko was the best coach imaginable. In labor, you're supposed to "visualize" beautiful vistas, so you don't notice that the pain makes you want to claw somebody's face off. Still, no one could help me do that better than a guy who'd known me, and the places closest to my heart, for all of our lives. He held me, and when the pain was at its worst, he held me harder; and he told me the story of our first kiss, that day I scraped my hand falling off Jade in his front yard. He told me about the night in the mud fort, when we first realized we were in love. He told me how we'd teach our baby to ski and to swim and to bike and to ride a horse. He made me laugh when he told me that he'd bought sparkling cider to toast the occasion with his nonalcoholic bride. As an Italian man, tender and funny by nature, and sort of a charmer by design, Miko was known around the hospital for making all the patients, especially the elderly women, feel comfy and safe. And I'd always known that beneath his jokey surface, he had huge emotions. But that night, when we saw our daughter for the first time, alone together in the room except for the doctor and nurse, Miko began to laugh and then to sob like a little boy. That moment was so powerful, it all but fused us into one being in a way even our marriage hadn't. That sounds kind of pukey, I know. But there are moments in life that really feel that way.

Starting that night, bouquets arrived in my room nonstop—from Clare and my parents, from my friend Emma and her husband, from my cousins. Miko's colleagues kept coming in every hour on the hour to slap him on the back and to say she looked just like him (she didn't). And what little time we got to sleep, we slept squeezed together in a hospital bed, with Mika between us. We took her home after only one day. Maybe it was hormones, but I felt like royalty as I lay down on my bed. When my mother arrived the next morning and insisted upon waiting on me, making me my favorite desert foods, a milder version of her tortilla soup and cornbread as only she could make it, I felt even more the princess. I suppose every young mother who's happy feels that way.

And we were happy.

We are happy.

I don't know that I'll ever be as completely happy as someone can be who's never been creased through her center by
agony; but I don't think I'm altogether the worse for it, either.
I'll never know, because I'll never be anyone else. I know this.
In my work, I'd already had and would always have to live with
seeing things that would make my cousin Bridget, for example,
run away screaming. And in my life, well, there would always be
a "despite" in my happiness. But at least I lived with a man who
knew it.

Epilogue

$\mathcal{A}$ first-year intern feels as though she's been standing up, almost steadily, for five straight years. I don't care what kind of shape she's in, how many miles she logs on the road or the treadmill. She becomes so deadly exhausted, so depleted, that she can literally catch a few moments' real sleep in the interval it takes for a nurse to bring a fresh tray of instruments and dressings. I'd mastered the art. I could even use one part of my mind to respond to the questions of patients who were chronic or sick with things only a psychiatrist could help—and who were in no immediate danger—with what sounded like sensible answers, while another part of me actually was asleep. An ER doctor in training, who faces impossible demands but also impossibly exhilarating rushes of salvation, is doubly blessed, or cursed, by the unrelenting velocity of the forward motion. Shifts end, but patients arrive. Hours are devoured. I'd thought that the four years of medical school would never end; and back then, I'd had time for the occasional run or workout or movie or . . . sit-down meal. Now, I looked back on those years as an oasis. Students go *home*. For me, a three-to-eleven can end with the sunrise. Everybody tries not to let it happen, but it does. You get involved with a patient, and even with an attending on, you don't want to leave until you know the outcome.

   That night was Christmas Eve.

Millie Aberg brought everyone hot chocolate with home-made marshmallows.

I was dreaming of my home in the Pine Mountains, of the Sissinellis' fifteen-foot-high tree near the fireplace. I couldn't be there, but later, after I put out the presents from Santa, including a rag doll Mama had made, with long straight brown hair, I would curl up on my futon with my cat, Athena, and call them. I'd listen to my brother's beautiful soprano as he sang "O Holy Night" to me from far, far away. Rafe had inherited his singing from Heavenly Father, not from Mama or any of us. Only an hour and I would trudge the mere block from Seattle Mercy to my home. I was getting ready to sign out when I was interrupted by a harsh whisper from one of my medical students. I expected the students to be grouchy—Christmas Eve in an emergency room is something I would wish on no one—but, as I always told them when times got rough, they knew that going in.

"It's always like this, Christmas or Easter or Halloween, when they bring them in," I heard Anita Fong tell Stacey Sweeney, one of the nurses. "Can't they tell if a kid has strep that bad *before* nine o'clock at night?" Anita was brilliant, but edgy and impatient, too impatient, too often. I was afraid that the people behind the green curtain would hear Anita's complaints. Parents sometimes *did* hesitate too long, but I thought that was often because they had gone to the pediatrician so many times too *promptly*, only to be told that their child had a virus and needed orange juice, not antibiotics. But as I waited, Anita came out with the five-minute swab and said, "Well, *she's* got it good. Merry Christmas. The pus in that kid's throat looks like stalactites."

Anita disappeared back inside the curtain, where I heard her telling the parents, over their murmurs, that they needed to be aware, and sooner, of their child's symptoms, because strep could potentially lead to serious complications. Anita said, "This little girl is going to have a throat that feels like she swallowed glass." This was over the top. I could have let her handle it on her own. Not every doctor has to have the patience of a Martha. But I swept back the curtain and, trying to lift my cheekbones into the semblance of a bright smile, asked, "Is everything all right in here, Doctor Fong?"

Juliet was, what, nine by then? She was still so exquisite, I had to catch my breath as much from admiration as surprise. She had long straight blond hair and eyes that I could tell would change from blue to green, depending on the color of the sky or the color of her clothes. She sat up in bed, with a red Popsicle in one hand and the other clutching a cold pack to her throat. I tried to back away, close the curtain before they turned around. But they turned too quickly, and Scott looked into my eyes for what seemed like all of time but what was probably ten seconds. Kelly tried to throw a blanket over the face of her baby, no more than eight or nine months old, asleep on her chest in his front pack, as if to shield him. But then she let the blanket drop, and tears shimmered at the corners of her eyes, and it seemed as if she would speak. I knew she mustn't speak.

"I see you're all in good hands," I said. "And if she takes her medicine, Juliet will be fine to open her presents Christmas morning. But make sure she stays away from her sweet little brother there."

The little girl sat up straight and pointed at me with her Popsicle. "How do you know my name is Juliet?" she asked.

"Santa told me," I said. "I have a little girl of my own."

"What's her name?"

"Mika."

"That's a pretty name. Why's her name Mika?" Juliet asked. "Is she nine?"

"She's two. It's a combination of her daddy's name and mine," I said. "Merry Christmas." As if sensing something in the room besides the six of us, Anita Fong fell silent. I stepped back and let the curtain drop.

There are no coincidences. If something happens and we don't understand the reason, that doesn't mean there is no reason. It means that the reason will later be revealed, likely not in this life. There were twenty cubicles on the ER at Seattle Mercy, and officially my shift was over. Why should I have walked into that one? It was obviously because there was something I was meant to discover. Not all parents who bring their children to the emergency room on the night of Christmas Eve are neglectful or neurotic. Some are only busy or tired or extra careful or have a child who's not a complainer. At least, the ones who come are concerned and not ashamed of it. The ones who never bring their children at all are the ones who worry us. Juliet was immaculate, well nourished, bright. Scott and Kelly had cared for her well. They had been the parents she was supposed to have. For me, that meant I was forgiven. In the locker room, I knelt at the bench and prayed that Becky and Ruthie, in celestial bliss at the celebration of our Savior's human birth, would bless Juliet, and the baby boy, and their niece, my little girl, and their little brothers.

I had never known where Scott and Kelly moved after they left San Diego. I'd never wanted to know. The unavoidable explanation for our meeting at Seattle Mercy was that it was essential, not only for the three of us, but for someone greater than the sum of all of our lives, to make us aware of what we had made of them.

I got up, lifted my coat from its hook, and, taking care not to glance back at the cubicle directly across from the charting station, crossed my name off the board. Wrapping Sister Barken's mohair scarf around my neck, I stepped out into the misty night.

The chilly rain that had soaked Seattle all that day had finally ended. I looked for the Big Dipper. Through a remnant smudge of cloud, I could see only part of the ladle, like a broken cage of stars.

Reading Group Guide

Q & A WITH JACQUELYN MITCHARD

Q. What was the spark that ignited the idea for this novel? Is it based on any real-life crime?

A. Only twice in my career have real-life crimes suggested the "opening notes," if you will, of novels I later wrote. Both incidents were so haunting I could never escape them. I thought about one of them for years before I ever wrote fiction. Thirty years ago, when I was starting college, a boy named Stephen Stayner was kidnapped on his way home from school. After seven years, he was returned to his family, when the same man abducted another boy—a boy roughly the age Stephen had been when he was taken. The man was a pedophile, who alternately abused and "fathered" Stephen. In 2000, two of the five children of a family named Carpenter were murdered when a stranger armed with a pitchfork attacked the children, who were at home in the care of their oldest sister, fourteen-year-old Jessica. In my novel *The Deep End of the Ocean*, Ben, the boy who was abducted, had an older brother, Vincent, who became deeply troubled and delinquent after the family's loss. Though I never knew this, Cary Stayner, the older brother of Stephen—who became a motorcycle police officer and died in an accident in his twenties—became, not a troubled teen who stole a teacher's car, but a killer. Cary Stayner murdered a mother and daughter and their guest, a foreign exchange student, in Yosemite. Even more strange is the fact that both the original crimes took place in the small town of Merced, California, a fact I did not know at the time I began my research.

Q. You said on your Web site (www.jacquelynmitchard.com) that *Cage of Stars* was a "chance to grapple with a character's moral struggle, and with those ancient questions (such as, do two wrongs make a right?)." Why did you make the main character, Veronica "Ronnie" Swan, the sister of the victims, rather than one of their parents? Was age a factor?

A. Age was a factor. Barely more than a child herself, Veronica didn't have the maturity or even the full security of her religious faith to help her through the stages of grief. Even her parents, who were both devout, barely functioned in their family and community for years. I saw Ronnie's age as giving me a protagonist who was both more vulnerable and liable to take risks—both of which were important to the story. However, those questions of moral rectitude and the efficacy of revenge bedevil all of us, no matter what age we are.

Q. Why did you choose to make the family Mormon? Since the novel does discuss a great deal about the Church of Latter-day Saints and the beliefs of its members, where did you get your insights and information?

A. First of all, it's not intended to be an exposé or even to entirely factually re-create the life of a real Mormon family, as some rituals and beliefs among Mormons are private. I chose to make the family Mormon because I wanted their faith to set them apart from the world, but also to allow them to be *of* the world—in a way that would not have been possible had they been part of a more "cloistered" religion, such as the Amish faith. I have long-time friends who are Mormons, and I went to live with them in their home and attend their church for a short time in Provo, so that I could render much of at least the sense of the LDS faith in a genuine way. Mormons also have a strict code of behavior. They believe that deeds and not only words of contrition are necessary to atone for a wrong. And yet, my friend knew a couple whose child had been killed by a negligent driver, and they lived in torment until they were able to forgive him. Like the Swans, they were faithful but unusually liberal Mormons, which is not the norm.

Q. A love story runs parallel to the novel's theme of retribution and justice. It, however, presents another conflict for Ronnie. Did you have a particular message in mind, such as "love is blind" (as is justice)?

A. It is, of course. But what I was actually thinking more about was the axiomatic belief that love can overcome anything—even grief and death.

Q. There is great emotional pain in this novel. Do the content and themes of a book you are in the process of writing affect you? How do you handle the transition from the world of your novel to your daily life?

A. It's excruciating. I don't write about these things to manipulate the emotions of my readers, or to torment myself. I have seven children, and the loss of one of those children is probably the only thing on earth that would drive me mad—as I've lost a mother, a brother, a husband. I write about these emotions sometimes, because they become so compelling to me that I can't handle them—process them—in any other way than writing.

Q. How much do you consciously use symbolism in your writing? For instance, why did you choose "Swan" as Ronnie's family name?

A. If a writer is entirely conscious of the symbols he or she chooses, the reader is going to feel a heavy hand on the back of the neck, saying, "Look here!" I suppose I simply believed it was a pretty name; but I know what swans symbolize in terms of transformation and, moreover, how fiercely protective they are of their young.

Q. Fate, more than choice, determines many events in this novel. Are you telling readers that life's seemingly random events do happen for a reason? Or is it simply one of the joys of writing that an author can give meaning to senseless tragedy and coincidence?

A. The latter. I think it is true that fate tips the balance. But we are in the presence of our fate in part because of the choices we've made. The children's death was a random event; but Ronnie's choice was determinant and intentional. What happened as a result of that choice was a combination of fate and choice. I think Ronnie would believe that all of the events had happened for a reason, as part of God's plan.

Q. Will you share some of your creative process with us? How do you go about developing a story? Do you base characters on real people? How carefully do you plot your novel before you write it?

A. I plan and outline my story before I ever sit down to write the first sentence. It must have a title and a general shape, though the way I will "color in" the lines is a huge part of the creative choice. Down to the number of chapters and almost to the nature of the ending, and even the last sentence, I know generally where the story is headed. Some characters, such as Anne Singer in my second novel, *The Most Wanted*, are entirely based on real people. Gordon McKenna in *A Theory of Relativity* was almost completely based on my brother's stories of himself in his early twenties—Gordon is even his middle name. Most of them are like vegetable soup—a little of this and a little of that—and all of them are, of course, to some degree, the author.

Q. You began your writing career as a journalist, and you still write a nationally syndicated column. How has that influenced your discipline as a writer? Would you advise aspiring writers to find a job that requires them to write for their daily bread?

A. Being a reporter helped me to learn discipline, how to make language precise, and to make choices quickly. I think it helped me be concise in writing (though some would argue with this). It helped me learn how to go to the sources of information I needed. But personally, I think more lawyers and physicians successfully make the transition to writing fiction than we reporters do.

Q. Since you were and are a journalist, how did that shade your depiction of the journalists in this novel? How do you feel about the "feeding frenzy" of media coverage created by a sensational crime?

A. Naturally, I find it disturbing and so do all reasonable reporters. But the frenzy is self-perpetuating; the media presents it, and the public drives it by hungering for more and yet more. The most upsetting component of that kind of news coverage is the way it catches families in the headlights, unshielded and unprepared.

Q. You also wrote on your Web site that besides *The Deep End of the Ocean*, your best known work, you have written other bestsellers, and some were even better than the one that made you famous. Which is your favorite book and why?

A. Without being coy, I think this book is the best—the leanest and most precisely told. I didn't "kitchen-sink" this book by overstuffing the plot. However, my favorite is probably *The Most Wanted*, which also is the most flawed of all my books, probably because of the obsessions it explores.

Q. You travel quite a bit, it seems. What are some of your favorite places? Have they appeared or will they appear in your books?

A. It seems that way, doesn't it? It's usually always for work or research. But I wrote the novella *Christmas, Present* while in Italy researching another book not yet written, and the British Virgin Islands will figure hugely in my next novel. Italy is undoubtedly my favorite place on earth; and I've set parts of novels on the east coast, which has been another important place to my family. I've been to Australia only once, but I'm mad to go back.

Q. What's in your near future? Have you another novel "in the works"? Is there anything developing in your personal life that you can share with us?

A. There's certainly not another child, I can assure you! Seven is the limit! But a new novel about four women in the most unlikely jeopardy is upcoming, as well as possible stories that have as part of their underpinnings conflicts over Mexican immigration, artistic theft by a husband of a wife's ideas, a twist on the desperation of infertility and on the psychic closeness of twins . . . I don't think I'll run out!

DISCUSSION QUESTIONS

1. Why do you think this book is titled *Cage of Stars*? It's a wonderful visual image, but what might it mean?

2. What real-life case does the situation in this book evoke for you? Do you believe that mental illness is a legitimate defense when a person commits a terrible crime? Is justice served if the person is released from an institution?

3. Who is to blame for this crime? Could it have been prevented? Can a random act of violence ever be prevented? Do any of the survivors feel guilty? Do they bear any responsibility in the deaths?

4. At one point, after reading a letter from Miko, Ronnie says, "I was the only one still . . . stuck." Do you think this being "stuck" is related to Ronnie's choice of vengeance over forgiveness? How else does her quest for "justice" affect her life?

5. Ronnie does not carry out her plan for revenge, but if she had, how would you rewrite the end of this story?

6. Talk about Ronnie's relationship with her parents. Do you think she is closer to her father than her mother? Why?

7. Ronnie says, at the beginning of chapter fourteen, that "I think every religion must have been started by a person who loved someone who died." What is your response to that? True or false?

8. Looking at Ronnie's life and that of her parents, do you believe that someone can love and hate at the same time? Do you think a person can go beyond grief and tragedy, even when the loss is as great as the murder of two innocent children? If yes, what behaviors can help that happen—carrying out an act of vengeance or offering forgiveness?

9. How much does the Swans being Mormon influence this story? Would this story be radically different if the family had been Jewish, Muslim, Roman Catholic, or Friends (Quakers)? Would a family without any strong religious affiliation have responded to tragedy in the same way as the Swans?

10. The names of the characters in this book are unusual. Do you think any of them have symbolic meaning? Which ones?

11. Ronnie has an exceptionally close friendship with Clare. Talk about its importance in Ronnie's emotional life.

12. What do you think ultimately stops Ronnie from carrying out the kidnapping of Juliet or from letting Scott Early die?

13. Ronnie's landlady, Mrs. Desmond, assesses Ronnie's character at their first meeting. On what does she base her judgment? Is she right? What traits or behaviors are the truest reflection of character?

14. Why does Ronnie fall in love with Miko and vice versa? Is true love a choice or an act of fate?

15. The story has a happy ending, and a symbolic one. Discuss what happens in the final chapter, when it happens, and what message it conveys.

JACQUELYN MITCHARD
ON JACQUELYN MITCHARD

The danger, gentle reader, of what I'm about to say is that you will believe that I am comparing myself with Ernest Hemingway, William Carlos Williams, F. Scott Fitzgerald, Ruth Rendall, and Barbara Kingsolver.

And that is that I am a self-taught writer.

Now perhaps you are thinking—well, that's obvious! And perhaps you're thinking I'm not fit to stand in line to get my driver's license renewed in the same building as those people named above.

But, while it doesn't mean I'm a good writer; and it certainly doesn't mean that I'm a *better* writer than authors who learned their craft early and well at Middlebury College, the Iowa Writers' Workshop, or Smith or Carleton College, the thing is that there are a good deal fewer of us around these days than there once were.

Although such wonderful mystery writers as Martha Grimes and Tess Gerritsen (Tess Gerritsen was a physician) have learned this thing we do (did you know that's the real meaning of the phrase "cosa nostra"?) on their own, and these are only the ones who quickly spring to mind, there are more carefully taught writers than ever before. Creative writing majors and graduate programs at universities and colleges have sprung up exponentially, as has the phenomenon of the writers' workshop. I teach at two writers' workshops each year. I'm never sure when I'm finished about a couple of things: whether I did anyone any good, and why yet another person wants to be a writer.

Once I was in a theater production with two of my sons, who were both very good actors as young people; one still is. All I had going for me was a love of the story (*A Christmas Carol*), experience in playing a mother of many children, and a histrionic personality disorder.

But for the role, I had to learn to sing, really to sing; and so I took lessons for four months.

And though no one came up to me afterward asking me to ink a contract for a recording deal, I ended up doing quite a good job, if I do say. I also had the best abs I've ever had in my life from learning the discipline of proper breathing. The point of this is that my friend and coach, who's an opera singer, told me, "I don't know why, but it seems everyone really wants to sing."

And I don't know why, but increasingly, it seems everyone really wants to write.

I don't know why.

I suppose it's the same impulse: It's a performing art; and it would seem that those who could do it *would* do it. But it's also very difficult and the likelihood of anything ever coming of it is also very small. On the other hand, if the force that propels it won't be denied, then people have to do it. I admit I've met my share who probably ought to try something different. But since there are so very many, many more books being published now than when I wrote my first novel ten years ago, the possibility may not seem so far out of reach.

Nor is writing, as so many of my colleagues and students tell me, the thing I love most in life. It's the *work* I love most in life; but I would give it up yesterday if it threatened my family. And so I suppose I am not a genius or truly passionate, not enough to sacrifice my full life as a wife, mother, sister, and friend, or my life in my lumbering house on the prairie, to follow this calling. It's never prompted me to use drugs or drink myself silly, either; and I suppose that is a hallmark of greatness.

My point about being self-taught is this: As the first person in my family ever to graduate high school, much less college, I had an obligation to support myself and, quite soon, a family; and I was first a high school teacher and then a newspaper reporter who never imagined that I would take up "creative writing."

And yet, all my life, I had schooled myself in writing sentences by literally copying out sentences that were beautiful to me—from books by McKinlay Kantor and Betty Smith and Truman Capote and Andrea Barrett—and then writing sentences of my own in the way they did, until I could do that. I was never afraid, as are so many young students I meet, that doing this would cause me to lose "my own voice." I didn't have one, so how could I lose it?

But when it finally came time to do something bold or succumb to despair—when my husband died young and I, a mother of three young sons, was left with sketchy employment—I did what my dear friend Jane Hamilton told me to do. She told me to tell the story as I would tell *her* the story.

And to a great degree, I did, though that is harder than it sounds. I found that I did indeed have the beginnings of a voice.

For several of my earlier novels, I was very mindful of not having learned this craft properly and at an Ivy League school; and I tried a great many verbal pyrotechnics that only left my fingers burned. With this novel, with *Cage of Stars*, I achieved what I always wanted to achieve: a story that mattered, told simply, with the fewest possible and right words.

I hope you love it.

That will mean that I taught myself at least well enough.

#1 *New York Times* bestselling author

Jacquelyn Mitchard

takes readers on a breathtaking journey
of suspense and high adventure . . .

Please turn this page
for a preview of

Still Summer

Available in hardcover

Day One

The three men finished with the small boat before nightfall. The painting had to be done quickly and it was difficult. So afterward they rested and smoked in the drawing dusk, their backs against a massive rock. The boat was called a *yola*. They had spotted it bobbing near an island on a buoy in the natural harbor formed by the embrace of two small spits of land and hauled it ashore. With thick smears of black paint, they covered up its pale blue gray color, its name, *Bonita*, and the white numbers of its registration. Over the lights, they spread a thinner coat. At sea, even if perchance they ran with lights to avoid a reef, this silty covering would make the lights indistinct and fickle; and someone might mistake them for a phosphorescent curiosity of the sea. Now they needed only to replace the engine with the larger one left for them the night before, beneath a tent of canvas concealed with branches and brush. The two older men had lived more than forty years in the same village in Santo Domingo. The younger man, an American barely twenty years old, could understand only some of the words they said. He might have been fluent by now but preferred not to be. Still, he could tell that they were talking about the way the sea always eventually gave up her fish, as well as other things. He heard the words for "weather" and "soup." He knew these men as Ernesto and Carlo; but he suspected these were not their true names. He knew that for these jobs, the men lived for a few weeks each year in Honduras, at the homes of people whose names they were given. They were different people each time, cousins of acquaintances of men who knew *these* men by other names. At each place they stopped for food or rest, they would meet other people with no names. There seemed to be an endless supply of people who would forfeit names and memory for fifty American dollars. He had met them only once before. He did not expect to meet them again.

The young man drew in the sweet smoke, laid his head back and thought of his sister. The last time he had seen her, she had been seven years old, dressed for Halloween as a carousel horse, in an outfit their mother had made of black tights and papier-mâché. He remembered his father saying that the young man did not need a costume to look like a freak. His mother pivoted on his father and defended him, a reflex retaliation of a mother on the part of her cub. But the young man knew that he had disgraced her, too, as his brother, still in high school, had honored her. He had failed to finish high school. His brother brought home trophies and fine grades. His own experiments with drugs and drunkenness had nearly put him in jail and cost his father considerable money and even more shame among his circle of wealthy friends. He did not like sports. After the time for playing baseball in the park was over, he had turned to quieter things. His mother had not minded; but his father spoke of him as a quitter. To the young man, the handsome, rough boys with their wide red mouths were embarrassing, almost frightening. He was not like the sons of his father's friends. Long ago, they had gone off to Brown or Michigan State. His brother would go to a fine college one day also. Still, his brother did love him. And his mother loved him no less than she loved his brother.

His mother thought he would come out of the ways he had never expected to go.

The young man sometimes believed this, too.

His thinking of it was interrupted when Ernesto said something conspiratorial to Carlo about offering a puff of their smoke to the owner of *Bonita*. This amused Carlo so much he deliberately fell over on his back, laughing as only a servile man can, like a dog performing for its master. Carlo was stupid, which the young man did not believe made him any less dangerous than Ernesto.

The owner of the little *yola* sat some distance away with his back also propped against a large rock. He made no comment on Ernesto's offer because he was dead.

Like a rare heron displaced from her environment, Olivia Montefalco high-stepped regally into the heat and blare of O'Hare International Airport. Though it was June, she wore a white wool suit with her high-heeled white sandals and huge diamond-stippled sunglasses. Those she passed were certain they had seen her before, perhaps in a magazine photograph. They fell back to make way. A grandmother rushing to meet her daughter for the Sunjet to Vegas thought that Olivia was that actress, the one from that movie about the artist whose boyfriend was a ghost . . . ? It had been a sweet movie, without all the sex, sex, sex. She had short hair, like Olivia's. A pilot who jumped down from a hotel shuttle—a little too athletically, but in a way he hoped would impress the flight attendants—was sure this woman had been on a charter he'd once flown to Crete. Unlike the gambling grandmother, he was correct.

Oblivious to the stares from fellow travelers and haggard morning smokers, Olivia stood on her toes and scanned the ranks of limousines, SUVs, and police cars. Where was that huge thing Tracy drove? The last time she'd seen it, it had been filled to exhaustion by Cammie and about a dozen of her soccer mates, all chittering and smelling of sweaty socks. Olivia was amazed that Tracy could work full-time and cook for Jim and visit her parents and send letters and coach soccer as well. Perhaps now that Cammie was grown, she had a different car.

Two skycaps trailed behind Olivia, like yoked oxen straining to push the teetering towers of Olivia's turquoise Henk van de Meene luggage. Olivia stuffed their hands with crumpled wads of dollar bills and gave them a smile so candent that they felt something more than a tip had been bestowed. Olivia had shipped most of her belongings, but the bits and essentials that comforted her after twenty years in Italy came with her, in fourteen matching pieces.

Olivia bit her lip—a gesture that, when she was married to Franco, guaranteed jewelry within days—and wondered if Tracy had forgotten her. Olivia hadn't written for months and months, not since Tracy's flurry of phone calls and offerings of help during Franco's illness. She didn't wonder if being left at the airport would serve her right. That was the kind of pondering that Olivia censored.

With a sure hand and her cousin Janis riding shotgun, Tracy piloted her huge van around the arrivals tier.

"There she is! There's Olivia! Behind that weird luggage!" Holly Solvig shrieked from the backseat. "Wonder how much extra *that* cost! I've never seen someone with so much baggage!"

"We already knew that," Janis said dryly.

Tracy remonstrated softly, "Jan. Hols. Come on. If it is

Olivia, it's *Olivia*. You knew she was wealthy. What I hope is that I have the right airline and the right day."

Olivia had returned to the United States only twice in twenty years, once for her brother's wedding, once for her father's funeral. Each time Holly and Tracy had come to fetch her, the encounter had been the same: Olivia changed her entire appearance the way other women changed the color of their nail polish. But since neither Holly nor Tracy Kyle ever changed, she never failed to recognize them; and she did not now.

"I told you it was her, Trace," Holly repeated triumphantly. "Look, she sees us! She's giving the Godmother wave." Tracy glanced back, nearly colliding with a Saab. It was their wave, the American Sign Language letter y, an extended forefinger and thumb. "Look at those sunglasses. She looks like Mario San-Giaccamo's mother at the country club pool in 1970! She's Westbrookian all over! Now it's going to take a half hour to come back around again to get her!" Holly felt like a fool, a forty-two-year-old woman making the "Y" sign out the back window of a van. She tried to cover by making other ASL signs she'd picked up over the years at the hospital, those for "Not true" and "Talk to me," so onlookers might actually think she was talking to someone who was deaf.

"No way!" Janis cried now. "Whoever that woman is, she's at least ten years younger than we are!" Suddenly, all three women, as if each heard a gunshot at the starting line, covertly found something reflective in the car and began the kind of inventory reserved for buying a bathing suit. Each was thinking variations on the same theme: If this *was* their old friend, then her appearance was more magical than surgical.

"But it is so too her!" Holly insisted, reverting to adolescent language now, up on her knees and peering out the back window. "That's Olivia Seno, the Duchess Montefalco—"

"It's countess," Tracy corrected her. "And you haven't seen her in eight years, Hols."

"She could be the Count of Monte Crisco for all I know," Holly said. "All I know is, she's trying to get you to back up!"

Abruptly, Tracy braked and, through sheer General Motors muscle, with Holly yelling, "There's a very sick woman back there! We need to get her to help! Move!" backed her van through a bleating horde of protesting vehicles toward Olivia. She jumped up and wrinkled her nose in delight. The rest of them smiled with various degrees of moxie. Olivia's shiny appearance, like an advertisement for the benefits of folic acid, made all of them aware of their damp armpits and Thursday morning hair, Jan's and Tracy's yoga pants and Holly's cutoffs, so tight she would have dislocated her thumb trying to put her hand into the pocket.

Twenty-five years ago, the four of them had been inseparable, a fighting unit with black fishnet stockings under their navy plaid school uniforms, imitation black leather jackets from J. C. Penney's thrown over their shoulders. Unholy innocents, they'd stalked the halls of St. Ursula High, cracking gum and cracking wise. Tough girls, who'd never thrown a punch, they posed as scofflaws but never missed their curfews. Twenty-five years ago, they'd baptized themselves the Godmothers (in homage to the movie everyone had seen at least ten times). Even Holly—who, unlike the others, didn't have a drop of Italian blood—had to dye her naturally flaxen hair to the color and texture of a witch's hat. In ninth grade, they'd run a double-D cup up the flagpole. They'd watched from their third-floor math class as Sister Mary Vincent fought the March wind to pull it down, without allowing the flags of the order and the

United States to touch the ground, because the janitor, a meek man called Vili, was too abashed to touch it. In tenth grade, once Janis and Tracy had their driver's licenses and Saturday night use of their grandfather's Bonneville, they'd gone to Benny's Beef to pick up rough, bright boys from Fenton High and go parking in the delivery lot behind the golf course, four couples on two leather bench seats. On a dare, they drank whiskey Janis had pilfered from behind the bar at her father's steakhouse as they sat on Alphonse Capone's grave in Holy Innocents Cemetery. In eleventh grade, they'd sprayed across the principal's parking space "We're the crew that brought the brew to the roof of St. U!" By senior year, Olivia was so madly involved with a college boy from Loyola that Tracy got horrible hives, scoring her arms into tracks of welts, because she needed to do both hers and Livy's term papers for Honors English and civ. Then the Loyola boy fell for Anna Kruchenko; and Olivia used scissors from art class to cut off Anna's twenty-inch braid a week before prom.

A week after prom, Olivia's mother had a hysterectomy. While the adult women murmured darkly of "C.A.," Olivia came to live at Tracy's house for a month, during which Olivia lost twenty pounds, opening huge hollows under the cheekbones that framed her huge eyes. Girls back then wore five, seven, and nine—not two and four. Plu-skinny as rote was not yet ordained. But Olivia's wraithlike beauty drove boys to fight over her like rutting elk, sometimes on the sidewalk in front of Tracy's house. And though Livy had almost never again allowed herself to be anything but concave, she confessed to Tracy that she had made a holy vow to eat nothing but bread if her mother would live, that she had been shoveling peas and pork chops into her table napkin every night. Those nights had been the only time Tracy had ever seen Olivia cry. She had not cried even in the hospital in Florence.

Their principal, Mother Bernard, had to explain to her young sisters (and there were young nuns then, though fewer each year) that there were two kinds of bad girls. One kind did not possess the DNA to turn out bad, and one kind did. The Godmothers were the former. They would grow up to be teachers, parents, and professionals. Perhaps one of them would even have a vocation.

The young nuns prayed that if one of them did, she'd be a Benedictine and cloistered for life.

But in everything but this one matter, Mother Bernard had been exactly correct. Holly was a nurse and the mother of twins. Janis stayed home with her two daughters until they reached high school age, and was only now resuscitating her event-planning business, which she ran from home. Tracy taught gym classes in the gym where she'd learned to play basketball. And Olivia! Olivia had made of herself something remarkable, although only by dint of looks and luck. When they spoke of Olivia, it was always Holly who pointed out that Olivia had not discovered radium, she had simply married up.

Still, despite Holly's protests, it was true: The others' lives had been cut from a single pattern—different only because one might have chosen short sleeves, another a scooped neck.

They'd all grown up in Westbrook, a bumper suburb on the hip of Chicago that Holly once called the town without a soul.

All their parents were ten-minute immigrants from the west side, with nothing but blue-collar grit and the best intentions for their children. Janis's father built the Grub Steak and threw in on founding a golf club even before he and the other town fathers got around to building their own church. All the girls were bused to St. Ursula in Belleview one town over, all the boys to Fenton in Parkside. An elementary school was built the second year that Westbrook was incorporated. But no one would have considered anything but parochial school for his or her children.

Janis's and Tracy's fathers were brothers who'd married cousins. Among the two families' six children, Janis and Tracy were the only girls and were raised essentially as sisters. The eight Loccario grandchildren still celebrated their birthdays at Tony's restaurant, the Grub Steak. After a martini, he would re-call for them when Westbrook had no strip malls or coffee joints: It was a cluster of houses surrounded by forlorn prairie, with distant moans and grumbles from the freight trains that rat-tled the china in everyone's hutch and the bewildered hoots of owls perched on bulldozers. There were prairie fires and muskrat. Janis always said Grandpa made the children believe they'd been pioneers in North Dakota.

When the time came, Tracy went to Champagne on a bas-ketball scholarship. Janis went to Triton Junior College and toyed with marketing, as well as with every boy in a twenty-mile radius. So winsome with her thick auburn blunt cut and her perky rear end that Tracy couldn't believe they'd come from the same gene pool, Janis turned Dave on and off like a faucet until, in dental school, he made a play for a sassy class-mate.

Rapidly, Janis had given her hand, but unlike Tracy, not her last name. Dave's surname was Chawson. "It might be dental," Janis opined, "but it's not musical." Olivia, meanwhile, had turned a junior-year-abroad romance in Italy into a romance. Even the ending had been appropriately tragic, hence Livy's triste return to her homeland.

"She's going to have to sit on my lap if we're going to fit that stuff in here," Holly groused as Olivia began the prodigious task of overseeing the loading of her luggage. *Put that there—no, no, that has glass in it—on top, that's right . . .*

"At least you won't feel her," Janis said. "Do you think she weighs a hundred pounds?"

"*Why* are *we* taking *her* on a cruise?" Holly asked sotto voce.

As only a teacher could do, Tracy gave Holly the Look. She whispered, "Because she's a widow, and we love her, and for your information, she paid for everything except the airfare! Be nice!"

It was Tracy's loyalty, not Olivia's royalty, that inspired this devotion, which drove Holly mad. She had been by far the more affectionate friend, the one who never failed to write Tracy when Tracy was downstate at school, who went to see her play, and fail in the quarterfinals, at state, who welcomed baby Cammie home with a hand-smocked cradle skirt and coverlet, who never forgot a birthday, who co-hosted Tracy's Christmas open house. Yet nothing was too good for Olivia. Holly understood, but she did not accept . . .

Tracy's daughter, Cammie, would later say that had it not been for the tendency of *everyone* except Holly to oblige Olivia's noblesse, things might have turned out another way. Lives might have drifted on, uninspired perhaps, but unscarred.

But in that moment, as the three of them piled out of the car and engulfed Olivia, the umbrella of years collapsed over them and bound them close. They were again a complete set. The ineradicable tenderness and surplus of memories they shared were all that mattered.

"Do you believe I've just flown nine hours and I'm going to turn around and fly nine more tomorrow?" Olivia asked. "All because of you nutballs?"

"Is that an Italian word?" Holly asked.

"Nuttaballa," Olivia said.

"But you're a jet-setter," Janis said. "You used to fly to Paris for a weekend to shop."

"Europe is teeny. The sea is big," said Olivia.

"You were always profound," Holly said with a grin.

And they pranced and hugged again.